"ARRESTING A
FAST-PACED
—San Francisco Chronicle

"MOVES AT THE SPEED OF LIGHT AND KEEPS READERS FRANTICALLY TURNING THE PAGES—A THRILLER WITH AN UNDENIABLE AIR OF AUTHENTICITY."
—Orlando Sentinel

"SMART AND SKILLFUL"
—Kirkus Reviews

POINT OF NO RETURN

Lara Sanderstone staggered to her car. Razor-sharp pains shot through her side, and she leaned over the steering wheel gasping. She was alive, she kept telling herself. But she could still see herself dead—she had been that close.

She should have taken the gun when the cop had offered it. If only I had, she thought, imagining the weapon in her hand, her finger on the trigger, the explosion reverberating inside the underground garage. Finally, after all her years of dealing with violent crimes and violent offenders, Lara fully comprehended how a person could reach that point beyond reason. If she had taken the gun, she knew what the outcome would have been. There was absolutely no doubt in her mind.

She would have killed him. . . .

Lara Sanderstone had always been a brilliant judge. She had always been a brave and beautiful woman. But now she was even more. She was a target out to turn the tables on terror.

"THIS STORY IS GOOD! GRIPPING, INTERESTING, BELIEVABLE—TRUE FEEL OF AUTHENTICITY. YOU GET HOOKED FROM PAGE ONE."

—South Bend Tribune

"An edge-of-the-chair legal thriller."
—San Gabriel Valley Tribune

"Fast and furious. . . .Compelling."
—Virginian-Pilot and Ledger-Star

"Belongs at the top of your must-read list."
—Sunday Oklahoman

"Moves at the speed of light and keeps the reader frantically turning the pages."
—St. Paul Pioneer Press

"Fast-paced . . .with a stunning conclusion. . . .Enough twists and turns for an amusement-park ride."

—*Sunday Montgomery Advertiser*

"Another success . . .Masters the art of misdirection and sleight-of-hand."

—*Richmond Times-Dispatch*

"Introduces a fascinating new protagonist, a brilliant woman judge. . . .Written with authenticity and authority for added impact."

—*Magazine* (Baton Rouge, LA)

Nancy Taylor Rosenberg

INTEREST OF JUSTICE

A SIGNET BOOK

To my mother, Laverne Taylor,
and in memory of my father,
William Hoyt Taylor,
and to my father- and mother-in-law,
Hyman and Doris Rosenberg.

SIGNET
Published by the Penguin Group
Penguin Books USA Inc., 375 Hudson Street,
New York, New York 10014, U.S.A.
Penguin Books Ltd, 27 Wrights Lane, London W8 5TZ, England
Penguin Books Australia Ltd, Ringwood, Victoria, Australia
Penguin Books Canada Ltd, 10 Alcorn Avenue, Toronto, Ontario,
Canada M4V 3B2
Penguin Books (N.Z.) Ltd, 182-190 Wairau Road, Auckland 10, New Zealand

Penguin Books Ltd, Registered Offices: Harmondsworth, Middlesex, England

Published by Signet, an imprint of Dutton Signet, a division of Penguin Books USA Inc. Previously published in a Dutton edition.

First Signet Printing, June, 1994
10 9 8 7 6 5 4 3 2 1

Printed in the United States of America

acknowledgments

I would like to acknowledge all the many people who assisted me in the development of this novel. First, I offer thanks to my wonderful agent and good friend, Peter Miller, of PMA Literary and Film Management, for his constant support and tireless efforts on my behalf; and to Jennifer Robinson, also of PMA, who assisted me greatly. I am particularly grateful to my editor, Michaela Hamilton at Dutton Signet, who offered her brilliance and insight. Without her this novel would not be what it is today. Elaine Koster, my publisher, has been wonderful, as well as the entire staff at Penguin USA.

Additionally, I would like to offer thanks to Dr. George Awad for his expert advice in the field of pathology. And last, I would like to thank my long-suffering and supportive husband, Jerry, and my wonderful children: Blake, Chessly, Hoyt, Amy, and Nancy for allowing their mother to become a writer and follow her dream, and for handling a lot of their problems without me. Nancy, I would particularly like to thank, since she sacrificed her summer vacation to assist me in editing this novel.

Chapter 1

Judge Lara Sanderstone had a ritual. When she was pondering a complex legal matter or was about to make a judicial ruling, she would spin her high-backed leather chair toward the American flag on the left side of her mahogany desk. It seemed to give her inspiration. As for the California flag right next to it, well, she didn't put much stock in its ability to inspire her—or anyone else, for that matter, although she certainly wouldn't voice this opinion publicly.

Many of the judges didn't have flags in their chambers. She had inherited the flags, the furniture, her chambers, even her secretary from the judge she had replaced when she was appointed to the superior court bench two years prior after eleven years as a prosecutor. The weekend before her swearing-in ceremony, she had driven to the courthouse in her jeans and lovingly sanded down and refinished the marred surface of the once magnificent desk. There wasn't much she could do about the chair, however. The judge she had replaced was a heavy man, and the innersprings had collapsed with his weight. They had promised her a new chair, but it had never appeared. It was like sitting in a bucket.

She glanced at the clock. It was almost time to return to the courtroom. The matter on the afternoon calendar was a pretrial motion. These were generally routine and uneventful, carried out in an almost empty courtroom. But unfortunately, this particular motion could destroy the people's case completely, and it had carried over to a second day. The motion should have been heard at the preliminary hearing, but then the defendant had been represented by the public defender, a man sympathetic to the prosecution and buried the case. Now the case had been taken over by Benjamin England, a Rhodes scholar, a man established enough to devote himself full-time to this case and none other.

The case involved the rape and murder of twenty-year-old Jessica Van Horn. She had left her home in Mission Viejo after a weekend visit en route to the UCLA campus in her 1989 Toyota Camry. The car was later found abandoned alongside the freeway with a flat tire. An exhaustive two-month search for the pretty blonde had culminated in tragedy. Her defiled and decomposed body had been found in a field near Oceanside, about forty miles from where her car was discovered. All those involved had hoped against reason that she was still alive. By the time the body was discovered, the officers, reporters, the entire community, had Jessica's image firmly implanted in their minds: the curly blond hair, the shy smile, the big blue eyes, even the white blouse trimmed in lace that she was wearing in the thousands and thousands of flyers they had distributed.

Judge Sanderstone was no longer facing the flag. She had her chair turned to the right side of the desk, where she had a large framed portrait of her great-grandfather, a tribal chief of the Cherokee nation. She took in the proud posture, the sculpted cheekbones, the penetrating eyes, the wisdom. This was where her eyes rested when she was looking for strength.

The courtroom was packed and noisy. Almost every seat was taken, and several reporters had been forced to bend on one knee in the aisles with their notebooks and pens ready. At least a dozen police officers were present, some in uniform, some plainclothes.

One of the clerks whispered something to the bailiff. The judge was on the way. Two additional bailiffs entered, escorting the defendant, a small, thin man in his thirties, to the counsel table. He kept his head down, holding his cuffed wrists to his face, actually sucking on one finger. He took small steps, the shackles around his ankles jangling like an enormous charm bracelet. On the top of his head was a shiny bald spot glistening with perspiration from the overhead lights. His bright yellow jumpsuit had the words ORANGE COUNTY JAIL on the back.

"All rise," the bailiff said, stepping to the front of the bench once the defendant was deposited next to his attorney. "Remain standing. Superior Court of Orange County, Department Twenty-five, is now in session, the Honorable Lara Sanderstone presiding."

Lara entered the courtroom through the small door behind the bench and ascended the stairs in a swirl of black robes. People told her there was a deceptive delicacy to her face: pale, soft, unblemished skin, the kewpie doll mouth, the high protruding cheekbones, the long eyelashes that fluttered behind her glasses. Her black hair was held back in a fancy gold clip, her one attempt at femininity in what was traditionally a masculine role. Young for the bench at thirty-eight, she had to work to appear authoritative. Not too long ago, someone had commented that she looked like a member of a church choir instead of a judge.

The A.D.A., Russ Mitchell, bolted through the double doors. He was late and had jogged from another courtroom and another matter. Slightly out of breath, he rushed to the counsel table and slapped a thick file down, adjusting his tie and glancing up at the bench.

Lara's gaze was firm and her voice laced with annoyance as she reprimanded him. "I'm pleased that you were able to join us today, Mr. Mitchell, but we are already in session and you are late as usual. I'll give you a few minutes to collect yourself, and then we'll begin."

Her eyes found the victim's parents while Mitchell frantically shuffled papers. They were seated in the first row, side by side like two parrots on a perch, their faces somber. They held each other's hand, the man and woman, both in their early fifties. Whatever was going on around them they didn't see or hear. They stared straight ahead, waiting. What they were waiting for now was justice.

Seated next to them was a dark-haired twenty-year-old boy, the victim's boyfriend. Lara recalled his face from the newspaper articles. He was wearing a black suit, probably the one he had worn to her funeral. He had dated the victim for the past three years. This was their first year at UCLA, and they had been living together in a small apartment near the campus. He'd told reporters he had been saving to buy her an engagement ring.

Finally the district attorney looked up. He was ready.

"*People* versus *Henderson,*" Lara said, immediately calling the case, accepting the file from the clerk's hand as the courtroom fell into silence, all eyes on the bench. "We will be continuing with the defense's motion to suppress evidence. Specifically, the defendant's confession. Mr. England, I understand you have another witness."

"Yes, Your Honor," England said, already on his feet. His dark hair was laced with gray, but at forty-three he was still a youthful, handsome man.

Once the witness was sworn in, he stepped up to the stand. He was in uniform. Yesterday they'd heard testimony from the arresting officers. Lara felt certain they'd perjured themselves. Today she could hear more of the same—more concocted lies. After the officer stated his name for the record and his position as a correctional officer assigned to the Orange County Jail, England stepped from behind the table and approached the witness box.

"Officer White, when did you first see the defendant on the night of June fifteenth?"

"I believe it was about three o'clock in the morning. I was due to get off at three. He was in a holding cell, on a bench."

"I see," England said slowly. "Was he alone in the cell?"

"Yes, he was."

"And what was the defendant doing when you entered the holding cell?"

"He was sleeping."

"Sleeping?" England said, cocking his head. Turning to face the spectators, he walked to the table and picked up something.

"I-I thought he was sleeping," the officer answered.

"Is it possible he was unconscious?" England's eyebrows went up. The witness's eyes were locked on the items in his hands, tracking them as England waved them around as he spoke.

"Probably," the officer replied. Then he scooted closer to the microphone. "I thought he was drunk."

"I see," England said. "So, you tried to rouse him?"

"Yes. When he didn't respond, I got another officer and we moved him to the cell."

"How did you move him?"

"We carried him under his arms."

"Did you look at his face during the time you were carrying him or dragging him to his cell?"

"Of course." The man scanned the faces in the audience, trying to find the arresting officers and possibly some of the correctional officers he worked with, grab some moral support.

"And you didn't notice the bruises on his face, his right eye swollen shut?"

"I don't remember."

The D.A. was squirming in his seat, tapping his pen annoyingly on the table.

England's momentum was building up like steam inside him. With the next question, Lara could almost hear the hiss. "You didn't possibly notice that his left arm was broken, did you?"

"No," the officer said, perspiration across his brow.

"Officer White, did you think for even one moment that the defendant was in urgent need of medical treatment, that he was in fact unconscious, that his arm was severely broken, so severely broken that it was flopping back and forth like a piece of rubber? Surely that's something you would notice?"

"No," the officer said. "I thought he had been in a bar fight or something. It's the booking officer's responsibility to see that a suspect gets medical treatment if he needs it. I'm just a jailer."

England spun around. "Officer White, did you beat the defendant, cause the injuries?"

He jumped in his seat. "No. I didn't lay a hand on him. I simply put him in the cell bunk and left."

"Well, that's very interesting. The arresting officers testified yesterday that he might have incurred, I quote, 'a few bruises' when they were placing him under arrest, but nothing more. I guess that means you broke his arm, right? I mean, if they didn't break his arm, you must have been the one who broke it."

The officer's face was bright red. He wasn't about to take the fall. "No way. His arm was broken when he was booked. I certainly didn't break it."

A flurry of commotion rang through the courtroom. The D.A. was ashen. England attacked. "You mean by the arresting officers? Right? Not during booking but prior to booking?"

The witness became silent. He dropped his eyes. "I guess so," he finally said.

"And you," England said, pointing a finger at him, "you left this man, this injured and unconscious man, in a cell where he could have died. Why? I'll tell you why. Because you were about to go off duty and you didn't want to be bothered. You didn't want to mess with the paperwork, the trip to the infirmary, all that time-consuming stuff. Isn't that right, Officer White?"

The officer's head dropped. He didn't answer.

"Objection," the D.A. spouted. "He's badgering the witness."

"Sustained," Lara said.

"No further questions, Your Honor," England said, taking his seat, his point clearly scored.

Lara looked at the D.A.; the tension in her neck was increasing, and she rolled her head around to relieve it. "Your witness, Mr. Mitchell."

The officer was gulping water from a glass placed in

the witness stand. The two arresting officers were seated in the back row, their eyes black daggers. White had far more to fear now than Benjamin England, Lara thought. He had rolled over on his own. The future months wouldn't be easy.

The D.A. stood, adjusting his jacket, his voice low and soft. "Officer White, are you absolutely certain that the defendant didn't fall out of his bunk and break his arm? Your preliminary statements were that you didn't notice any injuries. Are you now recanting that testimony?"

This time the witness met the arresting officers' eyes. He was beyond all that now. He just wanted out, off the stand and out of the courtroom. As a correctional officer he didn't testify on a regular basis, and for him this was grueling. "Yes. I noticed his arm. His arm was broken when I went into the holding cell."

"And you're absolutely certain of this now? Your earlier statement was false?" Mitchell swiped the hair off his forehead, shaking his head. He knew it was bad. He didn't know it was this bad.

"Yes," he said, blinking rapidly, more perspiration appearing on his forehead, his upper lip, little beads of it rolling down his cheeks.

"Isn't it possible, Officer White," the D.A. said, going for the last escape hatch, "that he could have fallen off the bench in the holding cell and incurred this injury before you arrived?"

White thought a moment. He apparently made a decision to come clean, spill his guts, make a feeble attempt to make amends in the eyes of the court and possibly his own conscience. "I guess he could have, but he didn't. Everyone knew he was roughed up before he was booked." He cleared his throat and continued. "He killed and raped a girl, you know?" With this last statement he looked confidently at the spectators, as if they would all understand, that if they had been given the opportunity, they too would have wanted to make this man suffer, to break some bones, draw a little blood.

The D.A. wasn't touching this one. Actually, he'd gone too far and there was no road back. England didn't bother to object to the speculation that the defendant was guilty. "No further questions, Your Honor," the D.A. said. He didn't simply take his seat, he fell into it.

Mitchell turned to the victim's parents and met their gaze. Lara felt the tightness move from her neck to her chest. The parents hadn't moved. They were still sitting ramrod straight, their shoulders touching, their hands tightly clasped. They looked like statues, bronze replicas of suffering. They had as yet to realize the magnitude of what had just occurred.

From the look on the face of the young man next to them, however, he had.

"Very well," Lara said, peering down at the witness. "You can step down," she told him. Then she turned to the courtroom. "We will recess for fifteen minutes before I deliver a ruling. Mr. Mitchell, I'll see you in chambers." She tapped the gavel one time lightly and slipped from the bench. As soon as she was through the door, she pressed her fingers down over her face, pulling her skin, wishing she would wipe the stench of this off her face and hands. It was poison—clear and simple.

She walked rapidly to her chambers. The D.A. was right behind her. She began speaking without looking back at him, and she entered her outer office with only a nod at her secretary. "Are you going to file on Madriano and Curtis?" she said, referring to the arresting officers. Not only had they beaten the defendant within an inch of his life, they had obviously perjured themselves the day before.

The D.A. answered, "I assume. I haven't given it much thought." He appeared more concerned about his case, or what was left of it, than pressing charges against the officers.

They were in chambers now and Lara stepped behind her desk, taking her seat and tossing her glasses, swiveling her chair to face the young D.A. "These officers should be prosecuted, relieved of their positions on the force, and frankly, taken out and shot. I've never seen such a fucked-up case in my life." She was so angry that her hands were trembling as she fingered a piece of paper on her desk.

The D.A's chin jerked up in response, but he didn't speak. It was obvious that he'd like to do the honors himself as far as the officers went. Crestfallen, he finally said, "He's guilty, you know?"

Lara didn't respond to this statement. Her hands were tied. Even if she was to blatantly deny the defense's motion to exclude the confession, any conviction would be overturned in appeal. "A layman would have no trouble figuring this one out. You simply cannot beat a person and then garner a confession." She watched as the D.A. slid farther down in his seat.

"You rule to suppress this, we're dead meat," Mitchell said. "He knows it," he continued accusingly, referring to the defense attorney. "Our primary witness died last week. Without the confession . . . well, we're looking at dismissal."

None of this was news to Lara. They'd been agonizing over this for three weeks. In a slurred voice on tape, the defendant had admitted the crime. The tape had suddenly ended. Lara was certain the defendant had collapsed from the injures inflicted by the arresting officers. They had worked the case all along, speaking daily with the family. They both were mature investigators with teenage daughters of their own.

They had simply lost it.

Without the eyewitness, and the absolutely vital confession, the prosecution had nothing. Lara had called Mitchell into chambers only to allow both of them a few minutes to accept the inevitable, present a unified front. The D.A. would withdraw the charges and regroup. If they took a case as weak as this to trial and ended up in acquittal, it was finished. They were better off withdrawing now and praying for more evidence to construct a more concrete case. The biggest problem was the public outrage sure to follow and the fact that a dangerous killer would be walking the streets while they built a better case. Instead of the public venting its anger on the real culprits in this case, the police officers, it would all fly in Lara's face.

"Are you going to withdraw today?" She hoped not. That would be the worst: for her to suppress the evidence and the defendant to walk out of jail a few hours later a free man.

"I don't know. England's going to press for dismissal." He leaned forward in his seat. Then he slapped back, throwing his hands in the air. "We have no case. We have shit . . . nothing but dog shit."

Lara stood to return to the courtroom. Mitchell took her cue and stood as well. A few seconds later, he was following her down the corridor.

Once back in session, Lara addressed the court. "After careful consideration," she said, the weight of the words she was uttering causing her to compress in her seat so that only her head could be seen from below, "the defendant's motion to suppress is granted." She braced herself for the onslaught and continued, looking out over the courtroom, "From the evidence presented in this courtroom, the defendant was severely battered, the confession was issued under extreme duress and is therefore determined to be inadmissible."

England sprang to his feet. "We move for dismissal, Your Honor. Without this evidence the case against my client is non-existent."

The defendant looked up, a blank look in his eyes. Lara had read in the files that he was on psychotropic medication. The noise in the courtroom was getting louder with every second. The D.A. had turned around in his seat and was speaking with the victim's family. The woman was crying, the father holding her head against his shoulder. He was whispering to her, stroking her hair, making a feeble attempt to comfort her. The victim's boyfriend's mouth fell open in shock and he jumped up. The D.A. yanked his jacket and he sat back down.

Mitchell stood. "The people withdraw the charges, Your Honor."

Now the courtroom was in an uproar, and the defendant's eyes were darting wildly around the room. Who would he rape or, God forbid, murder while the D.A. scrambled for more evidence? Lara thought. Was he thinking about it right now? Was his sick and tortured mind right this very minute hungering for another kill, his eyes searching the courtroom for another victim? Lara tapped the gavel loudly again and again, standing and leaning over the railing. The bailiffs started moving toward the victim's family, eyeing them and then the defendant. Finally the noise died down and Lara took her seat. "Let the record read that the charges have been dismissed at the people's motion," she said, sighing deeply, keeping her eyes on the file in front of her. "The defendant is remanded into custody; however, the sheriff will be notified to release the defendant posthaste. Monies posted as bail shall be released in the appropriate fashion through the court clerk's office. This court is adjourned." She didn't bother with the gavel. No one would have heard it anyway.

Reporters were running from the courtroom, pushing and shoving one another to reach their editors. Lara was rooted to her seat, her eyes locking on the victim's parents, her chest swelling with compassion. The D.A. was conferring with them, sitting next to them on the bench. The woman was holding a tissue to her eyes, then blowing her noise. People were leaving the courtroom; the court reporter was folding up her machine. All the police officers had vanished before the ruling. They weren't stupid, Lara thought. They knew how it would fall. By tomorrow the D.A. would file charges against the two arresting officers. The bailiff was chatting with one of the clerks. England was packing his briefcase, his job over.

Suddenly the victim's boyfriend stood, his face a twisted mask of rage. "How could you do this?" he screamed at Lara. "He killed her. He raped her and killed her. He deserved to be beaten. He deserves to die." He was panting, his face flushed crimson, leaning over the back of the seat in front of him. His eyes were enormous and blazing with hatred. A bailiff was rushing toward him, the D.A. trying to pull him back in his seat. "You're letting him get away with this. Someone should kill you . . . rape you, strangle you. You fucking bitch . . ."

The bailiff put his hands on the boy, and the two other bailiffs were moving in that direction. They were watching both his hands for a weapon. "Someone should kill your whole family . . . slaughter them . . . then you'd know about justice and your stupid laws. What do I have to do, kill the mother fucker myself? You're not a judge. You're no better than he is. . . ."

Lara just sat there, consumed with his sense of injustice. He had looked to the courts to avenge the death of the girl he loved and had met a brick wall of law. Those that should have upheld it had destroyed it. The bailiffs looked at her, waiting for direction. One nod and they would cuff him. They had him in tow and he was twisting, saliva dripping down one corner of his mouth, trying to wrench his arms away, ready to cross the floor and rip her apart with his bare hands. She shook her head at the bailiffs and left the bench. He had every right to vent his hostility. She hit the door and once through it, she leaned against the wall in the corridor, her eyes glazed and fixed, her chest rising and falling with the hatred that had been directed at her, so intense that she could feel the heat of it even now. She glanced up and down the hall, but all she could see was a misty fog of red. Images of the victim's decomposed body appeared in her mind, and she tried to suppress them.

Pushing herself off the wall, she straightened her robe and shuffled down the hall. Twenty-five homicides had occurred the past weekend in Los Angeles. One weekend, she thought in despair. One lousy weekend and twenty-five deaths. The city was being buried in an avalanche of violence, and she had just set a murderer free in the community. "Great," she said bitterly. "Just what you wanted to do all your life, Lara—set killers free, give them their walking papers." Heading toward the door to her chambers, she stopped in front of her secretary's desk.

"Did you say something?" Phillip asked, spinning around from his word processor. He was a slender, well-groomed man in his late twenties with sandy blond hair and dove gray eyes.

"What are you doing tonight, Phillip?"

"Tonight? I-I have plans. Why?" he said self-consciously.

Lara studied his face. She didn't think she could handle eating alone tonight, going home to an empty house. All she needed was a little companionship, some light conversation, something to purge the day's events from her mind. Before she could ask him to join her for dinner, he continued.

"I'm seeing someone later, ah, about nine. But if you need something typed, I can stay late."

His face flushed. Lara wondered if he had a new girlfriend, or any girlfriend, for that matter. She'd never heard him mention anyone. "No," she said, changing her mind, thinking she would try someone else, feeling foolish for even thinking of asking Phillip to have dinner with her. "Forget it. Go on home. It's nothing."

"What happened in there? How did you rule?"

"I suppressed the confession. The D.A. dismissed, so Henderson will walk."

"God," he said, arching his eyebrows and resting his chin on his hands. "Because the officers beat him up, right? They really punished that guy, didn't they? I guess they got carried away. The crime was heinous. You almost can't blame them for what they did."

"Well, I hope they enjoyed punishing him," Lara said flatly. "It might be the only punishment Thomas Henderson ever receives in this case."

With that, she entered her chambers and closed the door behind her.

Chapter 2

For over an hour Lara had sat behind her desk and stared into space. She'd given thought to calling the victim's parents and telling them how sorry she was, explaining to them how she was left with no choice but to make the ruling she had. But she realized that would be inappropriate.

Phillip buzzed her on the intercom. "I have the *Daily News* on line one. They'd like a statement from you about the Henderson matter."

"Tell them I've left for the day," she said, knowing she was only stalling. She'd have to give them a statement tomorrow.

Hanging her robe on the hook and grabbing her purse, Lara told Phillip good night and made her way down the back corridor to Judge Irene Murdock's chambers. Lara spotted her head bent over her desk. "Still at it, I see," Lara said, stepping into the room.

"Oh, Lara," Irene said, "you startled me." She looked up and removed her glasses, tossing them on her paper-padded desk.

Irene was approaching fifty but few would ever know it. She was tall and fashionably thin. Except for a few lines that shot down from her mouth and darted across her forehead, time had been kind. She wore her muted blond hair in soft feminine curls that framed and flattered her narrow face. Her lips were always lined and coated with fresh, moist lipstick, a bright coral, but her eyes held the key to her strength. They were an emerald green. "How did it go today?" she asked. "You know, the Henderson case?"

"You haven't heard?" Lara didn't sit down. She leaned against the back wall. "The D.A. dismissed." Raising her wrist, Lara glanced at her watch. It was after five o'clock. "Henderson should be walking out the door of the jail any minute. Free as a bird."

Irene didn't respond. They had all anticipated that it would fall this way. She sat there studying Lara's face. She had been on the bench far longer than Lara. As Irene had told her again and again, a judge's role was to interpret and rule on the law. She couldn't allow herself to become emotionally involved.

"This was a rough one, Irene. The parents . . . the relatives . . . I can't imagine how they feel right now. She was so young. And those frigging cops—"

Irene cut her off. "Have you heard about Westridge?"

Charles Westridge was a municipal court judge, known to be impassioned and ambitious. "No, tell me."

"He filed today on the sheriff for violating court orders in releasing prisoners prior to the completion of their terms."

"But the sheriff's under court order to release or close the jail down due to overcrowding. What does Westridge possibly hope to gain?"

"Attention maybe. Press. Who knows? I've heard he wants my position, is planning to run against me next year. He reviews every one of my decisions and probably stands up and cheers every time I'm reversed on appeal."

Lara took a seat, shaking her head. "Don't we have enough problems around here without going after each other? And the sheriff . . . that's inane. I swear, Irene, it seems like the system is falling down around us. It's like walking in rubble. The violence, the corruption, the ambiguities in the law . . ." Lara paused and then continued, "It gets worse by the second, and we're simply powerless to stop it. Sure, those officers were assholes for what they did to Henderson, but the cops are walking time bombs. They're just sick of it all. I mean, are we even civilized anymore? I'm not sure if you can call this civilization."

Irene looked at a spot over Lara's head. "Aren't you the voice of doom today?" Then she dropped her eyes to Lara's and smiled. "Things are bad. But even at the end of the world, Lara dear, someone's got to sit in judgment."

"Right," Lara said, making a feeble attempt to return Irene's smile. "I'd prefer it wasn't me, though." She added, "On a lighter vein, how about dinner tonight? I guess you may have plans with John, but . . ."

Irene pushed the auto-dial button on her phone. While the rapid tones rang out, she said, "Let me call him. If he isn't home, sure, I'd love to join you. To tell you the truth, I'm starving. I skipped lunch today." A few seconds later, she was listening to her own voice on the answering machine. She left a message for her husband, a prominent physician, and then hung up. "John's working too many hours, Lara. I have no idea why. Last year he told me he was going to scale it down, let his new partner carry more of the load, but he seldom comes home before eight o'clock every night. He's—" Suddenly she stopped herself. Irene Murdock did not make a habit of talking about her personal life, not even to her closest friends.

Now the roles were reversed, and Lara was watching the concern on Irene's face. John Murdock was in his early sixties, and Irene worried about him all the time. There was a long history of cancer in his family. His father and grandfather had died of it, plus several of his uncles, and just last year his brother had fallen victim as well. Even though Irene was a rock of strength and conviction, it was like she was waiting for the other shoe to fall, certain her husband would be next. A lot of people viewed her as strident and overbearing. Generally her speech was laced with all kinds of terms of endearment: honey, baby, darling, and dear. Lara knew she had cultivated this habit intentionally to tone herself down.

Her husband was as docile as a lamb, a sweet, gentle

man. She even towered over him in height, particularly with heels. There was never any doubt who wore the pants in the family, Lara thought.

Irene closed the file in front of her and stood, collecting her briefcase and purse, and turning out the lights. She walked with long, rapid strides down the corridor, and Lara almost had to run to keep up with her.

"I was thinking we could eat at Bob's Big Boy," Lara said, "What do you think It's only a block away, and they have this great special."

"Lara darling," Irene said, cracking a smile and turning to face her, "You're incredible. No, I will not eat at Bob's Big Boy. If you insist on your disgusting diet of junk food and greasy fried food, you'll have to eat alone. I don't know how you live like that. I really don't."

"All right," Lara said. "We can go to that new seafood restaurant down the street."

"Better," Irene said. "I'll follow you."

A few minutes later, they were both in their cars and heading up the ramp from the underground garage.

It was late, but Lara was still awake. She'd been thrashing about in bed for hours trying to sleep, details of the Henderson case playing over and over in her mind. First, she heard her neighbors' little terrier yelping. Then the other dogs on the block joined in, and Lara held her breath and listened, pulling the sheet up to her chin and staring at the ceiling. It was a quiet residential neighborhood in Irvine, but she was a woman who lived alone. She knew all the normal sounds of the night well: the ambulances and police sirens racing by on the nearby thoroughfares, the jets passing overhead, the occasional couple coming home from a late night and the familiar crank of their garage door. But when the dogs started howling, which they seldom did, it usually meant someone was out there prowling around.

Then she heard it: a soft tapping at the front door.

The tapping turned into a frantic pounding. Lara glanced at the clock and saw that it was after one. Thinking of calling the police, she reached over and put her hand on the phone. Then she heard a familiar voice calling her name through the bedroom window. It was a hot summer night, and she'd left the window open to get some fresh air.

"Lara, it's me. It's Ivory. Let me in."

Grabbing her robe, she padded barefoot to the door and listened to make certain she wasn't imagining the whole thing.

"Lara, open the door. Please open the door. It's Ivory."

She punched in the alarm code, and after releasing the double dead-bolt locks, she found herself face to face with her younger sister.

"Honey," she said, taking her in her arms as she walked through the door, "what's happened now?" She brushed a strand of dark curly hair off Ivory's face and looked for bruises. "Did Sam hit you?"

Ivory kept glancing over her shoulder at the street, her chest rising and falling, gasping for breath as if she'd been running. "No, no . . . it's not Sam. Someone's following me, Lara. Shut the door. Quick."

Lara slammed the door and slid the dead bolts back into place, quickly resetting the alarm, her own heart pounding now. "Who's following you? Where's Sam?"

Ivory was agitated, her dark eyes darting around the room. "Listen, I can't explain. I need to call Sam. I just need to use your phone."

"Stop right here, okay?" Lara said, placing her hands on her sister's arms and holding her. "Tell me exactly what's going on. If someone is following you or trying to hurt you, we'll call the police. Maybe he's still out there and they can pick him up. What kind of car was he driving? Give me his description." Lara started across the room to the phone.

"Forget it," Ivory said. "I'm not calling the stupid cops." Flopping down on the sofa, she grabbed the phone from her sister's hand.

Lara stared at her, thinking how beautiful she was, even now when she was frightened and upset. She was a striking brunette, with shoulder-length curly hair that framed her almost perfect face. Whereas Lara's eyes were gray, Ivory's were a brilliant blue. But it was her skin that was her finest feature. Her skin was absolutely flawless.

"Sam," Ivory spoke rapidly into the phone, "I'm at Lara's. Please, come and get me. Something's happened. Someone's following me." She paused and then her voice rose another octave. "I said I'm not leaving until you come and get me. No, I'm not driving home by myself. I don't care what time it is." Then she slammed the phone back on the hook.

Lara turned on the lights in the living room and sat on the sofa across from her sister. "Now," she said, her voice firm, "tell me what's going on. Is this about money?"

"Sam's coming," Ivory said, avoiding her sister's eyes. "He'll be here in about twenty minutes."

Lara felt her anger and frustration growing with each passing minute. She'd always been the one who protected Ivory, made certain no one hurt her. Ever since they were children, only a few years apart in age, Lara had been the one she always turned to when she had a problem. But since she'd married Sam Perkins, everything had changed.

"Ivory, you must tell me what's going on with your life. Don't you understand that I'm concerned about you? You can't just bang on my door at this hour and tell me someone's following you and then refuse to tell me what's going on."

Ivory stood and started pacing. "I can't," she said emphatically, tossing her long mane of hair, jerking her head around to look at her sister. "Don't worry, okay?" she snapped. "I won't come over here and bother you anymore. I won't even call you anymore. You can just forget you have a sister."

Lara put her head in her hands, and then peered up at Ivory through her fingers. "I never said I didn't want you to call me or come over here when you need something. You're not being fair, Ivory. I love you. It's Sam, isn't it? All of this has something to do with Sam."

"Leave Sam out of this. All you ever do is bash him, tell me what an asshole he is. He's my husband, Lara." She suddenly started tossing her arms around wildly. "Look at you, your whole life. You want me to end up like you, alone, with no one, living for nothing but a job, a career? Sam and I are going to make it, and we're going to make it big time. Then we're going to move away from here, start all over."

Lara tried to let her sister's words roll off her back. Every time they were together, they ended up fighting like this. What Lara wanted was to repair the relationship, help her sister put her life back on track. "What about your child, Ivory? What about Josh? You shouldn't uproot him, make him move. He's lived in that house all his life. He lost his father. And what about the pawnshop? You said if I loaned you and Sam the money for the pawnshop, you could make it. Not only that, but you haven't made one payment. You know, Ivory, I have financial obligations too."

"Josh is fine . . . just fine. What do you care, anyway? You haven't seen him in years."

It had been a long day. Lara was exhausted and couldn't handle a screaming match. But the issue of Josh was a sensitive one, and with each second her control was slipping. "And why haven't I seen Josh in years, Ivory?" she shot back, flopping back against the sofa and crossing her arms over her chest, locking them together and digging her nails into her skin. "Because you won't allow me to see my own nephew. You've poisoned him against me for absolutely no reason." She inhaled and her chest swelled, her gray eyes blazed. "I thought the deal was that I loan you the money for the pawnshop and we put the past to bed. What happened to that promise?"

"You," Ivory spat, still pacing, still frantic. "You tried to take my kid away from me. My own fucking sister tried to steal my kid. You know what Sam said? He said you were just bribing me with that money so you could get your hands on Josh and take him away because you don't have any kids of your own." She went to the window and peeked through the blinds and then returned to the center of the room.

Lara slumped on the sofa. No matter what she did, she couldn't get beyond this. "We've been over this a million times. After Charley got killed, you were drinking, using cocaine, bringing one man after another into the house. I never tried to take him away. I was only concerned for him. And I was concerned for you."

Lara had been so concerned about her nephew that she'd threatened to call Social Services if Ivory didn't get her act together. She'd only wanted to shock her, get her attention, make her realize what she was risking with her reckless behavior, but Ivory had never forgiven her.

Suddenly she noticed how Ivory was dressed. Was this the latest fashion? She looked like a tramp, a streetwalker. Once she had married Sam, Lara had thought the bar-hopping was over. When her first husband had been alive, Ivory had been a contented wife and mother. Lara knew that grief could destroy people, even strong people, and Ivory was far from strong, but her descent had been radical. Lara had arrived at the opinion that life had finally caught up with her sister and then simply passed her. Ivory was a child in a woman's body. She had been classified as learning disabled as a child, and had an emotional and mental age far below her chronological age. Within a closely structured and protected setting, she could survive. But alone, or with a negative influence like Sam, Ivory was in serious trouble. Then when alcohol and drugs were mixed in, the arrows all pointed to disaster.

Lara then noticed her sister's breasts, and her eyes expanded. Ivory had always been shapely, far more shapely than Lara, but not like this. Now her sister looked like Dolly Parton. Lara hadn't seen Ivory in two or three months. She must have had breast implants. It was complete absurdity. Sam and Ivory were always calling for money, claiming they needed it to meet the mortgage and survive, and now Ivory was sporting silicone breasts.

"If you won't tell me anything else, at least tell me why you're dressed like this," Lara said, her eyes narrowing. "And when did you get your breasts enlarged?"

"Fuck you, Lara. How do you want me to dress? Like you? You've never known how to dress. And look at your stupid hair. No wonder you can't get a man. You're jealous. That's what Sam says. He says you've always been jealous of me."

Now Lara was really angry, about to explode. Ivory was immature and ignorant, but this time she had gone too far. She simply couldn't take it anymore. "You've taken money from me," she screamed, her body trembling, "refused to let me see Josh, and you—you've pissed it away on cosmetic surgery and God knows what else."

"You're a bitch, Lara. You're cold now. You're not the same person you used to be. . . . You're heartless. You've turned to stone." Ivory walked over until she was only inches from her sister's face, her breath foul with beer and cigarettes. "I don't give a shit if I ever see you again," she said. "How do you feel about that? Why don't you stick that up your judicial rear?"

Lara stood there with her hands at her sides. She was beyond anger. The whole day rose up to meet her. Everything she did, everywhere she turned, she met hostility and rage. But this was her home and this was her flesh and blood. "Ivory, let's stop this . . ." Lara paused. Someone was knocking on the door.

Ivory's face became animated. She raced over and released the dead bolts, waiting for Lara to turn off the alarm. After Lara had done so, she flung the door open and leaped into her husband's arms. "Oh, Sam," she said. Then she took his hand and led him outside to the doorstep, where she started whispering and gesturing.

Lara strained to hear, but it was impossible. She

walked over to close the door, hoping she could go back to bed and get at least a few hours' sleep before the sun came up.

Sam Perkins stepped over the threshold. Lara back-stepped into the house.

He had dark, unkempt hair that fell over his collar and forehead and a thick black mustache. Even though he was only in his thirties, his face was heavily lined from hard living and years of drinking. He was dressed in a wrinkled red polo shirt and faded Levis, with about fifteen keys dangling from a metal clamp attached to his belt. He could have been handsome in a rugged, masculine way. To Ivory, he was handsome. But the only way anyone would agree with her was to see him in the dim light of a bar with about five drinks under their belt. To Lara, he was the scum of the earth. Even though she was several feet away, she could smell the alcohol. He put his hands together and cracked his knuckles, causing his biceps to bulge and his tattoo to appear from under the sleeve of his shirt. It said EASY RIDER. There was nothing easy about this man.

"I don't want you upsetting my wife anymore," he said, the words hissing between clenched teeth, stained from tobacco. "We've had about all we want of you. You may be a big-shot judge, but you ain't a fucking thing as far as we're concerned. Here," he said, throwing a handful of bills on the floor. "There's your payment. You happy now?"

"Get out of my house," Lara said. "And don't ever ask me to cover for you again, Sam, because I won't." She glanced at the bills on the carpet. Most of them were ones. He owed her over a hundred thousand dollars, and he had just paid her back maybe ten—she was counting—no, twelve dollars of it.

Ivory was standing right next to him now, one arm flung around his shoulder, her silicone breasts spilling over the cut of the tank top. "We don't need your money," she said proudly. "We're going to have plenty of our own. Soon too, real soon."

Lara blinked back tears. She couldn't possibly let this man see what he had done to her family, to her sister. Before her mother had died, Lara had promised she would look after Ivory, make certain that she and Josh were taken care of. But they were out of her hands now.

"Get out of my house," she said again, her voice firm.

"Come on, baby," Sam said to Ivory. "Let's let the old maid get her beauty sleep. Way she looks, she sure as hell needs it."

He yanked on Ivory's arm and she followed him to the door. Then she glanced back over her shoulder at Lara. For a moment their eyes met and the clock stopped ticking. Lara glimpsed the sadness in her sister's eyes. She saw Ivory's lips move, but no words came out. It was as if she could see the past projected on her sister's face, both of them fresh-faced little girls walking home from school together. Sam's laughter was time-delayed; it burst through the silence and the clock was ticking again, faster than before. Then the door slammed shut and they were gone.

chapter 3

Three weeks had passed since Thomas Henderson had walked out of the Orange County Jail a few hours after Lara's ruling. But he hadn't been on the streets long, thank God, she thought now, heading briskly down the corridor to her chambers during morning recess, and as far as they knew, he hadn't raped or killed anyone. This morning Russ Mitchell had called to tell her that Henderson had been institutionalized at Camarillo State Hospital, a state-operated psychiatric facility. Maybe tonight she could sleep instead of thrashing about until one or two o'clock in the morning and then waking at four.

The prosecution's case was still in limbo. They'd dredged up one good lead, a service station attendant who thought he'd seen the victim and Henderson together. But the twenty-year-old man was an extremely poor witness. He couldn't recall the date, the time—was such a stoner that he hardly remembered his own name. They would keep at it; eventually something would surface.

Even though the defendant had signed himself in as a voluntary admission and could walk out anytime he wanted, just knowing he was behind locked doors right now and heavily medicated made them all breathe a sigh of relief.

The press had been horrendous. In the local papers, the officers had been raked over the coals and had taken the brunt of the responsibility. They were both under suspension from the force and facing prosecution. In years past, the case might have folded, but the officers would've never been held to answer for their actions. Things were different today. This incident had fallen on the heels of the Rodney King fiasco, a notorious case of police brutality that had ignited riots in south central Los Angeles—angry crowds burning down one building after another, random and senseless acts of violence. Some speculated the area would never be rebuilt.

Lara looked up and saw Irene Murdock headed in her direction. "Are you coming to see me?" she said.

"Lara," Irene said, trying to contain a chuckle, "I'm going to give this to you, but only if you take it with a grain of salt and have a nice laugh over it."

Lara looked at the other woman's hands. She was holding a thin newspaper. Lara looked closer and saw it was the *National Tattler.* "What is it?" Lara reached out, but Irene pulled the paper away.

"Promise me you won't get all worked up over this, okay?"

"I promise. Let me see it, Irene." She did. The headline was a story about a horse with a human head. It was the strangest-looking thing Lara had ever seen. "Pretty funny. Is this what you want me to see?"

"Page three, Lara," Irene said, the smile disappearing.

On the third page was Lara's picture with the caption: "JUDGE RELEASES VIOLENT RAPIST AND MURDERER ON TECHNICALITY." "Gee," Lara said facetiously, "I'm a star. I'll go home and put this right in my scrapbook." But it wasn't really funny. This was a national publication. Even if it was made up of sensationalism and ridiculous stories, everyone read it at one time or another.

Irene pushed a strand of hair off her forehead and touched her friend on the shoulder. "I guess I shouldn't have even brought this to your attention, honey. I don't know why, but I thought it was funny. I mean, the whole paper is ridiculous. Look at the cover story. Who would believe anything these people say?"

Lara looked up into those deep green eyes. "Well, it is true, Irene. I did release him on a technicality."

"Hey," Irene said, stepping close and draping an arm around Lara, "we all release people on technicalities at one time or the other. You're not still agonizing over this case, are you?"

"No, no," Lara said softly, smiling at her friend. "Thanks for showing the paper to me, Irene. It's better than having people gang up on me at the grocery store."

Lara stood with the smile glued on her face until Irene had turned and headed back down the corridor. Then the smile evaporated and she too headed back to her office.

She was in between trials, something that seldom occurred. With the dismissal of the Henderson case, her calendar had been left wide open, and the presiding judge, sixty-seven-year-old Leo Evergreen, had zapped her into the felony arraignment calendar for vacation relief. Everyone called it the zoo.

Walking by Phillip, she gave him a nod. He had earphones on his head and was typing on his word processor. At least she thought he was typing. She took a few steps back and glanced at the screen. Once she had found him playing video games. But no, he was typing something. What, she didn't know. Probably his homework from law school.

Once she was inside, she slammed her door. It was a satisfying feeling. Besides, Phillip couldn't even hear it. Collapsing in her chair, she felt her buttocks slide into the hole. The least the county could do for me would be to buy me a cushion, she thought. Then she let the frustration go. It was counterproductive. So she wouldn't go to the grocery store for a few weeks until the newspaper article was cold. Irene was right. The article wasn't something to get upset about. All she ever bought anyway at the store were TV dinners and things that could be heated in the microwave. She didn't cook. She'd never learned how and simply didn't have the inclination. She ate simply to survive. She could live on hamburgers and nachos without a second thought and never gain a pound. Maybe that was why her ex-husband had divorced her, she thought now, because he had wanted a home-cooked meal.

Everyone else might go on coffee breaks during these recesses, but most of the judges worked. They pored over briefs, motions, read probation reports, returned phone calls, conferred with attorneys. If they were fast, they could go to the bathroom. She looked around her paneled office at the bookcases crammed with law books. Even though they had as yet to replace her chair, the office itself had been recently redecorated and was actually nicer than her home in many ways, with new mauve carpeting, two studded leather chairs facing her desk, a conference table off to the side in one corner where she sometimes worked when she was in the midst of a big trial. She had to rely on artificial light since there were no windows. She hated overheads and glare. On her desk were two matching lamps with green lucite shades that she had purchased herself. They gave the room a different look, an almost surreal atmosphere, casting shadows in the corners and across the faces of those who sat in front of her. Instead of looking like an office, it looked like a study or library in a stately home.

She opened the enormous file on her desk and then closed it. She was preparing herself for a trial that she would begin next Monday, but before she did anything, she had to pay her bills. She took out her checkbook and thought about the Adams case. It was another thorn in the side of the criminal justice system. As a senior district attorney, she had handled only the most serious cases. She really preferred it that way. When things didn't go right, however, as a D.A., there were a lot of whipping boys. Sometimes she'd cursed the judge. Now she was the judge.

The only person she had to vent her frustrations on was Leo Evergreen. He assigned all the cases. He was, in effect, her boss. But the man was the essence of professional perfection, his judgment impeccable, his knowledge seemingly endless. Getting angry and shaking her fist at Leo Evergreen was seldom justified. Most of his case assignments were well thought out and fair. If he advised her on something, his advice was solid and almost always on the money.

In actuality, Leo Evergreen was one of the most intelligent men Lara had ever known. His long-term management of the Orange county superior court had earned it the lowest percentile of judicial error in the state. The higher courts thought he was a god. He could have easily won a position on the appellate court, or any other higher court, for that matter, yet he preferred to remain here. From what she could tell, he was firmly rooted in his little domain, a creature of habit. He had also told Lara one day that he would never move from Orange County. He considered it one of the most beautiful places to live in the world. In many ways Lara agreed with him. There was nothing like it.

Orange County was south of the Los Angeles city limits. The courthouse was located on Civic Center Drive in Santa Ana, not far from Anaheim and Disneyland, the crest of the county. Once into Irvine, Newport, Laguna Beach, or Mission Viejo, the population was made up of WASPs and yuppies, wall-to-wall BMWs and those little Mercedes Benzes, the ones for baby professionals who wanted to show everyone they were on their way to the big time.

Past Mission Viejo was the quaint fishing village of Dana Point, right on the ocean with a lovely marina; farther south were San Juan Capistrano and San Clemente, authentically Spanish. San Juan Capistrano was where the swallows returned each year to the mission. A few years ago, they hadn't returned. Lara thought the swallows knew what all the people building huge homes there didn't realize: Los Angeles was sprawling outward, the crime following.

Miles of uncluttered beaches stretched beneath towering glass and metal structures housing high-tech companies. Orange County was only an hour drive by freeway to Los Angeles, but the air was cooler and cleaner here, the breezes full of the salty scent of the sea. Crime, street gangs, and crack were escalating in Santa Ana, Anaheim, and Costa Mesa, but elsewhere criminal activity was still moderate. People wore shorts and polo shirts and drove convertibles. This was California suburbia at its best.

Even though Lara was in chambers, she was still wearing her robe. She liked her black robe. It was a symbol of justice. When she slipped it over her clothes every morning, usually a simple white shirt and black skirt, she felt the weight of it, the yoke of responsibility she'd undertaken. She wasn't in this position for the money or the status. The satisfaction, the sense of accomplishment, the feeling that she was making a valuable and necessary contribution to society, were her motivations. She was idealistic, stubborn, compulsive. Some people thought she was a fool, clinging to values that no longer existed, seeking reasonable and fair solutions in an unreasonable and cruel environment.

They were probably right.

She slapped the stack of bills on top of the mounds of paper already covering the top of her desk, and started adding the columns of figures in her checkbook on an electronic calculator. Her salary was ninety-nine thousand per annum. In the beginning it had seemed like a fortune, but with taxes, retirement, insurance, it wasn't really that much. Most families relied on dual incomes while Lara was solo. And this was also Southern California, where the cost of living was particularly high. A decent house could run as high as three hundred thousand for something that would sell in the Midwest for eighty or ninety, and of course, in L.A. everyone drove a nice car, even if they lived in a shack. It was hard to plead poverty when making a hundred grand a year, but Lara's standard of living was far from the lap of luxury. Besides, she had always been a civil service employee. Most of the other judges who lived in spacious houses in the best of neighborhoods and had second homes in Palm Springs had left thriving private practices and amassed fat nest eggs before they took to the bench. Lara had been saddled with student loans from college and law school that she'd only satisfied a few years before. Her parents had been simple people. She had paid for her own education.

Thumbing through her checkbook, she saw all the checks made out to Ivory over the past two years and winced. She could kiss the savings account goodbye, she thought. No need for an IRA this year. She had also counted on the payments Sam had contracted to make on the loan she'd made for him to buy the pawnshop. She'd never see that money again.

A thought suddenly crossed her mind, and she punched numbers into the phone with her pen, getting Judge Evergreen's secretary. "Is he in, Louise? This is Lara Sanderstone."

"Yes, just a moment, Judge Sanderstone."

"Lara," an older male voice said, "I was just thinking about you. Why don't you come down?"

"Uh, Leo, I just wanted to call and see how you were feeling," she said in soft tones. "I heard you were out last week with the flu."

"Well, that's very nice of you to think of me," he said. "I'm feeling much better, actually. Come to my chambers and we'll talk."

Before she had a chance to tell him that she was due back in court in less than ten minutes, he was gone. She grabbed a handful of case files for the afternoon session and rushed out of the office.

"Here," Phillip said, "give me those and I'll take them down in the cart with the others."

"No," she told him. "I've got to review them." Juggling the cumbersome files in her arms, she opened one and began reading as she walked.

Although D.A.'s, public defenders, and clerks roamed around in these halls behind the courts, no one else was allowed back here and the area was sealed off with closed-circuit television monitors and manned security behind locked doors. Too many times defendants went crazy and came looking for judges with a loaded gun. Still walking and reading, she glanced up and saw the placard on the door and stepped inside. Evergreen's secretary nodded and she entered his chambers.

At sixty-seven, Evergreen was well preserved. He evidently worked at it. His hair was dyed. What color he had wanted it to be really didn't matter, because it had turned out a funny artificial shade of red. It was almost blood red, but not new blood. More like old blood that tends to darken. His face was soft and fleshy. Never was there even a hint of a beard. In some places his skin had a sheen to it as though he lathered it each morning with expensive wrinkle creams.

His lips were full and his eyes small and wide-set, a watery gray. Behind those eyes was a great legal mind, a mind Lara coveted.

"How do you stand on the Adams matter?" Evergreen said. He didn't stand but swiveled his high-backed leather chair to face her. "This is an important case, Lara. There's been a lot of press."

"Press," she said. "I've had enough of that for a lifetime." She didn't want to get into a discussion of the tabloid article even though she was certain Evergreen had heard of it. "No one's requested a continuance yet. It should go off as planned." A tremendous amount of coordination and organization went into Evergreen's position as presiding judge. This required real finesse, for attorneys were known for delays, and delays clogged down the system like wads of toilet paper in a toilet.

Glancing at her watch, she knew she had to be back in court any minute. "I'm preparing now. I thought I might review it with you before we open next week. When's a good time?"

They settled on a day and time, and Lara started to leave when Leo began speaking again. "There's a case on your calendar this afternoon. Hold on a moment," he said, moving a few papers around on his desk while she waited, making sure they were all perfectly aligned in a neat little stack in one corner.

Unlike Lara's desk, Evergreen's was so neat she could actually see the polished surface. He was a perfectionist, and every item on his desk had a designated place. According to Phillip, he didn't allow his secretary to touch it. He even dusted and polished it himself.

Evergreen was speaking, "Let me confirm the name. Here it is: Packard Cummings. The charge is possession of a concealed weapon."

"Yes," Lara said, wondering if old Packard had been conceived in the backseat of a car. With a name like that, he had to have been. She'd seen the file on her walk down but hadn't as yet reviewed it.

Leo continued in that monotone of his, so low she had to strain to hear him. He did that on purpose. He wanted her to work, have to listen closely. "We've been contacted by a local law enforcement agency about this individual. They informed us this man's been working for them as a confidential informant on a very large narcotics case. They alluded that this might be the reason he was armed. If I'm not mistaken, he's appearing on a bail review. As a courtesy, they've asked that we release him on his own recognizance."

"Just a minute, Leo. I have his file right here." She juggled the files in her arms, setting the others on the floor and dropping to a chair. Flipping through the top sheets to the computer printout of the man's criminal record, she quickly scanned it and looked up. "My God, Leo, this man has a five-page rap sheet of extremely serious offenses. He's been sentenced twice for rape, was suspected of stabbing another inmate at Chino, and he's even on parole. The district attorney's made a note right in the file that they intend to prosecute him as a career criminal. He's a member of the Aryan Brotherhood." This was a white-supremacist prison gang, basically neo-Nazis, extremely violent. "We can't release him O.R. even if he's working for the CIA."

Evergreen was silent. His mouth fell open and he breathed heavily, something he did often when he was thinking. Finally he said, the words barely distinguishable, "Well, of course, that's your decision, but we always try to cooperate with law enforcement."

Lara bit a corner of her lip, sucking it right into her mouth and sinking her teeth into it. One of the reasons she had fought for this appointment was to make independent rulings, decisions she felt were fair and just, but that kept men like this one off the streets. She started to speak up, but visions of another stint in the zoo should the Adams matter be continued flashed in her mind. "Fine," she said, pushing the words out of her mouth. "I'll grant him O.R."

"Very good, then," he said, his mind shifting to something else right before her eyes. "You handled yourself quite well with that Henderson matter, Lara. How is the prosecution's case developing?"

"Not good, Leo. Not good at all. But I'll keep you posted."

Lara snatched the files off the floor and headed down the corridor. As to the man he wanted released O.R., Lara thought she had probably overreacted. She was a diehard. The man's parole agent should put a hold on him anyway, so the issue of bail would be redundant.

She wasn't looking where she was going and ran right into Phillip on his way to the court. The files fell from her arms and scattered all over the carpeted hallway.

"I'm sorry," Lara said, looking at the mess she'd made and glancing at her watch. She bent down and picked up a few papers and tossed them into the cart. For a few moments, her eyes searched Phillip's face. Dark circles were etched under his soft eyes, and he seemed unusually tense. She noted a slight tremor in his hand as he picked up the remaining file off the floor. "Are you feeling all right, Phillip?" she asked, wondering if he was coming down with the flu.

"Oh," he said, standing. "No, I'm fine. Why do you ask?"

For the past two years Lara had made every attempt

to get to know this young man, but she had as yet to break the ice. "I just thought . . . I mean, you look tired."

"Law school," he said, looking away, clearing his throat. "It's not easy when you have a full-time job."

"Hang in there," she said, giving him a warm smile.

Following him down the hall, Lara unclipped the bow at the base of her neck and pulled the unruly strands back before she snapped it into place again. What she had to do was get on Leo's A-list, become part of the inner circle of judges that ruled the county. Irene had made the team years ago. She and Evergreen were close friends, but Lara was still on the outside. Then, she thought, she could make any kind of rulings she wanted.

"Get me a fucking beer," Sam Perkins yelled from the living room, "and put up my TV dinner."

"Get your own beer," Josh yelled back from the kitchen, his own dinner already in the oven. "What do you think I am, your slave?"

"You little punk. You're nothing but a skinny little punk. Get me that beer and fix my fucking supper, boy, or I'll beat the ever living daylights outa you."

"Go ahead," Josh said, just as his stepfather rose from the big easy chair in front of the television and headed in his direction, his face a mask of drunken rage. "Hit me. Go ahead."

His stepfather met his challenge and punched him right in the face with his fist. Then he pulled back and punched him several more times, connecting with his cheek, his forehead, the strength of his blows almost knocking the boy out of the chair. Suddenly he stopped and looked at Josh. He knew just how far he could go. He didn't want the school reporting Josh's injuries to the authorities. He had other ways to punish him. Ways that didn't show.

He forced Josh to sit at the table and eat the TV dinner he'd made for himself. "Since you're such a hot shot, too good to make your dad something to eat, I want you to eat the whole thing, even the fucking tray. Eat it," he demanded. "Now!"

"Don't you ever say you're my dad," Josh blurted out, blood trickling from his nose where Sam had slugged him. "My dad's dead and you're nothing. You're a bum, a loser, a pervert."

"Eat it," Sam said, laughing. He reached over and grabbed Josh's hair and shoved his face into the TV dinner. "Eat the foil, the tray, the whole damn thing, you wise-ass puny punk."

Josh's entire body was shaking with anger and humiliation, his face smeared with mashed potatoes and gravy. "I can't eat the foil. It'll kill me if I eat it. Please, Sam, I'm sorry."

"You ain't sorry. You're nothing but a spoiled pussy boy, a momma's boy." He leaned over and yelled at the top of his lungs. "Eat that fucking foil. You ain't getting up from that table until there's nothing left of that dinner."

Josh ate it.

He ripped the foil into small pieces and began swallowing them along with chunks of the food, tears streaming down his cheeks. He would run away . . . never come back. He missed his father. Since his mother had married Sam Perkins, their life had become a nightmare of humiliation so awful that he wouldn't even tell his closest friends.

Sam had returned to the chair in the living room. He yelled back at Josh, "If I come in there and see one speck of foil, I'll put your fucking little pecker in the garbage disposal."

Josh tore off another piece and ate it, listening to Sam's laughter from the other room. With his eyes glued on Sam's back, he grabbed what was left of the foil tray and shoved it under the waistband of his jeans to dispose of later. This was his home, had always been his home for as long as he could remember. If he ran away, where would he go, how could he survive? Before his father died, the house had been filled with laughter and the wonderful aromas of his mother's home-cooked meals. But in the past two years she'd almost completely stopped cooking, and she'd certainly stopped cleaning. Now the house was a pigsty. Beer cans and newspapers were thrown everywhere. Dishes were piled in the sink. Every night his mother went out, always telling Josh some stupid story about a club meeting, spending time with a sick friend. Tonight she'd told him she was going to the PTA meeting at his school. It was Tuesday night. Josh knew the PTA meeting wasn't until next Wednesday and his mother had never gone to one in her life.

Night after night she would leave him there, alone in the house with Sam, with nothing to eat but TV dinners. She thought he didn't know what was going on, thought he was still a dumb little kid. But she was wrong.

He knew everything.

Chapter 4

After the Henderson case had been disposed of, Benjamin England had called and asked Lara to dinner. Fluttering with schoolgirl excitement, she had rushed out and bought a new dress, got her hair cut, even fiddled with her makeup so she could be as attractive as possible. And the relationship was developing nicely. Tonight was their fifth date. They'd just finished a lovely dinner at a fine restaurant, sipped a sweet red wine over a pale pink tablecloth and fine china, chatting about books they had read and people they both knew.

"Why did you take Henderson's case?" Lara suddenly asked him. "You haven't taken a criminal case in years." When they had first gone out, Lara had issued a no-shop-talk policy, but they were running out of other things to talk about. She'd heard all about the sad days of his wife's illness, her death from breast cancer, heard all about his son at Stanford. Her own personal revelations had consumed no more than thirty minutes of conversation before being exhausted. Her marriage had lasted six months; she couldn't stretch it that far.

"To be honest, his mother is a client of mine and she asked me to represent him. Not only did she ask me, but she paid me. I feel sorry for the woman. She built a successful business, a chain of small hotels, but her son is a fucked-up lunatic. Besides, I love criminal law."

"I see," Lara said. "Didn't it bother you to know you were involved in releasing a dangerous man, a probable killer?"

England swirled his wine in his glass and gazed at Lara with those magnificent eyes. He sat forward, leaning over the table. "Do you doubt for one moment that even the public defender would have pushed for dismissal and suppression of that confession? Those cops beat him until he collapsed. They broke his arm. They . . ."

Lara nodded in agreement. England was right. Even though the P.D. had let it slide and the defendant was so whacko that he didn't realize his rights had been violated, it would have all come to light in the end. They were all just doing their jobs. England had done his well; the cops had not.

"I can't really believe you even asked me that," he said, raising his eyebrows in a questioning expression. The waiters were yanking off tablecloths and setting up for the next day. They would have to leave soon.

"It's just sad for the family when something like this goes down," Lara said. "I feel for them, you know."

He was a little abrupt, somewhat shocked at her emotional involvement. "Then you might be in the wrong profession," he said.

Lara smiled. "Just a little feminine regression. I love my position, but that doesn't mean it's easy. Anyway, I think they're about to throw us out."

England draped an arm around her walking to his Mercedes in the parking lot. When he suggested they continue the evening at his sprawling home in the Tustin hills, Lara eagerly agreed. Five dates was a respectable amount of time. It was obvious where the evening was heading.

He had thick candles burning around the large Jacuzzi; two chilled glasses and a bottle of wine were set on the stone ledge. Soft music filtered out of two stereo speakers designed to look like boulders positioned among the greenery. It was overcast and the air was heavy and moist. He slipped her sweater off her shoulders with thin, tapered fingers. She inhaled his scent, something musky and masculine. She really didn't need the wine; she was already intoxicated by the moment—ready, willing.

"Look at you," he said, "even your shoulders are beautiful. I don't know why you always cover them up." He bent down and kissed each one, moving his mouth to her neck and tugging on her sweater until her breasts were exposed, encased in her bra. He slipped his hands behind her and unsnapped the hook. Tossing the flimsy bra to a dark corner of the patio, he quickly seized her breasts in both hands and squeezed them like lemons.

"Don't squeeze too hard," she whispered in his ear. "They're sensitive. Be gentle."

He ignored her and locked his mouth on one and started sucking, moving his teeth over the nipple like he wanted to take a bite. She unzipped his pants and let her hands slide over his hips, pulling him closer to her body.

"God, you feel so good," he said in a raspy voice. "I want you."

She could tell; he was eager, his eyes heavy-lidded with lust. His erection was pushing against, her, strong, solid, his hand making its way up the inside of her thigh and ending up between her legs on the crotch of her panty hose. "Are we going to get in the water?"

"What water?"

"Your neighbors will see us. Let's go inside."

"No one will see us. I want you here." The panty hose was down and she was exposed from the waist up, her sweater being swiftly removed and tossed like her bra. He groped under her skirt, his fingers probing inside her. She moaned, trying to let the pleasure take her, but then she jerked away.

"What's wrong?" he mumbled, undaunted, his breath hot and fast, his fingers back again, more insistent than ever.

"You have a hangnail."

He didn't reply and removed her skirt, letting it fall to the ground. "Bend over. I want to take you right here."

"Protection . . ." she said. This was the nineties: safe sex, condoms.

"I have it," he said. His arms were already turning her around, and he moved in close behind her, pushing gently but firmly on her back until she bent over and placed her hands on the cool stone surrounding the Jacuzzi. In seconds she felt him push himself inside her, and her body began to respond. The strokes were long and smooth. Her mouth fell open and she moved with him, almost in time with the music, a soulful Kenny G tune, while her long dark hair tumbled over her head and brushed the ledge, several strands floating on the water. She tried to shut out everything but the feeling, the sounds, the excitement. It was going to be good, and she needed it desperately. They would make mad, passionate love all night, and she would sleep in his arms, warm and secure, waking to make love again in the early morning hours before the sun came up. They would take vacations to Las Hades and Palm Springs and spend Christmas and Thanksgiving together. She would buy a string bikini and a dozen off-the-shoulder slinky black dresses with hems four inches above her knees. His hands gripped her around the waist and the pace quickened. She began panting with mounting desire and anticipation of the sun-filled days ahead.

Then it stopped.

He didn't cry out or moan or sigh. He just stopped. She waited, thinking it would continue but she could tell it was over. Inside her body he was retracting, shrinking.

"That was wonderful," he panted, pulling her to a standing position and kissing the back of her neck. In seconds the panting stopped. "Want to get in the Jacuzzi now?"

She stuttered, "I . . . oh, we could . . ." She watched as he stepped into the swirling water and reached for his wineglass. It was no use suggesting that they go inside to continue this in the bedroom, continue it to the point where she too could enjoy it. Mission accomplished, she thought. Case closed. Another notch on the old belt, already heavily notched with all the willing secretaries and law clerks and divorcees that had gone before her. He was leaning his head back with his eyes closed as if she were already gone.

"Boy, today was a bitch. I'm dead. One of my clients came storming in today threatening to sue me because he has to pay fifty grand to his ex-wife. The nerve of these assholes. Never fails to amaze me. Without me, he would have paid a hundred grand. Believe me, if it weren't for the money, all my cases would be criminal. But the crooks can't pay, so . . ." He sipped his wine, opening his eyes momentarily and then closing them again. The other wineglass remained empty. He made no move to fill it.

Lara stood there naked, her arms wrapped around her breasts. It was always chilly at night in Southern California. She glanced around her. The yard was enclosed with a white picket fence—charming, probably his wife's idea, but not capable of affording them privacy. She imagined the neighbors watching them through the slats of the fence, looking at her standing there exposed. Had they seen her bending over the jacuzzi a few minutes before?

"I think I'll go home now," she told him. "I had a long day too." She started searching for her clothes. Some of them were wet, having been tossed in puddles of water splashed from the Jacuzzi. She picked up her soggy bra and shoved it into her purse.

"Now?" he said, his eyes springing open, the muscles in his face, previously relaxed, tense. "You want me to drive you home now? Right now?"

"Well, you said you were tired. The evening's over." She didn't look at him. She was stepping into her skirt.

"Just sleep here. I can drive you to the office in the morning. I'm too tired to drive anywhere right now." He leaned back in the Jacuzzi and closed his eyes again.

She was frustrated and angry. "I said I'm ready to

go home, Benjamin. Will you please have the common courtesy to drive me?"

"Can't you take a cab?" he said without opening his eyes.

Impulsively she kicked the empty glass into the water and exploded. "You're an asshole, a self-centered asshole." She stomped into the house and called a cab, waiting on the doorstep until it arrived. So much for this fantasy, she told herself. The cab pulled up and she limbed in the backseat, giving the driver her address.

Thirty minutes later the cab pulled up to her modest ranch house in Irvine, a far cry from England's palatial spread. Lara was sound asleep in the backseat, and the cabbie had to wake her. Then she had to search the littered contents of her purse for enough money to pay him, dumping out all the change and counting it out into his palm.

The house was dark. She had her shoes in her hands, her feet were killing her, and she now had a throbbing headache. Postcoitus syndrome, she thought. Postnothing syndrome was more like it. She was about to put the key in the door when she saw a small card stuck into the slit. She pulled it out and tried to read it, but it was impossible in the dark. Dropping her shoes on the porch, she unlocked the door and flipped on the light.

Her heart started racing and she almost screamed. Quickly she glanced at the card and saw it was from the sheriff's department. She'd been burglarized. The police had responded around seven-thirty when her alarm had gone off, only a few minutes after Benjamin had picked her up.

Her eyes took in the damage. Everything she owned was dumped in the middle of the floor, and the place was a total shambles. Even the cushions on her new sofa were slit, and the stuffing was scattered everywhere like thick balls of snow.

She just stood and stared. Although a residential burglary probably occurred every second in Los Angeles, she had never been hit. She felt violated. They had gone through her things. Her head was pounding so violently that she knew she had to sit down. But she couldn't disturb anything. She went to the garage, hoping the doorknob wasn't the only one in the house with fingerprints, and called the sheriff's office from the car phone in her Jaguar. Then she hit the garage door opener and sat in the dark until they arrived.

An hour had passed. Lara stood on the back porch with one of the police officers while evidence people were still working inside the house. One of them was hammering a piece of plywood over the broken window where the intruder had entered. Lara was picking dead white roses off a rose bush, oblivious to the thorns. "What?" she said, glancing up at the officer, barely able to hear him over the racket. "You really think it was more than a burglary?" It was three o'clock in the morning, and she was so tired she couldn't think.

"Well, nothing was taken of value and the place was ripped apart." The officer was a well-groomed man in his late thirties. His uniform was tight across his midsection, almost too small. She could see the outline of his bullet-proof vest. "Not many burglars do this type of damage and walk off without taking the TV, VCR, stereo, or something. Just doesn't make sense." He had a bag of peanuts squeezed in his pocket and was cracking them open and tossing them into his mouth. "Want a peanut?" he said, offering one to Lara.

"No, thanks," she said. "Then what were they after, what was the point?"

"How do I know?" he said nonchalantly. He had a handful of shells now and shoved them into his other pocket rather than toss them on Lara's porch. "Looked kind of vicious to me. Like maybe someone was looking for you, didn't find you, and went a little bonkers in there. You know, cushions slit with a knife . . . stuff like that. The only time I see a crime scene like this one is in a drug deal. When they're looking for the stash."

Lara was deep in thought. Jessica Van Horn's boyfriend came to mind and his hurled threats in the courtroom. With Henderson safely locked away, there was only her or England to strike back at. Could the boy have followed her from the courthouse one day and come here to act on his threats? She wrapped her arms around her body and shivered. A young man like that, so deeply in love, so devastated by his girlfriend's death—it was possible.

"What should I do?" she said.

"Anyone got a beef to pick with you?" He wasn't looking at her. He was looking up at the sky. Some of the fog had lifted and he could see the stars. "Didn't you handle the Henderson case?"

So, she was notorious. "Yes . . ." Of course, she had tried hundreds of people, both as a D.A. and as a judge. If a person wanted to count her enemies, they'd have to have a lot of free time.

"Judge Sanderstone, if I were you . . . you know," the officer continued, "I'd find somewhere else to stay for a while. At least until we process the evidence and see what we can find. I'd hate to come out here one night and find you cut up like your sofa." He had finished the peanuts, and he dusted his hands off. He was deadly serious, his eyes on Lara's face. Then his vision drifted and Lara realized she wasn't wearing a bra. With the sheer sweater she had on, her nipples were protruding. His eyes lingered on her chest, and he took a few steps closer. Lara stepped back, putting her arms around her chest again.

"I have an alarm. I even have a panic button."

"Yeah," he said. "Well, those are worth jack shit. See, how it works is the alarm company calls us when they get around to it, and then by the time we get here, the perp's long gone. I'd lay low if I were you. I personally think someone's got a hard-on for you. They'll probably come back."

"Great," Lara snapped, jerking her head to the side in anger. That's all she needed—some off-the-wall lunatic stalking her.

"Can I go inside now?" She glanced around the yard, all the tall trees and greenery. Even with the officer beside her, she was afraid. They might still be out there, hiding. They could have a gun and start shooting any second. Even before this had happened, she sometimes got frightened in the middle of the night, hearing strange noises, letting her mind wander. She handled so many heinous crimes that they came back to haunt her, always in the twilight hours before dawn. She sometimes had nightmares of autopsy pictures, bloody crime scenes, imagined her own image in the place of the victims.

Lara didn't know what to do or where to go. "Don't you think I'm safe here tonight? I mean, why would he come back the same night?" They went into the house. Lara stopped and made sure the sliding glass door was locked.

The other men had loaded up their equipment and left. The officer was eager to leave as well, and he moved toward the door. "Probably won't tonight. But if I were you, I'd get out of here by tomorrow and keep a low profile."

"Thanks," Lara said. Once he was gone, she locked the front door and slid the dead bolt in place. Like she could really keep a low profile. She was beyond logic at this point, into the area of absurdity. I can go to work tomorrow, she thought, and wear a hood over my head. The unknown judge, they could call her.

She staggered to the bed, certain she would be asleep in minutes. She was wrong. A dog barked, and she jumped, her heart racing. A car backfired and she leaped out of the bed and fell flat on her face on the carpet. By the time the gray light of dawn filtered into the bedroom, she had decided to move out.

She went through the day in a haze of exhaustion. It was Tuesday and her night to teach at the University of Irvine. Several times she picked up the phone to cancel and then decided against it. She was going to check into a motel that night until she could figure out what to do. I might as well teach my class, she decided, and then hopefully I'll sleep through the night.

The evening was pretty disappointing. She taught a class on field officer legal liability, more or less for students majoring in police science and aiming at a career in law enforcement. She'd offered to teach the class, thinking it might be a way to stop police brutality before it even started, telling these soon to be cops what could happen if they stepped out of bounds. Tonight, only about six students showed up. Right after the Henderson matter, the class had been packed—standing room only. The students had wanted to know exactly what was going to happen to the arresting officers. Would they be sued by the defendant? Could they actually go to jail? Would they ever get their jobs back? Tonight, she thought, they must be studying for a big test in another subject.

After the last student left, Lara headed to the computer lab to pick up her friend and fellow instructor. Emmet Daniels suffered from Lou Gehrig's disease, or ALS, amyotrophic lateral sclerosis. The disease caused disintegration of the nerve cells in the spinal cord and the section of the brain that regulates voluntary muscle control. It doesn't affect the mind, thank God, Lara thought, peering into the lab and seeing the small man sitting in a wheelchair before a computer terminal. Emmet's genius was renowned, particularly in the area of computer science. UCI was extremely fortunate to acquire him, although he did require a teaching assistant to handle the class. Every year his ability to talk diminished. Soon he might not be able to speak at all and would have to rely on a voice synthesizer. His actual profession was designing computer software for major corporations across the country. Except on Tuesdays, when he taught his class, Emmet worked in his condominium not far from the courthouse. A heavyset woman who lived in his complex drove him to the campus every week, and Lara drove him home.

For a minute she just stood there and watched him, recalling the day she had met him three years before.

They had both been attending their first faculty meeting and ended up sitting right next to each other. Emmet had struck up a conversation about the death penalty once he'd learned that Lara was a district attorney. He had such an analytical mind that she had followed him to his car and ended up in a heated conversation for almost an hour. Back then he had been in a wheelchair, but his ability to talk had as yet to be impaired and he was a ferocious debater. Over the past three years she had sadly witnessed this devastating disease consume him. But never once had she heard a complaint.

"Ready," she said, bracing herself in the doorway.

He hit a button on his wheelchair and it spun around. His glasses were so thick she could barely see his eyes. They were magnified many times over—large milky orbs that seemed to hold all the mystery of the universe. Although they had really never discussed his age, Lara thought Emmet was in his early thirties.

"Yes," he said. "I'm . . . ready. Tired . . . tonight."

The longer the day, the more strenuous it became for him to talk. Most of the time he spoke in short, choppy sentences, his eyes drifting here and there uncontrollably. When they were in his lab or his home, however, he used the computer, tapping out rapid-fire messages faster than Lara could read, using a metal-cage type of device that he slipped onto his head, allowing him to use a pen instead of his weakened fingers.

He already knew about the Henderson case. He knew about all her cases. Lara loved talking to him. Not only was he brilliant and sensitive, completely logical, but he was a great listener. Possibly his disease was partly responsible, yet Lara was certain he would have been a great listener anyway. He not only listened, he weighed each word. She filled him in on the burglary and the officer's belief that she was in danger.

"Doesn't . . . sound good," he said. "Stay . . . with . . . me."

"Oh, Emmet," Lara said, "that's really sweet of you, but I wouldn't impose on you like that. Besides, I really think I'll do what the officer said. You know, lay low for a while, get another place to stay. I'm just going to check into a hotel tonight." She pushed the chair across the campus parking lot to the Jaguar. At the car door, she opened it and helped Emmet into the passenger seat.

She shut the door and folded the wheelchair, placing it in the trunk. Once she was behind the wheel and they were on the road, Emmet turned to her again. "That's . . . silly. Let . . . me return a . . . favor. You've . . . driven me all these months. Stay . . . with . . . me, Lara."

She sighed. Of all the people she knew, Emmet was without a doubt the nicest. "Just tonight, then," she said. "Tomorrow I'll figure something else out."

Once they were inside his condominium, Emmet motioned for her to follow him to his office, and he slipped on the metal contraption and started tapping on the computer. Words flashed across the screen. "There's a place for sale in this development. It's been on the market for over a year, and they're now looking to rent. We can call them and see if they'll allow you to rent it for a few weeks, a month, whatever. It's furnished . . . a model."

"Great," Lara said, leaning over the back of his chair. "That would be perfect." Emmet's complex was only a few blocks from the office, and all she'd have to do is go home and bring over some clothes. "I'm sure this whole thing is nothing anyway. Maybe the burglar didn't take anything because he was scared off by the alarm."

"Better to be safe than sorry," Emmet typed.

They said good night and Lara collapsed in the little twin bed in Emmet's spare bedroom, his huge computer terminal whirring and blinking in the dark a few feet away. He had to have enough equipment in this place, she thought, to launch a rocket. It looked like NASA.

Tomorrow she'd try to rent the vacant condo. Tonight she was safe—the frail little man in the next room her sentinel. His very presence was reassuring even if he didn't have the strength to fend off an attacker. At least she wasn't alone. In minutes she was asleep, the soft tap-tap-tapping of Emmet's pen on the keyboard like a lullaby as he worked far into the night.

Chapter 5

Josh looked up the hill in front of him and sighed, letting his feet slide off the bicycle pedals to the asphalt. Every day he had to ride his ten-speed to school and back. Mornings were the best, because he could coast down the hill, wind whipping his face, and imagine he was on a motorcycle instead of a bike. His father had ridden a motorcycle, a big, roaring 450 Harley. But that didn't matter, he thought, stepping back onto the pedals and beginning the agonizing climb up the mile-long hill leading to his house. He'd never ride a Harley or any other motorcycle, for that matter. Not as long as his mother was still around. Not since the accident and his father's death. He'd be lucky if she let him drive a car in two years when he was sixteen and could get his license.

When he'd gone to the bathroom that morning, the toilet had been filled with blood from the sharp edges of the foil he'd been made to swallow. Crying to his mother wouldn't solve anything, even if he told her what Sam had made him do last night. She wouldn't do anything about Sam. All she talked about was how they were going to move away, how their ship had finally come in, or something dumb like that.

Halfway up the hill, he removed his T-shirt and tied it around his waist. It was already damp with perspiration and he was only halfway home. His mother screamed at him at least once a week because he was so thin. Maybe if she rode six miles a day, two of them up Mount Everest like he did, then she'd be skinny too. Besides, he thought, flexing his muscles by gripping the handlebars and seeing the veins and ridges, he wasn't skinny anyway, he was cut. That's what they called it in the gym—when someone's body fat was so low that skin merely stretched over the interior musculature like a piece of transparent fabric.

Josh had trekked along to the local health club when his father was alive and watched him work out, bench-pressing twice his body weight, grunting and groaning, jostling and trading jokes with the other men. But they couldn't afford to belong to a gym anymore. Josh worked out alone in his room every night, lifting again and again the few weights he'd got for Christmas, dreaming of the day he'd be as strong as his father, strong enough to defend himself against any man.

Even a man like Sam.

Reaching his block, he froze. Sam's truck was in the driveway. Glancing back over his shoulder, he thought of coasting back down the hill and maybe hanging out with one of his friends until dinner. He just couldn't take seeing Sam this early in the day—not with so many hours left, not when he might already be drinking, cursing, and looking for trouble. But Josh knew if he rode down and goofed off until dinner, he'd just have to go back up the killer hill and then he'd be too tired to work out. Better to sneak in through the back door and try to make it to his room before they saw him.

Quietly opening the side gate, he left the ten-speed leaning against the brick wall of the house, pushed aside the two trash cans, removed the key above the ledge, and entered through the door into the kitchen. It was quiet, still. God, he thought with relief, his eyes surveying the room. This was the biggest mess he'd ever seen. Everything was thrown out in the middle of the floor. They'd either had one of their screaming fights where they hurled anything they could find at each other, or they really were packing to move. Sam probably hadn't made the payments on the house and they were being evicted. That's all they needed right now, to be thrown out on the street.

He hated Sam Perkins. There wasn't anything in the entire universe he hated more than he hated Sam Perkins. He didn't care if the whole world blew up in a nuclear explosion as long as Sam Perkins blew up with it. "Pow," he whispered, seeing it in his mind: old Sam's body blown to kingdom come.

He snatched a can of Coke out of the refrigerator and headed to the back of the house. To get to his room he'd have to pass the master bedroom. He prayed the door would be closed. Sam had probably come home early to stick it to his mother. What other reason could there be? He was probably right this minute in there doing disgusting things to his mother in broad daylight. It made Josh want to puke right on the beige carpet and leave it there where Sam would step in it when he came strolling out of the bedroom.

The door wasn't closed. It was open.

Josh glanced inside the bedroom: his lunch rose in his throat and his heart stopped beating. He knew what he was seeing. His mind was screaming, trying to tell him what he knew he was seeing, but he just saw the images without thought or comprehension. Far away someone was screaming—it couldn't be him, it had to be someone else. There was a clawing, scraping wild animal inside his body, poking at his eyes through his forehead, eating through his stomach, squeezing his heart with huge hands until he knew it was going to burst. Then he heard it. His own voice. Time-delayed.

"Mom!" the scream rang out and reverberated in the air like an echo, the sound going forward and then returning. He placed his hands over his ears. He didn't want to hear it. His eyes were frozen on the scene before him, but he didn't want to hear the awful sound coming from his own mouth.

Department twenty-seven of the Orange County Superior Court was still in recess, but the clock was ticking. The fifteen-minute mark had passed, and it was now approaching almost twenty minutes since the gavel had come down. A few feet away, the courtroom was packed and noisy, everyone talking at one time, attorneys still rushing in and slamming their files on the table, quickly conferring with their clients, some who they'd never met until that very moment. Phillip walked into Lara's chambers and stood quietly in front of her large, paper-strewn desk. Her eyelids fluttered, but she didn't look up. He stood and waited.

"Yes," she said finally, removing her glasses and fixing him with her slate gray eyes. "What have you got, Phillip?"

"I know you're working on the Adams matter and you asked that I not disturb you. It's Sergeant Rickerson with the San Clemente Police Department on line one."

She didn't speak. He stood still, hands by his sides. Her eyes returned to the brief in front of her. Long moments passed.

"I'm sorry, but do you want me to tell him to call back?"

"Please, no calls," she mumbled, eyes down, deep in thought. "I only have a few more minutes. No calls."

He left. Then a few seconds later, he returned, a grimace on his face. "It's imperative that he speak with you. He says it's about your sister." He paused, waiting for her to look up, his face a mask of concern.

She set her hands on the desk. The fingers spread and pressed hard into the papers, her back rigid. "Okay, Phillip, I'll speak to him."

As he hurried for the door, she picked up the receiver. "My secretary said this was about my sister . . . Ivory Perkins . . . Is that correct?" Her voice was controlled. No need to panic. It was probably not even about Ivory. Generally it was Sam's name they mentioned when they called. "Mr. Perkins said to call you regarding this ticket," they would say. "Mr. Perkins said to contact you regarding this complaint that he's receiving stolen property."

The officer was speaking. She was looking at the second hand on the large wall clock. She was late. A few minutes could equal several arraignments. "I'm sorry, Officer, repeat what you just said."

"There's a problem here. It's bad. Your sister and her husband have been killed. It looks like a double homicide."

"Double homicide?" she repeated, as though she'd never heard of such a thing. "Ivory?" Not Ivory. Sam Perkins, yes. But not her sister.

"We're here at the house. Guess her son came home from school and discovered them. Pretty bad scene." Sergeant Rickerson paused. "He was hysterical when we got here, but he's calmed down somewhat and we sent him to a neighbor's house."

"I . . . he . . . she's dead." She stood, holding the phone, her mind blank, her hands sweating profusely. Gripping it with both hands, she stuttered. "When d-did it happen?"

"Medical examiner won't have an exact time of death until he does the post. Maybe a few hours ago from the looks of the bodies."

She had already started walking around the desk, heading to the door. She suddenly reached the end of the phone cord, dragging the multi-line phone over the top of her desk, knocking over her coffee and several files, which scattered on the carpet. In a state of shock she was going to walk out the door with the phone still in her hand. Finally realizing what she was doing, she dropped it and it crept back across the carpet. Then she turned around and bent over and picked it back up and said in a hoarse voice, "I'm on my way."

She didn't pick up her purse. She didn't speak to her secretary. She simply walked out of her chambers, still wearing her black robe, and kept walking until she reached the end of the hall, where the security console was set up. She stopped and stood, staring into space.

"You okay there, Judge Sanderstone?" the black guard said, leaning over the console. "You look real pale."

She slipped off her robe and handed it to the guard. "Call Phillip and tell him to have someone bring my car keys to the parking garage and cancel my afternoon session. Hurry," she yelled, walking fast as he pressed the buzzer on the security doors. "My sister . . ." She walked through the doors, talking to herself. "My sister's been murdered."

She punched the button and got in the elevator. It was reserved for judges only and led to the underground parking garage. The doors shut. The elevator didn't move. She fell against the back wall and then screamed: "Ivory! God, no! She can't be dead. I won't accept it." She was screaming and spitting at the same time, her fists clenched into tight balls, the emotionalism an alien and terrifying feeling as it consumed her. Her chest rose up and down, and she knew she was on the verge of hyperventilating.

The doors opened and Phillip stepped inside, handing her purse to her. "Is there something I can do? Has there been an accident? Do you want me to drive you somewhere?"

Pushing herself off the wall, she looked down. Tears were streaming down her face. She could feel them.

"No," she said. "Just cancel my afternoon session, please. My sister's been murdered." She reached over and punched the button for the garage level, flipping Phillip's hand off the elevator door. For a moment their eyes met.

"I'm sorry . . . so sorry. Call me if there's anything I can do."

"What could you do?" she said as the doors closed, his face disappearing an inch at a time. What could anyone do when someone was dead? Breathe life back into them? Make their heart start beating again and their blood circulate?

Nothing else really mattered.

She didn't remember the thirty-minute drive over—the traffic on the freeway, the exit to San Clemente, the steep hill to their house. She was approaching the house. It was real. It was a living nightmare.

Police cars lined the block, wheels turned to the curb

so they wouldn't roll. One black-and-white, probably the first to arrive, had run up over the curb. She pulled her green Jaguar into someone's driveway four houses down and left it there, keys in the ignition, engine running, her purse on the seat, and ran the short distance. Several officers had placed a yellow police tape across the front lawn and were standing there, blocking neighbors and kids from entering. The curious were pressing against one anther, trying to see, their faces flushed with excitement. One small child managed to slip his hand out of his mother's and duck under the yellow tape, jumping up and down in glee on the grass. An officer grabbed him and lifted him back over the tape to the sidewalk.

Lara didn't see the tape. She walked right into it and kept walking, her eyes focused on the front door of the small adobe house, nothing else in her line of vision.

"Hey, you," a burly voice yelled. "You can't go in there. Get back." A large arm reached out and managed to catch the edge of her sleeve.

She jerked her arm away and glared at him. "My sister," she said. She kept walking, flinging the tape aside and stepping over it. "My sister."

At the door she was again met with resistance. A uniformed officer placed an arm in front of her, blocking her entrance. "Can't go in there, lady. This is a crime scene."

"My sister," she said again, trying to push him aside. His eyes got large and he looked behind him and then back to her face.

"Judge Sanderstone, right?" he said, standing a little straighter, adjusting his gun belt. "Listen, wait here and I'll get Sergeant Rickerson. He's in charge here. You don't want to go in there."

She saw the compassion in the man's eyes. It didn't help. She stepped in front of him. The tiny house was crawling with people. Some were in uniform, others in suits. A few wore dark pants and white shirts with name tags pinned above the pockets. Those were the ones from the white van that she now remembered seeing parked at the curb with the rear doors open. The van that said the dreadful words on the side: MEDICAL EXAMINER.

A good-sized man wearing a shiny gray suit with unruly red hair and penetrating eyes, his face scarred from acne, walked up to her through the sea of bodies. He came close, too close. "Sergeant Rickerson . . . Ted," he said. He started to extend his hand and then realized it was an inappropriate gesture and dropped it by his side. "We met, but you probably don't remember. It was when you were still a D.A."

"Where is she?" Lara's eyes blinked rapidly as they searched the room, seeing nothing but bodies, hearing nothing but a cacophony of jumbled words.

"Look, I don't think it's a good idea for you to go in there." He flicked his red mustache and leaned ever closer. "Why don't we step out in the backyard and talk a minute? Let the people do their job."

"I have to see her. Please, Sergeant, let me see my sister." She brushed her hand over her head as though swatting a fly. Too many people were in the small room and not enough air. An officer tried to squeeze past them, and his nightstick became lodged obscenely between her legs, pushing the hem of her skirt up, exposing the top of her panty hose. She didn't notice.

Rickerson pulled her gently aside, dislodging the nightstick and giving the officer a dirty look.

"Sorry," the man said with a slight smile, raising his shoulders and moving on, unaware who the small, dark-haired woman was or what she was doing here.

"Come on," Rickerson said softly. "Let's go out back. You need some fresh air."

"Where is she?" She waited, counting seconds in her mind: one, two, three, four, five, six. It was coming. She knew it. It began somewhere in the pit of her stomach and rose with a fury as she opened her mouth and screamed, "Get these fucking idiots out of here and let me see my sister. Now!"

Almost every noise stopped. Everyone dropped what they were doing and stared at her. Some who were kneeling down stood so they could see what was going on. Sergeant Rickerson started waving his hands toward the front of the house and whispering in people's ears. One by one, they headed for the front door, and soon the living room was empty. "In the master bedroom," he said. "The medical examiner is in there now."

She was in a black tunnel. The bedroom door was at the end. In front of her on the end table was her own image in cap and gown at her graduation from UCLA. Next to it was a picture she and Ivory had taken at one of those booths at Knotts Berry Farm years ago where they were both dressed in costumes from the Old West. Ivory was holding a toy rifle.

She saw the door frame passing over her head as she entered, almost as if she was being moved forward by a conveyor belt or a moving sidewalk at an amusement park. Somehow she had moved to this point without awareness of her body. She immediately placed her hand over her mouth to stifle her screams, digging her fingernails into the soft flesh of her cheeks. The walls were splattered with blood in strange designs like an abstract painting. Sam's body was sprawled half on, half off the bed, face down, his head an unrecognizable mass of bloody tissue. The room smelled of death: coagulating blood, human excrement. The vision of what had occurred in this tiny space hung like a cloud of ash over them all. They all saw it, felt it, denied it was real.

She didn't see Ivory at first, and her heart leaped. They'd made a mistake. Ivory was alive. Someone had murdered her despicable husband, but Ivory was still alive.

Then she saw her.

Her body was on the floor by the bed. She was nude from the waist down yet wearing a flimsy bra. Her legs were spread obscenely. Both eyes were open and bulging. Her lips had a bluish tinge. Her mouth was tightly shut with a death-like grimace. Her black hair was matted with blood. The flawless skin was gray-blue, and streaks of blood ran down her forehead, her cheeks, covered her upper torso. Lara's eyes jerked from her face and rested at her feet. She was wearing worn-out tennis shoes, the laces not tied.

A man was crouched over the body; another man was snapping photos. The first one stood. He was wearing a white mask and surgical gloves. She focused on his busy eyebrows, bypassing his eyes. She was exhaling and then swallowing. Every time the camera clicked, Lara's body twitched, almost like a spasm. She forced herself to inhale. She was sensitive to odors. This was death she smelled. Death and fear. Ivory's death, her fear.

"From what I can tell at this point, she was probably suffocated with a pillow. If you will note the bulging eyes, the red and blue hemorrhage streaks across the white conjunctiva, the bluish and contused lips. These are all indications of suffocation. The blood you see is his." He glanced at Sam's body on the bed. "I think we have the murder weapon for this fellow. Looks like someone bludgeoned him from behind with a twenty-pound free weight. Cracked his skull wide open. This cheesy stuff here is his brain tissue," he said, picking up a glob of something off the bedspread with tweezers and dropping it into a plastic bag. To Lara, it looked like oatmeal.

He stepped over Ivory's body and moved to the other side of the bed. Lara dropped to her knees and tried to force her head down to her sister's face. She could not. She stared at the man in the mask and gloves, now bending over Sam. Ivory's hand was cold and limp, but soon it would be as rigid as a statue. Lara picked it up without looking at her and then dropped it. She had started tying her shoe laces when she felt someone's hands under her arms, lifting her slowly to a standing position.

"Let's go now. There's nothing you can do here," Sergeant Rickerson said softly, his eyes full of compassion.

"I need to wash her face," Lara said, seeing the

splattered blood, knowing she was being irrational but powerless to stop it. Ivory had always had such beautiful skin. Since birth, actually. Most infants have ruddy complexions, but according to their mother, Ivory's was perfect from day one—smooth and white. It was why their mother had named her Ivory. Ivory wouldn't want anyone to see her this way, Lara thought. She was proud of her lovely complexion. It was one of her best assets.

"No, no," Rickerson said. "That's not necessary. Please, let's go outside. Someone will get you a glass of water or a cup of coffee. Get some fresh air. You'll feel better." He was speaking low. He placed an arm around her shoulder as if he might embrace her.

Lara looked up into his eyes and then looked away. She couldn't remember anything . . . couldn't think. She walked straight out of the house, the sergeant hurrying after her, her mind completely blank. She didn't see the people still gathered in front of the house, the crowd growing larger and larger as people came home from work. Some of them had gone home and returned with cold sodas or beer cans—refreshments—as in the movie theater. She didn't see the news van and camera crew that were there shooting her very image as she walked out the front door, her blouse soiled and stained, her face wet with perspiration, her face almost as rigid as marble. She didn't hear the voice of the reporter speaking into a microphone only inches from her face.

"We're here in San Clemente, where the sister and brother-in-law of Orange County Superior Court Judge Lara Sanderstone have been brutally murdered. Judge Sanderstone," he said, pointing the microphone at her, "can you give us a statement?"

She walked by without even glancing in his direction and headed for her car. Rickerson stopped on the sidewalk and watched her until she drove off. Then he turned in the direction of the house. It was useless to try to interview her now anyway, he thought. She was in another world.

The collection of investigators and uniformed police officers who had been standing on the front lawn in a tight group, some smoking cigarettes, others making notes on clipboards as they waited, turned and followed the detective back into the house.

Judge Lara Sanderstone had forgotten all about her nephew. But so had Detective Sergeant Ted Rickerson. When an officer came in from the boy's bedroom with a box of dumbbells, the same brand as the murder weapon, a matched set, all accounted for but one, the murder weapon, Sergeant Rickerson still didn't think of fourteen-year-old Josh. Affixed to the outside of the box with Scotch tape was a torn piece of Christmas wrapping paper and a little tag. "TO JOSH, FROM MOM," it read. One glance and Rickerson's head jerked to the officer standing closest to him.

"Get the kid," he barked. "Get the fucking kid."

Chapter 6

Lara drove without thought. Finally she pulled up to the thirty-year-old cottage in Dana Point where they had grown up and parked the car. It didn't even look the same. The new owners—several, actually, in the ten years since their mother's death—had added a second story and remodeled the one-car garage, making it into some type of playroom. It looked like many different houses all pieced together into one. Gone were the beautiful rose bushes her mother had tended to every single day, wearing her wide-brimmed hat and cloth gloves. A wrought-iron fence and a padlocked gate had been installed in front of the house to keep transients out. All beach communities had their share of transients and homeless. Dana Point, San Clemente, and San Juan Capistrano, only a few miles apart, had more than their share. Inside the fence was nothing but concrete. No grass, no flowers, no walkway to the door. Everything was turning to stone: Ivory's once lovely hands, the front yard where they used to play. All stone now.

She gunned the Jaguar and sped away. The past was over. Both of their parents were dead. They had waited too long to start a family; the children had been almost an afterthought. When Lara was born, her mother had been close to forty and her father in his mid-fifties. They were up in years before Lara even graduated from college, and her father didn't live to see her complete law school. Now Ivory was dead too. There was no one to even remember the sunny days of years gone by, the happiness, the laughter, the hopes and expectations.

Ivory was going to grow up and become an actress—a movie star. Everyone really believed it, even Pop, and he barely believed Lara would make it through college when she'd made straight A's since the first grade. He was far from an optimist, but he truly believed his gorgeous younger daughter, the light of his life, would one day be on the silver screen. She was so pretty, so fun-loving, so eager to please people. She loved to pose for the camera. How could the world not love her as much as they did?

Before Charley died and after their mother had passed away, Lara used to call Ivory and suggest they meet somewhere for lunch. She wanted to stay close, keep the family together. Ivory would always say, "I'll have to call Charley and call you back." They had argued. Lara was so independent, so strong, so opinionated. Even though she liked Charley, had even had a big crush on him in high school before Ivory started going out with him, she couldn't tolerate the fact that her sister let him control her entire life, that the woman couldn't make a simple decision to have lunch without consulting her husband. She knew her sister was immature and not terribly bright, but every adult had to have opinions of their own, some sense of their own identity. All Ivory espoused were Charley's opinions. When Charley died, she was like a lost child, easy prey for a man like Sam Perkins—for any man, really.

In only a matter of months Sam had squandered every dime Ivory had: Charley's life insurance money, the savings account he'd had for Josh's education. He'd even taken out loans on their little house in San Clemente that Charley had purchased when he and Ivory were first married.

Lara was now on the freeway headed north to Santa Ana. At lunch, she'd made arrangements to move into the condominium across the courtyard from Emmet's. Before she went to work, she'd gone to her house and tossed a bunch of clothes in the trunk. She hadn't even told the detective about the break-in, the threats in the courtroom. The two incidents couldn't possibly be related, she told herself. How would anyone know Ivory was her sister? Her mind was spinning, still awash in blinding sorrow and denial. She was only blocks from the congested civic center area that housed the courts and other city and county office complexes as well as dozen of private law firms.

Then she thought of Josh.

They had no relatives. An aunt maybe in Georgia, but she had to be in her eighties now, a few cousins somewhere.

She would have to take Josh.

She gripped the steering wheel until her knuckles turned white and almost rear-ended the car in front of her. The poor kid. They hardly knew each other. Ivory had forbidden her to even see the boy for at least two years. But Lara had no excuse for what she'd done. She'd walked away and left him there without so much as a word.

Her eyes searched for the exit ramp in the string of cars in front of her. They weren't moving. Traffic was so congested that they were practically standing still. She couldn't go back to the house in San Clemente. Some things a person just couldn't do, and this was one of them. She forgot the exit ramp and seized the car phone from the console. Who should she call? The police, of course. She'd tell them to bring Josh to the condo. Then she'd figure it all out tomorrow.

Funeral arrangements had to be made. People had to be called. Plans had to be formulated. Although the sun was still out, the sky had clouded over and her vision was blurred. Like a nightmare, a case she'd handled or heard in the courtroom, Lara told herself someone else's sister had been murdered back there. Not her sister. The tears started to fall. They felt like hot acid, etching themselves into her face, the skin far from flawless, nothing at all like beautiful Ivory's.

She called the police station on her car phone, but Rickerson hadn't arrived. She asked the dispatcher to get him on the radio and find out where her nephew was. The girl put her on hold. She waited.

"He said the boy is being brought to the station here. He wants to know if you're coming to pick him up."

"Tell Rickerson to call me." She'd have them bring him to the condo. She gave them Emmet's phone number and the number of the car phone. "If he doesn't reach me, I'll call him back."

She replaced the car phone and took the First Street exit to the condo, glancing at the fast-food restaurants as she drove, her mind jumbled and unfocused. He'd have to eat. She needed food. She had nowhere for him to sleep. The place she had rented was a one-bedroom condominium. She'd have to go back to her home.

No, she thought, she couldn't go home. Not now, not after what had happened to Ivory and Sam. Fear seemed to be surrounding her. She felt trapped, paralyzed. Maybe they were after her, wanted to kill her and her entire family. It could be the boy who had threatened her in the courtroom . . . anyone. She was terrified, completely panicked. You have to stop it, she told herself. She had to find her inner strength, put her sister's pathetic body out of her mind long enough to find the condo, figure out what to do about her nephew.

How old was he anyway? She didn't remember. He was a sweet kid. He reminded her of Charley, but she hardly knew him.

She'd always wanted a child of her own, dreamed she would someday have a family. In some ways Sam had been right when he told Ivory that Lara was jealous. She'd envied Ivory for having a child, a family. Finally, a few years ago Lara had reconciled herself to her childlessness by telling herself she was doing the things that had to be done in the world to keep it safe. Ironic, she thought. Ivory's death made it all seem like smoke. Blown away. Just like that. Gone. The whole premise she had based her life on had been eradicated. If she couldn't keep an unknown person from snuffing out her sister's life, it was all a big zero.

She crossed the parking lot to Emmet's condo. That morning she hadn't even looked to see if the place she had rented had a phone. She was certain it didn't. It was a small complex, only about forty units. Emmet's unit was on the ground floor, a quick walk to the parking lot. The one she had rented was right across the grassy courtyard. It wasn't even a security building, and the area around here was riddled with crime. She looked around her, behind her. She cursed herself for not carrying a gun. A lot of the judges did. She knocked on Emmet's door and waited.

He didn't answer. She started beating on the door. He still didn't answer. She was trembling, shaking. She didn't know whether to go to the condo across the courtyard or drive to the San Clemente P.D. Finally the door clicked open and she entered, closing the door behind her and leaning back against it. "Emmet," she yelled, "are you in there?"

He appeared in the hallway. "Sorry," he said. "I . . . was in the . . . bathroom." Then he saw her tear-stained face, the look in her eyes. "What's . . . wrong?"

Lara put her hand to her mouth. For a few moments she couldn't say the words. Emmet hit a button on the wheelchair and crossed the room to her. Reaching out, he touched her shoulder. Then his hand fell away. "Tell . . . me."

"My sister, Emmet," Lara stammered. "My sister and brother-in-law were murdered."

"Murdered?" he repeated. "Oh, no . . . How . . . terrible."

She told him all that she knew, rattling off the details in a manic series of jumbled sentences. She rushed to the window to peer outside. "It could be over me. They may want me, Emmet. They may have even followed me here and be out there right now." Her heart was pounding, pressing against her chest. She didn't even ask. She simply grabbed Emmet's phone and called the police station again. This time she got through to Sergeant Rickerson.

She spoke rapidly, standing in Emmet's living room,

turning around in small circles. "I didn't tell you that someone broke into my house the other day. The investigating officer thought they were looking for me, that it was more than a burglary. And I was threatened about three weeks ago . . . a case I handled. The Henderson homicide. You may have read about it."

"Calm down," the detective said. "Where are you?"

"I'm at a friend's house in Santa Ana. I rented a small condo in his complex. The officer told me to move out until this blows over, not to stay at my house. I'm not sure, but this could all be related. They could have killed Sam and Ivory to hurt me."

"If you feel you're up to the drive, you can come to the station. I have your nephew. You can give me all the details."

"Do you think this is related to what happened to my sister and Sam?" Lara had wrapped the phone cord around her and had to turn in the opposite direction to get free. Emmet was sitting quietly a few feet away.

Rickerson answered, "It could be, but then you might have been a victim of an ordinary burglary." He was trying to reassure her.

"I'm coming there to get my nephew."

"That sounds like a good idea. We have to interview him, and we'd like to interview you. I was going to wait and do it tomorrow, but if you come—"

"I'll come," Lara said, her hands trembling on the phone, grasping it with both hands to keep it steady. "He's just a kid. This is so terrible for him. I forgot all about him. I didn't think."

She decided that the one place she'd like to be right now was a police station. Besides, she should have never left without Josh. This was all that was left that she could do for her sister—take care of her precious child, arrange her funeral.

"Judge Sanderstone . . ." He paused, his voice tense and uncertain. "Do you mind if I call you something else?"

"Lara," she said.

"Lara," he said, pronouncing it as Laura. Everyone

did. "Let me tell you something here. Your brother-in-law was killed with a dumbbell. That dumbbell belonged to your nephew. And let me tell you something else, your nephew isn't exactly a little boy. This kid is almost as big as me. Do you know what I'm saying?"

She had no idea what he meant. So, Josh wasn't a little kid anymore. What bearing did that have on all this nightmare? "Who killed my sister? Did the neighbors see anything? Did you find anything in the house?" Her voice started to rise, even though she tried to contain it. She had pushed these thoughts to the back of her mind, too painful to begin to deal with now. She couldn't suppress them any longer.

His voice was low and measured. "Take it easy, Lara. I know this is a terrible time for you, and please accept my deepest sympathy—the whole department's, in fact—but surely you understand that we have to do our jobs here. We have to cover all the bases."

She was silent, thinking. What he had tried to say diplomatically now clicked into place. He had implied, in a roundabout way, that Josh could be responsible. That was absurd. Sure, patricide wasn't uncommon. As awful as it was, it did occur. But her own nephew? Outrageous! Just the thought made her already churning stomach turn over and over like a ferris wheel.

"Why don't you come down and we'll discuss all this in person?"

"Fine," she said.

"What . . . did . . . he say?" Emmet asked once she had disconnected. She was just standing there staring into space.

"He . . . oh, Emmet, I-I have to go and get my nephew. He thinks my nephew . . ." She just couldn't say it. She walked over to Emmet and kissed his forehead and then rushed out the front door.

The San Clemente Police Department was housed in a small, older building. It wasn't a large department. San Clemente wasn't a large town. Even if Richard Nixon had once resided here and people had heard the name, it was still what some people called the boonies, stuck in the middle between Los Angeles and San Diego. New housing tracts and shopping centers were springing to life here and there, but the town itself still looked like a small, beachy city, almost like a town found along the Eastern Seaboard.

Rickerson had a cup of coffee in one hand and a soda in the other. The coffee looked disgusting, but he needed it. As long as it still moved in the cup, it was drinkable. The soda was for Josh, waiting alone in the interview room. He hoped like hell it wasn't the kid who was responsible for the bloodbath in that bedroom. He had two kids of his own, and he hated it when he had to arrest young people on serious crimes. Oh, a little bust now and then for possession or drinking in public or a curfew violation didn't bother him, but not a crime like this one. And this one was going to be big. It was going to make all the papers. The deceased weren't notable. The female was a housewife; the husband owned a small pawnshop in the center of old San Clemente. But the relationship to a judge would do it, particularly since this judge had made all the papers already only a few weeks before. It was a red flag to the press. And if they got wind that the boy was a possible suspect, all hell would break loose.

"Hey, Josh, brought you a soda, guy," he said, knowing his smile would not bring another from the grim young man who sat in front of him, his long sandy blond hair falling onto his forehead and almost obscuring his eyes. He was a fairly attractive kid—clear skin, nice features, blue eyes. Under the circumstances, it was hard to tell what he was really like.

The can of soda remained on the table. The boy didn't reach for it. His body was angled forward in the chair, his shoulders slumped, his eyes glazed and puffy.

"Okay, let's start at the beginning. I know this is painful, son, and I'm sorry we have to do this, but we do. As soon as we're through here, you can go home with your aunt and try to get some rest."

Josh blinked and licked his lips. "My aunt? I haven't

seen my aunt in . . ." He stopped himself and focused on a framed poster on the wall.

"So, let's get this over with. You came home from school and saw your stepfather's truck parked in front of the house. You told the other officer that this was an unusual event—that he didn't generally come home from the shop that early in the day. Is that correct?"

"Yeah."

He looked at the boy with compassion. "Sorry, kid." He continued, "You entered through the back door into the kitchen. Was it open or did you use your key?"

"I used my key. We hide it above the door ledge."

Rickerson was reading from the officer's notes and looked up at Josh. His eyes were wide, his mouth open. "You went to the refrigerator, got a soda, and then walked down the hall to your room. When you passed the master bedroom, the door was open and you saw the bodies. Is that right?"

"Yeah." Josh leaned forward in the chair, getting even closer to the table. His hands found the soda and he popped the cap, but didn't take a drink. With a jerky movement he swiped the hair out of his eyes and continued to stare at the poster.

"Tell me about the weights?" He looked directly into the boy's eyes and tried to read his reaction. Nothing. Even the tone of his voice was almost flat.

"The weights? What're you talking about?"

"You know, the set of weights your mom bought you for Christmas last year. Do you work out, Josh? You've got a nice build there, guy."

A small flicker of light went on in his eyes. "My dad was a body builder. My real dad. Yeah, I work out. How'd you know my mom bought me weights for Christmas?" He swallowed, choking up at the mention of his mother, almost ready to cry.

"We found them in your room, son. One of them was missing—the twenty."

Josh turned to the detective and spoke without blinking. "The twenty?"

"Yep, the twenty. It wasn't with the rest of the set."

"Oh, yeah. What does this have to do with my mom?"

"Why don't you answer my question first and then I'll answer yours. Sound fair?"

"All my weights were in the box in my room where they always are. I kept them in my closet 'cause Mom—" he stopped and coughed, a glint of moisture appearing in his eyes.

"Please, go on."

Tears streamed from both his eyes. He made no move to wipe them away, and Rickerson pretended he didn't see them. "My mom didn't like them all over the floor in my room, see. She made me keep them in the box in the closet."

"So, the twenty was in your closet this morning when you left for school?"

"Yeah, sure. I guess. I mean, I didn't look. It was there the night before." He sniffed. "I could have left it on the floor. I don't remember." The tears stopped and dried on his face. His face had been dusty and now there were streaks where the pale skin showed through and the dust had changed into muddy lines.

"Well," Rickerson said, "we didn't find it there. We found all your weights in your closet, the twenty missing. But we found the twenty in your parents' bedroom."

Josh's gaze was penetrating, his reply sharp. "My mom's bedroom. That wasn't my dad. I told you. My dad is dead. That was my stepfather."

Rickerson leaned back in the chair, rubbing his stomach. It was popping and churning. He'd have to check on how the real father died. Something about this kid was beginning to make him wish he'd taken his vacation this week like he'd planned. But no. Joyce had seen to that. After almost twenty years of marriage, she had jumped up one morning and told him that she wanted to go back to college and get her engineering degree. Then a few months later, she had moved into her own apartment and left him with the two boys. But she kept insisting she didn't want a divorce, and she called him every night and told him how much she missed him. She even made him promise that he wouldn't tell a soul at the department. Women, he thought, twirling the gold wedding band on his left hand. Fucking woman. Right this very minute he could be stretched out on a beach in Hawaii instead of sitting here facing off with this kid.

"Okay, Josh," he said, "just answer this for me. Why would your twenty weight be in your parents'—excuse me—your mother and stepfather's bedroom?"

"Dunno."

"Can you think of any reason someone would do this to your mother and stepfather?" He certainly wouldn't want to use the word *parents* again. One look from this kid was enough to make a clear impression on that one.

"Because Sam was a bastard! I hated him, man. Everyone musta hated him 'cept my mom." Now he reached for the Coke and drank half the can in one swallow, setting what was left back on the table with a thud.

"Did you kill them, Josh?" the detective said softly, knowing he was treading on shaky ground. He could question him about the murder as a witness, but he couldn't interrogate him as a suspect until a parent or guardian arrived. But the opening was there and Rickerson found the temptation irresistible.

"No," Josh said, looking him straight in the eye. "I wish I'd killed Sam, though."

Rickerson sighed and leaned back in his chair. "Your mother? Know anyone that might have wanted to hurt your mother?"

"Dunno. Sam maybe. He was always screaming at her."

"Did you ever see anyone at the house you didn't recognize? Can you give us a list of their friends?"

"I can't remember, okay. They didn't have a lot of friends." A dark shadow passed over his face. He refused to look at the detective.

"Did you see anything at all amiss or different when you came home today, before discovering the bodies?"

"All I saw was Sam's stupid truck. He never comes home in the middle of the day. And everything was all torn up like we were moving out or something."

Rickerson was tired and he was hungry. He was getting nowhere fast. The poor kid either didn't know anything, or what he did know, he wasn't telling. He stood and shoved the metal chair away from the table, placing his hands behind him and stretching his aching back. "Let's go, kid. That's it for today. Your aunt should be here any minute. She's on the way to pick you up."

Josh stood as well. Rickerson walked to the door, then turned and glanced back. The boy just stood there. "Come on," he said again. "Don't want to stay in this room all night, do you?"

"Why do I have to go to my aunt's house? She's a bitch. Why can't I go back to my house and stay there? I need my bike . . . and my clothes—my things."

Rickerson just shrugged his shoulders. Tough situation, he thought. Nothing's going to be easy in a case like this one, not now, not later. "It's either your aunt's house or juvenile hall until we find a foster home. Take your pick." He didn't wait for the boy to answer. The answer was evident. He walked out of the room and waited in the hall, leaning and resting his back a few seconds against the wall. A few minutes later the boy came out and shuffled behind him to his office. Did he kill the stepfather he hated, Rickerson asked himself, and then suffocate his own mother? Hard to tell at this point. He had enough doubts, however, to generate plenty of sleepless nights in the days to come. As far as Judge Sanderstone's fears that someone was after her, he personally doubted it. A residential burglary was a far cry from a double homicide. He had officers canvassing the neighborhood, and hopefully forensics would come up with something they could sink their teeth into and run with. If not, it was going to be a bad one.

In his own little world, he started when the young boy next to him spoke.

"That's her, isn't it?" he said, watching as a bedraggled woman made her way down the hall.

Rickerson looked up and saw Lara Sanderstone. "Don't you even know her, son?" he whispered, wondering if the boy was okay. Surely he recognized his own aunt.

"Yeah," he said. "I know her. I just forgot what she looked like, it's been so long." He cut his eyes to Rickerson. "I told you she was a bitch. That's what my mom always said. She said we weren't good enough for her. That she thought we were white trash and that's why she stopped coming around."

"Oh, yeah," Rickerson said. "Well, she's a pretty smart lady. Why don't you give her a chance?"

As Lara got closer, Rickerson looked up and shook his head. He felt sorry for the woman. Nope, he sure didn't want to be in her shoes right now. Sister and brother-in-law murdered; this gangly, bitter kid to deal with. She was a pretty woman, he thought, looking her up and down. Even under this kind of strain, there was an ethereal, unusual quality about her. But she looked small, vulnerable, broken. Not like the tough little prosecutor he remembered from her days in the D.A.'s office.

"Josh," she said, seeing him and running to embrace him. "I'm so sorry, honey. I'm so sorry." Then she finally pulled back and stared at him. "You're so big . . . my God." She put her hand over her mouth. He looked just like his father. It was like spinning back in time, back to the days when they were all in high school, the days when . . . She stopped herself, seeing the black look in his eyes, a look that passed right through her.

Josh just stood there. He didn't say a word.

Chapter 7

At the police station, Sergeant Rickerson called Lara aside, sending Josh down the hall to look at mug shots of possible suspects, anyone that he might have seen in the neighborhood or at his parents' house. It was really just a way to diffuse the situation—the friction between the boy and his aunt. Josh had flatly refused to go home with her. "It might have been a mistake for you to come down here," Rickerson said. They were standing in the corridor leading to the lobby. "This has been really tough for him, obviously. Why don't you go home and I'll talk some sense into him? Then I'll either bring him to your place later or find a placement for him."

Lara still felt the sting of her nephew's look. What she had seen in his eyes was pure hatred. She glanced at the detective and then looked away. Maybe he was right about the placement. "I don't know anything about teenagers," she said. "I'm not married, you know."

Rickerson ran his fingers through his already unruly red hair and then braced his back against the wall. "Yeah, well, I'm not sure I know that much myself, and I've got a few of my own. A kid's a kid. That's about it."

Although she was tempted to turn Josh over to Social Services, she couldn't. "Please convince him to stay with me. Tell him I care. He's my sister's only child. I have to take him." Lara reached into her purse for the rental receipt, gave him the address, and then something flashed in her mind—the last night she'd seen Ivory alive. "Someone was following my sister," she blurted out, stepping into a doorway as an officer walked by. "She came to see me about two months ago, late at night. She was excited, frightened, but she refused to tell me what was going on."

"Did you call the police, get a description of the car or whatever?" Rickerson was alert and standing only inches from Lara, his breath and clothing reeking of cigar smoke even though he wasn't smoking.

"No, she wouldn't tell me anything." Lara looked down at the worn and scuffed linoleum. The floor must have been white at one time. Now it was an ugly shade of yellow. "We had an argument. I have no idea what was going on. I asked her to leave."

Ivory had been in trouble two months ago, the night she'd come to her house. In what way or over what she had no idea. She knew Ivory had problems. She should have understood. She should have tried to figure out what was going on. If she had, her sister might still be alive. Rickerson was staring at her. Beads of perspiration were popping out on her upper lip. She blotted them with her hand.

"I'll call the sheriff's department and see what they made of the break-in at your house," he said, concerned about the woman standing beside him, more worried about her emotional state than any physical threats right now. "Nothing missing, huh?"

"No, not that I could see," Lara said, leaning back against the whitewashed wall. "I mean, I didn't go through everything. They told me to move out, so I moved out."

"I heard some of the details of this Henderson case, but not all. You said someone threatened you, one of the family members?"

"The dead girl's boyfriend," Lara said, the words reverberating inside her head; she kept seeing Ivory on the floor in that room. Would someone refer to her as the dead girl's sister? "I don't remember exactly what he said. I mean, he called me a fucking bitch . . . said someone should kill my family or me . . . something like that. We weren't on record then, so we don't have it documented, but the D.A. was in the courtroom, the bailiff. A number of people were present." Lara paused, not looking at the detective, her voice low. "I thought he was just distraught. It was a difficult situation."

"The medical examiner believes your sister was sexually assaulted prior to the suffocation." He hated to say it, but she had to know.

Lara looked up in shock. "No . . . Jesus Christ . . . she was raped. Ivory was raped." Then she quickly pressed her lips together into a hard, thin line. Ivory was dead. That she was raped was incidental. But it went to the suffering, the agony she had endured in her final moments of life.

"Wasn't the Henderson girl raped?" Rickerson asked.

Lara's head shot up at the big detective. "God, yes . . . You can't possibly think that the boyfriend would rape and murder Ivory to strike back at me? That would be insanity. All I did was rule on the law. My hands were tied." The muscles in her face were twitching. She no longer cared what Rickerson or the officers passing them in the hall thought about her. Facing the wall, she pounded it with her fists. She then thought of something and spun around to face him. "Are they certain it wasn't consensual? Maybe she and Sam had sex before she was killed."

Rickerson dropped his eyes. "Lara, the medical examiner said it was a rape. Pretty brutal from what he said. Numerous rips and tears in her vagina." He paused, his eyes full of conviction. "Whoever did this, we'll nab them. They'll pay. Go home now. Call someone . . . a friend, a relative. There's nothing you can do here."

Tears gathered in Lara's eyes. She thought of Thomas Henderson. He hadn't paid. He was sitting in a loony bin, free to walk out the door whenever he felt like it. She pushed herself off the wall and headed out of the building to the parking lot. All these years, all these cases, the endless faces. They were like a blur now, moving so fast before her eyes that she couldn't remember any of them. How many enemies did she have? Were there hundreds, even thousands? Was someone right this minute lying in wait for her, bent on revenge? Was someone so full of hatred that they would kill her sister and brother-in-law just to hurt her?

She heard herself arguing in court during her days as a D.A.: "The people believe the maximum sentence is both appropriate and justified in this case, Your Honor. The defendant is a sociopath, a danger to society, an animal. . . ."

These people had wives and children, mothers and fathers, brothers and sisters. For all she knew, she'd made mistakes. Could she have been responsible for sending an innocent person to prison? The system wasn't infallible.

Lara Sanderstone had a reputation for being tough, unmerciful, always leaning toward the longer terms, stacking the penalties as high as they would go. No one ever mentioned her name and the word leniency in the same sentence. Leo Evergreen had even called her into his chambers and read her the riot act only months after her appointment.

"You aren't a prosecutor anymore, Lara," he had said. "The bench has to consider other factors in imposing sentences. You can't send every single offender to prison. In some cases there are calculated risks. We have to take them."

The truth was obvious. She had enemies, probably far more than even a scum bag like Sam Perkins.

Lara glanced at the clock. It was late now, almost eleven o'clock. The little condo she'd rented looked like the typical model. Every other wall was mirrored to make it look more spacious. The furniture was small, deceptively so, also in order to create the illusion that the rooms were larger than they were. She wanted to hear noise, so she went to turn on the television. It wasn't real; it was a black plastic box that just looked like a television. She felt like she was in Disneyland.

She was still waiting for the detective to deliver Josh.

Although there was no phone, someone had placed the Yellow Pages inside the doorway. She picked up the book and flipped through the section listing funeral homes, but quickly found her fingers trembling on the thin paper pages. Dropping the large book on the floor, she decided Phillip could take care of it all tomorrow. She'd tell him what she wanted and he'd make the calls.

That's when the stark reality of death really hits a person, she thought. When they call a funeral home and purchase a casket to put their loved one in the ground, under the dirt. She stared at the door and tried to swallow the morbid thoughts like a pill without water.

On the drive back from San Clemente, she'd called almost everyone she could think of on her car phone, mostly the numbers she had committed to memory. Wasn't that what you were supposed to do when someone died? She'd called Irene Murdock. Irene was a rock of strength—just what she needed right now, she thought. Irene's machine had answered. Lara hung up.

Then she'd called Benjamin England. Even if he was a pig in bed, he was a man and she needed someone. She got his machine too. She'd forgotten that he was going to San Francisco on business. She didn't leave a message. She wanted to, but she just couldn't get the words out of her mouth. Telling a machine that your sister had been murdered was almost obscene.

She'd called Phillip. He'd listened, tried to console her, told her not to come to the office in the morning. He'd make the notifications, he'd said, arrange things, call Evergreen. He asked her if she wanted him to come over, but she told him no.

She'd started to call her ex-husband, Nolan, a prominent entertainment attorney, but decided against it. The short-term marriage had ended in a bitter divorce a number of years ago. They didn't have the same goals. He worshiped the God of money; she had a thirst for justice. Anyway, she thought, Nolan had a new wife now and a mansion in Beverly Hills. She doubted if he was willing to drive all the way over here just to help her bury her sister.

She went to the windows and peered through the drapes. On the coffee table was a little card that said the drapes were a decorator item. They didn't come with the condo. Although a light was burning in Emmet's condo, it was close to midnight. It wouldn't be right to wake him. His illness drained him and, besides, she thought, what could he do?

She was getting scared—more so with each passing minute. She heard sounds, sounds different from the ones at her house: cars on the nearby freeway, sirens, horns honking, people talking, their voices far away but audible. Was someone out there, waiting, just waiting for her to shut her eyes so they could come in and bash her head in or suffocate her with her own pillow as they had Ivory? They could have followed her even here.

She collapsed on the sofa. It was small, more like a loveseat. She'd sleep here, give Josh the one bed. Thank God, Rickerson had managed to talk him into staying with her. He'd called an hour ago saying that he was bringing the boy to the condo. He was big, as big physically as most men. They would be together.

Slouched on the sofa, consumed with exhaustion and grief, she vented her anger at Sam. In her eyes Perkins was a borderline criminal. Although it was mandated by law that a pawnshop operator report any property taken in to the local police, Perkins seldom did. If the police found him in possession of stolen property, he simply suffered the loss and paid the fine, claiming that the paperwork got lost in the mail. He also used his connection to Lara and the bench to escape prosecution and loss of his business license. Three times she had bailed the bastard out. She knew better—it had gone against everything she believed in—but she had done it for Ivory. Besides, all the judges granted favors at one time or another, and she had loaned him a hundred thousand of her hard-earned dollars to buy that business.

Finally there was a soft knock, and she jumped up and ran the short distance, flinging the door open without looking to see who it was. Rickerson stepped inside the condo and Josh followed.

"You're so late. I was worried," she said, her eyes locked on Josh. Even though she knew he was fourteen, she couldn't believe how big he was, how much he'd grown since the last time she'd seen him. He had to be at least five-ten and his body was developed like a full-grown man's, with bulging biceps and broad shoulders like his father's on a lean, wiry frame. "Are you hungry?" she said. "Have you eaten?"

He didn't answer. After a few awkward moments at the door, he walked into the room and looked around. Rickerson asked her to step outside.

"Look, I would suggest that you don't open the door next time without finding out who's there."

"I know," she said, embarrassed. "I've been waiting all this time, that's all . . ."

"And maybe you should get a gun if you don't have one."

Lara looked up. "You really think I need one?" He was compounding her fears, making her crazy. Why couldn't he just lie and tell her she was perfectly safe—that this had nothing to do with her?

"I think that's a definite possibility. I talked to the S.O. Your place wasn't burglarized, Lara, it was ransacked, rifled. Someone was looking for something. And they were looking for something at your sister's as well. They tore that place apart."

"But what? . . . I don't have anything. I have nothing anyone would want. I don't even have much worth stealing."

"How about a case?" he said. "Do you bring work home, evidence, police reports . . . things like that."

"Certainly," she said, "but not lately. I'm starting a trial next week, but even if I brought the whole file home, I can't see any reason for someone to steal it. All they have to do is walk into the records department and fill out a slip, and they can see it themselves. Unless the file is sealed, it's accessible to the public."

He shrugged. "Get your nephew to some type of psychologist or something. Of course, I'm sure you know that. He didn't eat. And here," he said, giving her a halfhearted smile, "don't say I never gave you anything."

Lara stared at the object in his hands. Light reflected off the blue steel of a small-caliber revolver.

"Go on, take it," he said.

"No," she said, "I don't want it. I hate guns. And Josh is here. . . . You know how dangerous it is to have a gun in the house with a child." Especially with this child, she thought. He was so big that even the word child was a misnomer. And Rickerson's suspicions could be valid. Josh could have come home and found his stepfather standing over his mother's body and bashed his head in. All she needed to do was give the kid access to a gun. Just the thought made her shiver.

"Yeah," he said, letting the word linger, looking deep into her gray eyes, almost as if he could read her mind. "You might be right."

Rickerson stepped even closer. The detective had a bad habit of invading her personal space. If he knew what was good for him, he'd step back. He didn't. He put the small handgun back in the pocket of his jacket.

A siren was blasting on the freeway a few miles away. Lara held her breath and thought of Ivory, the last night she'd seen her. "The night she came to my house had to have been July seventh," Lara said. "I thought I'd just tell you. It was the night before my birthday." Ivory hadn't even remembered her birthday. She'd gone out to dinner with Irene and some other women in Los Angeles. "What kind of evidence did you collect at the house?"

"We . . . I . . . we'll have to get back to you tomorrow. We've got to sort through everything, see what we've got. The crime-scene unit is still working there now, and I'm on my way back. Then we're going to start on his pawnshop. We've secured it as well."

It was chilly and Lara wrapped her arms around her body to stay warm, but she was still freezing, her teeth actually chattering as if she were in sub-zero temperature instead of a California evening in the sixties. The chill was not in the air, she decided, it was inside her.

"That has to be it, you know?" she said to Rickerson. "The pawnshop. Of course. What else could it be? They're not after me. If they wanted me, why didn't they kill me instead of them? Someone got pissed at Sam over something and came to his house and murdered them. He probably made the guy a loan and then sold the property out from under him. The guy could have been a criminal. Sam wasn't exactly a sweetheart, you know."

"So I've heard. Your nephew told me."

Lara jerked her head up. "What did he say? Does he know anything?"

Rickerson didn't want to upset the woman by repeating his suspicions. Of course, on the other hand, if the boy was a psycho, he was putting her in a pretty risky position. "How close were you to your sister?"

"Not very." She cracked the door and peeked inside. Josh was on his stomach on the sofa. She closed the door again. "Not close at all in the last two years. I didn't approve of Sam. She wouldn't leave him. Kind of like that, you know?"

"Yeah, but the kid? What do you know about the kid?"

"Nothing." She looked away. She was embarrassed by the truth.

"Your brother-in-law was killed with a weight, a dumbbell. The weights belonged to the kid."

"You already said that. Are you saying what I think you're saying?" Another resident of the complex walked by, and Lara and Rickerson stepped back, letting him pass. He nodded at the man; Lara ignored him, tilting her face up at the detective.

"Looks that way. Can't rule it out. Not yet." He rubbed his fingers across his face, feeling the acne scars.

"Jesus," she said, shaking her head, trying to convince herself as much as the detective. "I won't buy it. That's an aberrant thing, for God's sake. Don't even think it, and listen—"

"Yeah." He was reaching in his jacket. A few seconds later, he was rolling a cigar around in his fingers. He didn't light it.

"Please, have the decency not to spread this around about my nephew's possible involvement. He just lost his mother."

Rickerson grimaced. "It won't be in the press release, but it's not confidential information. I mean, there were dozens of officers at the scene today, and they all know the murder weapon was a dumbbell and the dumbbells belonged to the kid. We found them in his room."

She was indignant. "What kind of cops are you?" She flushed. "I'm sorry. I just can't see the rationale behind this. Just because the murder weapon is a dumbbell and the child owns a set of dumbbells doesn't mean anything. That would never fly in any court I sit, or anywhere else, for that matter. You're grasping at straws here, Rickerson." She turned and put her hand on the doorknob. "I want every officer you can round up to start tearing that filthy pawnshop apart. Call every single person he's ever made a loan to and run them every which way for criminal history. There's where you'll find your killer."

"I'm sending a man over tonight to watch your place."

"Thanks," she said. At least she could sleep. She opened the door and started to enter. Rickerson headed down the walk to the parking lot. He turned and spoke over his shoulder, "No forced entry. Whoever killed them knew them or had a way to gain entrance to the house."

She heard him. She couldn't think about it now. Seeing Josh on the sofa was something she'd have to get used to. But there were a lot more difficult things to get used to in this nightmare. That he might have been involved was one.

"Josh," she whispered, placing her hand lightly on his back, bending down over the sofa. He didn't raise his head, but he turned his face. The sofa was so small his long legs were protruding from the other end. She could see he'd been crying. He looked grown up, but he wasn't. He was still a child. And this child had been royally screwed, she thought, by the forces that be. He'd lost his father on that blasted motorcycle, and then Ivory had brought Sam into their lives, a situation she was certain had not been pleasant. Could it have made him bitter enough to kill?

"I'm sorry, Josh," she said. "I know how much you're hurting. I loved your mother very much." Instinctively she stroked his hair as her mother had done when she and Ivory were children.

He fixed her with those penetrating eyes, eyes so like his mother's. "Just . . ." he snapped, knocking her hand away, "leave me alone? Okay?" Then he turned his head toward the back of the sofa.

Lara got up and walked around the condo. It was so small. It was confining, like a box, like a coffin. She had to get out. "Josh," she said softly, "I'm going to drive over to Taco Bell and get something to eat. They're open all night. Are you hungry?"

He sat up on the bed and rubbed his red eyes with his hands. "I want to go home," he said flatly. "I'm not staying here with you." He got up and headed for the door. "I'll walk if you won't drive me. I've gotta get outa here."

Lara leaped in front of him and put her body in front of the door. "No, Josh. Listen to me. You can't go home. You have to stay here with me. The police won't let you back in the house, and you're too young to stay alone."

"Get out of my way," he snarled. He was looming

over Lara, glaring down at her like he was going to pick her up and toss her across the room. "You can't keep me here. This isn't a jail."

Lara felt tears on her face and wiped them away with her hand. Keeping Josh with her wasn't going to work. He was too disturbed and she didn't have a clue how to handle him. But no matter what happened, they had to get through tonight. She took a deep breath and turned to him, her voice firm. "Look, Josh, I know you resent me. But that was my sister that was murdered there today. It wasn't just your mother. It was my sister. I'm going to get myself something to eat. If you want, you can go with me. If you don't, you can starve. It's your decision."

"I'm hungry," he finally said. "I'll go."

"Good," she said. She found her purse and headed to the door, mumbling to herself under her breath, "We have to eat or we'll get sick." That's what her mother always said.

She had planned on going through the drive-thru and then returning to the house with their food, but she couldn't face the condo now. "Want to go in?"

He was staring out the passenger window. He didn't answer.

Lara parked the car and got out. Josh followed a good distance behind her. They got their food. He had ordered all kinds of things. "I'm glad you came with me, Josh," she told him. "I didn't want to be alone."

All he said was "I'm hungry."

Walking to the table, Lara noticed his face had softened somewhat. She figured it was the law of survival. They had been thrown into this situation. Neither of them could change it.

"You a real judge?" he said, unwrapping a large burrito and shoving it into his mouth.

Lara glanced at his hands and saw that his fingernails were dirty. "Sure I am. Didn't your mother ever tell you that I became a judge?" She studied his face, his eyes.

"I didn't think hot-shot judges ate at Taco Bell."

"Well, now you know the awful truth." They were talking. His tone was still sarcastic, but it was a start. "I'm a fast-food junkie. I'll probably die of a heart attack from all the chemicals and cholesterol one of these days, but I like the quick fix. No muss, no fuss. You know?"

The burrito was gone. He tossed the paper aside and began on the taco. "I don't like health food," he said, his mouth full of food."I lift weights and I'm supposed to eat right. Never do, though. I hate that bean curd stuff. That's sick."

"Uh-huh," Lara said, munching her taco, thinking he'd actually managed to complete an entire sentence without lashing out at her. "You'd think sick if you knew what was in that taco. I don't think about it. I just eat it."

No, she thought. He couldn't be involved. If he'd done this abominable act, it would show in his face. He couldn't have killed someone and a few hours later sit here and consume a burrito, a taco, and a complete plate of nachos. What she saw was grief, disbelief. It was etched on his young face, shot from his eyes. Like her, he was struggling for strength, trying to see through the horror to the other side.

"What will I do about my school?"

Lara almost choked on her taco. She'd never thought of his school. She certainly couldn't drive to San Clemente and back to the office every morning. "I don't know, Josh. We'll have to figure everything out. Tonight, let's not worry about anything. Tonight, let's just get by."

"Yeah," he said, his eyes drifting away, gazing out the window, filling with recognizable sadness.

Lara shoved the rest of the taco aside and looked at her nephew. Then she turned to the window and soaked up the night. Darkness and death were intrinsically compatible. Two spotlights illuminated the parking lot, but the vacant lot behind was completely black. The killer could be out there in the shadows, ready to pull the trigger the minute they walked out the door.

Placing her hands on the Formica table, she inched her fingers toward Josh's until she finally made contact. He didn't pull away, but he didn't look at her. Lara removed her hands and slid out of the booth. "Ready?" she said.

"Who killed my mother and Sam?" he said, finally turning to face her.

"I wish I knew, Josh."

"But you don't, right?"

"No, I don't," Lara answered, looking down at him. From this perspective, he looked small and helpless. His body was slouched low in the seat, his hair tumbling over his forehead and obscuring one eye. She wished she could wrap him in her arms and comfort him. What she really wanted was some miraculous way to assuage his grief and stop the pain. "Right now, Josh, we're going to go home and get some sleep. Tomorrow I'll start searching for the answers."

Running it through her mind, Lara decided the place to begin was with the victim's boyfriend who had threatened her in the courtroom. Then she would review her past cases to see which defendants were back on the streets possibly bent on revenge. Finally, she knew they would have to sift through the pages of Ivory and Sam's life: the pawnshop, the house in San Clemente, friends, neighbors.

Deep in her thoughts, she headed to the front of the restaurant. Josh passed her and stepped outside. By the time Lara saw him, he was halfway across the parking lot and a man in dark clothing was walking toward him from the direction of the vacant lot.

"No," Lara screamed, lunging at the doors, completely panicked. Racing across the parking lot, she seized Josh from behind and toppled them both to the ground. "Don't move," she whispered, her heart pounding, her eyes jerking to the man she'd seen. The man glanced at them and then walked away.

"Get off me," Josh yelled. "You're crazy. You're a nut. The whole world's crazy."

Lara stood and dusted herself off. "I saw that man

and I became frightened," she said quickly. "It's late. This isn't such a good area. I don't want anything to happen to you. Anyway, I'm sorry I knocked you down."

"You're sorry. Yeah, sure. Everyone's sorry." Josh stood there with a sullen look on his face while Lara unlocked the car. When they were both inside, he continued, staring straight ahead, his voice as sharp as a knife. "You know how many times I've heard that I'm-sorry bullshit? Every day, man. That's all my mom used to say to me, how sorry she was about everything. And when my dad died, that's all people said to me." He turned and moved his face close to Lara's. His breath was hot and sour. "Do me a favor, okay? Forget the sorry stuff."

They rode home in silence.

chapter 8

Lara lay on the sofa, the floral bedspread from the bedroom thrown over her. She had insisted that Josh take the bedroom. He was just a child, she had determined, and he had lost his mother. Right now all she could offer him was a bed and a burrito. In a deep, fitful sleep, she heard someone tapping gently on the door. Her pulse quickened and she rolled off the sofa to the floor, certain this was it, expecting someone to start shooting at her through the door. The clock read five in the morning. She seized it and listened to it. It was real. It wasn't just another prop.

"It's Officer Ringers," a man yelled through the door. "Judge Sanderstone . . ."

Her heart started pounding. Why in the world would they wake her this time of day?

"Sorry to wake you," the young officer said when Lara opened the door, his face haggard from lack of sleep, "but Detective Rickerson wants you to come to the house in San Clemente." He looked away. "You know, your sister's place. He's been there all night and he said there are some things you should see."

"Now? You want me to drive there now?" Lara whispered. "My nephew's asleep. Look, Officer, is this really necessary?" Her voice was sharp. She felt her sweatshirt and it was soaked with perspiration; damp strands of her hair fell across her face. Nightmares she couldn't remember, she thought, pulling the wet shirt away from her body. Even in sleep, the mind kept fighting, trying to accept the unacceptable.

"Sergeant Rickerson said so."

"You really think I should go?"

"Yeah." He looked around as if to say, What do I know, lady? I'm just following orders.

"There shouldn't be any traffic. Tell him I'm on my way. You're not going to leave, are you?" she asked the officer. She didn't want to leave Josh alone.

"I get off at six o'clock. They're sending a relief. Someone will be here."

"Fine," she said, closing the door in his face. She didn't know what to do about Josh, so she left him a note and some money on the kitchen table. McDonald's was right across the street. He could walk there for breakfast. She left him the spare key to the condo.

It was still dark when she left, but the darkness slowly changed before her eyes to a misty morning gray. The freeways were empty, particularly heading south away from Los Angeles. Bile rose in her throat. What had they found? A body. Something more gruesome than she could imagine, more gruesome than what had already occurred. Maybe Sam had killed someone and dissected them, burying their body parts under the house, and then someone had come looking for them and killed Sam and Ivory. Her mind was boggled; she was letting her imagination run wild.

From the moment she'd met Sam Perkins, she'd known he was nothing but trouble. She had an eye for things like that. But Ivory had been so alone and despondent, sliding into a haze of alcohol and drugs, dragging strange men home from bars. At first Lara had thought the marriage was for the best. One dirt bag was better than a dozen.

When she arrived at the house, three cars were in front. All the lights were still burning even though the sun was up and the day was evidently going to be a clear, sunny one. She hadn't brushed her teeth, hadn't combed her tangled hair, and she was wearing the sweatshirt and jeans from last night. She had slept in them.

Inside the living room, Rickerson pointed at the bedroom and she followed him reluctantly. The other officers continued working. Every drawer and cabinet in the house was open and everything out on the counters, the floors, everywhere. She cringed, stepping over an old photo album and a football trophy from years back, one of Charley's. Ivory's whole life was being invaded. Not only was the medical examiner about to invade her poor lifeless body, already ravaged and defiled, these strangers were snooping through every inch of her existence. The were touching her underwear, going through her toiletries: her Tampax, her Midol, her laxatives. It was disgusting, disrespectful, but Lara knew it had to be. Get yourself murdered and you're an open book, part of the public domain.

As she entered the bedroom, the bloodied walls pressed forward, surrounding her. She felt faint. Her body swayed back and forth, her stomach tumbling. Remnants of last night's taco were about to come spewing out.

Rickerson saw her and came over, extending his arm in front of her body. "Hold on. Take some deep breaths. Don't pass out on me. I guess I should have taken these things out in the living room. I'm sorry. I thought, though, that you should see them where I found them."

"I'm fine," she said weakly.

He opened a panel on the floorboard of the closet that was covered by a piece of cut carpet. It led to the crawl space under the house. Then he removed a large plastic storage box filled with various items. Some were clothes, others magazines and newspapers—some were photos. She tried to look at them, but her gaze kept returning to the walls, the blood, the nightmare in living color. She reached over and picked up a photo. Rickerson had spread them out on the dresser.

Her hands started trembling. She couldn't believe what she was seeing. "God," she said, "so he was taking pictures of her like this—the slimy bastard." She picked up another one. Ivory was wearing a black corset or something and thigh-high black boots, the same silly boots she had worn that night when she came to

Lara's house. She was wearing a mask and holding a riding crop. They were stupid pictures. They were disgusting. To Lara, they weren't even sexy. "So, I don't understand the importance of this, Rickerson. Certainly not to make me drive all the way over here at five in the morning just to see my sister like this. It might be disgusting, but lots of men take suggestive photos of their wives."

She gave him a look that said he should know about that type of thing. He was a man. Even old Nolan had once taken a picture of her naked when they were first married.

"Can you wait a minute?" Rickerson barked. "It's far more than the pictures. Your sister and brother-in-law were evidently into bondage, S and M, stuff like that. Did you know that?"

She stepped back in shock. As appalling as it was, her mind was adjusting to the bloody walls. "Of course I didn't know that."

"Well, if you'll look at these magazines and pictures, you'll see that they were more than a little interested in this stuff. Your sister was working in the trade, advertising for clients."

Lara's face turned white and her mouth fell open. The way Ivory had been dressed that last night she came to the condo . . . the phony breasts. "My sister was a prostitute? Is that what you're saying?" He was holding a thin newspaper, and she snatched it from his hand. He had circled a number of small ads. She tried to read them, but the print was too small and she didn't have her glasses. Her eyes were dry and scratchy from crying. She should have known. She shoved the paper back in his face. "I can't read it. I don't have my glasses."

Rickerson moved in close. Lara stepped back. "She wasn't a prostitute," he said. "Not exactly. She was a dominatrix and a submissive. Meaning, she would be whatever they wanted for a price. If they wanted to be whipped, she'd whip them. If they wanted to whip her, she'd let them. Most working girls choose either one or the other, but some play both sides of the fence to make more money. That's evidently what she did."

"No," Lara said, dragging the word out in disbelief, to the point where it almost echoed in the room. "No way. I can't believe this. She was a mother. She had a child. Surely you're not saying she brought strange men over here with her teenage son in the house and dressed up like this and whipped them." She still had the photo in her hand and was waving it foolishly in the air in front of him.

Worse than that, Rickerson thought, avoiding her eyes. He had no doubt whatsoever that this would be the most sensational case of his career. "Okay, let me just tell you what we've found. We've been working all night here." He looked at her, expecting sympathy, approval. "We found two private phone lines in this house, one of them in this bedroom with no extensions. Several of these ads had pictures of your sister with the number to call. We verified that it's this phone number. It rings in this room. Another answering machine had to be here to pick up these calls, but it's gone. We think the killer took it."

Lara started chewing on a hangnail, her eyes darting around the room, the walls and the blood back again in full horror. "How do you know there was an answering machine?" she asked in a small voice.

"There was a power pack and a plug that fits an answering machine. They took the machine but left the electrical cords. If you look under the bed there, you can see an indentation in the carpet where it sat. It must have been an old one, like a Record-a-Call. Big, you know. When they first came out, they were larger than they are now."

Here they were discussing progressive electronics and Ivory had been selling her body to anyone that wanted it. More than her body, actually, she had been selling her will, her dignity. "Then she probably did it a long time ago and then quit. The pawnshop was floundering with the economy. She told me. Possibly she did it once or twice and then stopped."

"Doesn't fly, Lara. This ad"—he raised the newspaper in her face—"was current. They renewed two weeks ago. We checked. And all these clothes and things . . . they're all costumes. You know, B and D costumes. I don't know if she had them over here to the house. She might have done out-calls. Or she could have serviced them while the kid was at school."

"Don't use that word!" she spat.

"What word?"

"*Serviced.* That's disgusting. You're talking about my sister."

"Sorry, okay. Like I told you, I've been up all night. We had to track people down on this and call them at home. The phone company, the paper . . ."

She followed him into Josh's bedroom. Clothes were strewn everywhere, and the contents of the drawers and closet were in a pile in the middle of the room. Not only was Ivory's life spread out for all to see, her son's was also. She saw little army men from when he had been a small child, a few stuffed animals, a few toy trucks. Then there were motorcycle magazines and *Playboys,* some of the pages ripped out. Lara bent down and began picking up a few items of his clothing to take back to the condo.

She suddenly dropped the clothes back onto the floor and fell onto Josh's twin bed, on the bare mattress now that they'd stripped it. She placed her hand over her mouth. Then she began sobbing. She couldn't stop. Her shoulders started shaking. It was all too much, just too much. This was all some sort of a dream, a delusion. She was cracking up, her mind unable to absorb this . . . the whole thing.

Could the poor kid have done this horrid thing? Could he have discovered what was going on and possibly killed Sam and then had to kill his mother when she walked in and saw him? Rickerson was talking to her. She couldn't concentrate on his words; they were floating around over her head somewhere like black birds or vultures.

" . . . do you think? It could be that Josh came home

and found your sister dead. He saw Sam Perkins over the body and went to his room for his weight. Or maybe he had it in his hand and heard noises and then saw the body, assuming Perkins killed her, which of course, he may have. Josh then bashed him to death in retaliation. That works."

Rickerson was talking to her as though she were another investigator. Her sister was dead and her fourteen-year-old nephew about to be accused of murder. "I don't know about any of this, but I know that animal she was married to was behind it all. That's all I know. Josh isn't a killer. I'd bet my life on it." She started walking to the door. Even if she had her own doubts about Josh, she owed it to her sister to defend him. She'd never felt so overwhelmed and horrified in her entire life.

"You are betting your life in a way," Rickerson said in a soft voice, almost taunting.

"What . . . what are you talking about now, Rickerson?" Then she saw the clothes she wanted to take and picked them up and held them to her chest.

"Well, you're living with him, aren't you?"

She didn't answer. She would probably have to pay to bury Sam Perkins. Now she might have to hire an attorney for her sister's child to defend him against a murder charge, possibly for more than just killing his stepfather, which might be feasible under the circumstances, but even his own mother, which was beyond comprehension. She shuffled to the car, tossed the handful of clothes in the backseat, and left.

Once Lara had left, Rickerson stepped outside the house and fired up his cigar. Then he reached in his pocket and took out the stack of Polaroids that he'd found inside the box in the crawl space held together with a rubber band, ones he had not shown Lara Sanderstone. One photograph was of a young boy, naked, posing suggestively with his buttocks to the camera, glancing back over his shoulder. He couldn't be certain, the boy was younger, but he'd bet his last nickel that he was looking at Lara Sanderstone's nephew. He'd found other photos as well, photos of children having sex with an adult male, his back to the camera. The man might even be Perkins himself. He shook his head and looked at the sky. He had started to tell her, but then decided against it. If the district attorney did prosecute the boy, these photos could be trump cards, and she was too close to the boy to play their hand. Judge or not, this was a criminal investigation and he was holding valuable evidence.

From the other photos he had found, along with this one, he assumed the boy had been exploited and more than likely sexually abused, how recently or to what extent he didn't know. But it was certainly a reason to kill someone, and it might not have been just his stepfather.

"Hey, Rickerson," another officer yelled, sticking his head out the back door. "Someone's on the phone for you. It's a reporter from the *Orange County Register.* Do you want to take the call or not?"

"I'll pass," he said, lost in his thoughts. Reporters were a pain in the neck anyway. They were going to be crawling all over his ass on this one.

"What do you want me to tell them?"

"Tell them it's a black day, buddy. Their weather report was all wrong and I don't want to talk to them. The sun's out, but it's just not shining. Know what I mean?" He shoved the photos back in his pocket and returned to the task.

chapter 9

Screeching into the parking lot and taking up two spaces, Lara rushed to the condo and threw open the door. Then she hurried to the bedroom. "Are you all right?" she asked. "I left you a note. I had to go out and take care of some things."

Josh sat up in the bed, rubbing his eyes. They were swollen and red.

"How did you sleep?" She wanted to take that back. How did she expect him to sleep?

He glared at her. "I slept."

"Okay, this is the plan," she said, trying to act like this was a normal day, a normal situation. "You go for breakfast across the street at McDonald's and I'll take care of some things at my office. Get a pen and write down the number. If you need me, you can call me from the pay phone on the corner. I'll be home by lunchtime." She tried not to let the strain show in her voice. It took a concentrated effort.

"I don't live here, remember?" he said sarcastically. "I don't know where a pen is?"

"I left one in the kitchen. Forget it, I'll write it down for you." She headed to the kitchen and then thought better of her plan. She needed to keep an eye on him. She went back to the bedroom. "Listen, scratch that plan. You'll go with me to my office."

"What for?"

"Don't worry about it. Take a shower now. I have some clean clothes." Again she searched his face, his eyes.

"My clothes?" He was standing up by the bed now,

holding the sheet around his waist. He must have been sleeping in his briefs. He wasn't wearing any other clothing.

"I went to the house and picked up some of your things."

His eyes expanded. "Did you get my bike?"

"No, I didn't. Take a shower." They were a pair to draw to, as Pop would say. She wasn't very wordy herself. Even though she wanted to get to the bottom of this kid, she actually didn't mind his brevity. It made things easier right now.

She glanced at his sinewy chest. She'd have to get him a robe. This wasn't appropriate. He was too big to walk around half naked. She threw the handful of clothes at him, and he headed to the bathroom. She was thankful that at least there were two bathrooms. While he was showering, she ran to Emmet's and called Phillip.

"It was on the news last night. Everyone's been calling. The phone's been ringing off the wall ever since I walked through the door at seven-thirty. They all send their condolences."

"Has Evergreen called?"

"Not yet. What can I do?"

"Call Evergreen. Explain to him what's happened and tell him that I'll need my calender covered for at least three days, possibly five. They'll have to get someone in there today. Maybe a pro-tem." A pro-tem was a local attorney willing to sit on the bench when the need arose. Since they had several judges out on vacation, it would be a mess. "Do that first and I'll be there in about twenty minutes."

Once she hung up, she turned to Emmet and let her shoulders fall. "I can't talk now," she told him. "But I'll try to come by later this evening."

"What . . . can . . . I do?" he said, his head rolling to one side in his wheelchair, gazing at her through his thick glasses.

"Just be my friend, Emmet. That's all anyone can do right now."

She left him sitting there by the window and ran back to the condo. Josh was on the sofa, dressed and waiting. He was fast, she thought. It didn't take him an hour to take a shower and put on his clothes like a lot of people.

"Are you going to your court like that?" he asked her.

She looked down at her clothes and blanched. She was still wearing the sweatshirt and jeans. An unusual feeling filled her stomach, and she reached over and impulsively threw her arms awkwardly around Josh's neck. His body was stiff. "That was nice that you mentioned that to me. I would have looked like a fool." She stepped back and looked down at her feet. "You should never let people see you when you aren't in control, not at your best. Not if you can help it. Do you know what I mean?"

"Yeah," he said, a blank look on his face.

She went to the bedroom to get dressed. It took her only five minutes and she looked about the same as she did every day: a hint of lipstick, her hair tied back at the base of her neck in one of the identical black bows, a simple blouse and skirt, practical shoes. "Better, huh?" she said, attempting a smile. It didn't work out well. The concrete of her face cracked only a hair.

"No," he said. "You look the same to me." He raised his shoulders and then let them fall.

"Oh," Lara said, thinking that he had expected her to walk out looking gorgeous, as his mother had when she was alive. It must be hard for him. There were resemblances, but not many. Ivory was lovely, almost glamorous without really trying. Even if her clothes weren't expensive, they were always colorful and flattering. Lara was pretty but plain, unnoticeable in a crowd. Her sister was always smiling and laughing, at least in the past, before Charley died and Sam Perkins took over her life.

She wasn't smiling now.

"We'll go through the drive-thru on the way to the office. McDonald's okay?"

He nodded. They left.

* * *

Returning to his home in San Clemente before his boys awoke, Rickerson dropped a sack on the kitchen counter and took out a loaf of bread, some lunch meat, a container of fresh orange juice, and a sack of apples that he had purchased on his way home. He threw open the freezer and removed some hamburger meat so it could thaw for dinner. Then he went to the sink and rinsed off a few dishes, placing them in the dishwasher. "There," he said, wiping his hands on a paper towel and looking around at the kitchen. He'd have to get one of the kids to mop the floor this week, but otherwise the place looked pretty good. Joyce had thought they would fall apart without her. They missed her, no doubt about it. But they were not about to fall apart. Not if he had anything to do with it.

Walking down the hall, he took his fist and banged one time on each boy's door. "Time to get up," he said. "Rise and shine in there, guys." Rushing back to the kitchen, he started a pot of coffee. Then he went to the laundry room and tossed a load of laundry in the washing machine.

His seventeen-year-old son, Stephen, stuck his head in the door yawning. "Got any clean underwear in here, Dad?"

Rickerson opened the dryer and yanked out a pair of Jockey shorts, tossing them to his son. "Be sure to turn on both the dryer and the dishwasher when you get home today."

"Sure," he said. He was a tall, muscular redhead like his father. He was also an outstanding student, under consideration for a full scholarship at Stanford and a member of the varsity golf team at his high school. "Hey, did you just get home or what?"

Rickerson leaned back against the dryer and rubbed the thick stubble on his chin. He was about to drop on his feet. "Yep, you got it, bud. Caught a bad one yesterday. It's going to be rough sailing around here for a while."

Stephen stepped into the doorway. "How 'bout a clean shirt? Anything like that in there?"

Rickerson took the entire load of clothes out of the dryer and dumped it on the tile counter behind him. "Be my guest. Looks like we mixed the whites again, kid. Got to be more careful in the future."

Looking down at his underwear, Stephen started laughing. They were a pale shade of blue. Not only that, but everything else in the load of laundry was blue. His fourteen-year-old brother had washed his brand-new Levis with all their underwear. "I kind of like it, you know. At least it's not pink like last time." He started to walk away and then stuck his head back in the door again. "Don't worry about anything, okay, Dad? I'll keep a lid on things around here for you."

Rickerson smiled at his son. He loved this kid. Without him, he would have never made it after Joyce moved out. But together they were doing a pretty damn good job, if he did say so himself. "I might not be home tonight. Just put that hamburger meat in the Hamburger Helper and read the instructions on the box. And make sure your brother does his homework."

"No problem," he said from the hall. "If he doesn't, I'll kick his butt."

Rickerson made his way down the hall to the master bedroom, his shoes clanking on the hardwood flooring. Sunlight was filtering in through the blinds, and the entire house had a warm yellow glow. He fell face first on the bed and then rolled over onto his back, staring at a streak of light and the minute dust particles dancing in the air. It wasn't such a bad house. It was small and it needed work, but for many years it had been a comfortable home. The kids had ridden their tricycles right outside on that sidewalk. They knew every single person on the block. They had watched the trees grow from tiny saplings to towering oaks.

But Joyce didn't want to live here anymore. She had said she wanted more from life. Evidently that meant more than he could give her. At first she'd insisted she only wanted a career, an education, and pleaded that if he could just bear with her until she graduated from Long Beach State with her degree in mechanical engineering, then they could start a new life. He didn't understand what was wrong with their old life. There, he thought, right there, that's where she had completely lost him. They'd raised two fine young sons. They owned their own home and had managed to save enough money for their children's education. He had his pension with the department, and when he retired, he could enter private security. They had planned their whole life from start to finish, and she had simply tossed it away.

"Dad," Jimmy said from the doorway, "can I talk to you a minute?"

Rickerson sat up and swung his feet to the floor. He wanted to light up a cigar, but he never smoked in the house. The boys hated it. "Sure, guy. Come here. Have a seat. What's on your mind?"

"When is Mom coming home?"

Rickerson draped an arm around his younger son, and they both leaned forward over their knees on the edge of the bed. Whereas Stephen looked like his father, Jimmy looked exactly like Joyce. He had her sandy blond hair, her full lips, her clear skin. And like Joyce, he had a tendency to put on weight. "Jim-boy, I wish I could tell you, but I just can't."

"But she's been gone three months now, and we never see her."

"Well, she's in college and she's working hard. One of these days you'll be in college, and you'll see how hard it really is."

"Is she ever coming back?"

Rickerson sighed. He asked himself the same question at least fifty times a day. "I just don't know, son."

"Are you going to get a divorce?"

About eighty percent of all the cops in the department were either divorced or remarried. Rickerson had always thought he would be different. His parents had been married for sixty years. In some ways he was old-fashioned. He thought marriage meant forever, thick or thin, rich or poor, until death—all that sappy stuff. "Divorce? I-I don't think so, but we can't rule it out.

Whatever your mother decides, we'll just have to accept. But look, if we do get a divorce, she's divorcing me. She's not divorcing you."

His son cleared his throat and stood. "I'm going to be late to school. Are you coming home tonight?"

"Maybe not for dinner, but I'll try to stop by before you go to bed."

Jimmy stood there for a moment. He was a sensitive child. He had such a full face and soft, expressive eyes, it was almost a baby face. "Be careful, Dad," he said.

Rickerson stood and ruffled his hair. Then he pulled him roughly to his chest and hugged him. "I'm always careful. Now get the hell out of here and let your old man get some sleep."

He slept until about noon and then leaped out of bed when the alarm sounded. The house was quiet, the kids at school. He felt stiff as a board and ached like hell.

Years ago, he'd been writing a speeding ticket alongside the highway when a car came along and plowed into him, pinning him between the two vehicles and breaking his back and right leg. He could have retired on disability, but he had wanted to stay on. In retrospect, he considered it the worst mistake of his life. Now, no matter how much he complained, they'd never give him disability. He'd proven that he could work with the pain.

The number of homicides that occurred in San Clemente were nominal. This one, he thought, staggering to the bathroom, was surely going to kill him, both emotionally and physically. He hated to see women and children exploited. It did something to him, made him absolutely crazy. No matter how long he worked at the job, there were some things a person just couldn't stomach.

How many loans had that guy Perkins made anyway? Would there be thousands of tickets to dig through and try to track down? It would take them years to even make a dent. And now with the woman working the trade, turning tricks, and the implications of child pornography or sexual exploitation, the possibilities seemed endless. Judge Lara Sanderstone had demanded that every man in the department sink their teeth in this case, but that just wasn't going to happen. Someone had to cover the streets, the stolen cars, the drunk drivers, the injury accidents. The department wasn't that big, and this was a humongous case.

He stood under the shower, letting the hot water pound his aching back. All the bending and stooping last night and this morning had taken its toll, and it was only the beginning. By the time he waded through the pawnshop, he'd be hurting so bad that he would barely be able to stand upright.

After a short conversation with the medical examiner last night, they were both of the opinion that two separate killers could have been involved. It didn't make sense to bash in one person's head and not bash in the other's as well. Two distinct m.o.'s usually meant two killers. The manner in which a person committed a crime was almost as exclusive as their fingerprints.

It was simple, exactly like he'd told Lara Sanderstone. Kid came home from school, found the stepfather in the bedroom with his mother's body, and then smashed the fucking hell out of him with his twenty weight. He'd outright admitted that he hated the man, and it looked as though he had good reason.

Or, he thought, maybe after years of abuse Josh had simply gone over the edge and killed them both. All they had to do now was prove it, and once they did, the kid would probably get off with little more than a slap on the wrists and Rickerson would finally get his promotion to lieutenant.

There was no forced entry—another fact that pointed the finger at the boy. Even though Josh had said there was a hidden key, it was doubtful if they entered that way, using the key, killing the two people and then being cool enough to remember to put the key back exactly where they found it. If that was the case, he'd be dealing with a sophisticated killer, one he'd probably never catch, more than likely a person who did this type of thing for a living.

The biggest problem was the kid's clothes. Not a speck of blood on them. It was the first thing they'd checked. They'd torn the house apart and didn't find any blood-stained clothing. No one could beat someone as savagely as this man had been beaten and walk away without a speck of blood.

He grabbed the towel, wrapped it around him, and studied his image in the mirror. Seeing a blemish, he stood close and picked at it. Then he chastised himself. The dermatologist had told him years ago that the scars he had were from picking at his face. Old habits die hard, he thought. He smeared shaving cream on his face and started shaving.

Of course, the kid could have killed them and then buried or tossed the stained clothing somewhere before he called the cops at four o'clock that afternoon. They'd have to search the entire area on foot. Then they'd have to check with his school and determine if he was actually present in the last class of the day. Once they had the established time of death, they could start formally building the case. He needed help. He'd have to go to the chief today and get every possible body they could find.

They were wasting their time with the pawnshop. The boy had been exploited, sucked into the life-style of his mother and her new husband more than likely as a money-making proposition. Whether the boy was aware that they were selling his photographs or not was up for grabs, but Rickerson bet they were. With everyone cracking down on child pornography from local authorities to the feds, perversion of this type must have a high price tag.

They might have been selling more than just Josh's photographs. They could have been selling the boy himself.

* * *

Lara had Josh situated down the hall in the law library. She'd tossed a stack of magazines on the table and left him there. He'd talked her into ordering a Sausage McMuffin for breakfast, and it was burning a hole through her abdominal wall. Besides, she was running now on adrenaline: tense, shaky, but flying. And she was running on a razor-sharp edge of bitterness toward whoever had committed these heinous acts.

"Did you find Evergreen?" she asked Phillip. "Is my calendar covered?"

"Finally," the young man said, looking Lara in the eye. As soon as their eyes met, he pulled his away. "He's sitting for you himself."

In her chambers, she went over what she thought she wanted for the funeral with Phillip. "Call the morgue and find out when they're going to release the body." She gave him the name of the cemetery where she'd bought the other plots for Charley and their parents. "Buy two cemetery plots instead of one." She paused, sipping her coffee, scanning the spines of the books on the shelves in front of her, looking at anything but Phillip's face etched with sympathy and concern. This was so hard. He was staring at her and she felt like melting in an oily puddle all over the floor. Anything, she prayed, anything but tears. More tears she couldn't stand. The extra plot wasn't for Sam Perkins, it was for her. She didn't feel the need to explain that to Phillip, but she and Ivory would one day be side by side, next to Charley and their parents. Ivory would like that, just like she knew Ivory would like a white casket with brass fittings. She liked pretty things. "I want a white casket with brass fittings. As long as it's under ten thousand, buy it. Do that and come back when you're finished."

Lara bent down and was starting to make notes on a yellow pad when she noticed that Phillip was still standing in front of her desk, a strange expression on his face. "Yes?" Lara said.

"I-I never realized you had a sister until the police called the day of the murders."

"Well, we weren't very close. Not in recent years."

"You look . . . I . . ." The young man's face turned parchment white. "I'm sorry. I'll make those phone calls now."

Before Lara could continue the conversation, Phillip went out of the room and closed the door behind him. He was an extremely private person. Sometimes she wondered about him, about his social life. Today he looked awful, as if he were the one who had lost a loved one. Maybe he had, she thought, shaking her head. Possibly he had lost someone recently and had kept it to himself.

She had no earthly idea what she should do about Sam Perkins. Ivory had never mentioned family of any kind, but someone would probably come crawling out of the woodwork in the next day or two, thinking they would be inheriting a going business with the pawnshop. Thank God, she thought, she had insisted on her name on the title. Even if the business was shit, she'd have some means of covering her loss. She'd sell the damn building.

As to Sam, she'd just let him sit in a meat locker until some of his own clan claimed him. After what he'd done to Ivory, she gave thought to calling one of those cheap cremation places, where they charge only a few hundred bucks. If no one surfaced to claim him, she decided, he was on his way to the flames.

She went through the files on her desk and found those on the morning calendar were gone. Evergreen must have taken them. She wondered how long it had been since the old goat had handled the felony arraignment calendar. The position required some preparation but not much. Most of the day was consumed with the parties entering pleas, setting matters over for trial. The bail reviews required some judicial renderings, and she always read the reports generated by the probation department outlining the defendant's criminal history, if any, and at least scanned the police reports on the crime. Releasing someone into the community was a significant decision. Not only did a judge have to weigh the factors indicating whether or not the defendant would flee, but they had to determine the risk of recidivism. And the victim's safety had to be considered. In violent offenses this was particularly germane. Sometimes while suspects were pending prosecution, they went back and finished the job, actually killing someone. Lara made every attempt to keep violent or sex offenders in custody pending trial, even if she had to put her neck on the line to do it.

Most of the cases scheduled for that day she had already reviewed. She took out each file scheduled for the afternoon session and made detailed notes to Evergreen. Then she called Phillip and had him carry them to the court.

Alone in her chambers, she relished the cloistered privilege of her position. No one walked in unannounced except other judges, sometimes a D.A. Today, of all days, this mattered. She glanced at the lights on the phones and saw they were all blinking. The bell was turned off in her chambers. When Phillip was busy, the main reception center picked up the excess calls. In her hands were at least twenty pink message slips. She shuffled through them.

Irene had returned her call from the night before. She'd obviously heard the news by now. Lara tossed that slip in the trash, thinking she'd call her tonight or try to catch her in recess before she left the building.

Most of the other callers were condolences and offers to help. Benjamin had called and left a number at a hotel in San Francisco. She placed that one in her purse. The others she read, committed the names to memory, those who had taken the time to call, and then tossed them too. Nolan had called. Probably because she made the papers. Press. He loved it. If she'd thought of that aspect, he might have actually come last night. He liked that kind of thing. It was Hollywood, right up his alley. His message she didn't simply toss. She took the time to rip it up. It made her feel better.

She hit the intercom and Phillip answered. "I'm

speaking with the funeral home now. They're on hold. The casket's going to run at least fifteen thousand or it won't be waterproof."

She'd been through this before. She'd buried her father and mother. She had made all the arrangements when Charley was killed. She knew all the scams and sales techniques in the most unscrupulous industry in the universe. "Tell the guy I don't care if it's watertight. She's dead. She can't drown. Ten thousand and not a penny more.

"Fine," he said. "Anything else?"

"No," she said, the word barley audible.

As soon as the light went off, Lara called Phillip back on the intercom and asked him to send for the Henderson file. She wanted him to give Rickerson the name and address of the boyfriend who had threatened her, let him track the kid down, find out where he was yesterday. She had to put some of this fear to rest or she would lose her mind, and she wanted to move out of the condo and back into the house. She couldn't spend that many more nights on that sofa.

Her mind kept returning to Ivory and the photos she'd seen. What her poor sister had been made to do. She couldn't bear to think of it. Sam must have coerced her into prostituting herself just as he coerced her into asking Lara for money. She felt like taking a match and cremating the bastard herself.

It was the only explanation, she told herself. Ivory certainly didn't think this one up by herself. It had slimy Sam stamped all over it. Of course, even before she'd met Sam, Ivory had been drinking and experimenting with cocaine. "It makes me feel so good," she had told Lara. "It makes me feel smart and confident. I've never felt that way in my whole life." Maybe having men pay her for sex made Ivory feel powerful and confident too. Possibly she actually enjoyed whipping them and degrading them.

Lara felt like taking every single paper and file off her desk and hurling it at the wall. Why hadn't she seen it? Why hadn't she stopped it? She was her sister and she was a goddamn judge. Wasn't she supposed to be intuitive and observant? Hadn't she seen what was happening to her own flesh and blood? The night Ivory had come to her house, she was dressed like a streetwalker.

Lara suddenly found herself gulping air. Quickly she spun her chair around to face her great-grandfather's portrait. When she was little, her grandfather used to come and visit and tell her stories about the past, about her ancestors. Not from history books had she learned how white men had taken away their precious land and moved them to reservations. She had learned these things as a tiny child sitting at her grandfather's feet, listening to him drone on and on in his deep voice, her eyes locked on his leathery skin. The one thing she had learned early in life was that a person sometimes had to accept the unacceptable.

It was time to get Josh and leave before people started trying to get in to see her and shower her with sympathy. Besides, she had to get him to a psychologist and start checking into schools. If he hadn't killed Sam, or anyone else, he was going to need therapy to get through this. If he had to live with her, which she was fairly certain was going to be the case, then he'd probably need a shrink until she packed him off to college. She didn't know if she had what it took to raise a teenager. It was going to be a long, long haul.

Then a thought flashed in her mind: boarding school. Perfect. She didn't know why she hadn't thought of it before. Not now, she thought, passing Phillip, still on the phone, and heading down the carpeted corridor to the law library, but soon. As soon as the psychologist thought he was ready. At least with this thought in mind, she could see an end in sight. She doubted if he wanted to be with her anyway.

"Let's go, Josh," she said softly. He wasn't reading magazines. He was just sitting there staring into space.

Under the right circumstances, he might even be a nice companion, Lara thought as they headed down the hall. What he needed was stability, structure. He needed hot meals on the table, someone waiting when he got home from school, someone to wash and iron his clothes. Lara just didn't have the time, and unfortunately, she didn't have the inclination. What did she possibly know about raising a teenage boy? Nothing, absolutely nothing.

Again her eyes drifted to the shaggy-haired young man walking next to her. He didn't cry, he didn't complain much, he didn't say much. He seemed to like junk food. If she could find a man like him, she might consider getting married again.

They entered the security level, and he pushed the button for the garage. "What're we going to do now?" he said.

"We're going to go home and arrange for you to see a doctor, a psychologist. Someone you can talk to. And I'm going to stop off and buy a portable cellular phone."

"No way," he said, his face frozen into hard lines. "I'm not going to some crazy person's doctor."

Lara was five-three in her stocking feet. She never wore heels. Josh was looking down on her inside the small space of the elevator. "Well, you have to go," she told him. "I'm not that good of a listener. You need to talk this out. Who knows, maybe I do too. Maybe we'll both go." It was a tactic. She could see immediately that it wasn't going to work.

"You're not going," he snapped. "You're just saying that to get me to go. Right?"

"Right. Pretty astute there, kid," she said and brought forth a weak smile. "But I might, let me tell you." The elevator doors opened and they headed to her car.

"Can I drive?" he asked, his voice echoing in the underground garage. "I can drive, you know. Sometimes Mom lets me drive to the store and back for things like milk."

Both of them froze. He'd used the present tense. These were the kinds of things that took getting used to. They were like nails in a coffin. They just kept on pounding at you long after the person was gone. She knew. He started sniffing and breathing heavy. Lara didn't know what to do or say, but she couldn't let him continue. If the boy broke down, she'd break down with him. She handed him the car keys. "Drive." Then she narrowed her eyes and peered up at him. "Were you telling me the truth? You really know how to drive a car? If you don't, we'll get killed."

For the first time she saw her sister's son smile. She felt like she'd won a Nobel prize. It didn't really matter if they got killed, she thought. What mattered was that he smiled.

They went careening out of the underground parking tunnel, barely missing the concrete wall. Lara almost wet her pants, but she didn't. Instead she checked her seat belt and gripped the dashboard, preparing herself for the impact—if not the wall, the way he was driving, they were going to hit something. And they were going to hit it with the most extravagant possession Lara had: the Jaguar, her pride and joy. The smile on Josh's face was enormous. He was sitting up close to the steering wheel and licking his lips with excitement.

"A Jaguar . . . I can't believe I'm driving a Jaguar. Man, wait till my friends hear about this. How much does a car like this cost?"

So what if he bashed in the Jaguar? Lara thought. She was insured, maybe not for an unlicensed driver, but right now she didn't care. It was only a car, an expensive collection of metal and glass and chrome. And sometimes rules had to be broken, exceptions made. Just keep smiling, she said to herself, glancing at him. Just keep smiling, kid, and we'll get through this and make our way to the other side.

chapter 10

About two blocks from the government center, Lara asked Josh to pull to the side of the road and let her drive. He'd run a red light and almost had a head-on collision.

"Why are you living in that place?" he asked her. "There's nothing in there at all. I thought you had a house or something."

"I do," Lara said. She certainly didn't want to scare the kid to death, tell him someone might be stalking her after what he'd been through. She cleared her throat, preparing herself to lie. "See, Josh, they're doing some remodeling at my house, so I rented the condo. It was close to the court."

He was silent. That took care of that. The car phone rang and she let Josh answer it. It was Rickerson. He handed her the phone.

"Thought I would just touch base with you. We're going through the pawnshop tickets now. Then we're going to start on his books."

She wanted to ask about the autopsy, find out if it had been completed yet and the findings, but it wasn't the type of thing to discuss in front of Josh. "Call me later this evening when you've talked to the M.E. What about prints?" Josh wasn't paying attention anyway. He was staring out the window. The smile had been a momentary thing.

"Lab's working on it as we speak. We lifted all kinds of prints, but who knows who they belong to. . . . I wanted to point something else out to you. There was no forced entry, remember? That means that either the killer or killers were inside the house to begin with, or they were known to the victims and were allowed to enter. Don't you think that rules out someone Perkins made a loan to here at the pawnshop? Just doesn't make sense that they'd open the door to someone like that and let them walk right into their house."

"Look, Rickerson, Ted . . . you already told me that last night. Aren't you the man who informed me that we had to cover all the bases? I want every single pawn ticket checked out."

"There's got to be at least a thousand of these tickets. Some of them go back a number of years. We're only going to follow through on the ones going back six months or so, or we'll be here digging through this shit forever. And we're in the process of tracking down all the phone records."

Lara glanced at Josh and gripped the phone, steering the car with her other hand. "Well, then I guess you'll be busy. Don't you agree that we should pursue this at least? The pawnshop."

"Lara," he answered, a touch of sarcasm in his husky voice, "you seem to think there are hundreds of officers available to sift through this stuff. There's three of us right now. I'm trying to round up more men, but we can't produce what we just don't have. If we get another serious case in this city, there'll be two of us, and then as time goes on, there'll only be me. We also have to get over to the house again and comb the neighborhood looking for evidence the killer could have discarded, like bloody clothes—"

"Tell you what. You have someone box up the pawn tickets and bring them to my condo. I'll personally start going through them in the next few days, and your people can work on the phone records. Let's trace every call from that house and give me a list of the names after you run them through the system for wants and warrants."

Josh was tugging on her sleeve. "Ask them to bring my bike, okay?"

She looked at him and felt her heart melt. All he had

of his old life right now was a few clothes. His parents were dead, his home was a shambles, and he was stuck with a woman he hardly knew. "Forget that, Rickerson. I'll come and get the pawn tickets myself. But do me a favor, okay? Go to the house and get the kid's bike and meet me at the pawnshop in San Clemente. I'll be there in about forty minutes."

She could hear Rickerson breathing. He didn't answer. The breathing was loud. She started to hang up when he finally spoke. "I can't release evidence in a homicide."

"Let's set things straight right now, Rickerson. I more or less own the pawnshop. My name's right on the deed of trust. I provided the funding for them to buy it. You've got to make a decision here. Are those pawn tickets valuable evidence or merely pawn tickets? You seem to think they're merely pawn tickets and that the whole thing is a waste of time. I'm offering to give you a hand."

"I'll get the bike," he said. "And Lara, let me tell you something, you need to get that boy to a shrink right away. Don't wait. I'm telling you. That boy needs treatment."

Lara glanced at Josh again. At least the detective had expressed a genuine concern. She appreciated that. "Oh," she said, "did Phillip call you with the information on the Henderson case? . . . You know, what we discussed last night?"

"Yeah," he said. "I've got a man trying to track him down now. Once we find him, I'll interview him." With that, he hung up.

Rickerson was right. She'd have to find a psychologist for Josh today. She slipped onto the freeway and, for the third time in less than two days, headed to San Clemente. She wondered about Josh's friends, his school work, reestablishing his life, but it was too early for that. Now they had to tread water and deal with the sorrow, the funeral, the black days ahead of them—days Lara knew would get worse before they got better. The awful truth that his mother had been murdered would start to sink all the way to the bone soon enough. Lara already felt it coming. Her own subconscious was packed with reality as sharp as a machete, about to slice its way into her every thought and cut her heart into ribbons.

"Isn't that the exit to San Clemente?" Josh said, looking out the window. "You just passed it."

"Oh," Lara said, lost in her thoughts. "I'll take the next exit."

"You're going to miss this exit too," Josh said, all excited. "Hurry, get in the right-hand lane."

They were soon on the city streets, approaching the pawnshop. Lara felt tears gathering in her eyes and bit the inside of her mouth. If a person could only rewrite history knowing what was ahead, more or less stop the wheels of life from turning the wrong way. But of course, that wasn't reality. A child with no parents, she thought, glancing at Josh, Ivory's body in a tiled autopsy room—that was reality.

First they lugged the two huge boxes to the condo filled with records from the pawnshop, and then Lara sent Josh back down to bring his bike up from the trunk of the car. Lara took out the portable phone she had purchased and called Irene Murdock. She caught her in recess.

"Lara, darling," Irene said, "I've been frantic. I've been calling your house since I heard this on the news. Are you all right? Your sister and brother-in-law. How horrid."

"I guess you've heard it all by now," Lara said, collapsing on the sofa.

"Well, I don't know if I've heard it all. I've heard what's been on the news. What do they have? Do they know who did this despicable thing? Do they have any witnesses, leads?"

"No," Lara said. "They have next to nothing." She then gave her the cellular phone number and told her why she wasn't staying at her own house. "What do you think, Irene? Tell me the truth. Do you think I'm in danger, that these crimes are related? Could it be the young man who threatened me?" Lara got the words out of her mouth just as Josh returned.

"Obviously, it doesn't sound good. Did you know that a man once stalked me? It was about five years ago. I had sentenced him to prison on an armed robbery. When he got out, he followed me home from the courthouse and parked outside my house. It was terrible. By the time the police unit would get there, he would flee. We finally got a restraining order. Then we had to wait for him to violate it. Eventually he ended up back in prison, but it was an agonizing ordeal. After that I bought a gun. I carry it in my purse everywhere I go now."

"I didn't know that, Irene," Lara said, and she really didn't want to know it either. Sometimes a person just wanted to pretend everything was all right even when it wasn't. "So, you don't think I should go back to my house?"

"No, certainly not," she said. "Where are you now? You said you're staying in Santa Ana in a condo? Possibly John and I can come by tonight. Why don't you give me the address?"

"No," Lara said quickly, "but thanks." She looked around and saw Josh standing there, practically breathing down her neck. "Tell you what, Irene, I'll call you back later. I have my nephew here now. I can't really talk."

"If we don't come over tonight, we'll come over tomorrow. I'll bring you some food—some things you can heat in the microwave. That poor child. This is just so terribly sad."

"I'll let you know. Hold on." Lara turned to Josh and asked him if he could step into the other room a minute so she could talk to Irene privately. Once he was in the bedroom with the door closed, Lara carried the portable phone to the kitchen and whispered, "I need a good psychologist for my nephew. Maybe John can recommend someone?"

"I know someone myself. Wait a minute . . . I have

his number right here in my Rolodex. He's a psychiatrist. That would be better, don't you think? They can prescribe medication. His name is Dr. Frederick Werner." She rattled off the number.

"You know, Irene," Lara said, cupping her hand over the phone and peeking around the corner to make certain Josh was still in the bedroom, "I'm at a loss with this kid. He's bitter. He's obviously disturbed. There might even be a slim chance that he was involved in this nightmare."

"What do you mean? Did he see the killer? Was he an eyewitness?"

"No, I . . ." Lara paused and inhaled. "Maybe he killed my brother-in-law. It's possible. He was killed with a dumbbell and it was Josh's dumbbell. There was no love there, let me tell you."

Irene didn't answer. At first Lara thought they had been disconnected. "Did you hear me?" she said.

"Put that out of your mind, Lara. That's a terrible thought. Just get him to a psychiatrist and pursue this boy who threatened you. Call me later and we'll talk in greater detail."

Lara was about to tell her about Ivory's occupation and the awful things they'd found in the crawl space when Irene said she had to return to the bench. Just as well, Lara thought. She didn't really want anyone to know.

Josh's bike was leaning against the door in the entryway. With the boxes and now the bike, the condo was beginning to feel no larger than a walk-in closet. She quickly contacted the psychiatrist and arranged for him to see Josh at six o'clock that evening. Then she clicked off the phone and leaned back on the sofa with her eyes closed. She might really have to do what she told Josh and see this man herself, she thought, maybe get some sedatives so she could sleep.

She opened her eyes and looked at the boxes. It would take her forever to go through all those pawn tickets. Not only that, but she had no idea what she was looking for. Even if the poor kid hadn't killed them, he might know a lot more than he was telling. There was only one way to find out. Start asking.

"Josh," she said, having told him to come out of the bedroom, "come here and sit down on the sofa with me." She patted a place next to her. "Let's have a little talk. There's the sodas we bought in the refrigerator and some chocolate chip cookies on the counter. Why don't you get them?"

It was almost lunchtime. Cookies and Coke would have to do. Tonight she'd try to find him something halfway healthy. Maybe she'd buy a roast chicken from the deli department at the supermarket before they went to see Dr. Werner. If the poor child had not shared her affinity for junk food, he would be starving to death. At least she didn't have to worry about malnutrition yet. Not for a few days anyway.

They were sitting side by side on the sofa munching cookies and sipping soda from cans. They weren't looking at each other. Finally Josh said, "What do you want to talk about?"

Lara sighed, a long one. "What were things like at home?"

"What do you mean?" He set the sack of cookies aside and brushed his hair out of his eyes.

"What were things like with your mom and Sam? Were they fighting? Was he drinking? Was your mother drinking?"

"Dunno." His back became rigid and he stared straight ahead.

Lara touched his arm and he looked at her. "It isn't going to work this way, Josh. You lived in that house. You're a smart boy. You would have known if they were drinking or fighting."

He was silent and unresponsive. She could almost see the memories flashing in his eyes. They weren't happy ones. That Lara knew for sure.

"Please, Josh, for your mother's sake, you have to help us. You were there yesterday. You saw what happened, what someone did in that house. I know you want them to pay as much as I do, as much as we all do."

"Sam was a bastard."

"You're not going to get an argument from me on that one. Go on . . . there has to be more than that."

Lara had not opened the drapes in the condo and it was dark. Some light was filtering through from the small kitchen window behind them, but their faces were bathed in shadows. She started to get up and open the drapes and then thought better of it. Somehow it seemed to work better for both of them to discuss this in the shadows.

"Sam drank at least a six-pack of beer every night. He'd get drunk and then start fights with us—Mom and me. They had fights over money, things like that. Sometimes Mom would tell me to go out somewhere on my bike. Then when I came back home, they'd be in the bedroom with the door closed. The next day they'd be fine."

"Josh, did Sam ever hit your mother? Did you ever see him hitting her or hurting her in any way? Did anyone else ever come over to the house? You know, strange men. Think hard. Anyone you didn't know?"

He looked sharply at Lara. "I don't remember, okay? Everyone keeps asking me all these questions, and I just don't remember." He stood and looked at his bike by the door. "I don't want to talk about this anymore. Can I go out on my bike?" His face was set, his lips compressed. She'd touched a nerve.

"Wait just a minute and then you can go out. I'm not going to hold you prisoner here." She paused. She'd have to let him out of the house. They'd go crazy for sure if they just sat hour after hour inside this dark hovel. Hopefully, if someone was out to harm her, they didn't know about Josh or where they were staying. He was several feet away, standing by the door, his hands on the bike.

No wonder he wanted that bike, Lara thought. It had been his only escape mechanism. When things got tough, he took off. Things were getting tough now. She spoke in a calm, matter-of-fact voice, not wanting to emphasize her words. "Did you ever see anything that you didn't understand? Maybe something relating to your mother?" The images from this morning flashed in her mind. Her eyes quickly returned to Josh when she heard the door open and saw him pushing the ten-speed out the door onto the sidewalk.

"Josh, wait," Lara said, heading to the front door. "Stay right in this little area here by the condo. I don't want you wandering off. And you have to help us, tell us everything you saw or heard."

He turned around and stared at her, his gaze intense, his eyes blazing with hatred. "You're a fucking bitch," he yelled. "Now you're all concerned about my mom . . . about me. Now that she's dead. You never gave a shit about us when she was alive. I'd rather go to juvenile hall than stay here with you."

Lara took a few tentative steps toward him. "You're wrong, Josh. I always cared about you, about your mother."

"Yeah, sure," he said, flipping his head back to get his hair out of his eyes. His voice went up several octaves. It was almost the little boy voice before going through puberty. His face twisted up like he was trying to keep from crying. "You used to come and see me, take me to the movies, buy me things. Then you just stopped coming . . . like we weren't good enough for you. We were just trash to you. You—"

His words stung. "Josh," Lara pleaded, "listen to me. Your mother wouldn't let me see you. It wasn't that I didn't want to . . . She got angry with me . . . It was her way to get back."

Glaring at her, he jumped on the seat and pedaled away, slamming the door to the condo behind him.

Lara went back to the sofa and sat there in the dark, leaning over onto her knees, her head in her hands. She'd had no idea that those earlier visits had actually meant something to Josh, that he'd missed her, even thought she'd abandoned him. He'd been a skinny, aloof twelve-year-old then. She'd always assumed he was bored silly on their little outings. She was wrong. He was bitter. Bitter at Lara, his mother and stepfather, the miserable world in general. Just how bitter she couldn't judge. Hopefully, she prayed, not bitter enough to become a killer.

For a long time she just sat there in the dark. She tried to think. She tried to rationalize. Her mind was so muddled that her thoughts were racing in a million different directions at once. She finally stood and went to the bathroom, thinking she'd take a shower, hoping it would help. Tossing the bedspread back on the bed, she saw something sticking out from under the mattress. She bent down and pulled it out. It was a backpack. She vaguely recalled Josh walking in with it last night. Starting to drop it back where she found it, she instead dropped to the edge of the bed and began rummaging through the contents. There were three textbooks, some notebook paper, a few pens. She took them all out and placed them on the bed. Then she saw it.

In her hands was a rolled-up T-shirt that had been shoved in the bottom of the backpack. On the T-shirt was blood.

Still holding it in her hand, she ran to the front door and flung it open. Why, she didn't know. Then she slammed it and went into the bathroom, sitting down on the toilet seat and staring at it. "No, God," she cried. "It can't be. It just can't be." She was shaking; her heart was pounding. Her palms were sweaty and she felt cold, really cold. She spread the T-shirt open all the way and tried to estimate how much blood there was. It wasn't much, just a long red streak. For a second she thought it might be paint. She held it to her nose and sniffed it. Then she tried to flick some of it off with her fingernails. It wasn't paint. It was blood.

She walked out of the bathroom and started pacing inside the bedroom. She felt like she was walking upside down. The room kept spinning and moving. Visions of Josh bringing the dumbbell down on Sam's head kept flashing in her mind. What was she going to do? She couldn't turn her own nephew over to the police, yet she couldn't allow him to get away with murder. No matter who Sam was, or what he had done, he was a human being. There was no way to reconcile herself to murder.

She thought of all the possible reasons for the bloody T-shirt. He could have fallen off his bicycle. That made sense. It could even be an animal's blood, like a dog's or a cat's. A lot of teenagers were into Satanism and cutting up cats. Suddenly a thought came to mind and she grabbed the textbooks, quickly reading the spines and then tossing them back into the backpack. Maybe he took biology, she thought, and he had dissected a frog. There was no biology textbook.

She was completely panicked.

Glancing at the door, she realized he could walk in at any moment. If he saw her with the T-shirt, he could even kill her. He was big enough. He could beat her to death, strangle her, suffocate her like Ivory. Terrified, she rolled up the T-shirt as she had found it and replaced all the items back in the backpack.

The phone rang and Rickerson started speaking. She'd left her new number with the switchboard operator at the San Clemente P.D.

"The S.O. just called and they lifted a few sets of prints from your house in Irvine. One set we can't match yet, probably one of your friends, but the others come back to a lowlife hoodlum by the name of Packy Cummings. He's got a record a mile long and even did a stint at San Quentin. He's been listed as a suspect on several homicides in the past. He's a bad actor, Lara. We're trying to pick him up now. No prints at the murder scene, though. They must have worn gloves."

Lara's breath caught in her throat and she couldn't speak. She hadn't heard half of what the detective had said. She couldn't tell him about what she had found. She wanted to, but she just couldn't. Not until she was sure. She owed her sister at least that much. They'd drag the poor kid back down to the station and give him the third-degree; the press could even get wind of it and Josh would be tried and convicted even if it turned out to be nothing. Lara knew too well how these things happened. Once they accused a person in print, even after a full trial and acquittal, the rumors and innuendos sometimes persisted for the rest of their lives. "I . . . I'm sorry," she said, "repeat what you just said."

He did. She listened and then something seized her. The name Packy Cummings. "Wait, Rickerson, don't hang up. What's his full name? Is it Packard Cummings?"

"Yeah," he said. "You know the guy?" Rickerson was a little shocked on that one, unless she knew him from the courts. He sure hoped he wasn't one of her boyfriends. That would be downright absurd.

"He was on my calendar . . . I think it was the day before Ivory was murdered. He's an informant on a narcotics case working with a local agency. I don't know which one, but I can find out." Lara had all these crazy thoughts in her mind right now, like maybe they had somehow confused her house with that of a drug dealer's. The investigating officer had said it appeared they were looking for drugs. Things like that did happen. Several times the LAPD had gone out with their battering ram, a big tank, and destroyed an innocent person's house.

"Nah," Rickerson said finally, "this guy isn't working for anyone inside the law. One of the people he was suspected of knocking off about seven years ago was an undercover cop. They'd be out of their minds. Who told you that?"

"Leo Evergreen. You know who Evergreen is, don't you? He's the presiding judge."

The line was silent. Rickerson was thinking. The sheriff's department had called him about this guy. They knew nothing about him. A drug case, of course, could mean the DEA or some other agency, but to use a man like this as an informant? Not unless he could help bust the Colombian drug cartel or something. Even if the man had been working as an informant, what was he doing breaking into houses?

Rickerson could smell something, and it was as rotten and foul as they came.

"I'll have to make some phone calls and get back to you."

"Look," she said, "why don't I just call Evergreen and ask him which agency the man is working for? They called him and asked him to release Cummings O.R. as a professional courtesy. I didn't want to do it, but he pressed. It could be a mistake, you know. Some type of crazy mistake."

Again Rickerson was quiet, reviewing things in his head. Judge releases a guy O.R. one day and the next day he pays her back by ransacking her house. Didn't make sense. "Lara, I don't like the way this thing is stacking up. Not one little bit. I'm sending my man back over there to watch your place, and believe me, I wouldn't do it if I didn't feel you were in danger. The chief's gonna have a fit when he finds out. We need every warm body to work this case, not sit around in a parking lot."

"What about Evergreen?" She looked at the door, thinking Josh would come back any minute, truly frightened now. She'd released this man. This man who had broken into her home. And her own nephew had a bloody T-shirt hidden in his backpack. What else could possibly happen? She was beside herself now. She wanted to throw herself on the floor and scream. "Look," she told him, talking fast, "I don't really care who broke into my house. What I care about is who killed my sister."

"If they are one and the same, then . . ."

Right now she prayed that they were one and the same. Anything or anyone but Josh. "Is that possible? You know that this Cummings man is the murderer?"

"Anything is possible," he said. "Keep this to yourself until I get back to you. Don't tell anyone anything. You know even at the top, things get around. Let's just keep a lid on this until I check some things out. And listen, Lara, I had to call Social Services. They'll probably be contacting you about the kid today."

"Ted, tell me something. When you picked up Josh from the neighbors' house the night of the murder, was he carrying anything?"

"I don't recall. Another unit drove him down to the station. Why do you ask?"

"Forget it," Lara said quickly. Rickerson hung up and she just sat there, listening to the dial tone. Surely the police would have searched his backpack looking for evidence. But then they might not have considered him a valid suspect at the time, and with all the confusion, searching his backpack might have slipped by them.

She'd let them take him, she decided. Then she wouldn't have to deal with him. In a way, she was relieved. Her breath was starting to come slower. If additional evidence surfaced that Josh was involved, then she'd come forward with the T-shirt.

Social Services would have to come out anyway, check out her place, make certain it was appropriate for Josh. It wasn't. She knew the rules. She had to have a bedroom for him. She didn't. Not unless she returned to her house in Irvine, which everyone was advising her not to do. And obviously, living with someone whose life could be in danger was not an appropriate placement for a child.

Of course, she thought, she could be in danger from Josh himself.

Then she thought of the Adams case set to open trial the next week. The entire Social Services department was in an uproar over it. The case was extremely controversial and had attracted extensive coverage by the media. It was a felony assault, with a G.B.I. enhancement, for great bodily injury. Victor Adams was a young white-collar professional, an Orange County yuppie, employed at McDonald Douglas as a high-level aerospace engineer. He was the father of two beautiful little girls. The victim was a female social worker. According to the police reports, the Social Services Agency had received information from the school psychologist that one of the little girls had been sexually abused by the father. On the basis of this information, the county authorities had obtained a court order and removed the minor children from the home, placing them in two separate foster homes while charges were being prepared against the father. The abuse turned out to be totally unfounded, but the family was destroyed. The defendant lost his job, his wife suffered a nervous breakdown, they lost their home, and the minor children spent six traumatic months separated from their parents, only able to see their mother during a weekly visitation.

The irony and tragedy in the case was the fact that the younger child, a five-year-old girl, was actually sexually assaulted while in foster care by an older teenage boy residing in the same foster home. On hearing this information, the father went crazy and chased the social worker to her car, punched out the window with his fist, spraying her with glass and causing severe lacerations to her face and neck. The entire case was a tragedy, a mockery of the system. The father had been wronged, the social worker who was only doing her job scarred for life, the children made to suffer, and the family destroyed. The clincher was the fact that the exact crime that was to be prevented had occurred. Sad case. Extremely interesting both legally and morally.

Lara deflated, letting her body compress on the sofa, sink lower and lower, like gravity was pulling her down. If the blood on the T-shirt was nothing—a spill from his bike or whatever—Josh would never forgive her for abandoning him again. But if Social Services took him on their own, then he couldn't blame her. She decided to wait it out.

She was vacillating.

If they did remove her sister's son and place him in a foster home, she thought, leaning in the opposite direction now, even more psychological damage might be inflicted on the boy. She just couldn't let it happen without at least trying to make it work. He might resent her, she thought, sniffing, holding back the tears, but all they had to call family was each other. And if there was any suspicion that he was involved, the way to find out would be to spend time with him, watch him, not send him away somewhere. She just couldn't wash her hands of him, no matter how much she wanted to.

The first thing she had to do was find out whose blood was on that T-shirt.

chapter 11

Dr. Frederick Werner's offices were only a few miles down the road in neighboring Costa Mesa. As Lara steered the Jaguar into the parking lot of a large medical tower with tinted glass windows, she turned to Josh, who was silent and withdrawn. They'd had another battle. He had stayed out past dark on his bike and Lara had panicked. Then when she'd told him about the appointment and he had pitched a fit, she had taken his bike and locked it in the trunk of her car. He hadn't spoken a word since.

"This is it, Josh," she said, cutting the ignition and placing her hands in her lap. She wanted desperately to ask him about the T-shirt, but now was not the time. "If you don't like this doctor, we'll get another one. But let's give him a chance, okay?"

Werner's office was on the tenth floor. From all appearances, the majority of the people employed in the building had already left for the day, and the enormous skyscraper was eerily empty. They were late. Lara glanced at her watch and hoped the psychiatrist hadn't given up and gone home. Josh was standing on the far side of the elevator, as far from Lara as he could get, staring at the control panel. If he'd been eight or ten years old, she might have had some clue how to treat him, but with a teenager she was completely lost. She couldn't spank him and send him to his room when he refused to obey her. All she could do was take his one possession away—his bike.

"I didn't mean that about your bike," she said just as the doors opened. "You can still ride it and all. But you stayed out too long, Josh, and you simply must see a counselor."

Six other physicians were listed on the door along with Werner. Lara stood at the reception desk and looked around, but there was no one in sight, just a labyrinth of halls and doors. Finally she yelled, "Hey, is anyone in here?"

From the back she heard a chair squeak on plastic, and a tall, handsome man in his late thirties or early forties came out and extended his hand. "I'm Dr. Werner. You must be Judge Sanderstone and this is Josh." He shook Lara's hand. His hand was cold and soft like a woman's. He tried to shake Josh's hand, but the boy wouldn't even look at him. "Come with me. We'll talk in here."

His office was quite elaborate, with a comfortable pale blue leather sectional with a sort of metallic sheen, a glass-topped coffee table in the center, and real art on the walls. Lara didn't ask about his fees, but she could well imagine. She looked for a desk and didn't see one. This room must be his session room. There were a few certificates on the walls. Lara walked over to gaze at them. Josh just stood there, refusing to sit down.

She took a seat and brushed an unruly strand of hair off her forehead, feeling the urge to excuse herself and slip into the ladies' room to put on some lipstick or some blush, maybe comb her hair.

"Uh, thank you for seeing us, Dr. Werner," Lara said. "Josh, as you can see, is not too happy about this, but he's been through a terrible ordeal." She looked knowingly at the psychiatrist.

"I see," Werner said slowly. "Why don't you let me speak with your aunt, Josh, for a few moments? There's some magazines in the reception area and some fruit juice. We'll come and get you in a few moments."

Josh looked relieved as he exited the room, almost slamming the door behind him. Lara sat nervously under Werner's penetrating gaze and crossed and uncrossed her legs.

"I'm somewhat aware of what this situation involves. I've seen the papers, and Judge Murdock called me this afternoon. In case she didn't tell you, we're neighbors. I know both Irene and her husband. Why don't you give me a rundown?"

Lara started speaking, tentatively at first, and then she couldn't seem to stop. She told Werner about her relationship with Ivory, the night she'd come to her apartment, the break-in at her place. Basically, the whole sordid mess. Dr. Werner sat attentively, nodding his head off and on. Whatever kind of demeanor psychiatrists affect to get people to talk, this man obviously had down pat. Lara had just spilled her guts and probably consumed most of the hour. Finally she stopped herself.

"I'm sorry . . ." she said, embarrassed. "It's Josh you should be talking to now. I'll go get him." She stood and headed for the door and then stopped. The real issue was trapped in her throat. She had to tell someone. "Dr. Werner, there is a slight—very slight—possibility that Josh could have played some part in my sister's and brother-in-law's death. I know this sounds awful for me to even mention something like this, but—"

"That's fine, Lara," he said. "May I call you Lara?" She nodded, and he continued. "From what I can see, you have a lot of unresolved conflicts regarding your sister and the circumstances surrounding her death. You're harboring a great deal of guilt and maybe even demonstrating a little paranoia." When Lara blanched, he quickly added, "It's all perfectly normal. When someone close to you is violently murdered, it's easy to become fearful and confused. I would like to see you again, not just your nephew."

"Dr. Werner," she said curtly, "I am not paranoid. I'd appreciate it if you would explore the possibility that my nephew was involved. Will you do that?"

"Of course," he answered calmly, leaning back in

his chair. "But I would like to counsel you on another occasion."

Lara stared at him. He was the typical shrink—more concerned with amassing an enormous bill than finding out if her nephew was a murderer. She couldn't afford twenty grand in psychiatrist's bills along with all the other expenses. "We'll see," she said. "I'll get Josh."

His eyes were penetrating, a rusty brown with flecks of yellow. Even with his comments about her being paranoid, Lara was enthralled by his eyes, his rich brown hair, a little black mole over the top of his full lips that looked like a beauty mark. Besides, he might be right. The bloody T-shirt could be a fluke. It could have been in there for months for all she knew. She asked herself if Werner was married and glanced at his hand for the wedding ring. It wasn't there.

Lara had a thick lump in her throat and tried to swallow it. Whatever attraction she had for this man suddenly vanished, and she felt all the blood drain from her face. In her mind, the Packard Cummings rap sheet appeared—the prior convictions for rape. She'd forgotten about his record when she spoke to Rickerson this afternoon. Ivory had been raped. Cummings had broken into her home. He could be the killer. That would eliminate Josh.

"Are you all right?" Werner said, a little flurry of concern in his eyes. "Why don't you sit back down and I'll get you a glass of water?"

"No," Lara said, heading for the door. "I'll get Josh. I just need to use your phone."

"There's one at the receptionist's desk."

As soon as she was out of the door, she jogged down the long hall, sent Josh in to see Werner, and stabbed in the numbers to the San Clemente P.D., standing up behind the receptionist's console, too nervous to sit down.

"He's not in?" she repeated. "Do you know how to reach him? This is Judge Sanderstone and I think it's urgent."

She read the number off the dial of the phone and

sat down, picking up a pen and tapping it on the counter. They'd said they could find him. A few seconds later, the phone rang and she grabbed it. "Rickerson," she said, hearing his voice, speaking rapidly, "that man Cummings has a history of rape, sexual offenses. Ivory was raped, so . . . he could be the one . . . the one that killed them. We have to find him."

Rickerson was unruffled. "No shit," he said. He was perfectly aware of Cumming's record. "I've had his description broadcast to every unit in the city and across the state. We're trying now to reach his parole agent and get his last known address. The agent's out of town, but someone else is checking his files."

The front of the reception desk was high. Lara could barely see over it. "And that girl's boyfriend who threatened me?"

"Look, Lara," he said, a hint of annoyance in his voice, "I know how you feel right now, but why don't you just let me do my job? It's not like we're dragging our heels right now. For this kind of case, we're working at breakneck speed. If you hadn't been who you were, we wouldn't even have the lab reports back yet. They've got stuff backed up for months both in forensics and pathology. They don't even have enough drawers for the stiffs downtown."

He was right. She'd been pressing, calling too much. "I just remembered his rap sheet. I wasn't certain you'd seen the whole thing."

"I've seen it all." He was abrupt, and then his voice softened. "Take is easy, Lara. Try to get some rest. Just lay low, stay in that condo, take care of your nephew and yourself. Leave the police work to me. I'm the cop. As soon as I know anything, I'll call you. Deal?"

"Deal," she said weakly. Then he was gone.

About thirty minutes later, Josh and Werner came out. It must have been his last appointment because Werner walked to the door of the office with them, slipping his jacket on. Then he followed them down the hall and got in the elevator with them. Josh was sullen. This time he stood next to Lara, however. Anything, evidently, was better than Werner.

At the condo, Josh told her he hated Dr. Werner, that Werner was nothing but a stuffy prick.

"Well, I don't care what you think about him," she told him. "You have to see him. That's all there is to it."

"You can't order me around. You're not my mother. My mother's dead. I hate this place. I hate you. I hate that stupid doctor."

Lara flopped down on the sofa. She was inches away from calling Social Services herself. He was standing in the middle of the room glaring at her. "Josh," she said, "have you fallen off your bike lately?"

"I don't fall off my bike."

"I see," Lara said. "Do you or any of your friends practice Satanism? You know, sacrifice animals or anything? Don't be afraid to tell me, but if you do, it's important that I know." She was trying to remain calm during this discussion. It was difficult. Her hands were trembling; she shoved them under her hips and sat on them.

He looked at her like she was insane. "You're crazy. I can't believe you're even a judge. All you do is ask me ridiculous questions."

Lara stood her ground. "You didn't answer my question, Josh."

"No," he yelled at her, his voice booming. "Do I look like a devil worshiper? What, do you want me to join up? Is that what you are? You look like a frigging witch."

Things were getting out of hand fast. His chest was rising and falling, and his face was turning red. "Okay," she said. "Let's have a truce." She stood. "It's late. We're both tired. Since you called me a witch, you can sleep on the sofa tonight."

Lara left him standing there and went to the bedroom and closed the door. A few minutes later, he tapped lightly on the door, a solemn expression on his face. "Can I at least have the bedspread?"

"Here," Lara said, snatching it off the bed and tossing it to him. Then she remembered the backpack and picked it up. For a moment she stood there with it in her hands and searched his face. "Need this?" she asked, curious as to his response.

Josh reached out and tried to grab the backpack out of Lara's hands. She stepped back and Josh sighed, dropping his hands to his sides.

"No, I don't need anything." Wrapping the bedspread around him, he walked the few feet to the sofa and collapsed.

"Good night, Josh," Lara said as she closed the door again. She opened the backpack and pulled out the bloody T-shirt. The only way to know for sure now was to have it tested, find out whose blood it was. She wondered if she could arrange something like that without anyone knowing. She didn't know. Back it went into the backpack. Tomorrow, she thought. Get through tonight and deal with it all tomorrow.

The room was dark and she watched the shadows, imagining flashes of the blood-spattered walls at the house in San Clemente. She held her breath, listening for Josh in the other room. He knew she had the backpack and might assume she knew about the T-shirt. He could come in while she was sleeping and bash her head in or suffocate her. Suddenly she felt desperately ill and bolted to the bathroom to hug the toilet bowl. All that was left in her stomach to vomit were the sodas she had consumed during the day. Josh had eaten; she couldn't swallow a bite without having it stick in her throat.

She finally stood and washed her face. Then she leaned her head under the tap and rinsed it with water. Dropping her clothes on the floor by the bed, she crawled under the covers and pulled them up to her chin and stared at the ceiling. She stayed that way for at least an hour, her body as rigid as an ironing board, listening for sounds in the other room, listening to the clock tick next to her on the nightstand. At two o'clock, she turned off the light, but still she could not sleep. She reviewed cases in her mind. She counted sheep. At four o'clock, her eyes closed involuntarily and her exhausted body fell into a deep, dreamless sleep.

Lara heard the phone ringing and opened her eyes. She was stiff and her head was pounding. She'd left the portable phone in the kitchen, and Josh had evidently answered it. He yelled at her from the living room, "Phone." Then he came to the bedroom door and stood there until Lara tossed on her robe and staggered over to take the phone.

"Lara," a woman's voice said, "it's Irene."

"Irene, I took my nephew to see Werner. Not bad. But you know, Josh doesn't like him."

"Isn't there anything I can do for you, Lara? And other people here at the courts have been inquiring. People are concerned. This is a tragedy. Such a terrible tragedy."

"No," Lara said, lowering her body to the edge of the bed. "There's nothing anyone can do. I'm arranging the funeral. I hope that you'll come. We don't have any relatives." Self-pity was evident in her voice and she tried to suppress it. "Irene, something horrible came to light. This man—this man," she started, stammering and gasping. Just the thought of this was more than she could bear. "This man who appeared on a bail review in front of me that day before Ivory and Sam were murdered. He's the one who broke into my house. I released the son of a bitch. And he has a prior for rape. Ivory, bless her heart, was raped. I'm losing my mind over here. Let me tell you."

"Why did you release this man?" Irene said. "You mean on an ordinary bail situation, right?"

"No," Lara said. "I would have denied bail completely—any amount. Evergreen himself told me to grant him O.R., said he was working as a C.I. for some police agency . . . big drug case or something."

"Well, dear," Irene said, "it sounds like nothing more than a terribly unfortunate situation. At least you know who he is and may see an end to this in sight. That's something, isn't it, Lara?"

"But I released the bastard. The man was standing right before me. I can still see his face."

"Honey, get a handle on yourself. You don't know this man was involved in your sister's death. Possibly he was released from the jail, needed money, and tried to burglarize all kinds of homes in that area or even did, for that matter. He might have hit ten places and it was a coincidence that he hit yours. You're not far from the jail over there. And from what I know, there's no definitive link between these two crimes."

"I don't believe in coincidence, Irene," Lara said flatly. Normally when Irene, who was considerably older than Lara, used all her little terms of endearment, Lara just sopped it up. But today it all sounded trite.

"Be rational. What kind of motive could this man possibly have? You released him O.R. You didn't sentence him to prison. When you were speaking of the Henderson situation yesterday, an outright threat, that was a different matter. This you must put out of your mind." She paused and then continued. "Honey, have you seen the paper this morning?"

"No, I just woke up. It was a rough night. I don't even know what time it is. What do they say? Do they have my picture in there or something?"

"Lara, it's far worse than that. I'd rather not be the bearer of bad news. Why don't you get your paper and read it and call me back? I'm reading the *Los Angeles Times*. Do you subscribe?"

"Yeah," Lara said. "Call you right back." Bad news, she had said. What kind of bad news could there possibly be now? She walked into the living room and saw Josh sprawled with one leg off the sofa. He'd evidently gone back to sleep. She opened the front door and then remembered she wasn't at home. Seeing a newspaper lying next door, she took it. The people were probably at work already. She'd replace it before they got home.

Paper in hand, she carried it back to the bedroom. Removing the rubber band, she used it to tie her hair back in a ponytail and stretched out on her stomach on the unmade bed. There was nothing in the cover story. Maybe Irene was referring to a case she had handled that had been overturned on appeal without her knowledge.

Then she saw it. It was at the bottom of the front page.

"SADISTIC SEX MURDERS IN ORANGE COUNTY."

She placed her hand over her mouth and glanced at the door. Then she ran over and closed it and returned to the bed, removing the paper and placing it on the carpet. She got on her hands and knees and read the text of the article.

"The sister and brother-in-law of Orange County Superior Court Judge Lara Sanderstone were brutally murdered yesterday in apparent sadistic sex-related homicides. Ivory Perkins, 36, and her husband, Samuel Perkins, 38, were murdered in their home in San Clemente by unknown assailants. The couple's fourteen-year-old son discovered the bodies on returning home from school. Insiders at the San Clemente Police Department advise that information has surfaced indicating the judge's sister was involved in sex-for-hire, specializing . . ."

She dropped the paper on the floor. Rickerson was to blame for this, and she was going to make certain he paid. Her eyes jerked to the clock on the nightstand, and she saw it was nine o'clock. Tossing on a pair of baggy jeans and an old shirt, she left the condo and jogged to her car in the parking lot, immediately calling the San Clemente Police Department on the car phone.

"Is Sergeant Rickerson there?" she asked the woman who picked up the phone.

"Yes, he just came in. I'll transfer you."

Lara hung up. She punched the gas and pulled out

into the morning traffic, honking her horn and screaming out the window like a madwoman when someone pulled in front of her. She didn't try to control her anger. She let it build like a wave far out at sea, knowing that by the time she got to the police station, it would be large enough to wash over the entire department and half the town of San Clemente. But it was Rickerson that she focused her rage on. He was responsible for leaking this smut stuff to the press, and she was ready to yank his head right off his body.

She parked illegally at the curb in a red zone. She flung the door open and marched into the police station, huffing and puffing like she'd just climbed six flights of stairs. Passing the receptionist without so much as a glance, she headed directly to the back of the building, where she knew the Investigative Bureau was housed. Rickerson was standing by a file cabinet in his shirtsleeves, drinking a cup of coffee and joking with another detective. As soon as he saw her, he moved in her direction, a look of concern on his face.

"How could you do this? Leak this stuff to the press?" Lara said, her body shaking, her hand moving back like she was going to slap him.

Two other investigators were sitting at their desks. They stood, momentarily not recognizing her, and one moved toward her rapidly, his hand on his weapon. Lara turned and faced him. The look in her eyes was enough to stop him cold. Realizing who she was, he turned and walked back to his chair.

"Let's go outside," Rickerson said. "There's no use screaming in here and making a scene."

Lara's chest was heaving and her face was crimson. She didn't take her eyes off Rickerson. "Why did you do it? My God, I didn't think I even had to mention this to you. Any damn fool would know not to leak something like that to the press." She tore her eyes away from Rickerson's and thought of Josh. Now he'd have to change schools. All his friends would know. The whole world knew now what his mother had been doing.

The detective was pulling gently on her hand, trying to lead her out the back door. She resisted, planting her feet on the ground, refusing to move.

"It wasn't me," he whispered, inches from her face. "If you'll just step outside with me, we'll discuss this like two civilized adults. Okay?"

Reluctantly, she followed. "Okay," she said, once they were standing on a little concrete porch with steps leading to the parking lot, "tell me and tell me fast. Who's responsible for this?"

"I don't know," he said, shaking his head. "One of the other officers must have said something to the press without thinking, or maybe he said something to his wife or kids and they got wind of it that way. It could have been a file clerk here. Anyone. But rest assured, it wasn't me."

She stared at him, trying to read his eyes, detect if he was lying. Her breath was coming slower now. "Retract it," she ordered. "Call them right this minute and make them print a retraction."

The sun was bright and he was squinting in the glare. "Do you really want me to do that? Think about it for a few minutes. If they print a retraction, which I'm not even certain they will, it'll only draw more attention. Do you really want that?"

She didn't answer. She looked out over the parking lot and the rows of police cars. It was a gorgeous day. The sun was bright, no fog. Even the air smelled clean and fresh, and there was a gentle breeze from the ocean. It didn't seem right in some way. Lara wished it would cloud over and pour.

"Mind if I smoke?" Rickerson said, reaching into his pocket for a cigar.

Lara didn't look at him. A few seconds later, she was waving the cigar smoke out of her face. He was right. The damage had already been done. Another article would simply fuel the fire. "No," she finally replied, "you're probably right." Then she pointed her finger at him. "I want that person, Rickerson. You find the person who leaked this to the papers and bring them to me. I'll handle the rest."

She turned and seized the door handle, yanking on the door. It didn't budge and she almost fell backward off the porch. Rickerson stepped behind her and inserted a key. "Locks automatically," he said, speaking with the cigar clamped between his teeth. "Let's go somewhere and get a cup of coffee. I'll meet you at Denny's across the street. After this, it's better that we don't talk in the office."

A few minutes later, they were sitting in a booth at Denny's. Lara was gripping her coffee cup with both hands. Rickerson had a large file folder that he placed on the table.

"We've been going over the phone records. I have a printout from the telephone company. I made an extra copy for you, in case you recognize anyone." He slid it across the table, and Lara stared at it without seeing anything but a white sheet of paper. "There's a lot of calls here to a lot of different people. I have records working on it now. As you can see, we've already tracked down most of the calls and listed the names and addresses beside them. Maybe we'll get lucky."

"I want copies of the entire file."

"I can't do that."

"You owe me."

"I told you I didn't leak anything to the press." He'd been moving the cigar from one side of his mouth and back to the other. Now he removed it and placed it in the ashtray.

She slapped the top of the table, jiggling the coffee cups and silverware. "Get me copies of that entire file. I'm not anyone off the street. I'm an officer of the court, for chrissake. I want that file."

Rickerson's acne-scared face was menacing. He wasn't a man to be pushed.

"Then if you're an officer of the court," he said softly, trying to calm her down, "you should realize why I can't hand over evidence in a homicide. You could decide that some innocent person was responsible for your sister's murder and go out and shoot them. The department could be sued."

She stood. "I'm going to follow you back to the station and wait in the parking lot while you copy that file. You have that stuff in my hands in fifteen or twenty minutes max, or you'll be the sorriest cop to ever work in this county. I'll make your life a living hell."

Rickerson remained in the booth and watched her stomp toward the door. "Like my life isn't already a living hell," he mumbled tossing a few bills on the table.

When he looked up, he saw her marching back toward him. As soon as she reached the table, she placed her hands on her hips and glared at him. Then she reached down and snatched the cigar right out of his mouth and tossed it on the floor. "And for your information, I hate these stupid things. I never said you could smoke." She spun around and left.

chapter 12

"Your suspect's on the run," the sheriff's deputy informed Detective Rickerson by phone. "We surrounded the place and went in ready for war. All we found was an empty room full of beer cans and cockroaches. No Packard Cummings."

"Fuck," Rickerson said, slapping the top of his desk. "Can you tell how long it's been since he was there?"

"Guy across the street saw him come in early this morning. Looked like he'd been out all night. Said he went upstairs, came down with a bunch of garbage bags, probably with his clothes and stuff in it, tossed them in the trunk of his car, and split. We must have just missed him."

"And the landlord?" Rickerson said. "Do they know anything? You know, maybe a forwarding address."

"Just that he owes them a couple months' back rent. This isn't the type of place that runs TRW's on their tenants, Sarge. This is a fleabag boardinghouse here. Landlord wasn't even sure what the guy's name was . . . said everyone pays in cash."

"Think he was tipped?"

"By me, buddy. Anyway, we did our thing. Word's out on the vehicle. Unless he dumped it, he'll surface."

Rickerson hung up and finally reached Packy's parole agent. The agent informed him that Cummings had basically absconded, had not reported for his weekly visit, and was presently in violation of parole.

"Were you aware that Cummings was acting as a snitch for some local agency?" Rickerson asked, knowing this was something a man like Packy would brag about to his parole agent.

"Not at all," the man told him. "Never mentioned a thing."

After confirming the description and license number of the vehicle Packy was known to drive, the agent suggested several other possible locations he was known to frequent. Rickerson hung up, turning to the young detective who had been assigned to work with him on the case, Mike Bradshaw. Bradshaw was the son of the chief of police.

"Here we go," he said, placing everything he had on Packy on his desk in a manila file folder. "You want to prove yourself, kid, this is the case to do it on. Get some patrol units to follow up on these locations where Cummings might be, then call every law enforcement agency in Southern California and find out if anyone's ever heard of this guy. He claims to be working as a C.I. Check it out."

Back at his desk, Rickerson took out the handful of Polaroids from his pocket and started shuffling them like a deck of playing cards. Then he studied each one. He'd waited long enough, he decided, stuffing the photos into a brown evidence envelope and jotting something on the front before he sealed it. It was time to go to the chief.

"Okay, Ace," he said to Bradshaw, "have someone get these to the crime lab downtown and fast. I want them hand-delivered to a Dr. Stewart and no one else."

Bradshaw placed his hand over the mouthpiece of his phone. "I'm speaking with the DEA now. What do you want me to do first?" he said, somewhat befuddled. "Try to find him, call the agencies, or get this to the lab?"

"Everything," Rickerson said, heading to the door. Then he stopped in the doorway and rolled a fat black cigar in his fingers. "The way it looks right now, hot shot, Cummings is our man. He ransacked Sanderstone's house for what reason we don't know, probably did the killings, and he's on the run. Let's bring him in."

After returning from her encounter with Rickerson, Lara was weak and shaky. She took the newspaper and shoved it in the trash can in the parking lot of the condo. How could she ever face her friends, her peers? Her parents were respectable people. Common people but respected. Thank God they were not here to see this. It was a disgrace, a complete disgrace.

She started to open the door to the condo and then decided against it. She crossed the grassy courtyard to Emmet's.

"Did you see the newspaper this morning?" she asked him.

"Yes, Lara . . . I did. I'm sorry."

Emmet had a fresh pot of coffee. He told Lara to help herself. Bringing a cup for Emmet, she followed him to his office. "I have a problem, Emmet. It's a serious one. I'm not certain there's anything you can do to help me, but I thought I'd try."

He hit a button on his chair and spun around to the computer console, slipping his head into the metal contraption. "Tell me, Lara," he typed. "I'll do anything I possibly can to help you. And Lara," he continued, "don't worry about the article in the paper. You must not concern yourself with what people think. If I worried about what everyone thought, I'd never leave my home. You have enough problems now." He turned the chair around and looked at her.

"No one else knows this, Emmet, but I found a T-shirt with blood on it in Josh's backpack. I don't want to turn it over to the police unless I'm certain it's valid evidence. After what happened this morning with the newspapers, there's no telling what they will do if they learn about this. I thought I heard you mention a friend one time who was a biologist at Strand Laboratories. Could you get him to type it, see if it is my brother-in-law's blood? I can check his blood type from the police records."

"Where . . . is it?" Emmet asked.

"It's in the condo, but I can get it."

"Get . . . it," he said.

"Then you think you can get it tested?"

"Yes," he said slowly. "Get . . . it."

"I'll bring it over as soon as Josh goes out on his bike. And Emmet, I'd like you to meet him. Pray that it's nothing."

The following morning, Detective Rickerson and Chief Bradshaw were walking down the corridor at the Los Angeles County Crime Laboratory after fighting the morning rush-hour traffic for over two hours. Chief Terrence Bradshaw was a very attractive man in his mid-fifties, with a full head of premature white hair and a deep tan. The only weak thing about him was his eyes; he wore thick glasses in heavy frames that magnified his eyes and made them appear enormous. To the men in the department, he was a diehard. The man jogged seven or eight miles a day every single day of his life, regardless of the weather, lifted weights, read every book he could get his hands on, and still managed to put in a fifty- or sixty-hour work week. As fit as a man twenty years younger, he was actually in better shape than his twenty-three-year-old son. Law enforcement was his life.

"Why in the hell did you insist on coming all the way down here for this?" the chief questioned Rickerson. "I mean, we have our own lab in the county. Everyone thinks they do outstanding work."

"Because of one woman," Rickerson said, peering through the glass doors into the offices. "She's fast and she knows her stuff."

"Who?" the chief asked.

"Dr. Gail Stewart."

"I think I've heard of her, but I'm not sure where."

"She's one of the foremost criminologists in the country. She can do it all. There's not one piece of equipment in this lab that she doesn't know how to operate, and her specialty is photographic evidence."

The woman stood when they walked in the door. Then she pumped both of their hands. It wasn't the kind of handshake you would expect from a woman. It was hearty. Everything about Gail Stewart was hearty. She'd been waiting.

"Gail Stewart," she said to the chief. "Follow me."

Both men followed the heavyset brunette in the white lab coat. She was in her late thirties, at least forty pounds overweight, and walked like a storm trooper. She was also impossible to dislike. Her skin was soft and clear, her eyes round and expressive, and she absolutely loved what she was doing. She spent so much time at the lab that some people thought she lived there.

"Give something to this gal," Rickerson whispered to the chief, "and she'll grind it between her teeth, chew it up, and spit back the answer. The woman's dynamite."

She marched them to a corner of the room where there was a screen and a slide projector. "I have slides of the enlargements," she said, "but they were Polaroids, which means the quality is extremely poor. I'll give you the prints when we're finished."

"Give me a rundown," Rickerson said.

"Well," Stewart said, "none of these are recent photographs. We've classified them in groupings. In group A, we estimate that these were taken approximately two years ago. We can denote age by the texture and rigidity of the photo itself, particularly instant print film. They tend to get more brittle as time goes on. Also, this is Kodak and they haven't produced this backing in at least two years. The photos in group B were taken with Polaroid SX-70 film and are probably about five years old or older." She paused and sighed, mumbling under her breath, "I wish we'd had the negatives." Then she dimmed the lights as an image appeared on the screen.

"This first slide is a solitary young man, as you can see. You can't see his genitalia, but he has no underarm hair. We estimate his age to be about eleven or twelve, prepuberty." She hit a button and the next slide fell into place. "This is not the same young man, although they do resemble. They could even be brothers. These are from group A. He's even younger than the first young man. Our pathologist believes he's no more than nine or ten. This is based on his size, musculature, and other factors."

"Is that your kid?" the chief asked Rickerson.

"Nope," he said. "I thought at first he was, but I was evidently mistaken. I'm fairly certain none of these photos are of Josh McKinley."

Once they had stopped talking, she clicked another slide into place. "These are from group B, so they're the oldest of the photos. Of course, it's obvious that the nude male standing behind the boy is an adult, probably in his forties or early fifties. He could be much older or much younger. We can't be certain, but his skin does appear to be sagging a little, therefore, we made a guess. As in just about everything, there are a lot of variables. The man could be a young man who had lost a lot of weight. Who knows? Anyway, the only distinguishable thing we can determine is that he suffers from scoliosis, or curvature of the spine. He's in all the photos—the same man. He never faces the camera. Someone else is taking the pictures," she said. "See, there's his hand reflected in the mirror."

"Did you enlarge that shot?" Rickerson asked. "That could be him. Josh McKinley. He might be the one taking the pictures."

"Certainly," she said, flicking fast through the slides until she came to the right one. "Here it is. From the looks of it, he's young. Note how slender and small his hand is. Of course, it could be a girl. We're just guessing it's a male because all the others are males."

Rickerson got up and walked up to the screen, studying the image. "Can't you do better than this? I need to know if this is the kid."

"Sorry, Charley," she said. "I can't give you something that isn't there. But if you'll just be patient, Ted, I do have something." She brought another slide into place, held it a few moments, and then replaced it with an enlargement of one section of the photograph. "This is where you got lucky. See this right here?" she said. "These weren't taken in a hotel room or something. They were taken in someone's home. This is an enhancement of a reflection in the mirror, probably on the dresser or something from the looks of it. What you're looking at is a photograph in a silver frame. It's a middle-aged woman and a young man. Hold on," she said, clicking another slide into place. "Now you're looking at the enlargement of the photograph itself. I know it's distorted, but if you try real hard you can see the similarities in their appearance. My bet is the young man is the woman's son. Looks about seventeen, doesn't he? Now, assuming the older man with his back to the camera in the photographs is the young man's father, we have even more to go on."

Chief Bradshaw and Detective Rickerson were mesmerized. They spent a solid hour viewing slide after slide, studying each one intently. "Had enough, gentlemen?"

She turned and faced them, leaning back against a desk and crossing her heavy legs at the ankles. The room was still dark. Only the light from a neighboring lab filtered through a glass window behind them. Dr. Stewart's voice echoed in the tiled room. "What you've just seen is the photo collection of a pedophile. As I'm sure you both know, most pedophiles prefer prepubescent children. Once the child passes puberty, they are no longer desirable and are frequently discarded."

She turned the lights back on and continued, "If you find him, we can positively identify him by the spinal curvature. No one's spine curves exactly the same way, to the same centimeter. We can prove this by photographing this man's back and superimposing it over the photograph you've just seen, studying and comparing his X rays and medical records, and we can back it up with the latest computer technology." She smiled and her full face creased with two large dimples. "All you have to do is find him. Piece of cake, huh?"

"Sure," Rickerson said, exchanging glances with the chief. "Pretty impressive."

"I saved the best for last. Follow me." They followed her across the tiled floor to another work space and a computer terminal. "Have a seat, guys. I've been working on this all night." She turned around and squinted at Rickerson. "And I mean all night, Ted. I haven't been to bed."

By the time the men had pulled up two chairs, Dr. Stewart had the computer up and running. "This is new software. We just recently got this whole system. It requires the use of high-speed computers." She waved her arms around the room. Behind a glass partition was row after row of huge computers, lights blinking and tape spilling out of printers. "I generated a computer composite of the young man in the photograph with the woman and a torso of the nude adult male. Working under the assumption that they are related, or even father and son, we developed another composite photograph of what this older man might look like. Of course, we've aged him as well." She tapped a few keys on the keyboard and an image appeared on the screen. "Here it is. What do you think?"

Both the chief and Rickerson leaned over and peered at the screen. The image was three-dimensional. While they watched, Dr. Stewart rolled a mouse around on the pad, tapped instructions into the computer, and the naked image actually walked, turned, and moved its arms and head.

"The technology you are seeing is called artificial reality along with computer-assisted design, or CAD. It's the latest thing. They even used something like this recently in San Francisco in the trial of that guy who murdered his brother. You know, the porno kings. They've been using it in the movies for a while now, but of course, it's extremely expensive, so we're just getting it."

"Isn't this fascinating?" the chief said. "It looks like a video game or an animated movie."

"See," the woman continued, "this is a very rough attempt here. That's why his facial features are so generic at this point. It actually takes weeks to make it perfect. If it's complex, it can take months. We can create a crime scene, put the suspects in the picture, and then move them around like the crime really occurred. This way we can tell if someone is telling the truth, match their testimony to what actually occurred. We can also tell the exact point a bullet would strike if fired from a certain location, which way the body would fall, and basically recreate every aspect of the crime. The possibilities are endless."

She glanced at both men and then turned back to the screen. "Now, watch this image walk. I didn't spend a lot of time on the face yet. We have no way of knowing that the young man and the older nude male in the pictures are actually related, and therefore I thought this was a little premature. If you will notice, however, this man has a noticeable limp on the right side of his body. We developed this from data entered into the program on the scoliosis. I can print this out, but it won't be three-dimensional like you're seeing." She hit a button and a printer generated a hard copy. She handed it to Rickerson. "I'm going to keep refining this, and eventually you'll have something pretty realistic to look at."

"You did good, Gail," Rickerson said, visibly excited. He turned to the chief. "Told you she was the best. There's no one around like her."

"Yeah," the chief said, rubbing his chin and addressing Dr. Stewart. "This is all intriguing, but you hit the nail on the head. Until we find him, we don't have anything. And this is all just speculation. To assume that the two people in the small picture were his wife and son is a mammoth assumption. They might not be related at all."

"Right you are," the woman replied, "but you've got to start somewhere. Let's watch this man move again, officers. A person's walk is a distinctive thing, and this man's spinal curvature is quite severe, enough to have an effect on how he moves all of his limbs." She started tapping like wild on the computer, and the figure on the screen appeared inside a room, with doors, furniture, walls. While they watched, she moved him to the back of the room and then brought him forward. "One hip is actually higher than the other, therefore, the limp. Also, watch how he moves his arms. That swing right there—" She stopped the figure and locked the image into place. "That's a compensation factor, meaning in simplistic terms, that he must balance himself, particularly since his body is physically imbalanced by his deformity."

Finally stepping away from the computer, she turned and punched Rickerson on the arm with a fleshy fist. "Hey, big guy, you promised me a steak dinner if I shelved everything else I'm working on and delivered. I delivered. When do I get my dinner?"

"You'll get it," Rickerson said, smiling. "I'm not sure you need it, though. You don't look very hungry to me."

"Asshole," she said, shaking her head and laughing. "Why am I so gullible? Next time you can wait your turn like everyone else."

"Thanks a lot, Gail. We'll be in touch." Rickerson headed for the door and the chief followed.

Dr. Stewart yelled to him, "You know what I'd do?"

"What?" Rickerson replied.

"I'd let Lois Anderson at the FBI take a look at these pictures. She heads the task force on missing children. One of these boys might be a runaway that's since been returned to his parents. I hope you catch this bastard. You know why?"

Rickerson just stood there and stared at her. Of course he knew why. Whoever this person was, he felt certain he was involved in contracting the Perkins homicides. Cummings might have been the hands-on killer, but Rickerson's assumption right now was that it was a contracted assassination.

"In an active pedophile's career, certainly one as old as this one, he can have hundreds of victims. Maybe it's time this fellow pays the price."

"Send them over to her now," Rickerson said, thinking of all the young lives this man had destroyed—children so devastated that they might never be the same.

"No problem," she said, plunking her large body down in a chair that looked like it was about to collapse beneath her and snatching a Snickers bar from her desk. She unwrapped it and then held it in the air. "Brain food," she said. "Secret to my success. Person just can't think when they're hungry."

"So what do you think?" Bradshaw said as they headed back down the hall, their shoes tapping on the linoleum.

"I think we've got one hell of a case on our hands, Chief. Someone killed that couple to get their hands on these photos. There's no doubt about it. I was hoping we could exclude the kid."

"I'm not sure you can do that. If the boy was being exploited or sexually abused, your motive is right there."

"I don't think Perkins and his wife took these pictures or even sold them as I originally thought. I think they found them. What do you think about that?"

"They just found them, huh? Interesting. Want to be more specific?"

They hit the double doors and stepped outside. It was overcast and muggy. The smog was so thick they could see it hanging like a foul cloud over the entire city. They stood for a few minutes on the steps, as officers and other law enforcement personnel passed them coming in and out of the building. "Can you believe this place?" Rickerson tossed out to the chief. "It's like Grand Central Station here."

"Yeah," the chief said, uninterested. "Lot of crime."

Rickerson looked at him. "Last weekend they had twenty-five homicides in L.A. County. We're talking one weekend, Chief—one lousy weekend and twenty-five lives."

The chief belched and looked at the detective. Every year the crime stats went up. Just thinking about it made his stomach churn. And crime was working its way out from the inner city to the suburbs, particularly since the riots. There wasn't much left in south central Los Angeles, other than burned-out buildings and rubble. "Want to tell me about the case?"

"Okay, Ivory Perkins was working as a prostitute, see," Rickerson said, leaning back against a spiral column in front of the building, "with heavy emphasis on S and M. I think she had a client that was a pedophile, liked to have sex with kids."

"Wait a minute," the chief retorted. "That doesn't make sense. Why would a guy who liked kids go to a hooker? That doesn't fit anything I know about pedophiles. They usually abhor sex with adult women."

Rickerson had thought of this and was ready with an answer. "I already talked to the S.O.'s staff psychologist. He thinks this man was masochistic, possibly out of guilt over his attraction to young boys. I mean, he could have been sadistic, but it really doesn't work as well. One day when the Perkins broad serviced him, she somehow came across his little X-rated photo collection, and that's when she and her husband decided to try their hands at extortion."

"Sounds plausible," the chief said, looking at the sky. "Think it's actually going to rain?"

"Never," Rickerson said, lighting a cigar. "Trust me. Weather is my specialty."

"How does Packy Cummings fit into this picture?"

"Well, that's the glue that holds this whole thing together. On September seventh, the day before the murders, Judge Leo Evergreen informed Lara Sanderstone that Packy was a police informant and insisted that she release him without bail. If he is, no agency in the state of California will claim him. And if you review his criminal history, I think you'll agree that they would've never used a guy like this one. Jesus, he was a prime suspect in a cop killing a few years ago, Aryan Brotherhood membership paid in full, prior convictions for rape."

"Really?" Chief Bradshaw said. "What happened to the case? The officer-related killing."

"Got off for some reason. They couldn't put it together. Anyway, I think Evergreen was lying."

The chief started down the steps. Rickerson followed, puffing clouds of cigar smoke into the atmosphere. "Go on," the chief said. "I don't understand why you think he was lying, but go on."

"I think he's our man."

Chief Bradshaw stopped halfway down the steps and looked straight at Rickerson, his mouth open, his eyes enormous behind his thick glasses. For a few moments he was completely speechless. "The presiding judge of Orange County? Really, Rickerson, isn't that taking things a little too far? We're only in the preliminary stages of this investigation anyway."

"Not hardly," Rickerson said, his voice laced with conviction. Not as far as he was concerned. "Have you ever met Evergreen?"

The chief was at the bottom of the steps and looked back up at the detective. "Not that I recall. I think I've seen his picture in the paper sometime in the past, but to be honest, I wouldn't know him if I saw him."

Rickerson moved the cigar to the other side of his mouth and clenched it between his teeth, the words snaking out of one corner of his mouth. "Well, I have," he said, his chest expanding. "I'll never forget that bastard. Years ago, one of my first big cases to go to trial was dismissed on a technicality. Evergreen was the judge."

"And . . ."

"Just listen, okay. What if Leo Evergreen was Ivory Perkins's client and had no idea she was Judge Sanderstone's sister? Obviously, the Perkins woman didn't broadcast this information to all her clients. Might tend to make a client a little nervous. Know what I mean? So, Evergreen sprang Packy Cummings to do his dirty work: get the pictures back, kill the people that had them. He knew from court records that Packy was down for a fall, headed straight back to prison, and this time he was going for the long haul. The D.A. was planning to prosecute him as a career criminal, tacking on all those five-year enhancements for his priors. Old Packy had nothing to lose and everything to gain."

"Hold on," the chief said just as a burly motorcycle cop bounded down the steps and almost knocked him down. "Once this man was out on the streets, why didn't he just split?"

"Bucks, cash, bread," Rickerson said, rubbing his fingers together. "Can't go too far without it, and I never saw anyone come out of jail or the joint with an abundance of green. Not only that, before this asshole could drive two feet, Evergreen could have every cop in town after him with handfuls of warrants. He's certainly in a position powerful enough to do a man a lot of harm, particularly if you're on the wrong side of the law."

"As I understand it," the chief said, "his prints were found in Sanderstone's house in Irvine. All you've got him on right now is 459, residential burglary. How do you put him into the homicides?"

The two men started walking to their car. This was typical L.A., Rickerson thought, glancing around him in disgust. Almost every building and every wall in sight were covered with graffiti. The names of rival gangs were spray-painted in fluorescent colors in large block letters.

"Let me give you my theory, Chief," Rickerson said as they crossed the street at the light. "Ivory Perkins came to her sister's house almost exactly two months before the murders claiming that someone was following her. Whoever it was, they were completely unaware that the house belonged to Judge Sanderstone. They probably thought Ivory lived there herself or something. Like I said, why would anyone in their wildest dreams connect these two individuals? One a prostitute . . . one a judge."

"So your theory is that Evergreen paid Cummings to kill the couple and get the pictures back when he couldn't find them in the judge's house. But when Cummings committed the homicides, he left the pictures there. Why would he do that?"

"Possibly because the boy came home and startled him, or he just never thought of the crawl space. The carpet obscured it pretty well, and there was a box of old clothes on top of it. He went through those, he just didn't think to look for the crawl space. Anyway, he ransacked Sanderstone's house thinking they were hidden there, and when it was a no-go, Evergreen got desperate and contracted the killing."

"A killing? You really think that's possible? A judge contracting a killing?"

Rickerson raised his eyebrows. Both he and the chief had been in this business too long not to realize that anything was possible. "Maybe Evergreen just wanted the photos back . . . and the animal he hired—Cummings—simply went nuts in there. Pretty, sexy woman. He's a sex offender. Then the husband walked in and he had to do him too."

"Well," the chief said, deep in thought, "if Evergreen is the man in the photos, he would certainly have a lot to lose. There's no doubt about that. Boy," he said, actually shivering, "that's a chilling thought . . . a fucking iceberg." The chief stopped walking and turned to the detective. "Do you have any idea, Rickerson, what it's going to take to go up against the most powerful judge in the county? Don't think for a minute you can put together a thin case and ever get out of the box."

The chief waited until Rickerson unlocked the police unit and then opened the passenger door. He looked up at the sky and held his hand in the air, smiling at Rickerson. "It's raining. Hope your ability to solve homicides is better than your ability to predict the weather."

They were looking at each other over the hood of the police unit, the sky spitting forth moisture but only enough to leave a few drops on the windshield. Rickerson drew hard on his fat cigar, and an enormous cloud of smoke appeared, almost obscuring his face. Just before it started pouring, the detective ducked inside the police car, leaving the chief standing there in the rain.

The first step in building a case against Evergreen, Rickerson thought, was somehow connecting him to the homicides. The problem was simple: lack of evidence. Once the chief was inside the car, Rickerson fired up the ignition and pulled out into traffic. "I blew a lot of hot air out there, Chief. Even if my gut tells me it's Evergreen, I'm gonna have a hell of a time proving it."

The chief had his glasses off and was wiping them from the rain. Rickerson stopped at the light and glanced at him. Funny, he thought, people look so different without their glasses.

"I don't think you've even broken ground with this case, Ted. What about this woman's tricks? What if this Perkins fellow was dealing in child pornography and stepped on the wrong people? That's a dirty business. These photos we just saw aren't even recent. There's no telling where they came from. And all you have to connect Judge Evergreen to these crimes is the fact that he asked Judge Sanderstone to grant Cummings an O.R. release. Why don't you interview Evergreen and find out who asked him to release this man?"

The chief had some valid points, but Rickerson certainly wasn't going to interview Evergreen and tip his hand. He liked the element of surprise, wanted his prey to move around freely while he stalked them. That way they might fall right into his hands. "There's one thing you are right about, Chief."

"Yeah, tell me."

"Even if our man isn't Evergreen himself, the person behind these killings has to be someone working inside the system: a judge, D.A., cop, someone with access to booking information and rap sheets."

"Thousands of people have access to that kind of information," the chief said, "even clerical people."

"Whoever arranged Packy Cummings's release is our killer, Chief. I might be wrong about Evergreen, but I'm not wrong here."

chapter 13

By the time Rickerson got back to San Clemente that afternoon, Lara Sanderstone was waiting in his office. She was sitting in the little chair by his desk in the detective bay. Her hair was down instead of pinned at her neck. It fell to her shoulders in a blunt-cut style that was extremely flattering. The jet black hair against her fair skin, the high cheekbones, the stress she was obviously under, all served to give her a look of vulnerability and touching beauty. She was wearing a tailored pants suit and little black shoes with studs on the toes. Josh was waiting outside in the Jaguar with the radio blasting. Rickerson had seen him on his way into the building.

Lara stood when he walked up, glancing at the other officer at the next desk. The man was on the phone, not paying attention to them. "I wanted to apologize for the way I acted yesterday," she said in a contrite voice. "I know you wouldn't have leaked that stuff to the press. It was all just too much and I took it out on you. I'm sorry."

He smiled at her. "Yeah, well, we all have our bad days. You've certainly had more than your share. Forget it."

"Do you have any news on that man . . . Packard Cummings?"

Rickerson loosened his tie and flopped into his chair, tossing his legs on his desk. "He split, but we'll nab him. Give us time. We're working around the clock."

"Did you find out who he's working for? What agency?"

He didn't want to tip his hand, take a chance on blowing the biggest case of his career. He looked away, avoiding her eyes. "We're working on it."

"Why don't I just ask Evergreen? Why all this subterfuge? You know, I want to go back to my house. The condo is too small for Josh and me. I want to go home."

"Listen to me. I'm going to repeat myself. I already told you this the other day. Don't open your mouth about this to a soul. Not a soul, do you hear me? If you want to find out who murdered your sister, do exactly as I say and don't ask questions. And as of this minute, I don't want you anywhere near that house. Got it?"

Lara flipped a wayward strand of hair off her forehead. "I went over there this morning and got some more clothes and things." Rickerson was glowering at her. "I didn't go to the condo from there, so don't give me that look. I came straight over here. If anyone followed me, they would have just followed me here. And I'm not going straight back to the condo."

"It's your neck, Lara," he said. "You lead the guy back to that condo and you can kiss safety goodbye. Not only that, but I can't spare the manpower right now to have someone sit there all night. As of right now, you're on your own."

"What about the autopsy and forensics? Is the report complete yet? I want to see it."

"No, they're still working on it. I told you no prints in the San Clemente house."

"No prints," she repeated. "Shit . . ."

"They're completely swamped down there. All the M.E. told me is that he thinks it went down this way." Rickerson paused, picking up his cigar, and then he remembered the scene in the restaurant with Lara. He dropped it back in the ashtray, turning his chair to face her. He spoke in a low, controlled voice. "Somehow the assailant managed to get into the house. He may or may not have intended to kill them. We can't know that for sure. All we know is that he was looking for something in that house, and from the looks of it, he didn't find it. She was there . . . he raped her, held the pillow over her face to keep her from screaming, drawing attention, and then he suffocated her. Maybe she was fighting; maybe he just likes to kill women, or maybe someone paid him to kill them both. Your brother-in-law more than likely walked into this scene. The suspect was hiding, probably in Josh's bedroom, and bashed Perkins in the back of the head as he went to your sister's side. Sam fell forward on the bed where we found him." Rickerson sat back in his seat. "At first we thought there were two separate killers, but now we're going on the basis of only one. Forensics has some pubic hair, not your brother-in-law's, some skin under her fingernails, and other than that, they're still looking."

Lara was trembling, her mind filled with the horror Ivory had endured. She hadn't heard half of what Rickerson had said. She kept seeing the bloody walls, Ivory's lifeless body, Sam's cracked skull with his brain exposed. "Isn't there something . . . that I can do?" she stammered. "I can't let this person get away with this . . . my sister . . . I simply can't."

"Not a thing. We're doing everything humanly possible to bring this man in and put this to bed. We've even called some men in from retirement, borrowed some men from the sheriff. We're doing it all."

"Nothing," she reiterated, her frustration escalating. "Just like that, I'm supposed to sit around and do nothing."

"Just like that, kid," Rickerson said, his rust eyes flashing with compassion. "I know you like to run the show, but this is one show you better stay out of or you'll end up the star. That's more or less what happened to your sister and she's dead."

Lara's chest was rising and falling. She stood to leave but didn't speak. She kept her eyes locked on the redheaded detective. He stared right back until she looked away. "The boy involved in the Henderson case? Have you found him yet?" she asked.

"He's coming home from UCLA tonight. I've already talked to his parents. I'm interviewing him later this evening. To be honest, I don't really think he's involved, but believe me, we're gonna give him a full tumble."

"I'm frightened, you know," Lara said. Her palms were sweaty and she was rubbing them on her pants legs. "And I keep thinking they're going to get away with this. Too many people get away with these horrendous crimes."

Rickerson came out from behind his desk. The other detective had disappeared. Phones were ringing. Outside the detective bay was a flurry of activity. He needed to get back to work. He put his large hands on her shoulders and stared her right in the eye, only inches from her face. "One of these days you're going to have to trust someone, Lara. Why don't you start with me? They aren't going to get away with it."

The detective dropped his hands, and Lara walked out of the police station. Packy Cummings was still out there somewhere. She tried to bring forth the image of his face from that day in the courtroom, but it was buried somewhere in her subconscious. Had he followed her here to the police station? Had someone hired him to eliminate her entire family? She saw the Jaguar and Josh still in the front seat. She should have never left him alone.

Once she was inside the car, Lara turned down the radio and smiled at Josh. "You hungry? I'm starving. Where do you want to go to lunch?"

Josh jerked his head away and stared out the window. With each passing hour the boy became more withdrawn and morose. Today he had barely spoken.

"Yes, Aunt Lara, lunch would be terrific," she said, hoping she might embarrass him into opening up, acknowledging how hard she was trying.

Slowly he turned toward her and stared at her with a black intensity. "I'm not hungry," he snapped. "And

I don't know why I have to go everywhere with you. I'm not your pet dog, you know."

"No, Josh," Lara said softly, trying to keep the exasperation out of her voice, "you're not my pet dog, but you are the only relative I have now. It would be nice if we could help each other get through this, don't you think?"

Josh didn't answer. Lara felt her fingers tighten on the steering wheel. As horrid as it might seem, she knew she could not eliminate her nephew as a suspect. While the police were combing the city for the killer, the killer could be sitting right next to her.

The men were assembled in the squad room at the San Clemente Police Department. It was three o'clock, time for the regular change-of-shift briefing, and the majority of the men were uniformed officers. Chief Terrence Bradshaw walked to the front of the room to address the men.

"In a few minutes I'm going to have Detective Rickerson go over where we stand in the Perkins homicides. He's heading the task force investigating these crimes, along with my son, who you all know." The chief paused and looked out over the men, seeing the fresh-scrubbed face of his oldest son. He'd been on the force two years now. This would be his first assignment out of uniform, his chance to prove himself to both the seasoned men on the force and his father.

"As you've all probably heard by now," the chief continued, "someone in this department leaked sensitive information to the press, and when that person is found," he said, his eyes scanning the room with authority and menace, "he will be dealt with appropriately. Now, I'll turn you over to Detective Rickerson."

The chief took a seat in the front row and Rickerson stood. "This is what we have," he began. "We have a man and a woman who were found murdered in their home in the San Simeon housing tract of our city. The medical examiner has placed time of death between 0100 hours and 0300 hours on Wednesday, September eighth. There was no forced entry into the residence, but the killer or killers could have managed entry through the rear door of the residence. There was a hidden key there. The murder weapon on the male was a twenty-pound dumbbell discovered at the scene. The female was suffocated. There are only two sets of prints on the murder weapon—the woman's and those of her fourteen-year-old son."

Rickerson paused and took a drink of water from a glass on the table. "We do, however, have a suspect, as you are all well aware by now. His prints were found in the residence of the murdered woman's sister, Judge Lara Sanderstone, which was ransacked only a day before the murders."

Rickerson stopped and picked up a large stack of flyers off the table that he handed to one of the officers to distribute. "This individual should be considered armed and dangerous. Use extreme caution if you attempt to stop him. I'm certain you've all heard earlier broadcasts and have been on the lookout for this vehicle. The suspect, a Packard Cummings, was on parole and recently arrested for carrying a concealed weapon. Right now he's wanted only for questioning and for violation of parole. If located, book him on the parole violation and contact me immediately. Do not interrogate the subject."

A commotion broke out in the room. Officers were talking among themselves and fidgeting in their seats. So far Rickerson hadn't told them anything they didn't already know, and they were eager to hit the streets. The senior Bradshaw stood and the pandemonium immediately stopped. He then sat back down. Rickerson continued.

"The murdered woman, an Ivory Perkins, was working the trades as a prostitute, specializing in S and M. We have reason to believe that she and her husband, Sam Perkins, were extorting money from someone, possibly a high-placed government official."

"Who? Tell us who," a voice from the back yelled out.

"No names will be disclosed at this point."

The younger Bradshaw raised his hand. Rickerson glanced at his father and then back to the boy. "Yes, Mike."

"What evidence is there implicating extortion?"

Rickerson's opinion of the chief's son was obvious from his expression, but he didn't let it show in his voice. "Next sentence, Mike. I was getting to that. Just be patient here."

"Sorry," the young man said, a flush spreading over his face. The men let forth a round of laughter. It wasn't easy being an officer in a department where your father was the chief. Every time the young officer opened his mouth, someone thought it was a reason to ridicule him.

"Shortly before the murders, Samuel Perkins started throwing a lot of cash around—paying for things with a thick roll of hundred-dollar bills. He was seen at the racetrack in Del Mar, where he dropped a bundle, and there was about forty thousand in cash in the safe at the pawnshop. We know of no legitimate means for him to come up with this kind of money. His pawnshop was failing. Before this date he was being hounded by creditors. In addition, he was apparently fencing stolen property through the pawnshop. Some of it we have recovered and returned to the rightful owners."

A burly cop in the second row spoke up. "I tried to pop this guy a number of times for receiving stolen property. He was connected. Judge Sanderstone stepped on me hard."

Rickerson coughed and looked at the ground. This was something he didn't want spread all over the department—that a superior court judge was using her position to cover for a small-time thief like Perkins. Of course, with the kind of cash they had found, he was evidently growing in stature and couldn't really be classified as small-time anymore. "Let's move along, okay."

Now the officer who had spoken up stood. His name was Connors. "No, let's not move along. I'm getting pretty fed up with the graft and corruption in this county. We do the work and some crooked judge throws it out or tells us to take a hike."

"As I said, Connors, let's move along," Rickerson said, again glancing at the chief. "We have the phone records from the residence and numerous other leads that we will be following up on. Anyone with any information regarding this case, please contact me at once." Rickerson started to walk off and then reluctantly returned, remembering the chief was in the room. "Or contact Investigator Mike Bradshaw if I'm not available."

Getting that out of his mouth took a lot. It was a bitter pill to swallow, getting stuck with the chief's inept son on a case as big as this one. As soon as he was out of the squad room, he removed a cigar from his pocket, bit off the end, and shoved it between his teeth. A few seconds later, the younger Bradshaw was right by his side.

Rickerson looked down at him. He almost wanted to laugh. The man was so small. He couldn't be taller than five-six. The chief was a giant of a man. Son must have taken after the mother, he thought, in more ways than one. Everyone knew he wasn't that sharp, was borderline to even be in the department at all. Rickerson headed to the detective bureau, the younger man hot on his heels.

"Some attorney has been calling here asking a lot of questions about this case," he said. "Says he's a friend of the judge."

Rickerson spun around and faced him. "Who? What's his name? Why haven't you brought this to my attention? Are you sure it was an attorney? Maybe it was a judge?"

"Uh, I don't know, but I'm certain he said he was an attorney. He was real pushy, wanting to know about any suspects we might have had. I mean, it isn't a lead or anything. Besides, I misplaced the guy's name. I have so much junk on my desk, I guess I threw it away."

Rickerson completely lost it and stomped right on Mike Bradshaw's foot. While the young man yelped and jumped around on the linoleum, he snarled at him. "You incompetent little fool. I want to know everything, do you hear me? Absolutely everything. And what did you tell this man, huh? What in the fuck did you tell him?"

"Nothing . . . You stepped on my foot, man."

Looking up at a spot on the wall, Rickerson sucked air into his lungs and then slowly let it go. That's all he needed right now was for this little shit to go running to his father. His voice became soft, as if talking to a child. "I'm sorry, Mike. That was an accident, but don't you think you should keep me informed? Isn't that what we agreed on from the start?"

"I think the lady judge is involved. See, what I think is this was a big extortion and crime ring. She was the inside contact, the protection."

"Yeah," Rickerson said, turning and walking fast down the corridor on his long legs, making the little man almost run to keep up with him. "Well, I'd keep my damn mouth shut if I were you. I think you've been reading too many crime novels or watching too much TV. She may have asked Connors to lay off a few times, but that's it."

"Can I see the pictures? Dad said there were some incriminating pictures."

Rickerson stopped again and the other man ran right into his back. He turned and faced him, purposely puffing cigar smoke in his face. "No, you cannot see the pictures. The purpose is to stop this type of activity, not promote it."

"But I'm on the case," he said, his voice almost rising to a whine. "Is there anyone in the pictures that we know?"

"Mike," Rickerson barked, "just do what I tell you and don't ask questions where you don't belong."

While the younger man stood there with a blank expression on his face, Rickerson entered the men's room. A few seconds later, Bradshaw followed him, and Rickerson spun around and grabbed him by the lapels. "I'm going to take a crap now. Do you mind?"

"Dad just said to stay with you at all times."

Rickerson shook his head. As if he didn't have enough problems. "Let me tell you something, Mike," he said, spitting the words into the little man's face, "I know who leaked that stuff to the press. If you give me any shit at all, I'll tell your daddy."

"But I . . ."

"You what? You thought it was fine, huh? You thought it was fun being the big guy, giving the press some juicy tidbits. Those juicy tidbits will make that kid's life hell. How would you feel if that was your mother? Now, get the hell out of here and leave me the fuck alone."

While Josh was out on his bike, Lara removed the bloody T-shirt from his backpack and took it to Emmet's. "I don't have Sam's blood type yet. The autopsy report isn't finished."

"Do . . . you have . . . Josh's?"

"Wait a minute," she said. "It's on his birth certificate, right? I saw it in all the documents from the pawnshop. They must have kept all that stuff in the safe."

"Good," Emmet said. "Then . . . we . . . have a start."

Lara ran back to the condo and found the birth certificate. For a few moments she held it in her hand, looking at the tiny footprints, wondering what it was like to give birth to a child. Then she walked over to Emmet's and told him the blood type. It was type AB.

He said it would take a few days. While Lara watched, he rolled the T-shirt up in a ball and slipped it inside a plastic bag. Then he addressed a Federal Express envelope and handed it to Lara, telling her to drop it in the bin when she left the condo. He'd already contacted his friend the biologist. Lara thought of driving it over herself, but she had to go back to her place and wait for Josh.

She'd set strict guidelines, telling him where he could ride his bike and how long he could stay out. He was late. The minutes clicked by and turned into hours. She kept walking to the window and looking out, then returning to sit on the sofa and stare.

Finally she got in the Jaguar and rode around the neighborhood but no Josh. She didn't know what to do. He'd gone out the other day and come back a few hours later. She was frightened, but she had no choice but to wait. Lara knew the reality of his mother's death was finally beginning to sink in. Either that or he was afraid. Afraid they were getting close to finding out what had really happened in that house.

After pacing back and forth in the condo for about an hour, she decided to leave him a note and check in at the office. No matter what Rickerson said, she had to see Evergreen. She could forgo discussing this man Packy Cummings, but Evergreen was her boss.

Phillip informed her that the funeral arrangements were complete. The funeral was to be held in three days, which fell on a Monday. The medical examiner had made a commitment to release the bodies to the funeral home today, and Phillip had prepared the obituary Lara had dictated yesterday when she was in the office. It was only a paragraph. "What do you think?" she asked him, knowing he'd seen the newspapers this morning. "Should I just forget the obituary after what's happened? Is everyone talking about it?"

Phillip looked down at his desk and started shuffling papers from side to side. "I mean, that's your decision. But maybe it would be better to have a small, dignified service and forget the newspaper."

"You're right," she said, dropping the paper back on his desk and entering her office.

A few minutes later, Phillip came in with an enormous stack of papers. "I need your signature on these documents. A lot of them are late. I've been holding them. I didn't want to bother you."

"Do you know where Evergreen is right now?" Lara

said, signing her name on each piece of paper without even reading it.

"I'll check. He got a pro-tem to handle the calendar. He's probably in his office."

"Forget it," she told him, turning another document over and starting on the next one. "I'll just go down there when I'm finished here. Any other calls?"

The young man sighed. "Dozens."

"Anything pressing . . . that can't wait?"

"Social Services called. They need to see you ASAP about your nephew. I didn't give them your new number."

"Good," she said. "I'll call them when I get back."

Only a few more documents were left to sign when Lara noticed a form she didn't recognize. Grabbing her glasses, she quickly scanned it and then looked up at Phillip. What he had given her was a bank form verifying his employment and salary. Phillip's annual salary was thirty-six thousand a year. On the form he had listed his salary at fifty thousand. "Didn't I sign another loan paper like this just a few months ago?"

"Ah, yes . . . I hope you don't mind," he said. "I'm having some financial problems. I really . . . need this loan. I have to pay my tuition at law school . . . and my car broke down last week."

"Aren't you afraid they'll contact county personnel and find out we're fudging on your salary? I don't mind helping you, Phillip. I mean, we all have financial problems from time to time, but it doesn't look good for me to be caught in a lie. I have enough problems right now."

"This bank doesn't go through personnel. They go directly to the employee's supervisor. I know, remember. I already got one loan from them."

Lara felt sorry for the young man. She remembered all too well how difficult it was to put herself through law school. She signed her name and handed him the stack of papers. "Just don't overextend yourself. It took me years to pay off my student loans."

Clasping the stack of papers to his chest, Phillip

said, "I don't know how to thank you. I really appreciate this."

"No problem," Lara said, standing. "If you need me, I'll be in Evergreen's office."

She walked down the back corridor to the older judge's chambers. It was silent in the windowless, carpeted halls. She glanced at her watch. Most of the courts were still in session, for it was only a little after three o'clock. "Is he in?" she asked his secretary. The woman got all flustered and refused to look at her. Lara assumed she'd seen the newspaper article about Ivory. She silently nodded and Lara walked in.

Evergreen stood. She could see the gray at the roots of his dyed red hair, but he was a dapper dresser and Lara admired his suit.

"Lara," he said. "Sit down. I heard the news and saw the papers this morning. This is a very unfortunate situation. Please accept my condolences."

"Thank you, Leo," Lara said, sighing. "It's been tough."

She remained standing, but Evergreen sank into his large leather chair and spun around to his mahogany desk. As always, it was perfectly clean, no clutter or papers whatsoever. She tried to imagine him in here at night after everyone had gone home, with his little can of Pledge and his feather duster. After a few moments of staring at him, she took a seat.

"I had no idea you even had a sister. You never mentioned her." Evergreen started tapping a pen on his desk and then dropped it. His eyes drifted down to the surface of his desk, and then he fixed his gaze on a picture in a mahogany wood frame. The frame was a perfect match to all the other wood in the room.

"How bad is it?" she said. "You know, the talk and all . . . about the newspaper article."

"Oh," he said, sort of jumping up a little in his seat as if she had startled him. "People are calling. They're concerned."

"I'm going to have the services Monday . . . just for the family . . . something small." She inhaled until her lungs almost exploded. She'd have to bury Sam. She hated him, but having him cremated was too extreme. And there was Josh—it just wouldn't look right. She exhaled and sank even farther in the chair. "I'll be back Tuesday to open the Adams trial."

"I see," he said. "Why don't you take some time off? Go away for a week or so instead of jumping back into all this work. Once you open this trial, Lara, it will be almost impossible for you to bail out."

Lara stood. She wanted to ask him about Packard Cummings, what agency had called him regarding this man, but Rickerson had insisted. She thought it was stupid. Why all the secrecy? "I need to work, keep my mind occupied. Don't worry, I can handle it."

"I'm not sure you are emotionally ready to return to the bench."

"I . . . Leo . . ." Lara grabbed the back of the chair and leaned forward. She needed to work, put her life back into some semblance of normalcy. She didn't need to run off somewhere by herself. They were shorthanded anyway. "I have my nephew, Leo. I can't leave town."

"Isn't there another relative who could take him? Your parents or someone?"

"No," Lara said emphatically. "They're both dead. The kid's mine."

"I see," he said slowly, licking his lips. "Social Services called this morning inquiring about you."

"God," she said. "Already, huh? They already called?"

"Yes, they did," he said, his brows knitting, "and they were concerned about some information they learned from the San Clemente Police Department."

"What information?" Lara said, searching Evergreen's dim eyes. Certainly, she thought, they hadn't already discovered that she didn't have a room for the kid. No one at the courthouse even knew where she was living.

"As they informed me, you evidently used your position to curtail investigations into your brother-in-law's criminal activities. I had to do some follow-up on this, and it's come to light that you are co-owner of that business—that pawnshop. Social Services expressed concern that you might be involved in this whole sordid affair. I, of course, assured them that you have an excellent record both as a prosecutor and as a member of this bench, but these are serious allegations, Lara."

"What?" she said, blanching. "What the hell . . ." She was shocked really, quite simply shocked. "All I ever did was tell them to lay off him a little. I never thought he was actually involved in criminal activity, Leo. I swear. I thought he was just sloppy, forgetting to report all the property he took in. He wasn't that bright." Lara had feared that this would someday come back to haunt her, but her statements to Evergreen were more or less the truth. Sam had never run a business before, and in the beginning she had attributed these incidents to sloppy bookkeeping. Probably by the last phone call the truth was beginning to sink in and she had simply denied it. All pawnshops took in a certain percentage of stolen goods. Everyone knew that. Even those that were scrupulously honest sometimes found themselves in that position.

Evergreen lifted his head and his chin jutted out. "Well, we've all made mistakes now and then, but it doesn't look good, particularly in light of what has occurred and all the attention this case is garnering in the press. This is an embarrassment to the bench." He cleared his throat and started speaking again in a firm, flat voice, one he usually reserved for the courtroom. "If you recall the *Canons of Judicial Ethics,*" he said, pausing, picking up his reading glasses and a large leather-bound book from his desk and reading from it: " 'A judge's official conduct should be free from impropriety and the appearance of impropriety; he should avoid infractions of law; and his personal behavior, not only upon the bench and in the performance of judicial duties, but also in everyday life, should be beyond reproach.' " He snapped the book shut and peered at her over his glasses.

Lara was speechless. Her hands on the chair were trembling, and she removed them and placed them at her sides, her back rigid. "Are you saying what I think you're saying?" He was blatantly accusing her of impropriety and unethical behavior.

"Yes, unfortunately I am. I consider it serious enough to warrant a full investigation. And of course, I'll have to relay this information to the Judicial Counsel in San Francisco."

Lara stared at him, but he didn't flinch. She thought at first he might have been attempting to scare her, teach her a lesson like a father, but the look in his eyes was not fatherly at all. How could he have the balls to do this to her, and now of all times? Her heart raced and she placed a hand over her chest. She was seconds away from letting it all go, asking him point blank about this Cummings man.

"I'm sorry, Lara, but you have to understand my position. Once something like this is brought to my attention, I would be remiss if I didn't follow through," he said softly, punching a button on his phone that was blinking. "If you will excuse me, I have to take this phone call. You look quite distressed. You should go home and rest."

Their eyes locked and lingered. A coldness was reflected there—as if she were gazing into two sheets of ice. Before this had all occurred, Lara had thought she was beginning to get to know this man, win his respect and admiration. Now she could see it all dissolving right before her eyes. Sure, she looked distressed. How else would she look when someone accused her of impropriety? Reaching her office, she walked right past Phillip and grabbed her purse off her desk and headed out the door.

"Judge Sanderstone," Phillip said, standing. "Don't you want your messages?"

"I'll call you later," she said, and then remembered Sam. "Buy another coffin, the cheapest one they have, and advise the mortuary to have my brother-in-law inside it by Monday." She didn't look back. She just kept on walking. She might be burying more than her sister and Sam come Monday. She might be burying her entire career.

chapter 14

Racing back to the condo, Lara felt certain Josh would be home, but he wasn't. Taped to the front door was a note from Social Services insisting that she call them at once. Rickerson must have told them where she was staying. She certainly couldn't call them now. She didn't even know where the kid was. Evergreen was accusing her of impropriety, and she'd somehow managed to misplace her dead sister's child. She went into the small kitchen and looked for a glass to get a drink of water. She was shaking and her throat was dry. There was nothing. All the cabinets were empty. She suddenly spun around in the small space, slamming all the cabinets as hard as she could, kicking the walls until she thought her ankle had broken, screaming, "Why? Why has this happened?"

Placing her head under the faucet, she let the water run into her mouth. Then she just stuck her head under and let it soak her hair, her face. She was in a tight little box—a box she couldn't escape from no matter what she did. It wasn't the condo. It was the whole thing. She had invested everything in her career, and now it was all going up in smoke. Never once had she been called on the carpet. Her record was impeccable.

Before long, it was going to be dark. She didn't know what to do about Josh. She'd seen Emmet's van in the parking lot and crossed the courtyard to his door. "Emmet," she yelled through the door. "It's Lara. Can I come in?"

She waited until he hit a button and the door unlocked. She found him in his office. Her hair was soaking wet, her eyes wild.

"Lara," he said, his voice as always weak, his head dropping to one side. "I called. Your nephew answered . . . and . . . hung up on me."

Sometimes it was hard to understand Emmet. His speech was slurred due to his illness, and people just didn't give him time to say what he wanted to say. "I'm sorry, Emmet. Have you seen him? He went out on his bicycle and hasn't come back."

"No," he said. "I've . . . been . . . working out."

Lara felt her panic subsiding. Just being here with Emmet made her feel stronger. If he could deal with the harsh reality of his illness, then she would have to find the strength to deal with her own predicament, her own sorrow. She suddenly noticed that his hair was soaking wet like her own. "Did you say working out, Emmet? Are you all right? Your hair's all wet."

"Yours . . . too," he said, managing a smile. "See, I . . . want to keep . . . my strength up, so . . . I crawl . . . from room . . . to room. Then I get . . . in my bed and then . . . out of my bed."

"Really?" she said. "You never told me you did that, Emmet."

"Look," he said, unstrapping a large pair of knee pads attached to his frail legs with Velcro, "did you . . . think I went roller . . . skating with these? Want . . . to borrow . . . them?"

Lara laughed. She needed to get back to work. Then, she thought, she could put some of this out of her mind. Emmet was always working, either on his physical therapy or his computers. Most people were put off by his appearance, his illness. Some even mistakenly thought he was retarded. But they were wrong, dead wrong. The frail young man with the wasted body and the thick glasses was brilliant. His software programs were unrivaled anywhere in the country. His disease was advanced but not to the point that he didn't have some muscle control. He could certainly work hour after hour, day after day, put in more hours than most healthy people.

But eventually he would die. He knew that fact well. He lived with it hanging over his head.

"Can I . . . do . . . something?" he said, his wrists jutting out awkwardly. "I want . . . to help you, Lara." He had spotted her distress. Emmet knew she was hurting.

Lara loved this man. There was something about him that exuded personal strength and power in the midst of physical infirmity—like a high-performance engine in an old, beat-up car. It shot right from his eyes. If people only took the time to look, they'd see it.

She looked around the room for a chair and then decided she should return to the condo in case Josh returned. "You could give me a hug," she finally said. She needed to touch someone, feel their body heat. She needed to borrow their strength.

She walked over to his wheelchair and leaned down and kissed his forehead lightly. He tried to raise his arm, but it fell back on the edge of the chair, too weak from his exercises even to hold her. Lara pressed her body against his and held it there. This was an Emmet hug.

"Thanks," she said. "I feel better already."

Emmet smiled with his eyes. Lara smiled back.

"I'm so . . . sorry . . . about your sister."

"Yeah," she said. "I'm sorry too, Emmet. About as sorry as a person can get." For a few moments he managed to maintain eye contact, and then his eyes drifted away involuntarily. She didn't have to explain pain and sorrow to him. Emmet knew all there was to know. She quietly let herself out of the apartment as he turned back to the computer. As she walked out the door, she heard the soft tap, tap, tapping of his pen on the keyboard.

Still no Josh. Lara was beginning to get very concerned now. God forbid, she thought, what if something terrible had happened to him? Did boys his age do this all the time—just disappear for hours?

She didn't touch the boxes of pawn tickets in the entryway, but she did start reviewing the copies of the phone records that Rickerson had given her.

The list of numbers and names of people who had been called from the residence in San Clemente was extensive and varied. The investigators had managed to get the names and addresses from the telephone company, and she studied the list carefully, trying to see if she recognized any of them as old friends of Ivory's or anyone she might have mentioned through the years.

A number of the names she did recognize, or at least, she recognized the businesses where the phones were located that had been called. A lot of the numbers were to hotels, some in Orange County, some in Los Angeles. Lara shuddered. Only one reason for these calls, she thought. Clients. No names were listed next to these numbers. Once the calls were transferred from the switchboard, they were impossible to trace.

The calls to public officials were puzzling, to say the least. There was a call to the man who was superintendent of the Orange County School District and a call to a man she recognized as president of the Anaheim Chamber of Commerce.

Then she started thinking, rubbing her forehead. One fact had to be the starting point for all speculation, a fact that Rickerson knew all too well. The fact that there was no forced entry. Whoever had killed Sam and Ivory was someone they knew well enough to allow them entrance to the residence. And she really couldn't stretch her imagination far enough to believe that Ivory had clients over and "serviced" them, as Rickerson had called it, with Sam in the house. But then again, she might be wrong. What did she know about this type of activity? Her mind was full of unanswered questions, not just about the murder, but the life her sister was secretly leading. What kind of man would allow his wife to do something like this? A cheap, slimy asshole like Sam, she thought, wishing that he were still alive so she could kill him herself. He had taken advantage of Ivory's lack of intelligence, her lack of self-confidence, her immaturity. He had probably plied her with drugs and praised her every time she turned a trick like a damn dog. He was a parasite, a predator. All her life, people had taken advantage of Ivory. As sad as it was to consider, her sister would do anything to win people's approval. Everyone's approval but that of her own sister. After Lara had threatened to take Josh away, Ivory had never sought her approval again.

Josh still hadn't returned, and Lara walked to the window and peered through the curtains. She was about to give up and call the police when the front door opened and in he walked, pushing his bike over the door frame.

"Where in God's name have you been?" she said, almost screaming at him. "I was worried sick. You should have left me a note or something."

He tossed his shaggy head of hair and glared at her; his skin was glistening with perspiration. "Well, I came back and you weren't here, so I went back out."

"Okay," she said, lowering her voice. "I'm sorry I screamed at you. I was just worried, that's all. You can't go running around in this neighborhood. You could get hurt."

"So what?" he sneered, suddenly erupting in anger. "What's it to you?"

Lara brushed her hair off her face and walked over to him. "Look, Josh, we have to make this work. You're all I have and I'm all you have. That's the way it is, whether you like it or not."

"You're ugly. You look like a witch. This place is a dump. I hate it here. I want my stuff . . . my friends . . . I want to go home."

As tough a facade as he was presenting, Lara could see his chest heaving and knew he was about to break down. "You can cry, Josh. Don't be ashamed to cry. I know how awful you feel." She paused, shuffling her feet around on the small entryway. "I made an appointment for you to talk to Dr. Werner again."

"I'm not going," he shouted. "I told you I'm not going to that stupid shrink. I hate him. I'm not crazy. You can't make me. I'll run away. I'll . . ."

He grabbed the handlebars of the bike and started to push it back out the open door. Lara reached for his shirt and accidentally ended up with a handful of his hair. "Stop right there," she ordered him. "You're not going out again. It's almost dark. There's a lot of crime around here. I won't allow it."

"Let go of my fucking hair. You're a bitch. You look like that horror woman . . . Elvira . . . Mistress of the Dark. Let go of me."

Lara took some deep breaths and held onto his hair. "I'll let go as soon as you promise me you won't go back out. Do you promise?" she said, pulling on his hair enough that his forehead fell backward and she could peer down into his eyes. If this was what it took to control a teenage boy, keep him from getting hurt, then this is the way it would have to be.

The door was still standing open and Josh was really yelling now like she was killing him. "Let go of me," he shrieked. "You're scalping me. Okay, I promise. Just let go."

Lara released him and he snapped his head back up. Then both of them stood there and stared, their mouths falling open in unison. Only a few feet away on the sidewalk, watching the whole scene intently, were two women. As soon as Lara looked at them, they stepped toward the door to the condo. One of the women had short blond hair and was as skinny as a twig.

"I'm Lucille Rambling," she said, extending her hand, "and this is Madeline Murphy. Judge Sanderstone, I presume?"

Lara felt her stomach do about five cartwheels and for a moment thought she was going to be sick. She shook the woman's hand and then dropped it. It was cold and limp.

"We're from the Social Services Department, Judge Sanderstone," the woman said. "We're here about your nephew."

* * *

Lara hadn't taken the time to make the bed or pick up the condo that morning. Josh had most of his clothes spread all over the floor in the living room. When the two women from Social Services walked into the room, the skinny blonde turned up her nose and stepped over the mess.

"Uh, Judge Sanderstone," Lucille Rambling said, "we need to see your nephew's bedroom, the place he will be sleeping while he's staying with you."

Quickly, Lara tried to think. This was it. She could let them take him. Letting them take him would certainly be easier than what she was going through. Josh was just standing there with a surly expression on his face. "In here," she said without even thinking. "His bedroom is right in here. Of course, I have a large house in Irvine. We'll be moving back in there in a few days."

The women walked into the bedroom and looked around, peeking into the small bathroom and then walking back to the living room. "Is there another room here?" the other woman said. "You know, another bedroom." She was craning her neck around toward the kitchen.

"No," Lara said self-consciously. "This is it."

"Humph," she said. "Then where do you sleep?"

"I sleep on the sofa . . . here. I let Josh have the bedroom."

"You did not," he said, narrowing his eyes, "you're lying. You didn't give me the bedroom except that one night. I've been sleeping on that stupid sofa. It's a bitch, man."

Lara's shoulders fell. If he'd just kept his mouth shut, maybe they wouldn't have known about the sleeping arrangements and would have overlooked the scene they walked into at the door. But possibly it was for the best, she told herself. The child seemed to despise her anyway, and she was a nervous wreck.

"Why don't we step outside?" Ms. Rambling said.

"Fine," Lara said, shifting her eyes to Josh. See, she wanted to tell him, see what you did.

"Look," Lucille Rambling said once they were outside and the door was shut. "We're certain your intentions are good in wanting to care for your sister's child, but there are certain criteria that must be met for us to allow him to remain here. One of these is that he has his own room. He's a teenage boy and he needs his privacy."

"I understand," Lara said, "but surely there's some flexibility in all rules." She kept glancing back at the door. For some reason she felt a tug on her heart. She didn't want to let him go. "I told you we will be moving back to my house in Irvine, and Josh will have his own room. In fact, we could do that now if that would rectify the situation."

"I'm sorry," the blonde continued, exchanging a knowing glance with the other woman. "Investigator Bradshaw at the San Clemente Police Department informed us that you were hiding out here, that they feel you are in some kind of jeopardy. I don't think that you should take your nephew back somewhere where he would be at risk."

"Of course not," Lara said quickly, wondering who this Bradshaw was. If he kept telling everyone where she was, she wouldn't be hiding out anywhere much longer. "I could possibly rent a bigger place in this same complex. It might take me a few days to arrange it, but I'm certain I could."

"We can't allow the boy to stay here. We'll have to find a placement for him, and then when your situation changes, you can contact us and we'll do another evaluation. Believe me, it's far better for all concerned that he remains with you, yet it must be within our guidelines." She paused and then continued, her face softening somewhat, her voice almost a whisper. "The Social Services agency is under close scrutiny right now, Judge Sanderstone. I know you're aware of the Adams case. The agency director has instructed us to enforce the rules with no exceptions. And that exchange we saw between you and your nephew . . . well, maybe you could both benefit from a cooling-out period."

Lara dropped her head. She thought of throwing her weight around, insisting that they leave Josh with her. But no, she decided, an exercise in authority would make these women even more determined to take Josh away. Lara might be a judge, but in this situation Lucille Rambling and Madeline Murphy held all the cards.

"Why don't you get his things together?" Madeline Murphy told Lara. "We'll be taking him now."

"Look, the funeral is Monday. Why don't you let him stay here until then, and I'll work on getting another place? Besides, they're looking right now for the man that did this. As soon as they find him, we can go home."

"I'm sorry," she said.

Lara refused to look at the two women, her eyes on the concrete walk. "Thanks. Thanks a whole hell of a lot." As soon as she said it, she regretted it.

"There's no reason for you to get snippy with us, Judge Sanderstone. We're only doing our job . . . surely—"

"Excuse me," she said to the woman, finally raising her eyes. "I thought possibly after all he's gone through, you might see the benefit of his being with a close relative. You know, bending the rules somewhat to fit the situation."

Madeline Murphy had mousy brown hair and thick glasses; her eyes were so small they looked like shiny black beads. "I wouldn't talk about bending the rules if I were you, Judge Sanderstone, not from what we've heard."

Sirens started squealing on the street in front of the complex. First, there were black-and-whites racing by, and then an ambulance raced by. The noise was so loud, they couldn't even speak. A few moments later, a fire truck rolled by. This was real impressive, Lara thought. All she needed now was someone to go running past her doorway with a sawed-off shotgun. Great neighborhood, she thought. Super place for a kid.

Finally the sirens stopped. "What do you mean to imply, Ms. Murphy?" Lara knew just what the woman was talking about, the fact that she'd talked law enforcement out of going after Sam, covered him inadvertently while he was involved in criminal activities. She remembered all too well her little chat with Evergreen.

"Never mind," the woman said. "Please, just get the boy ready and we'll be on our way. We'll wait out here. Send him out." The woman reached into her purse and handed Lara her card. "We are sorry about your sister," she said. "Call us when you get situated in a larger place."

Lara went inside and shut the door behind her, leaning back against it. Josh stuck his head out of the small kitchen.

"Are those old biddies gone?"

Lara sighed. "Those old biddies, huh?"

"Yeah, boy, were they ugly." He laughed and made a face. "Look, I'm starving. We don't have any food at all here, not even a cookie. You've got to go to the store."

"I thought I was the Mistress of the Dark?"

"Sorry," he said and gave her a lopsided grin. "I was in a bad mood, okay?" As soon as the smile appeared, it fell away.

"Well, unfortunately, Josh, or fortunately for you, depending on how you look at it, since you don't want to stay with me—"

"Wait," he said. A shadow passed over his eyes as he walked into the living room and plunked down in a chair. "I'll stay, okay? I told you I was just upset."

"They won't let you stay. I don't have the right situation for you . . . a room and all. And they saw the little argument we had in living color. I have to pack your things. They're waiting."

"No," he said, springing to his feet. "What're they

going to do to me? They can't take me away somewhere. I said I'd stay here with you."

He was blinking rapidly and Lara saw the tears gathering in his eyes. She started toward him and he disappeared into the kitchen. He really wanted to stay with her. She was shocked. More than anything, she was touched. "Josh," she said softly, "I'll take care of it. I'll figure out something, okay? You may have to stay in a foster home for a day or two, but I promise I'll get you as soon as I can. We're going to have the services Monday. Maybe I can have it arranged by then."

Josh had his forehead pressed to the refrigerator door. "You'll never get me. Why would you want to? I called you names. I . . . I'm not a good person."

Lara walked up behind him. "Josh, I understand . . . please believe me. I wouldn't give up on you simply because you called me names."

His body began shaking and Lara reached out tentatively to touch him, stroke his hair. When he didn't resist, she moved even closer, as if she were about to pet a wild animal. Now she was so close that she could smell his hair, his skin, his sweaty boy odor. He didn't move and kept his forehead against the refrigerator door.

"I miss my mom . . ." he said, his voice weak and frail now. "I keep having these nightmares that she's calling to me . . . begging me to help her and I can't find her. I look all over the house, in every single room, and she isn't there."

Gently, Lara turned him around and wrapped him in her arms. She felt a powerful surge of emotion, one so strong that she had to grit her teeth and lean into it, like a person walking in gale-force winds.

"Look," she said, pushing herself away from him, "look at me." She let forth a nervous laugh. She wiped her eyes with her fingers. "And I never cry."

All of a sudden his hand reached out for her, almost in slow motion, only touching a single strand of her hair as he studied her face. Then his hand fell away and dropped to his side.

As quickly as it had come, the moment was gone.

Josh walked out of the kitchen and started throwing the few things he had in a pile on the floor.

"I'll get you a sack or something," Lara said, heading back to the kitchen.

"What about my bike?" he said, glancing at it in the doorway, his one possession, his one means of escape. "They won't let me take it, will they?"

"Probably not, honey, but you can ask."

A few minutes later, he walked out the door, suitcase in hand, his shoulders slumped. He glanced back at Lara. They didn't say goodbye. He didn't return for his bicycle.

As soon as they left, Lara went back to Emmet's.

The complex wasn't really such a bad place to live, she thought, crossing the courtyard with the huge weeping willow, its branches brushing the ground. That is, if you overlooked the neighborhood surrounding it. A nest of sparrows lived in that tree, and every time she walked out the front door, she could hear them chirping. Today they were silent. But mature trees were scattered all throughout the complex, making it shady and lush. She thought the trees and grounds might be what had attracted Emmet. The structures were older, steeped in character, marked by time. Lara liked that type of thing. She'd always looked back instead of forward. Most of Orange County was so new, so shiny. Row after row of tract houses lined the streets, the trees all mowed down by developers.

She'd never felt so dejected in her life. She had to get Josh back. She had seen through that tough outer shell. He was just a frightened child—so alone, so full of pain. Sure, he was bitter. Who wouldn't be bitter? She had no idea what he had been through before the murders, but she knew it wasn't good.

She'd tried to call Irene Murdock, but she was out. Everyone seemed to be out. With the ever present sunshine, the seventy-degree temperature, the ocean always only a few miles away, people in Southern California seldom stayed inside their homes.

Every time she thought about Emmet, she smiled—even now when her heart was breaking. Almost from the night she had met him, Lara classified herself as an Emmet fan; she admired him so much. He struggled with his disease without ever slipping into self-pity. He lived independently and had built a successful business. And he was a marvelous companion, far more interesting than any other men she knew. He was witty, intelligent, sensitive. Many Friday and Saturday evenings when Lara didn't have a date—and there were many—she'd call Emmet up and come over here, have real discussions about philosophy, literature, science, Emmet typing out responses on his computer faster than she could read, Lara standing behind him sipping a glass of wine.

Emmet's condominium was sparsely furnished. When he'd purchased it, he'd had all the carpeting removed and discovered the original hardwood flooring underneath. Since the building was older, it had wide hallways and oversized doors, which made it easier for Emmet to navigate his wheelchair in and around the rooms. His front door was wired to the ever present computer. All he had to do was push a few buttons and the front door opened.

Lara plunked down in the one chair, a Lazy Boy recliner. When there was no one to help him, Emmet used a trapeze type of device to hoist himself into the recliner. Lara flipped it out of the way. Every evening between six and seven o'clock, a male nurse came to assist him.

"I don't know what to do," Lara told him after he'd joined her in the living room. "Even if I went against Rickerson's and everyone's advice and moved back into the house in Irvine, they still won't let me have Josh back. Of course, they probably have a point—that I would be putting him at risk. I told them maybe I could get a larger place, but I can't do it today or tomorrow, and I certainly won't be able to get one that's furnished like the model. I just have to get him back, Emmet. He needs me. He just can't be involved in the murders. I know it."

"I . . . have . . . an . . . idea," Emmet said, making an effort to squeeze out all four words. At the end of the day, speaking was even more strenuous. "Come . . ." He turned his electric chair around and headed for his office, the wheels rolling over the hardwood flooring. Lara followed.

Sticking his head back into the steel cage, Emmet started tapping out words on the computer. Lara stood behind him and read.

"You can have my place until you find another and I'll stay at your place. I have three bedrooms. We'll move some of my equipment and I'll be fine. I can come over here and work during the day when you're gone."

"Emmet," Lara said. "I can't ask you to do that . . . all this"—she looked around at the room—"this is your work. You need all this equipment. We'd have to hire someone to disconnect everything and reassemble it at my place, and my place is carpeted. No," she said, shaking her head. "I appreciate it, but no. I'll find something." She thought of the house in San Clemente—the obvious choice. It was doubtful if the killers would go back there, but she knew living in that house right now would be too painful.

"Yes," Emmet typed, "it will be easy. No big deal. I have a firm that will set up the things I need at your place in only a few hours and I can work here during the day. I'll call the phone company and have a modem installed. Because I'm disabled, they'll do it at once. Let me help you, Lara. It will make me feel good to help someone else."

He stopped typing and tried to look her in the eye. Every time his gaze drifted, he seemed to force it back with a concentrated effort.

"But, Emmet, I have carpet, remember?"

He spun back around to the computer and typed out another rapid-fire message. "We can have plastic runners put down. They'll work just fine. Besides, I won't need my knee pads when I exercise."

"All right," Lara said, putting her hands together and clapping softly and then clasping them together tightly in relief. "We can start making the arrangements right now. You're a hero, Emmet. You're a first-class hero."

His head rolled far to the side, almost to the armrest of the wheelchair. His eyes smiled behind his thick glasses. "I . . . know," he said. "I like being . . . a . . . hero."

Lara laughed. "You know, huh? Let's call these people and start getting things set up. I'm sure it won't be for more than a few days at the most. They're trying to find the man now, and then we can go home."

"I'll . . . make the calls," he said.

"Don't you want me to handle the arrangements, Emmet?" Lara asked.

"No need," Emmet said. "Let . . . me . . . do something."

Lara gave him an extra key and let herself out of the condo, crossing the courtyard. She'd let Social Services know that she had a place for Josh first thing in the morning.

Back in the condo, she placed a call to Benjamin England at his residence in Tustin. His message had said he would be returning this weekend. She simply could not be alone another moment. When she was alone the demons came out and stalked her. They were stalking her now.

She saw herself in a dark, deep well, clawing the walls to get out, screaming for someone to come and rescue her. Her sister's body kept appearing in her mind, Sam's exposed brain tissue, the gruesome blood-splattered walls. It should have been her, she thought. Ivory had Josh. She picked up the birth certificate and stared at the tiny footprints again. She had nothing. If she could change places with Ivory right this minute, she would. In the blackness there must be peace, she thought—an end to this chaotic existence that seemed to lead nowhere and was so full of anguish.

Even though she had never been religious, Lara fell to her knees by the little sofa. She let her head fall forward and prayed. She prayed for courage to raise her nephew, track down her sister's killer and avenge her senseless death. She'd let her sister down, failed to see the signs when her life was falling apart. By her own hand, a tap of the gavel, the man who had possibly done this had been set free. She prayed for strength and direction.

In the silence Lara listened. The answers came to her. She stood and pushed her shoulders back as a wave of calmness and resolve washed over her. Her mother used to say that you should never ask God for something you can handle yourself. Lara was the direct descendant of a Cherokee chief. She would not succumb to weakness and self-pity. Not now, not ever.

chapter 15

Rickerson and his two sons were finishing dinner at the long oak table in the kitchen. He'd finally had to take a little time off. He was completely exhausted and besides, he had to go back out to interview the young man who had made threats to Lara in the courtroom. Big case or not, Rickerson knew he had to go home every now and then. He did have a family to raise, and unfortunately, right now he was doing it alone.

Stephen and Jimmy had prepared the entire meal by themselves. They'd made a roast chicken, a salad, some lumpy mashed potatoes. "Not bad," Rickerson told them. "Next time, though, turn the oven up a little higher the last ten or fifteen minutes. That way the chicken will get nice and brown on the top."

Jimmy had the pot of potatoes set on his plate and was scooping out every last bite. "How'd you learn to cook, Dad? Mom never said you could cook."

"Oh, yeah, well, I know how to sew too. Think I'm a sissy?"

Jimmy started laughing. He had a little pot belly, and when he laughed, it jumped up and down. They would never in their wildest dreams consider their rugged father a sissy. "Tell," Jimmy said, sticking a spoonful of potatoes in his mouth.

"When I was really young, my parents lived in Ohio. We had a boardinghouse. So, I had to help my mama with the cooking. I had to mend things that needed mending. I always wanted you guys to know how to take care of yourselves. Never know when you'll be alone in this world. Can't always depend on other people to care for you all your life."

Stephen was listening intently. He knew the boardinghouse story. He also knew his mother had walked out on his father, and he simply could not forgive her no matter how hard he tried. If he was his father, he wouldn't take her back, no matter what she said or did. She was his mother and he would always love her, but she had just abandoned them. He could handle it. He would be in college next year, but it certainly wasn't fair to Jimmy. He was immature for his age and missed her terribly. Some nights Stephen heard him crying.

Rickerson was rolling a cigar around in his fingers, about to bite off the end and shove it in his mouth. "If you light that, Dad," Stephen said, "I'm leaving the room, okay, and you can clean up the kitchen. I can't stand that smell." Just then Jimmy reached over and grabbed another roll. Stephen slapped it out of his hand. "Stop that. What do you want to do, weigh three hundred pounds? You'll die of a heart attack when you're thirty."

Rickerson's eyelids fluttered and he dropped the fat cigar onto the table. "Any news on your scholarship?"

"Get up, asshole," Stephen said to his brother. "Now. Move it. I have to do my homework. I don't want to be stuck in the kitchen all night." As soon as his brother started clearing the table, he turned to his father. "My counselor said I definitely have a partial academic scholarship, but it won't cover my room and board in the dorm and all of my tuition. They're still reviewing it, so I could get more, but I don't know. It's going to be expensive, Dad. Stanford's an expensive school."

Rickerson looked at his son. He was so serious. Too serious almost. "What? You don't think I can afford to send you to college?"

Stephen dropped his head. "I don't know. With Mom in school now and everything, I—I could go somewhere else. Maybe I could go to UCI and live at home. That would save a lot of money. And I could help you with Jimmy if Mom doesn't move back home."

Rickerson leaned over until he was peering into his son's eyes. "I've got the money, kid. Just worry about your grades, okay? Let the old man worry about the dough."

"What about Jimmy? He can't stay here alone all the time when I go off to college. All he'll do is eat and get in trouble. He won't even do his homework."

"Hey, what are you, the diet cop? I'm the real cop and you're suddenly your brother's dietitian. Give the guy a break. And as to next year, we'll cross that bridge when we come to it."

Rickerson left the table to go into the living room to smoke his cigar. He flopped down on the sofa, leaned his head back, and closed his eyes, sticking his long legs out in front of him and kicking off his shoes. He let his mind wander to Lara Sanderstone. For some reason his thoughts drifted more and more to her every day. Something about her intrigued him, and it wasn't simply that they were spending a lot of time together, talking to each other several times a day.

It might be the fact that she was lonely.

Rickerson knew about that type of thing. He felt terribly alone sometimes, and the funny thing was, he'd felt that way long before his wife had left. Joyce had always had the kids, the house to keep up, her own set of friends and activities. Women married to police officers tended to get very self-reliant.

The only friends he really had were other cops, and all they talked about was the job. After all these years he just got tired of listening to the same four-letter words, the same pumped-up war stories, the constant complaints. It was hard, really, for people like him to socialize. What did he possibly have in common with a man who sold used cars like the guy next door, or a man who punched numbers in a computer all day in a room about the size of a closet? Most Friday and Saturday nights when friends got together to socialize were the nights of heavy business for Rickerson. That's when the natives really got restless, and violence and crime spewed forth like water from an untapped faucet.

Cops were a different species. Most of the time when he was with people outside the job, all they wanted to do was ask him about the job anyway. Being a police officer was like wearing a suit of clothes with no zipper, like the color of a man's skin. If you were black or brown, you were black or brown from the time you got up until the time you went to bed. That's what it was like to be a cop.

Sometimes he'd made love to Joyce and fantasized about other women. He told himself that after twenty years of marriage, even the best of things became stale. Oh, he loved his wife. In many ways she had been his closest friend, but the excitement had vanished. Both of them had felt the clock ticking. Their youth was gone. All that was left, as he saw it, was to grow old and die. Now it looked like he was going to grow old and die alone. He would have never in a million years thought he would be in this position. The past three months he had tried not to give up hope, but hope was slowly slipping away.

Last night he had fantasized about Lara Sanderstone.

He sat up on the sofa and slapped his thigh. It was those damn suggestive pictures that got him daydreaming, started the juices flowing in a direction that he just had to put a stop to, and now, right now. When he looked at the pictures of Ivory, he imagined he was looking at Lara.

He simply couldn't look at those pictures again.

Lara Sanderstone would never be interested in a man like him. He wasn't a fool. She was a classy broad—a judge at that—and a good-looking woman. He'd never had a way with the women. Joyce was the only one he'd ever seriously dated.

Dating. Just the thought made him cringe. If Joyce didn't come back soon, he'd have to start prowling around looking for someone to spend time with, someone to have sex with now and then. He might be forty, but he wasn't dead. He was a man. He had normal desires. Women didn't just hop into bed with anyone that walked by, not today, not with all the diseases floating around. And most of the single women in his age group were looking for security, a meal ticket, a man with a fat paycheck and a fancy car. He couldn't afford to wine and dine them. He just didn't have the money or the time.

"Dad," Stephen said, sticking his head out the kitchen door. "It's Bradshaw . . . you know, baby Bradshaw."

Rickerson sighed, bringing himself back to reality. "Tell him I'm off duty. Unless he's got another stiff, it can wait for tomorrow."

Stephen disappeared and Rickerson fired up his cigar. He was smoking way too many of these things, he decided, rolling it in his fingers. Even he was beginning to get sick of them.

A few moments later Stephen stuck his head back out. "Says he's got a stiff." The boy shrugged his shoulders. "That's what he said."

"Nah," he said. "He's pulling your leg. That stupid little prick. Just wants me to come to the phone. I'll kill him . . . I'll frigging kill him."

Rickerson shuffled across the living room, looking down at all the spots on the carpet. In some places it was almost threadbare. Such is life, he said to himself.

"Bradshaw," he barked, "if you don't have a stiff, you better take out your gun and point it at your head."

"I do, I do . . ." the officer said, so excited that he was panting.

Rickerson let the cigar fall from his mouth to the kitchen floor in a stream of saliva. "Give it to me. Damn you, who and where?"

"Dad," Stephen yelled, bending down to pick up the cigar, "that's disgusting. We just mopped the floor today."

"Packy Cummings," Bradshaw continued. "The S.O. found him a few minutes ago. In a car . . . wait . . . wait. It was his car—the red Camaro. I'm in the radio room. They're on the air now." He paused. In the background the dispatcher was talking and the unit at the scene responding.

"Okay, okay," Bradshaw said. "He was shot . . . in the head. Ambulance and rescue are en route, but they're certain he's dead."

"Where, Bradshaw?" Rickerson yelled into the phone. "Tell me where. I can't do a damn thing if I don't know where it is I'm going."

"Just a minute . . ." More voices could be heard in the background. "Santa Ana . . . First Street . . . parking lot of an apartment complex near the courts. The officer doesn't know the address. It just went down."

"I'm on the way," Rickerson said. If Bradshaw hadn't fucked up, the location he was describing was right down the street from where Lara Sanderstone lived. "Get me an exact location and advise me over the radio."

When his father hung up, Stephen was wiping his hands on a dish towel. "Guess he really had a stiff, huh?"

"Yeah," Rickerson said, walking rapidly toward the door. Then he turned around and returned and gave his two sons a quick hug. "Don't look for me tonight. It looks like a long one."

"Be safe, Dad," they both said, almost in unison.

"Always," he answered. In seconds he was out the door and backing out of the driveway.

The parking lot of the Sea Breeze Apartments was taped, barricaded, and surrounded by squad cars.

Rickerson leaped out of his vehicle, leaving the car door standing open, and jogged the short distance to Packy Cummings's red Camaro.

A uniformed officer stepped forward and stopped him. "Wait a minute, bud. This is a crime scene."

Rickerson sneered and flipped his badge, then placed it on his belt and made sure his coat was open. "What do you have?" he asked. "And who's the commanding officer here?"

"Lieutenant Thomas," the man said. "Over there."

Thomas was a big guy, six-five or more. He was young for the rank of lieutenant and carried as much muscle around as height. His light brown hair was neatly cut, and he was standing by the vehicle as the men worked. The doors were open and several men from the medical examiner's office and the sheriff's crime lab were photographing the body and poking around for evidence. Packy was in the driver's seat, his head back on the headrest, a bullet hole a few centimeters above his left ear. Blood had gushed out in brackish rivers down his neck and onto his white dress shirt. Most of it had dried now. His eyes were open and his mouth was gaping. From the expression on his face, Rickerson bet he'd never known what hit him. He was now wearing a permanent mask of surprise.

"Didn't expect it, did he?" Lieutenant Thomas said, having arrived at the same conclusion.

"Are you sure it's him?"

"It's the car"—the lieutenant jerked his head to the side—"and that guy over there is his parole agent. He identified him. The parole office is only five minutes away."

"What do you have?"

"Who knows?" Thomas said. "There's all kinds of prints in and on the vehicle, but who knows who they belong to? The killer may have never stepped foot in that car. See," he said, walking over to the vehicle, "the driver's window was rolled down. Shooter could have stood right here and pulled the trigger." Thomas took out a pack of cigarettes and offered one to Rickerson. He waved them away.

"What else is in there?"

"Hey, Stanley," the lieutenant yelled at one of his men. "Show the sergeant here what you took out of the trunk."

Both men walked a few feet away. On the sidewalk was what looked like most of Packy's belongings. They had been inside a large plastic garbage bag and were now spread all over the sidewalk on a canvas tarp.

"Let's see," Officer Stanley said, picking through the stuff with gloved fingers. "We've got some underwear—definitely not clean—a couple of white dress shirts from J.C. Penney, their own brand. And these," he said, laughing, pulling out something in little packets.

"Condoms?" Rickerson said.

"Yep. He might have gotten himself blown away, but he didn't die of AIDS. Smart guy, huh?"

All the men around them started laughing except Rickerson. The detective failed to see the humor of the present situation.

Packy Cummings was the string of crumbs leading to the prize. Whoever had offed him had known just that.

"Any witnesses?"

"Little lady over there," Stanley said. "She lives in the upstairs apartment, the one overlooking the parking lot."

Rickerson felt his dinner rise in his throat and swallowed it. If she saw the killer, the case could come together in a matter of hours. "And . . ." he said excitedly.

"She was a good distance away, and the car was partially obscured by these trees. She saw two people in the car about two hours ago. They might have been inside the car and they might have been outside the car. She's not certain." The man's lip was curling. "She was opening her curtains and casually glanced down and saw the Camaro. There was another car parked nearby that she didn't recognize as belonging to one of the tenants, and she'd never seen the Camaro before today. Good place for a homicide, huh?"

Rickerson looked at the trees. "Right. The other car . . . ?"

"She thought it was a green Mercedes, or a blue BMW, or a black Ford." He looked at Rickerson and smacked his chewing gum. "Get the picture?"

"Yeah," Rickerson said. "Did she hear the shots?"

"Yep," the other man said, spitting his gum out onto

the concrete. "Heard something . . . thought it was a car backfiring. We got the call when some kid saw this guy with a hole in his head inside the vehicle with the engine running. Killer was gone by then. We're just lucky he called. People don't like to get involved around here."

None of this was worth anything, Rickerson thought, greatly disappointed. The woman was a shitty observer. Many people were. He'd had homicides in which a person was killed not more than two feet from where people were standing and they didn't remember a blasted thing.

California, he thought. The land of the proverbial airhead.

"Nothing in his pockets, his wallet?"

"*Nada,* my man, no such luck," Stanley said. "All the dude had in his wallet was a five spot. If he had anything else, someone could have lifted it after the killing. Won't know if the killer took it or a neighborhood vulture. Fellow with a bullet in his head is a pretty unthreatening victim for a thief."

"Small-caliber weapon?"

"Hole's little . . . guess so."

The lieutenant had walked back to the car and was flicking his ashes in the nearby grass. He saw Rickerson and nodded for him to come over. "We're taking impressions of the skid marks. See," he said, looking down where a man was working. "I'd say the killer arranged a meet here, pulled up, and parked right next to the Camaro. Killer stood outside the window and they talked. That's when he pulled out a gun and blew him away. Cummings must have felt pretty secure with this person, because his own shooter is still in the glove box."

"The killer's prints could be on the door handle. This might have gone down inside the car." Rickerson knew the door handle was the perfect surface for prints. He could hope. "You guys didn't stick a dozen prints on top of it when you got here, did you?" he said, accusing the few officers standing around of destroying evidence.

"Hold on a minute, Sergeant," the lieutenant barked. "We aren't a bunch of backwoods cops. We know how to handle a crime scene."

The lieutenant was being a prick, letting him know he was the one from the small department. In their eyes, they were the pros. "Well, I guess you've got a handle on it, then," he told him. "I'll be waiting for the reports. As soon as your people write them, fax them to my office."

"No problem," the lieutenant answered. "Think this is your shooter?"

"Maybe you need to review the facts of this case yourself, Lieutenant," he told the man, already heading across the parking lot, tossing the words over his shoulder. "We never had a shooter. Cause of death was a blow to the head and suffocation."

Rickerson smiled. Let him blow that one out his asshole, he thought. Then he marched to his unit, threw the gear shift in reverse, and burned off backward onto the street.

Alone in the condominium, Lara tried reading the newspaper, but she couldn't keep her mind focused. She thought of returning to Emmet's, but his nurse was there now. All she could think about was Josh, and then the horrid conversation she'd had with Evergreen. Was he really going to pursue this? Pull out all the stops and place her entire career in jeopardy just because of a few words on the phone over Sam's pawnshop? It seemed incredible.

The phone rang and Lara seized it, thinking it was Irene or Benjamin. She'd left messages for both of them.

"He's dead," Rickerson said.

"Who's dead?" Lara said, her heart pounding.

"Cummings. Someone shot him this afternoon not far from your apartment."

"My God," Lara said, her spirits soaring. "Then I

can go home. If the man who broke into my place is dead, I'm safe." She wouldn't have to move into Emmet's condo. She could get Josh back.

"I'm right down the street," he said. "Can I stop by in a few hours? I'll fill you in on all the details. But, Lara . . ."

"Yes?" she said. She was sitting up straight. There was a God, she thought. He'd heard her prayers. Everything was going to be fine now. She couldn't bring Ivory back, but she could care for her son, resume her own life.

"You can't go home just yet, and . . . well, let me tell you everything when I see you. Right now I've got to go."

Before she could say anything, the detective had hung up. The way she saw it, this was a cause for celebration. She showered, dressed in clean clothes, sprayed herself with cologne. She went to the corner liquor store and bought a bottle of wine. Then she waited.

"You can come in," the woman said at the door to Rickerson. "Ian's expecting you."

He stepped over the threshold into a picture-perfect living room. The furniture and the decorations were nice enough to be on the cover of *House Beautiful*. Mrs. Berger was still standing at the door. She was in her mid to late fifties, well dressed and still fairly attractive. Her husband was a successful businessman. Finally she shut the door.

"I'll go get Ian. He's in his room." She turned and had started walking toward the back of the house when the detective called to her.

"No," he said, his voice low. "Rather than talking to him in here and disrupting the rest of the household, why don't I just speak with him in his room?"

The woman's eyes drifted up and then down. She shrugged her shoulders as if it didn't matter. She was worried sick about her son. It showed. "First door on the left," she said.

The door was open. Ian Berger was sitting at a small desk with several books open in front of him. He looked up. Dark circles were etched under his eyes. Rickerson let his gaze wander. At least six framed pictures of Jessica Van Horn surrounded him. On the wall was an enormous poster of the murdered girl, larger than life. Her entire presence seemed to fill the room.

Ian stood and shook Rickerson's hand. "Sit down," he said, indicating his bed. "Or you can sit here if you want. I mean, we could go in the living room."

Rickerson dropped to the edge of the bed. He'd wanted to see the inside of this room. When a person's mind was disintegrating, enough to do something rash, their surroundings generally reflected it. This room might be a shrine to the dead girl, but it wasn't the room of someone who'd gone over the edge. It was neat and appealing. The bed was made, everything was in its place. But, of course, he reminded himself, the boy lived in an apartment near the UCLA campus during the week. The lack of clutter and disorder in this room might mean nothing. His mother probably cleaned it.

"Do you know why I'm here?" he asked the boy.

"Sort of . . ." He coughed and leaned over his knees. "It's because something happened to that judge, isn't it?"

Rickerson changed the subject. He liked to switch things around, get a subject headed in one direction and then head off in another. "What are you studying at college?"

"Economics." The boy's eyes were locked on Rickerson's face.

"Good subject," the detective said. "Tough one, isn't it?"

"Yeah."

"I was never very good at math. There's a lot of math in economics. Right?"

"Look," Ian Berger said, "can we get down to what you wanted to talk to me about? I have a big test next week. I have to study or I'm not going to make it this year."

"Where were you on Wednesday, September eighth, between say twelve and three o'clock?"

The boy thought a few moments and then turned back to his desk, flipping through a calendar. "I was at school . . . in class."

"The entire time?" Rickerson stood, glancing up at the poster of the dead girl. Like the *Mona Lisa,* her eyes seemed to follow him around the room. He hadn't told the boy the crime had occurred in the afternoon instead of the morning, but Ian had known it had. Of course, he probably read the papers.

"From twelve to one, I was at lunch. I think I ate in the commissary. I eat there everyday. At one, I had a class in macroeconomics."

"I see," Rickerson said. He took a cigar out of his pocket and rolled it around. He had no intention of lighting it. "How long did the class last?"

"Until three. Look, why don't you quit playing around and just ask me what you want to ask me?" His face flushed and he sat up, his back rigid. "I threatened that woman judge. That's what this is all about. I certainly didn't do anything, though."

Rickerson stopped and glared at him, flicking the hairs on his mustache. "You did threaten her . . . tell her someone should kill her whole family?"

The boy looked down. "You know that. Everyone in that room heard me. I . . . didn't really mean it. I was upset, angry."

Slipping the cigar back into his pocket, Rickerson barked at him, "Maybe you were angry enough to carry through on those threats, make her pay?"

Ian Berger shook his head. Beads of perspiration popped out on his forehead. He was a nice-looking young man, with dark hair and penetrating dark eyes, but he looked older than his years now. He would never be a carefree young man again. "You can check with my classes. I was there. Not only that, if I wanted to kill someone, I would kill that maniac that murdered Jessica, not the stupid judge."

"But you didn't threaten Henderson. You threatened the judge. Right?"

"Right," Ian said. "I made a mistake, okay? I was acting like a fool. I know she was only doing what she had to do. It was just so hard to take . . . to accept. . . . Do they have anything new, or is he still out?"

"Not my case, son," Rickerson said, stepping toward the door. Henderson was out, but it wasn't something to tell the boy. "Write down the name of your professor and we'll verify your story."

The young man scribbled something on a piece of paper and walked over and handed it to the detective. "What if the professor doesn't remember that I was in class that day? It's a big class."

Rickerson searched Ian Berger's face. He couldn't tell if what he was seeing was grief or fear. Some of the classes at UCLA had a hundred students or more, and it wouldn't be surprising if the professor didn't keep track of attendance. Without something to substantiate his statements, Ian Berger would remain an active suspect. "Then I guess you're gonna have a problem, Ian. What about friends, other students? Surely someone saw you that day."

Ian's head dropped. He said without looking up, "Jessica was my best friend."

Could he have done it? Rickerson asked himself. The ingredients were all present. Again he let his eyes roam around the room. Thomas Henderson had taken more than one life from the looks of it. The boy standing in front of him might never recover. He could even end up in prison for murder. Rickerson hoped that wasn't the case. He felt an overwhelming sadness in the room and was anxious to leave. "We'll be in touch."

"Tell the judge I didn't mean it, okay? Tell her I'm sorry about her family."

"Sure," Rickerson said, taking several steps down the hall. Then he turned and returned to the bedroom.

"Son, let me give you some advice. Take down all these pictures. She's gone now. Let her go. Go on with your life. She would have wanted you to."

The boy had turned back to the desk. He spoke without turning around. "I can't," he said in a voice laced with emotion. "I just can't."

As Rickerson let himself out of the house, his own words echoed in his head. She's gone now. Let her go. Go on with your life. You're pretty good at giving advice, he told himself. Might just be time to take some of that advice for yourself.

It was almost ten o'clock before Rickerson arrived at Lara's condo. She had already consumed three glasses of wine.

She threw open the door and he strolled into the small living room. He didn't appear to be in the best of moods. "Don't open the door, remember? One of these days you're going to open that door and get a face full of lead."

For a moment she just stood there. "Thanks," she said. "I mean, I thought this was a celebration. The man is dead. Isn't that what you told me?"

He turned around and looked at her, letting his eyes roam up and down her body. "First, I believe this man was responsible for more than the break-in at your house. I think he might be our killer, but he was hired to kill them. The person responsible is still out there, and to be perfectly honest, the next person to go could be you."

Lara felt her heart racing. Up to this point it had been only speculation that the two crimes were related. Now the detective was confirming her worst fears. And she had released this man. "You think someone contracted these killings? But why? My God, why?"

Rickerson's voice was urgent, his face flushed. They were both still standing in the center of the living room, only a few feet apart. "He thinks you know something, maybe have something incriminating." He let his words sink in before continuing. He had to evaluate how much he was willing to reveal. "If I'm right, he's eliminated the one man who could identify him—Cummings. He's cleaning house now, Lara, tying up loose ends. You're a loose end or your house would have never been ransacked."

"But I can't identify anyone. This just doesn't make sense."

"Your sister came to your house claiming someone was following her. If the man who hired Packy Cummings was the man following your sister, then this man has to consider that you know something, that she told you something. I mean, you were her sister. If she was in trouble, why wouldn't she tell you?"

"Well, she didn't. I already told you why."

"I know that, Lara, but he doesn't. Think about it."

She did. The silence hung heavy.

"I see your point," she finally answered. "What now? And what about Jessica Van Horn's boyfriend?"

"Says he was in class at UCLA. We have to verify it."

"Do you think he's telling the truth?"

"To be honest, it's a tough call. He loved that girl and he's crazy with grief. Just how crazy I don't know." Rickerson paused, flicking the hairs on his mustache. "Oh, Thomas Henderson is back on the street. One of our men spotted him in Costa Mesa yesterday on their way to court."

"Shit," Lara said. "He was at Camarillo State the last time I heard. He's out?"

"You got it, kid."

"Well, Henderson should want to kiss me, not kill me. I certainly didn't do anything to him. It was my decision that set him free." Wonderful, Lara thought facetiously. Now she was setting all the killers free instead of locking them up.

"I agree," Rickerson said. "Just keep in mind that he's out there."

"What about all the other leads . . . all Ivory's clients? One of them could have killed her and Sam. Just because this Packy person broke into my home doesn't mean he was involved in the homicides."

Rickerson sighed. She was right on that one, even though he thought he was headed to pay dirt with Evergreen. "We've interviewed almost everyone on the list. Most of them were at work with dozens of witnesses. Remember, this crime occurred during the middle of the day. Of course, the calls to hotels and things are impossible to trace." Suddenly he remembered his conversation with Bradshaw. "I'd like to ask you something. Do you have a good friend that's an attorney?"

"God, Rickerson, all my friends are attorneys. Either attorneys or judges."

"This would be a male, Lara. It appears someone has been calling the station asking about suspects in this case. He claimed he was a close friend of yours and was attempting to pry information from the chief's son."

Lara stood there for a moment thinking. "The only person I can think of is Benjamin England. He represented Thomas Henderson. We've been dating, but he's been out of town and I haven't even talked to him since my sister's death. I think he's coming back tomorrow."

Rickerson took out a small notebook and scribbled England's name down. "I'll check it out. Henderson, huh? Lot of people connected to this Henderson case."

"It doesn't make sense for Benjamin to call and ask about the case when he hasn't even talked to me."

"Maybe he doesn't know where you are, Lara," Rickerson said. The man could also be a valid suspect, he thought. As a criminal attorney he would have access to courthouse information. This boyfriend of Lara's could have called Evergreen, claiming that he was with a local law enforcement agency, and easily arranged his release. Anyone who knew what to say and who to call could have pulled something like that off. The detective shook his head. This case was like chasing butterflies without a net. As soon as he thought he had something in his hand, it fluttered away.

Lara walked over to the sofa and threw herself on it face first. The wine, the disappointment, the stress of the past few days, were taking their toll. "I thought it was over," she said in a thin, high voice. "Now you're telling me I'm next . . . that someone really is out to kill me, that I released the man who killed my own sister. Jesus."

At that moment she felt Rickerson's warm breath on the back of her neck, his cool hand on her flesh. "Scoot over," he said softly. "What you need is a neck rub."

As he started kneading her neck, Lara stiffened. "Relax," he said. "I'm not the big bad wolf." This time he whispered, "I wouldn't let anyone hurt you, Lara."

His thigh was rubbing against her rib cage, brushing against her breast. She could almost feel his body heat through his clothing. And she could smell him. It wasn't strong cologne like most men wore. It was a masculine, earthy scent. Cigars, coffee, sweat. Tonight it didn't smell bad. This was the way her father used to smell when he used to hold her on his lap.

As he continued to rub her neck, she wondered what it would be like to have a man like this one. A man who carried a gun. A man who wasn't afraid of anything. Then she felt something else. His hands were soft and fleshy, like he was wearing velvet-padded gloves. She felt her body responding and imagined those hands on her skin: her breasts, her hips, between her legs. She shivered. What was wrong with her? This was insanity.

"I—I'm fine, Ted," she said, attempting to roll over. "I acted like a baby. I'm embarrassed. Let me up."

"Ssssh," he said. He moved his hands to her back and massaged her through her blouse. "Go to sleep," he said. "We'll talk tomorrow."

Lara shut her eyes. Several times she almost fell asleep and then her eyes sprang open. His hand was roaming. Either that or she was imagining it. She thought for sure she felt his touch on her buttocks. She wanted to feel his touch. That was the problem. "Ted," she said. "Thanks for the neck rub, but I think I'll go to bed."

His fingers were dropping down off the side of her back and grazing her breasts. He leaned over her back and lifted her hair off her neck. She inhaled, certain he was going to kiss her. And there, right there—the one spot she was so sensitive. She closed her eyes and waited. She held her breath. Her heart was beating so fast that she was certain he could tell.

Nothing happened. She heard the door close. Rickerson had left.

chapter 16

The following morning Lara headed to the hall of justice. It was Saturday and the parking lot was almost empty. She wanted to review the Adams case and make some phone calls. And she wanted to get out of that condo. All night long she had thrashed about in her bed, unable to sleep. Her thoughts kept returning to Ted Rickerson: what kind of lover he was, what he looked like without his clothes, what it would be like to have him inside her. She was certain he was married. He wore a wedding ring. She'd never known anyone to wear a wedding ring that wasn't married. Not only that, he was a cop. If she started seeking sexual gratification from the police force, she might as well kiss her career goodbye.

She was all nerve endings and quivering flesh. This morning she had felt as though she'd spent the night in an X-rated movie. If he'd just make a real pass at her, she thought, the fantasy would probably vanish. That was a funny thing about women. They always seemed to want what they couldn't have, and she, for one, was normally put off by real aggression. Men never seemed to realize that about her.

But the way the detective had touched her, it was so covert, so seductive. She shook her head, getting out of the Jaguar. She had to put this out of her mind. And fast. It was silly. She didn't have time for this type of thing. He must think she was hard up, desperate. Was she? It was one thing to deal with life alone when it was uneventful. But now she needed someone. She needed someone to hold her, to make the pain go away.

It couldn't be Ted Rickerson. She knew that for sure.

Since there was no security guard on weekends, she had to search in her purse for the key to get inside the hall leading to her chambers. On her way out this morning, she'd stopped at Emmet's and he'd informed her that he'd already made arrangements with a company that would move his things to her place today and set up his equipment. The phone company had installed his line yesterday.

The air-conditioning system in the building was either off or on some type of climate control that barely moved the air. This section of the complex had no windows, and it was stuffy and uncomfortable.

Once she was inside her office, she called the number on the social workers' card and left her number at the court. They could have at least notified her where she could call Josh, where they had placed him, she thought, feeling her frustration level rise about five notches. No wonder Victor Adams had flown off the handle and gone after one of these people. Their rules were too rigid, their attitude too superior. Yesterday she'd felt like punching them both in the face herself

She had to buy Josh something appropriate to wear. The funeral was Monday.

The phone on her desk rang and she grabbed it. It was Rickerson. "How did you know where I was?" she asked him.

"I know everything," he said.

"Oh, really."

His voice dropped to a low level. "How did you sleep?"

She cleared her throat. She would have slept a lot better if he'd been in the bed next to her. "Fine," she said. "And you?"

"Fine." After an awkward pause he continued, his voice all business now. "I want to ask you some questions about Judge Evergreen."

"Evergreen? Why?"

"Evergreen asked you to release Packy Cummings.

If I'm right, whoever arranged Cummings's release is our killer."

"But not Leo Evergreen. What possible motive could he have for killing my sister and brother-in-law? And he's an old man, Ted. Ivory was raped. What you're saying is absurd."

"Lara, I'm not saying he killed them himself. Like I was telling you last night, I think someone hired Packy to break into your house and then kill Sam and Ivory."

Lara's voice went up several decibels. "But why?"

"Try blackmail?"

"Ivory and Sam were blackmailing Evergreen? Over what?"

"Ivory was a prostitute," he said. He wasn't prepared to tell Lara about the photos or the cash they had discovered in the safe at the pawnshop. Not yet.

"And Evergreen probably hasn't had sex in years. None of this makes sense to me," Lara said, tapping her pen again and again on the desk. "Ivory had a list of clients a mile long. She and Sam could have been blackmailing dozens of people."

"Lara, your sister specialized in S and M. Her clients didn't always have sex."

Lara was silent.

Rickerson continued. "What do you know about Evergreen's personal life? Is he married? Does he have children?"

"I think his wife is dead. I really don't remember. She's either dead or divorced him years go. I think he has a son, though."

"How old is his son?" Rickerson asked.

"Gosh, Ted," Lara replied, "I don't really know. Grown, I'm sure. Come to think of it, I've seen a picture of his son on his desk. What does this possibly have to do with everything?"

"Stay right there, Lara. I'm coming over."

Before she could tell him that he couldn't get into the building, the detective had hung up. She'd have to meet him in the parking lot.

* * *

Rickerson followed Lara down the long carpeted hallway that separated the judges' chambers from the courtrooms. "But I told you I can't unlock the door to his chamber," she said. "I don't have a key. Every judge locks his door for security reasons."

"Does your secretary have a key to your chambers?"

Lara stopped and turned around. "Well, yes, he does. He generally unlocks it before I get here every morning. He has to have a key in case I leave a case file or something in there and someone needs it when I'm not around." Lara stopped for a few moments. The detective was making her a nervous wreck. She was in enough of a predicament as it was, and now he wanted to snoop around in Evergreen's chambers. "Look, I know what you're saying. Evergreen's secretary has a key too, right?"

He nodded.

She continued, "But she probably locks her desk as well. Phillip does. I'm not going to let you break in here, Rickerson. Don't even think it."

As soon as they got to Evergreen's office, Rickerson walked in, headed straight to the secretary's desk, and removed something from his pocket. A few seconds later, he was rifling through her drawers.

Lara stood there with her hands on her hips. "How'd you get that open?"

"With a lock pick," he said, holding it in the air. "These cheap county desks are a piece of cake. The door might be harder. Let's go." He had a large brass key ring jangling in his hands.

"Stop right there," Lara told him. "I don't like this at all, not at all. Now you've got me breaking into the presiding judge's chambers. They're going to throw me off the bench."

Rickerson had the door open to Evergreen's chambers and was already inside. Lara just stood there in the outer office shaking her head. He yelled at her, "You might get thrown off the bench, but it's better than being dead."

She walked inside.

"Is this the picture?" he said, holding up a snapshot of a baby-faced young man in his early twenties.

Lara nodded.

Rickerson picked the lock on Evergreen's desk and started digging. He found a stack of cancelled checks on what appeared to be the judge's personal bank account and looked up at Lara. "Don't just stand there. Do something. Take these to a Xerox machine and copy them, front and back. Do you have one that prints in color?"

"I think so," she said. "It's down the hall."

"Okay, take the picture out of the frame and copy it too. And hurry. He might come down here on weekends."

"Why do you need a picture of Evergreen's son?" Lara demanded.

The detective had been standing up. He now flopped down in Evergreen's leather chair. "Trust me," he said.

Lara snatched the photo and cancelled checks out of his hand and left the room, moving as fast as she could down the hall. All she needed was to have Evergreen catch her with the goods right in her hands. "Trust me," she mumbled, mimicking Rickerson. "Like I've never heard those words before." Finding the copy room, she slapped the checks upside down on the glass and hit the button. The machine whirred to life.

On Sunday, Lara drove to the address Madeline Murphy had given her. The house was a sprawling older adobe in a low-income section of Costa Mesa. Scattered all over the front yard were children's toys. Lara had to pick up a skateboard off the walk to even pass. The social worker had given Lara permission to take Josh out to purchase a suit for the funeral. He came to the door himself, pale, looking as if he hadn't slept all night, his hair dirty and limp. While he was standing in the doorway, a scruffy little boy tossed a Frisbee across the room and it struck Josh in the head.

"Knock it off, you crusted little toad," Josh yelled,

"or I'm gonna come over there and beat the shit out of you."

"Fuck you, asshole," the kid yelled back. He was only about seven years old, a street kid from the word go.

They drove in silence, Josh turning his head away and looking out the window.

"Honey," she told him inside the department store, "by Tuesday you'll be out of that place. We're moving to another condo in the complex. It's only temporary. It belongs to a friend of mine. You know, that man I told you about—Emmet."

"They're gonna keep me in that place forever. I hate those people. The woman is a porker and she stinks. The man wears his pants so low you can see his hairy ass all the time. I don't think they ever take a bath. There's six screaming little kids in there. I can't even sleep."

Lara jerked her head around. "I thought you had to have your own room. Are you telling me you're in a room with six kids?"

"No," he said. "I have a room about the size of a closet. I can sit on my bed and touch both walls. I can't keep the brats out. They bang on the walls too, and they throw things."

And these people were more suitable than she was, Lara thought. They were foster parents, people who made their living caring for kids like Josh. Unfortunately, most of them didn't do it for the kids. They did it for the cash.

Lara had been looking through the racks of suits while Josh just stood there, no interest whatsoever. "What do you think of this one?" she said, holding up a navy blue suit with a reddish stripe.

"I hate it," Josh said.

"Fine," Lara said. "Even if you hate it, will you please see if it fits?"

He snatched the suit out of her hands and headed to the dressing room. She really didn't know why she was going to all this trouble. No one was even going to be there except Irene and John Murdock, Benjamin England, if he'd received her message with the time and location, and Phillip. Then she thought of Emmet. Irene could drive his van and bring him.

The suit fit; she bought it, slapping her credit card on the counter. "I'll pick you up tomorrow about ten o'clock," she told him. He didn't answer.

As they were walking to the Jaguar in the parking lot, he turned to her. "Did you go through my backpack?"

Lara froze in her tracks. A car was backing up and she stepped aside. "I-I was looking for a pen, Josh. I'm sorry. I guess I should have asked you, huh?"

"Did you take my Metallica T-shirt?"

She couldn't lie. She unlocked the car door and got in. As soon as Josh was inside, she turned sideways in the seat. "Look, Josh, I want to be truthful with you. I took the T-shirt because it had blood on it. Now that it's out in the open, why don't you tell me whose blood it was?"

His eyes flashed with anger and he reached for the door handle. Lara grabbed the back of his shirt. "Don't run away. That's not going to solve anything. You've got to tell me, Josh."

"Get your fucking hands off me. I knew you were a bitch. I don't know why I thought you were different. You think I killed them, don't you?" The muscles in his face started twitching, and he leaned over close to Lara's face.

She drew back, thinking for a moment he was going to hit her.

"It was my blood. There . . . now you know. Are you happy?"

"What happened? Did you fall off your bike? How did you cut yourself?"

He turned away and stared out the window. "I can't tell you."

Lara reached across the seat and touched his hand. "Josh, please look at me. You can tell me. Honey, I have to know. This was a serious thing. I want you to be totally in the clear."

"I can't," he said, sniffing. "It's embarrassing."

Lara just sat there. Finally she started the car and made her way out of the parking lot. She had no idea what he was talking about. Why would it be embarrassing? "I have an idea," she said. "Could you write it?"

"Maybe." His voice was small. He wouldn't look at her.

They drove in silence to the foster home, both of them lost in their thoughts. Once she had pulled up at the curb, she reached into her purse and handed Josh a pen and a piece of paper. "I'm going to take a walk. Write down what happened and leave it on the seat. I promise I won't read it until you're in the house. Deal?"

She didn't wait for a response. She walked down the sidewalk and crossed the street. As soon as she saw Josh get out of the car and go into the house, she returned to the car. She looked but there was nothing there. Thinking it had fallen between the seats, she went to the other side of the car and opened the passenger door and searched for it. She glanced back at the house and saw Josh looking at her through the window. After standing there a few minutes, Lara left.

The first thing she did was call Emmet. "Did you get the blood type on the T-shirt?" she asked.

"Yes," he said. "I was . . . trying to . . . find you. It's type AB."

Lara pulled to the side of the road and put her hand over her chest. "Thank God, Emmet. I really appreciate this. I'm not certain why his blood was there, what he did to himself, but I guess it's all right. I mean, it's his blood type."

"Unless," Emmet struggled to say, "your brother-in-law . . . has . . . AB as well. Not likely . . . though. Only about four percent . . . of the . . . population has type AB blood."

"I'll find out, Emmet. And listen, thanks. I'll see

you in a few minutes." She rushed back to the condo. The place was a shambles, but at least he had found someone to handle the move on the weekend. Poor Emmet, she thought, heading across the courtyard to his door.

He was sitting in his office working.

"Are you all right?" she said. "This move was a bigger job than I thought it was."

"Fine," he typed. "I'm leaving my office the way it is. Look in the bedrooms. See if they put everything where you want it."

Lara checked and saw all the bedroom furniture from the model in one room and the other was as Emmet had left it. Emmet had left his computer equipment in both rooms, and the movers had placed all her clothes and things on top of them.

She went back in and hugged Emmet from behind. "I can never repay you for this. Never. No one's ever done something this nice for me before."

He didn't turn around, but words flashed on the screen as he typed. "Most people are jerks. I'm not."

Lara laughed. "You got the phone line in and everything?"

"Yes," he typed. "I had a modem installed yesterday. I seldom use the telephone. Oh," he continued typing, "if you want, you can talk to me that way. Just come in here and follow the instructions on this sheet. We can talk on the bulletin board. I have a lot of friends I talk to all the time. When they send me a message, a bell rings on my console."

Lara wheeled Emmet to her place, the chair hard to push on the grass.

"See?" he said, showing her his bed. He had a tray that moved his laptop computer back and forth from the desk to his bed. That way he could work at night when he couldn't sleep.

His nurse would be there shortly, so Lara left, going back across the courtyard. Madeline Murphy had promised they would come by Tuesday and check her new living situation. Then she could get Josh back.

Only Emmet's chair was in the living room and an end table with a lamp. It looked empty, stark. Lara sat down. She was completely exhausted. Tomorrow Ivory would go in the ground. Then it would all be real—too real.

Rickerson called her. A cacophony of noises rang out in the background; Lara wondered where he was calling from.

"I'd like to see you," he said. "Discuss some things. Can you meet me at that bar on the corner of Seventeenth and First Street? It's not far from your house."

"I guess," she said. "I mean, if it's important."

"I'll be there in fifteen minutes."

Before Lara could protest or ask questions, he'd hung up. What now? she thought. Did he want to tell her that she'd released someone else who was out there killing people? Lara felt like chucking it all in, taking Josh and moving to Kansas or something, leaving this whole smelly, disgusting city behind. She grabbed her purse and headed out the front door.

She beat Rickerson to the bar. It was a dive. She didn't see his unmarked unit in the parking lot, so she slid down in the seat to wait. She'd wait right here in her car until he arrived, she decided, locking the doors.

Approximately thirty minutes later, Rickerson drove up as a passenger in a black-and-white patrol car. He stuck his head in the window of the Jaguar and then waved to the officer. The man drove off. "Want to let me in?" he said. Lara unlocked the doors.

"What's going on? Why did you want me to meet you here?" Instead of smoking a cigar, the detective was smacking a huge wad of chewing gum. Lara looked at him and sniffed. "Have you been drinking?"

"Few beers," he said, his voice slurred. "Chief had a barbecue. Left my car over there. Caught a ride."

"Want to tell me why I'm here?"

"Your sister's trick book. We got it."

Lara gave him a questioning look.

"You know, every working girl has a book where

she keeps information on her clients. We've been looking for it. Somehow we missed it. It was in her car under the mat. Some fool just booked it into evidence. I was poking through the stuff and found it today. It might be good."

"Well . . ."

He shrugged his shoulders. "Have to check it out. Right now most of the numbers we already have, but you never know. One might be promising—a woman, probably another prostitute. Tried to find her, but she must be out working."

The space inside the front seat of the Jaguar was actually very small. For some reason Lara felt funny sitting here with the big detective in the dark with only a swatch of light drifting in from the bar. He was almost larger than life, and the air was thick with his very presence.

"Is that all?"

Rickerson's red hair was standing straight up. A fierce wind had picked up in the past thirty minutes, and he had his jacket collar turned up as well. They weren't that far from the ocean and Lara could smell the salty sea air.

"I think Evergreen is behind all this—that he contracted to have your sister and brother-in-law killed."

"Not this again," Lara said, frowning. "Leo Evergreen contracted to have my sister and Sam killed?"

"Yeah," he said. "Look, I've got to go inside. I need a bathroom." He glanced at her. It was obvious that he'd had more than a few beers. He was smashed.

"You're drunk," she said, disgusted. "I can't believe you called me out tonight to continue this ridiculous line of supposition—that the presiding judge of Orange County is contracting murders? What are you going to tell me next, that Mother Teresa is stealing money from orphans or the Martians are landing? Sober up, Rickerson. Go home." She started to turn the key in the ignition.

"I have to go," he insisted, reaching for the door handle. "I have to take a leak."

"Well, I'm going home," Lara shot at him.

"I'd like to talk to you. You want me to go behind a bush or something? The beer . . ." He belched, a hand over his stomach.

"My place?" she said flatly.

"Better make it fast," he answered.

Lara was staring at the road in front of her, her mind reeling. Rickerson was trying to talk fast through the fog of alcohol, his words almost running together like a foreign language, trying to explain to her how he had arrived at this assumption. Suddenly he yelled at her to stop the car and got out without a word and disappeared behind a building. A few minutes later, he returned. "Sorry," he said. "Couldn't wait."

Lara burned inside again. "Leo Evergreen a pedophile? He's an asshole, but a pedophile, a child molester? Never. I can't believe it. You're out of your mind, Ted. You've had too much to drink. Besides, he was married. He even had a child. You saw his picture today."

"Right," he said, inching his way toward sobriety with every passing second. "Thought you judges knew everything. Since when do pedophiles never marry and have children? You know, this is something that can surface any time in their life. It's not like the color of their hair or something they're born with. It's a sickness."

"Sure, and Ivory was seeing Leo? Ivory stole these pictures of Leo with little boys? Sure. All of this is a stretch." She craned her neck around to look at him. "And I mean a *real* stretch of the imagination. What possible proof do you have to support this preposterous claim?"

They pulled into the complex and parked. It was a lousy parking job. Lara had the front wheels of the Jaguar up over the curb. "I'm living over here now," she told him, slamming the car door, not bothering to lock it. "I had to move because of Josh. The social workers wouldn't let him stay with me if I didn't move."

Rickerson ignored her and walked behind her to the door.

She stopped on the sidewalk. "What evidence do you have? Are you going to tell me, or still keep me in the dark? Come in," she said, unlocking the door.

Rickerson walked in, looking around, and then flopped in the one chair, leaving Lara standing. Then he jumped back up and told her to sit down. He talked as he paced, slipping his sports jacket off his shoulders and tossing it on the floor. "You got any coffee in this place?" he said, looking around. Underneath his jacket he was wearing a blue knit shirt and casual slacks. The fabric was flat over his abdomen, then strained to cover his bulging biceps. In the neck of his shirt were tufts of strawberry blond hair. He took out a cigar and then put it back in his pocket and started working his jaws on the gum.

"I'll make some," Lara said, going to Emmet's kitchen and trying to find the coffee in the cabinet. Rickerson was still talking.

"Here's what I have," he said. "The lab enlarged and enhanced the Polaroids I told you we found at the house. There was a reflection in the mirror of another photo of a woman and a young man. I think it's Evergreen's wife and son. They're working to verify this as we speak. That's why I took the picture off his desk. If it looks good, then we'll find his son and talk to him, make certain it's him. His wife is dead. I saw her death certificate in his file cabinet. She died about five years ago."

The coffee was brewing, filling the small rooms with its fragrant aroma. One of those gourmet coffees, it smelled like cinnamon. She took a seat in the chair. "I'm certainly listening. Keep going."

"We found over forty grand in cash in the safe at the pawnshop. Does that smack of extortion to you?"

Lara blinked at the amount. "Forty thousand dollars? You're kidding. Sam couldn't amass that kind of money in a hundred years. You might be right on the blackmail, but I don't see how this implicates Evergreen."

Rickerson gave Lara a sidelong glance and then continued to pace. "We're going through Evergreen's cancelled checks, his bank statements, looking for the payout. In addition, every month Evergreen writes a check for a thousand dollars to Miramar Properties. He also writes checks to a mortgage company that I assume are his house. We checked and Miramar owns and operates apartment complexes. We couldn't contact anyone in their office today, but my guess is that Evergreen has a secret pad somewhere. That's where he met your sister for their little rendezvous and probably where he takes the kids he molests."

"Shit," Lara said, shaking her head. "You're crazy. He probably pays his son's rent or something. I can't believe any of this, can't believe you're wasting your time with this."

Rickerson stopped pacing and looked at her. "I think Evergreen killed Cummings. I think he's desperate now. Cummings wasn't working for any law enforcement agency we can find. Evergreen was lying or someone else inside the system arranged Packy's release. Any way you look at it, it comes back to someone with access to inmate information."

Lara's mouth fell open and her face was ashen, almost as gray as the upholstery on the chair. For a few moments she couldn't get her mouth to work. She opened it, closed it, opened it again. He was right. Anyone at the courthouse, even Phillip, could have pulled up Cummings's rap sheet and booking information on the computer and then simply called Evergreen and conned him into believing they were police officers. Lara herself had been contacted by local officers asking for special handling on cases. She'd never once verified the callers' identities.

"Evergreen told me to release Packy Cummings so he could murder my own sister? If this was true, why didn't he have one of the other judges release the man?

Why me? He would have been an outright fool to do that . . . and believe me, Evergreen is no fool."

"He didn't know, Lara," Rickerson said. "Use your brain. If he was seeing your sister, a prostitute, do you think for a minute she told him about you being a judge or that he would ever in his wildest dreams link the two of you?"

Lara was silent. At least this made sense even if nothing else did. Maybe the detective wasn't out of his mind completely. "So, what you're saying is that he didn't know we were related. They were blackmailing him and he needed a hit man, a strong arm. He went for this Packy animal for whatever reason and selected me only because I was sitting the arraignment calendar?"

Rickerson just stood there flicking the hairs on his mustache. "Looks that way."

"And I released the man who murdered my sister?" All roads led back to this. Lara knew she was obsessing, but she couldn't stop herself. She was about to come unglued. "Look, you said it could be anyone in law enforcement, even a clerk. How about my secretary? He knows the system like the back of his hand. Not only that, he's been getting loans lately, even falsifying his salary. And he's younger than Evergreen. Maybe he was seeing Ivory. He didn't know she was my sister. I never mentioned her to anyone at work before her death. We didn't get along, you know."

Rickerson started pacing again. "The man in the photos was an older man, Lara."

Lara was silent, thinking. "Maybe Phillip was one of the boys in the photos? You said several young boys were in those pictures and they were taken years ago."

Rickerson stopped and locked eyes with Lara. "I'll check him out, okay? But don't you think a pedophile has more to lose than a victim? I mean, people don't normally blackmail victims."

"You don't really understand this type of offense, Ted," Lara said, leaning forward in her chair. "What makes sexual abuse so insidious is that the victims often feel responsible. The offender convinces them that they incited their advances, even encouraged them. The victims are sometimes more contrite than the offenders."

"So you think your secretary should be considered a suspect?"

"Why not? He's in law school. If he'd been victimized in the past, he certainly wouldn't want anyone to know, particularly since you said the boys were having sex with an adult male. Maybe that's why he's been applying for all these loans—to come up with the extortion money?"

"I'll look into it," Rickerson said, obviously not enthusiastic. Just because he felt the killer was someone in the system didn't mean it was Lara's secretary. "Does Evergreen limp?"

Lara thought for a moment. "I wouldn't really say he limps, Ted. He has a distinctive walk, but so do a lot of people."

"The lab thinks they can identify the man in the photos due to some kind of physical disability."

Lara's mind wandered and she heard only snatches of what Rickerson was saying. Someone was playing a stereo a few doors down. It sounded like Etta James—a heavy blues tune. Cars were whizzing by on the freeway. If she didn't listen closely, she could imagine it was the ocean instead of the freeway. She'd let a vicious criminal walk out on the street, and he had killed her own sister. She leaned forward and put her head in her hands, pulling her hair straight out from her head. "I released him. I released him. I released the very man who murdered my sister."

Rickerson stopped pacing and walked to her chair, dropping to his knees and looking her straight in the eye. "Stop this," he said. "Blaming yourself isn't going to cure anything."

She ignored him. "I can't believe it. I just can't believe it. All my life I've tried to do the right thing. And now I've actually caused my sister's death."

Rickerson reached for her, touching the top of her

head gently and then drawing it against his shoulder. "It wasn't your fault. You did what Evergreen told you to do. How could you have possibly known?"

His voice was soft and low, and he was stroking her hair. She could smell the beer on his breath and the lingering odor of cigars on his clothing, but she could also feel his masculine strength. His body was solid, as hard as a rock. She let him hold her. Then she pulled away and pushed her hair out of her face. For a few moments their eyes met and he probed there—down where it was tangled and dark, a twisted maze of confusion and grief. She was beginning to lean on this man, she thought, allowing him to get close, see a part of her few people saw. She had to stop it. Their relationship was passing the level of friendship, even fantasy. Lara was about to take his hand and lead him to the bedroom. It wasn't the sex she really wanted. Not now. Right now she just wanted him to hold her, tell her everything was okay, tell her he would protect her.

"You're married, huh?" she finally said.

"Yeah," he said.

"Kids?"

"Two."

"Happy?"

He stood and looked away. If he was going to tell her, he thought, now was the time to do it. But he couldn't. He didn't know why, but he simply couldn't. And what would he tell her? That he was separated. That his wife had walked out on him after nineteen years of marriage. That he might or might not be getting a divorce. She was dating this Benjamin England, a prominent attorney. "Sometimes," he said softly, "but not always. No one's happy all the time, Lara. That just isn't the way it is. There are good days and bad days. You know?"

"Yeah," she said, wiping her nose with a paper napkin off the end table. "How well I know."

The room fell silent. They were both uncomfortable. He belonged to someone else, Lara thought. This type of discussion held no future for either of them.

"I know how you feel," he said. The neighbors had turned the music down, and they could now hear only the bass notes, a sort of thump, thump, thumping that almost vibrated the walls. "I killed someone one time."

Lara jerked her head up. "You shot them?"

"No, it was an accident—a young kid, a two-year-old boy."

Lara didn't know what to say. His face was etched with pain, the memories flooding his mind. They weren't good ones. With the one light on the end table, the other side of the room was bathed in shadows. He stepped to the back wall and stood there as they talked.

"I was working the graveyard shift . . . it was years ago. To be honest, I was sleeping in my unit, parked under a freeway overpass. This woman ran up to me screaming her baby was dying, that he wasn't breathing. I tried to administer C.P.R. I was determined I was going to save him. Back then I thought that was what the job was all about." He stopped speaking and she could hear him breathing, loud, raspy breaths that were like another instrument combined with the pounding bass.

"Go on," she said.

"He was so small, so tiny. My younger son was about the same age. The woman panicked, jumping on my back, beating it frantically with her fists. She was screaming that I was killing him, insisted that I get off. She was heavy. I was bent over the front seat of her car giving him C.P.R. I fell forward on top of the child and shattered his sternum. He died."

"It was an accident," Lara said quickly, not knowing what else to say. "Things like that happen. You were trying to save him."

"But I didn't," the detective said. "I killed him."

Lara was silent. He continued, "And I never got over it. That kid's face chased me around for years. I dreamed about it; I thought about it day and night. My philosophy back then was that a person has only one chance in life to do something great, heroic—like destiny or something. I thought you lived your entire life for that one specific moment. You know, to pull someone out of the path of a car, to save them from drowning, to tackle a man with a gun and disarm him before he hurt someone. And I was convinced that I missed that chance. I didn't think there'd ever be another one."

"Was there?" she said, her eyelids fluttering. They were going way off track, into another realm of familiarity.

"No, there wasn't. Not yet, anyway." He stepped out of the shadows. The past was receding. "But maybe this is it, you know. This case . . . helping you . . ."

"Tell me," Lara said finally, her voice weak and cracking, back to the present nightmare. "It's hard to picture a sixty-seven-year-old judge tracking down a guy like Cummings and putting a hole in his head."

"Picture it. That's what I think happened. I think Cummings wanted more money or saw how dirty this whole thing was—you being a judge, Ivory being your sister. Evergreen was terrified of exposure. Possibly he didn't even intend for Cummings to kill them, but just to get the pictures back. He could have gone crazy over that. You know, protecting yourself from exposure is a long way from murder. Anyway, I think he met Cummings in that parking lot and blew him away. It's only four blocks from the courthouse. He could have shot him, returned to work, and no one would have been the wiser. And it was a tree-shaded area. Perfect."

"Phillip could have done that, shot him and driven back to the courthouse." Lara couldn't help it, but the more she thought about it, the greater her suspicions were that Phillip might be involved. "He's a strange man, Ted. Believe me, I wouldn't be saying this if I didn't think there was something to it. And he's been acting funny lately, like he has some kind of personal problems."

"I keep telling you I think the killer is Evergreen, and you keep talking about your secretary," Rickerson said, annoyed. "Can I continue my line of thought here?"

Lara nodded.

"Okay, even if we prove Evergreen is a pedophile, we can't necessarily prove that he was responsible for your sister's death.. But if he does have an apartment we may find her prints there."

"Even that wouldn't be enough for a conviction," Lara retorted. "Hell, you've see the list. Being her client means nothing. Half the county was her client." Then she thought about it. "The only way to prove this is a direct link between Evergreen and Cummings, and you don't have it. Not only that but you don't have any proof that Cummings even committed the murders. There weren't any prints at the San Clemente house."

"But we may have evidence soon. Forensics is working on matching the pubic hairs we found on your sister to Cummings and the skin tissue under her nails. He had some abrasions on his face and arms. There was also semen in her vagina. And it wasn't your brother-in-law's."

"But not yet?"

"No," he said slowly, "not yet. So as a judge, you don't think we have enough yet for a warrant to go for Evergreen? If it came to you, you wouldn't sign it?"

"An arrest warrant, no," she answered. "But a search warrant to gather evidence? Possibly. You get everything you talked about put together, and you might be able to get that."

"You'll sign it?" he said.

"You've got to be kidding. I don't think any judge in this county will sign it, go up against Evergreen. This is serious, vile stuff we're talking about. He could sue everyone involved for every dime they have—defamation of character, false arrest, no telling what else. He's a powerful, influential man. He'll hire the best lawyers in the country. He'll . . ."

Rickerson rubbed his forehead and finally sat down on the wood floor. He looked funny there. He was so big. Lara got up and gave him the chair.

"Professionally," she said, "I'd say go for the child molestations. The statute of limitations has been extended on those type of offenses, so there's no problem there. But you need a victim. You can't have a crime without a victim."

"Right," Rickerson said, licking his lips, knowing what she was saying exactly. "We don't have a victim."

Lara stared at him. "What if Phillip is your victim?"

"Then Phillip would be the murderer," the detective said, shaking his head as if he didn't agree. He didn't say goodbye. He just walked out the door. Lara knew they didn't have anything yet. What they had was absolutely nothing.

A few minutes later, Rickerson returned and knocked on her door. Lara had already shed her clothes and tossed on a robe.

"There's a light on in your old place, the other condo. Who's there? I thought it was empty."

"I never said it was empty. My friend is staying there. The man who loaned me this condo." In a way it was ironic. Lara had lived such an uneventful, sedate life outside of the courtroom, and now she was moving every day like a gypsy, living out of a suitcase. Overnight her entire life had changed.

"That isn't such a good idea," he said. "We have no way of knowing if you're safe here. Evergreen could know where you're staying, maybe think those pictures are hidden over here now." His face became flushed. "You didn't tell him, did you?"

"No, no," Lara said. Then she recalled the social workers. "Did you give Social Services my address here?"

He shook his head. "Of course not. I told them to contact you at the courts. Why?"

"They came here today. They had all kinds of information. Claimed some officer named Bradshaw told them. They knew all about the pawnshop fiasco, me covering for Sam. They even knew I was hiding. Who in the hell is this Bradshaw?"

Rickerson was hot now. "Fucking Bradshaw. I'm

gonna kill that prick one of these days. He's the chief's son."

"Well, there's nothing I can do right now." She looked across the courtyard. There was only a small light burning in the bedroom. Emmet was probably asleep.

"I'll try to spring someone to watch the place."

"Fine," she said. "Thanks, Ted."

"Lara," he said, stepping into the doorway again, only a few inches away. His gaze drifted to the spot where her robe opened in front and her legs were exposed.

"Yes," she said, "what is it?" Please, she thought, don't let him ask to come back in, don't push this any further than it's already gone. Right at this minute she had absolutely no willpower. They'd just do something they'd later regret. She had enough regrets.

Suddenly the burly detective's face flushed bright red and he stammered, "No—no . . . never mind. Just be careful." After that, he left.

The bedroom Lara's furniture was in at Emmet's was the guest bedroom, and Lara had to pass through Emmet's office to get to the bathroom. It must have at one time been the master bedroom before he converted it to his office, she decided. It probably made it easier for him to get to the bathroom when he was working. Emmet was always working.

Then she saw it.

The computer screen was on and there was printing across it and a light on the console was blinking. She stopped and stared at it, thinking Emmet had forgotten to turn it off.

"Shit," she said, her eyes scanning the text, her stomach in her throat.

"sOMEone's in here with me. Im scared to move. they don't know Im here. can't call police . . . emmet."

Darting down the wide hall to the front door and flinging it open, Lara started screaming, hoping against all reason that the detective hadn't left. "Rickerson . . . Rickerson."

She saw movement in the shadows. He stepped out.

"You rang," he said, a funny, lopsided smile on his face.

"Jesus," she said, spurting out the words. "Someone's in the other condo. My friend's there alone. Do something quick. He's handicapped."

"Stay here," Rickerson said, jerking his gun from the shoulder holster with a snapping noise and a creak of leather. "Call 911 and have them dispatch some units. Tell them I'm here, or they'll shoot me."

Lara rushed back into the condo and did as he told her. Then she stood outside with her arms locked around herself and watched through the tree branches, her heart racing.

Rickerson arrived at the front door. He knocked and then flattened himself against the wall. "Police," he yelled. "Don't move or you're a dead man."

After only a few seconds, Lara could hear sirens. She held her breath. She prayed. Please, God, she prayed, let Emmet be okay. She'd kill herself if anything happened to him. She'd just go right out and kill herself.

Rickerson was kicking the door in. "Wait," she screamed, knowing he couldn't hear her, running halfway across the damp grass in her robe. Other people were coming out of their condos. Some were peering out windows. He was going in by himself like a fool. The backup units would be here any second. He should have waited. She couldn't bear to watch. Any second she thought she'd hear gunshots and the detective would be dead. This was all her fault. Everything was all her fault.

Time stood still. The sirens were getting closer.

"No," she screamed in total anguish. No one was coming out. Emmet was dead in there. Rickerson might even be dead.

She ran back to the condo and dialed 911 again. "Hurry," she yelled in the phone. "The detective is in there and he's not coming out. Something terrible is happening. God, please come . . ."

"Calm down," the dispatcher told her. "The units should be there any minute. Do you hear the sirens?"

"Yes," Lara said. They were even closer now. She dropped the receiver and ran back out into the courtyard. Still, there was nothing. She was panting now, terrified. She leaned over thinking she was going to throw up on the grass.

Then she saw him and a wave of relief washed over her. He stepped outside and waved at her to come over. She ran.

"He's okay," Rickerson said, his chest heaving, his face flushed. "In the bedroom. Go to him. I'll wait for the units."

Emmet was still in his bed, in his bedclothes. His bed was low, evidently so he could get in it by himself. "Okay," he said weakly. "They . . . left . . ."

Emmet's belongings were thrown out in the middle of the floor. His laptop computer terminal was broken and in pieces. She rushed to his side. "Oh, Emmet," Lara said, falling on her knees by the bed. "I'm so sorry. I should have never let you stay here. I'm an idiot, a fool. Please forgive me. Can I get you anything?"

"No," he said. "I'm . . . fine."

She stepped aside as Emmet scooted himself across the bed into his wheelchair and headed straight to the bathroom, the electronic chair making a funny sound on the plastic runner. The movers had installed a trapeze in the bathroom similar to the one by his chair. She didn't embarrass him by asking to help. A few seconds later, he opened the door and rolled back across the mat.

"Did you see them, Emmet?"

"Mask," he said. "He . . . wore a . . . mask. Big man . . . deep voice . . . very thin."

Evergreen wasn't thin and he wasn't that tall, but Phillip was tall and thin. Lara couldn't wait to tell Rickerson, but her primary concern right now was Emmet. "Did he hurt you? Oh, God, Emmet, I feel so bad. I don't know what to say."

"No . . . guess . . . didn't think . . . I was strong enough to . . . hurt him."

She pushed Emmet to the small living room, which was now filled to capacity with officers. Evidence men were checking for latent prints. Lara glanced at the front door and saw where the lock had been forced.

Rickerson was outside talking to one of the men, smoking a cigar. "Don't touch anything," he barked at her through his teeth, his nerves still frazzled. "Nothing. Do you hear me?"

"Nothing," Lara said, throwing her hands in the air. "Who did this? Surely you don't think it was Evergreen? Not the way Emmet described him—tall and thin. Phillip is tall and thin, and he knows where I'm staying. I told you I was on to something with him."

"I don't think it was your secretary, okay? Evergreen just got another goon," Rickerson stated.

"God," Lara said, pulling the robe tighter around her body, pulling on the sash. "Thank God you were still here." Then she raised her eyebrows and tilted her head. "Why were you still here, by the way?"

He grabbed her arm and jerked her aside. "Don't do anything from now on without checking with me," he said. "Don't loan your place out. Don't talk to anyone about anything. Don't go anywhere without telling me. Don't even take a piss without calling me. Are we straight on this, Lara? Are we perfectly straight?"

She looked down. She didn't answer. There was nothing to say. "Why did you stay?" she said.

"Who do you think was going to sit here all night and watch your place, Lara? You think I can just pick up the phone and yank one of our men off the street and have them sit here all night?"

"You were really going to stay here all night just to make certain I was safe? That's so sweet, Ted. I mean it, that was a really nice thing to do. And you weren't even going to tell me?" She shook her head. For some reason this really touched her. "Thanks," she said affectionately. "I don't know what I'd do without you, big guy."

"Oh, yeah," he said, yanking the cigar out of his mouth like it was poison and tossing it across the courtyard. "I hate these stinking things," he said, the anger gone now, a smile playing at the corner of his mouth.

Just then Lara remembered that they had driven her car to the condo, Rickerson riding over in a black-and-white. "I remember now, you didn't have a car."

There was a mischievous look in his eyes. "How'd you think I was going to get home? Walk all the way to San Clemente?"

"Oh," Lara said, narrowing her eyes, "so that's why you came back to the door." He must have felt like a fool and was too embarrassed to tell her. "That was a pretty big speech you just made," she said, smiling coyly. "Particularly since you just stayed because you didn't have a car. Like playing the hero, huh?"

"Just wanted to show you that you can be had, Lara. A lousy third-grader could have your pants down around your ankles in about five minutes." He paused and cleared his throat, gazing into her eyes with conspicuous longing. "And if you're not careful, one of these days it just might be me."

Then he turned quickly and walked back inside with the men.

chapter 17

As soon as the officers cleared at Emmet's, Rickerson got a ride to San Clemente and then leaped in his unit, checking his notebook for the address of Carol Montgomery. The address was an upscale apartment complex right off Pacific Coast Highway in Newport Beach, but Montgomery had a record for soliciting. No matter where she lived, she was a whore.

If he wanted to catch her, now was the time to do it. It was almost two o'clock in the morning. Even in her line of work, business was probably over for the day. Tomorrow was Monday. People had to go to work.

It was a security building, a high-rise. Rickerson called her from the phone in the lobby. At first she refused to let him in. Then he told her he was a cop and the buzzer sounded.

When she flung open the door, Rickerson felt a gush of air leave his body. She was gorgeous. The woman was tall, shapely, and blond—sort of a Nordic look. She was wearing a see-through silk robe and was completely nude underneath.

"Come in," she said, insisting first that Rickerson show her his shield. "I was asleep."

The apartment was luxurious. Business must be good. Rickerson gave thought to telling the woman to put on some clothes, then thought better of it. If he had to be out pounding on doors in the middle of the night, he might as well reap a few benefits. There weren't that many to be had. He walked over to a large wine-colored velvet sectional and collapsed. The woman strolled past him, fully aware that he was feasting on her body, flaunting it. She was wearing spiked heels, and her tan, smooth legs were tantalizing.

Once she was seated on the opposite side of the sectional, she reached for a cigarette from a pack on the end table and lit up, the flimsy robe falling open and exposing an ample white breast, the skin like buttermilk, the nipple a bright shade of pink. "So, what do you want?" she said, exhaling a thin stream of smoke.

"Uh, I . . . gosh," he said, thinking of how long it had been since he had made love to Joyce. Was it four months now . . . or five months? "Mind if I smoke?" he asked, pulling out a cigar.

"Not those. Want a cigarette?"

"No, I . . ." Her breast was still exposed. She was watching him squirm. "Why don't you cover yourself?" he finally said, feeling his face flush. "You know . . ."

She did. It didn't help much. He could see right through the fabric.

"Tell me what you know about Ivory Perkins."

"She's dead. I know that. It was in all the papers."

"But you knew her? Did you work together occasionally, turn tricks together?" He could smell her cologne all the way across the room. Something heavy and sweet. He wondered if it was really cologne or just her body that smelled so good. It looked good; it must smell good. No, he told himself, what he was smelling was Lara's cologne from last night and imagining what Lara would look like in a robe like that. He rubbed his eyes, thinking he needed a cold shower and a cup of black coffee.

"Yeah, we worked together a few times," the woman said. "Sometimes a client wanted a threesome or wanted to just watch a couple of women together. Men like that kind of thing. You know what I mean?"

He certainly did. She had those mile-long legs crossed and was swinging one up and down as she talked. He licked his lips and cleared his throat, trying to remember why he was there to begin with. "Did you know any of her clients? Anyone that might have wanted to hurt her? Anyone that she could have been blackmailing?"

She stabbed the half-smoked cigarette out in the ashtray and walked across the room to a mirrored bar, pouring herself a glass of vodka in a cut crystal glass. "Want a drink?" she asked. Rickerson shook his head. Then she left the robe completely fall open as she crossed back to the sofa. Her pubic hair was pale blond and sparse, inching its way between her legs.

"Ivory . . . poor Ivory. She had such an asshole for a husband. Did you know he turned her out, put her in the trade? What a prick. Chick never got to spend a dime of the money she earned. Not a fucking dime. And the nose candy, man. He fed it to her like it was chicken soup or something. When she was high, she'd do just about anything and anyone. And let me tell you something, this girl liked it. She liked it a lot."

"Were they dealing cocaine? Anything like that?"

"No, not to my knowledge. Most of it Ivory got from her johns or I guess her man bought it for her on the street. He was a boozer. He didn't even use, but boy, did he make sure she stayed high."

"You didn't answer my first question," Rickerson said. "Did you know anyone that might have wanted to kill her or her husband?"

"When I first read about it in the papers, I was certain he'd killed her, but of course, he's dead too. So . . . as to her clients, I didn't know many of them. She did a lot of B and D calls. I don't handle those. Sometimes the clients get nasty. My clients like it straight—just sex, a little fun. Most of them are professionals."

"She never mentioned anyone in particular . . . perhaps a regular client, someone she saw all the time? Maybe someone with a big job like a judge?"

Carol Montgomery tossed her head back and laughed. It was a wonderful sound, like tinkling bells. "A judge, huh? I don't remember her mentioning a judge, but I know she had a client she saw a lot. He was a regular. Good tipper too, from what she told me. She kind of liked him. But a judge . . ."

"I see. Know this guy's name?"

She shot Rickerson a knowing look. "No one has names. Not real names anyway." There was an awkward silence. "Sorry, I can't help you, Detective . . . what was your name again?" She smiled. Her teeth were straight and white.

"Ted," he said slowly. "Ted Rickerson. Tell me about her other clients. Anyone other than this guy who was a regular, someone she mentioned?"

Carol Montgomery twirled a strand of her blond hair in her fingers, bringing it to her mouth and draping it provocatively across her lip. "Let me think here a minute, okay? Sometimes these people just blur after so long. I can't remember who was her client and who was mine," she said, leaning forward and crossing her arms at the waist so that her cleavage was even more pronounced. "I mean, you'd think if you fucked someone you'd remember them, but believe me, Ted, after a few thousand or so, you wouldn't recognize the sucker on the street if you walked right into him. She had one real weird guy. He was also a regular."

"Tell me about him." Rickerson decided he didn't have to look at the woman to hear what she had to say. As soon as he looked away, he saw her pull her robe shut and slap back on the sofa. Evidently the game was no fun when no one was playing.

"White guy. Young. Skinny, she told me. He wanted her to dress him in diapers and feed him in a custom-made high chair. Then she'd spank him. He never had sex with her. Wouldn't even touch her."

"No name, right?"

She didn't even answer him. She just glared at him.

"Know what this guy did for a living?"

"Let me ask you something, Ted," she said. "If you went to a hooker and had her dress you in diapers and feed you, do you think you'd tell her your life history? Give me a break here. All I know is the guy didn't have any bucks. Sometimes when business was slow, she'd do him on credit. She used to call it a student loan."

"So he was a student? Was he in college?"

"How the fuck do I know? Look, it's late." She stood and walked up to him, purposely spreading the robe now, moving her body only inches from his face. "I mean, I might not be able to help you on your case, but maybe I can help you in another way." She had stepped over his legs and was standing with her own legs on either side of them. She reached a hand down and touched her genitals.

"No," he said flatly, standing, pushing her back. He shifted his jacket on his shoulders and headed for the door. Then he turned and glanced back over his shoulder. "Don't think I can afford you, sweetie. But if I were you, I'd be mighty careful. Don't want that gorgeous body to end up on a slab in the morgue."

For the first time he saw a crack in her self-confidence, a slight tremor in the slender hand that reached for another cigarette.

"Can I ask you something?" he said. "It's something that really bothers me. I don't know why, but it does."

"You've asked me everything else," she said. "Fire away. If you want to know how much I charge, it's two bills. That's for straight. Anything else is extra. Of course, I do have a police discount. For cops, I charge two fifty." Again she laughed.

"Aren't you even a little concerned about AIDS? People are dying out there, woman. Don't you want to live?"

Carol Montgomery's brows knitted and her mouth compressed into a thin, hard line. She seemed to age right before his eyes. Flicking her ashes on the carpet, she reached under the sofa and pulled out a large box and tossed it across the floor, where it landed right at Rickerson's feet. It looked like a carton of cigarettes. "Condoms, dick head. I buy them by the case at the Price Club. Trick doesn't wear one, he doesn't fuck."

Now he could see how hard she really was. The curtain fell on her little performance and she was fully exposed. "Everybody fucks, Officer," she snarled, her lip curling, "it's a basic instinct. And they're gonna just keep on fucking, AIDS or no fucking AIDS. As long as they fuck, I'm gonna make a living. And as long as I'm alive, I'm gonna make my living fucking."

She didn't show him to the door. Rickerson let himself out. No one on the list had been identified as a student. Then he recalled Lara's statement that her secretary, Phillip, attended law school. Carol Montgomery had described Ivory's client as tall and skinny. Lara said Phillip was tall and thin. Rickerson stuck a stub of a cigar in his mouth and lit it, looking up at the sky. A few seconds later he was coughing and tossed the cigar in a dumpster next to his car in the parking lot. This case was going to kill him, he thought, his back aching and his head throbbing. The last thing he needed was another suspect. He got into the car and pulled the door shut.

"Damn," he said, looking out over the parking lot and slapping the steering wheel with both hands. He wanted Evergreen, not some skinny secretary. Ever since Evergreen had dismissed that case when he was a rookie, Rickerson had been carrying a grudge against him. He didn't like the man. He was too smug, too cold. He'd raked Rickerson over the coals that day, right in the courtroom in front of his fellow officers. He'd blamed Rickerson for compromising the case. And bringing down the presiding judge—what a coup that would be. Had he slanted this investigation to fit his own agenda? Obviously he had.

"Can't bust Evergreen if he isn't guilty," he said, taking a deep breath and then letting it out. Cranking the engine on the big Chrysler, he roared out of the parking lot and headed home.

Monday was a beautiful day. A beautiful day, Lara thought, if you were going to the beach, or roller skating, or for a nice long walk. But this was the day she was burying her sister and Josh would say his final goodbye to his mother.

There was no such thing as a beautiful day for a funeral.

What she really wanted was for the sky to open up and soak them all, make it really lousy, make it seem like what it really was: a day of death, a day of finality. From this point there was no going back. Once you went in the ground, you didn't come back up.

But no, she thought, tilting her head up, the skies seldom darkened in Southern California, not just a few miles from Disneyland. The sun was shining and the temperature was in the seventies with a gentle breeze filled with the scent of the ocean.

The cemetery was in San Clemente, high on a hill. From some spots the shoreline could be seen, but most of this property was being overrun with developers. Less than a mile from where they were standing, they were clearing for a new housing tract, and huge bulldozers like dinosaurs gobbled up the foliage, turning what was once natural and green into barren, dusty earth.

While everyone was standing around, talking in hushed voices among themselves, Lara walked over to the plots where her parents and Charley were buried and gazed down at the simple markers. "She's with you now, Pop," she whispered. "You, Mom, Charley, and now Ivory. You're all together." She stopped and inhaled deeply, knowing that one day she'd be there next to them. Except for Josh, this spot of earth would soon cover her whole family. Out of the corner of her eye, she saw Sam's casket next to Ivory's on the berm, the man from the funeral home standing there solemnly in his black suit. "I'm sorry about Sam, that he has to be here too," she added. "But he was her husband."

She faced the small gathering. Only four people were present other than herself: Irene Murdock, Benjamin England, Phillip, and Josh. Lara had decided at the last minute that Emmet shouldn't come after last night and what he'd been through. The poor man had been scared out of his wits, and the police had kept him up half the night. Irene's husband, John, couldn't spare time from his thriving medical practice.

They all stood around in a tight little circle, and Lara bowed her head and said a brief prayer. Josh stood beside her in his new striped suit. "Lord," she said, not really knowing what to say, "bless these two souls. One of them was a wife and a mother, a sister. She was loved and we will miss her." As hard as she was trying, tears were gathering in her eyes behind her dark glasses. "They are in Your hands now." She paused and then said, "Amen."

Everyone was silent.

Lara had Josh's hand in hers. He walked over and placed a letter in an envelope on his mother's white casket with the brass fittings. He didn't cry, but his hand was shaking; Lara let go of his hand and put her arm around his waist. For a few long moments they just stood there, wind whipping their hair, leaning on each other.

Finally she turned back to her friends. "I guess that's it," she said. "We can go now."

Rickerson was sitting in his county vehicle on the little paved road leading to the area where they were having the services. He'd come today fully intending to pay his respects and see Lara, but once he was there, he couldn't force himself to get out of the car. She hadn't asked him to come, and in some ways it had hurt his feelings. It was a sign that she didn't consider him a part of her life outside of the investigation. He saw the BMW and the Mercedes. Fancy cars, he thought, thinking of the ten-year-old Ford parked in front of his house with the ripped upholstery. "She's out of your league, bud," he told himself. He picked up his binoculars off the seat and watched the little grouping of people. Seeing a tall, thin young man, he adjusted the focus. That had to be Phillip, he thought, searching the man's face with avid interest. He'd have to get his last name and address from Lara tomorrow.

Seeing that they were about to leave, he started the

car and pulled farther down where he couldn't be seen and again looked through the binoculars. The guy in the expensive suit had to be Benjamin England, the attorney she had mentioned. He watched as he embraced Lara. "Fucking prick," he said, feeling jealousy surge through his veins, an alien, ugly emotion. "You're a suspect too, buddy." Then he let the binoculars slide from his hands to his lap in frustration and locked his fingers on the steering wheel. It was time for him to leave.

Lara and Josh had driven to the cemetery with Irene Murdock. She'd arrived at nine o'clock with her BMW filled with food in plastic containers. She was always well dressed, generally something tailored and professional, something extremely expensive. Today she was appropriately dressed in black. Unlike Lara, she looked and acted like a judge even when she was outside of the courtroom. She had a presence about her that exuded strength and purpose.

"Please come to Lara's," she told the little group of people, taking charge of the situation as she always did. "I've prepared some food. That would be nice, don't you think?"

Benjamin England and Phillip followed them to the condominium in their own cars. Lara was bursting to tell Irene what Rickerson suspected about Evergreen and her own suspicions about Phillip, but with Josh in the car, she knew she had to wait. "When we get to the complex, Josh," she said, turning around to speak to him in the backseat, "we're going to go and get my friend Emmet so he can join us. He's in my old place now, you know. I've been wanting you to meet him."

"Why do I have to go with you to get him? Just call him on the phone."

"He's in a wheelchair, Josh. Didn't I tell you that?"

They rode in silence the remainder of the drive. Rickerson had said he didn't feel there was a risk right now for Emmet to stay where he was; they'd searched her house now and the condo. He doubted if they would come back. Stay maybe three more days until the evidence on Cummings was processed, and then he had told her, she could finally return to her house in Irvine. The killer, Rickerson supposed, was probably now under the assumption that Lara had done something with the photos: turned them over to the police, taken them to her safe-deposit box or the office. Whoever was behind this knew where she was and could obviously find her. Lara turned her head around and glanced at Phillip in the car behind them, feeling the icy touch of fear. Then she wrapped her arms around herself and remained that way until they arrived at the condo.

At the condo, Benjamin cornered her in the kitchen. "Lara," he said, "we need to talk."

She stared up at his face. There were dark circles under his eyes, and he looked awful. "Late night, huh?" she said, thinking he'd had some young secretary in his bed last night, someone who'd lie and tell him what a fabulous lover he was, hoping to end up with a ring on her finger and a membership to the country club.

"Not really. I've been sick with the flu, and let me tell you, it's cold as a bitch in San Francisco. The wind goes right through you." He stopped and Lara went back to what she was doing, transferring the food from the plastic containers to serving dishes. "Lara, can we talk about the other night, the last night we were together? I've thought about it and know you were angry with me. I shouldn't have asked you to take a cab home. I was just so tired."

"Forget it," she said. "It's done." After all that had happened, the night in England's backyard seemed like a lifetime ago. "Oh," she said suddenly, "did you call the San Clemente Police Department and ask for information on the homicides?"

He stepped back a few feet and his mouth fell open. "How'd you hear about that?" he said. "I was really upset when I read about the murders in the newspaper,

Lara. And to tell you the truth, I think it was rude that you didn't return my phone calls. I really thought we were close, you know."

He was right, Lara thought. She should have called him back. "There was a lot going on, Benjamin. Surely you can understand that. I think I called you once or twice, but I couldn't reach you."

"Are you going to see me again?"

She didn't turn around. "I don't think so. We can be friends, though. I need a few friends." It was almost as if she was talking to herself.

He turned her around. "But why? Don't you think you're being childish? Did I really do something that bad?"

Lara glanced through the kitchen door. Phillip and Irene were talking and sipping coffee. She didn't see Josh. She kept her voice low, almost a whisper. "That depends on how you look at it. I'd say satisfying yourself with no regard whatsoever to your partner is inconsiderate and obnoxious, but then I'm not a man." Lara had always been frank. If you asked a question, you usually got an answer.

"My God," he whispered, his lips compressed. "What are you going to do? Sue me for failing to comply with the terms of a contract or something?" He stopped and was silent. Finally he responded, "I'm sorry. I was inconsiderate. I didn't think."

"I have to take this in the other room, and I want to go and get Emmet now," she said, wanting to conclude the conversation. She started toward the living room when Benjamin stopped her.

"Can we try again? We'll go away somewhere or something, maybe to Palm Springs. Then my mind will be clear." He laughed nervously. "I'll read books. You can give me lessons. It's never to late to learn. . . . I was a real pig, huh?"

Lara smiled at him, the first smile of the day. She set the tray down and leaned back against the kitchen counter. "Yes, you were," she said. She thought of this elegant man standing before her: the manicured nails, the five-hundred-dollar suit, the starched lavender shirt with his initials embroidered on the pocket. He was a far cry from Ted Rickerson, but for some reason he just didn't stack up. The detective seemed alive, living on the cutting edge. He saw and felt her pain. And something soft rested inside Ted Rickerson, something incredibly gentle and compassionate. England was self-absorbed to a fault. "Let's go inside."

As soon as Lara walked into the living room with the tray of food, her eyes started searching frantically. "Where's Josh? she asked.

"He's sitting right there under the tree, Lara," Irene said, looking out the window.

Lara handed her the tray and went outside to Josh. "Want to go and get my friend now?" she said.

"Yeah, I guess. What's wrong with him anyway?"

Lara explained Emmet's condition as they crossed the courtyard. Once they were inside the condo, she introduced them. "Emmet, this is my nephew, Josh. Josh, this is one of my closest friends, Emmet Daniels."

Josh just stared at Emmet. Then he cleared his throat and looked at Lara as if to ask her what he was supposed to do now. Emmet hit the button on his chair and headed to his office. Lara placed a palm on Josh's back and they both followed.

"Do . . . you . . . like video games?" Emmet said.

"Sure," Josh answered, looking around the room and then back at the terminal. He watched as Emmet stuck his head into the metal contraption and started typing on the computer.

"If you want, you can come over and play later. I have almost every game. You're welcome to use my system anytime you want. I'm deeply sorry about your mother, Josh."

"Yeah, thanks," Josh said. "That's cool, you know. That thing you put on your head. And your wheelchair is cool too. Is that electric?"

They headed back across the courtyard, Josh asking Emmet about every question he could think of and Emmet doing his best to answer him. He asked him how long he had been sick, why he had to use the metal cage to type, how he went to the bathroom, what he did for a living, how fast his wheelchair would go. Lara was thankful when they finally reached the door. She wasn't certain Emmet appreciated Josh's interrogation. Some of these questions Lara had never even asked herself.

Once they were inside, they all just sat there and looked at each other. Irene and Phillip finally started chatting about office politics and one of the cases he was studying in law school. Benjamin England was brooding and obviously bored. Funerals and grief didn't appear to hold his attention. Josh sat on the floor; Emmet's wheelchair was right next to Phillip.

"Emmet," Lara said, "I thought your computer was broken last night."

"I . . . have . . . friends," Emmet said slowly. "They all have . . . computers."

"Oh," Phillip said, turning to Lara, evidently assuming that he must speak or interpret for Emmet just because he was sitting next to him. "I guess he's saying one of them brought another terminal over for him. Is that what you're saying, Emmet?"

Emmet nodded.

No one lingered. After they ate, Lara was silent and introspective, staring out the window until people got the hint and stood to leave. There weren't a lot of memories to share, she thought, looking around the room; these people were not her family. Her family was gone except for Josh. On his way out, Phillip jumped up and said he'd wheel Emmet back to the condo.

Josh gave him a nasty look. "It's an electric chair, dummy. He doesn't need anyone to push him." Then he stood and looked at Lara. "Can I go back with Emmet?"

"Sure, honey," she said, thankful that she might have a few moments alone with Irene.

While Irene stood at the sink rinsing off her plastic

containers to take home, Lara stood next to her. "How well do you know Phillip?"

"Me?" Irene said nervously, pointing a finger at her chest and facing her friend. "He's your secretary, Lara. Why? Isn't he doing a good job for you?" Irene seemed strained, tired. She looked at her friend with compassion.

"I don't know. He's worked for a lot of the judges. I thought he had worked for you once."

"No," Irene said. "He worked for Westridge. He even worked for Evergreen for a short time about two years ago. Very competent man from what I hear." Her face relaxed and she smiled. "I'll trade with you in a minute. Just let me know."

That said, Lara filled Irene in on the situation with Evergreen. She didn't tell her all the details. Rickerson had said to keep it under wraps, but she had to talk to someone and Irene was her friend.

The tall blond judge stopped and wiped her hands on a dish towel. "Well, that's just nonsense," she snapped. "Evergreen is a crusty old goat, but the most respected man I know. He's certainly not . . . a pedophile." Just the word seemed to be more than she could utter.

"What do you know about him, Irene?" Lara asked, leaning against the kitchen counter. Irene knew Evergreen well. They had lunch all the time. If anyone knew about Leo Evergreen, it would be Irene Murdock.

"What do you want me to say?" She was somewhat defensive. "He's an intelligent, decent man. His wife died, you know, a number of years ago."

"Do you know anything about his son?"

Irene arched her eyebrows and shoved her glasses back in place on her nose. "His son?"

"Rickerson wants to talk to him."

"We used to see him all the time but not lately. You know, we were all friends when Elaine was alive. He went to school at the conservatory in Santa Barbara. He's a musician. A flutist." She paused, her face stern. "You know, Lara, if Evergreen were a child molester, which I think is complete madness, how would he recruit his victims? He couldn't risk hanging out around schools or anything. He'd have to keep a very low profile."

"Most child molesters can't risk exposure," Lara quickly responded. That was the truth. In most cases they were respected members of the community, had good jobs, went to church every Sunday, paid their bills.

"Well, I can't see discussing this," she said. "I think it's absurd." She paused and her face softened. "I'm concerned about you, Lara. So is Leo. He thinks very highly of you. He would be aghast if he ever heard these insinuations."

"Thinks highly of me, huh? Sometimes he sure doesn't act like it." Lara didn't want to get into a discussion about her improprieties. Not today. Not the day she'd buried her sister.

"It could be Phillip, Irene. He has access to court information. He's been borrowing a lot of money lately and acting strange. What if he was victimized by a pedophile years ago and Ivory and Sam got their hands on the pictures? The man who broke into the condo last night was tall and thin." She paused, staring out into space. "Phillip could even be a pedophile himself. I don't know anything about his personal life. Not once has he mentioned a girlfriend."

Irene kept looking at Lara and blinking her eyes. "I think you're getting paranoid, Lara. The stress . . ." She stopped and cleared her throat. "Maybe you should get Dr. Werner to prescribe a tranquilizer for you."

Lara grimaced and looked away. Irene thought she was cracking up. Maybe she was right.

"How's it going with the boy?" Irene said, changing the subject, deep concern in her eyes.

"Josh? . . . Oh, Irene, it's been tough. And I mean really tough. It was almost a relief when Social Services took him, but I know underneath it all, he really needs me. I just don't know how to reach him." Lara took a sponge and started wiping down the countertops. "Hey, you raised two sons. You know all about teenage boys. Is there some trade secret or something?"

Irene smiled and her face came alive. She loved her two sons and was extremely close to them. If you ever wanted to see Irene Murdock smile, all you had to do was mention them. "With my boys, I always tried to keep them busy, involved in something positive. You know, Little League, things like that. Matt played golf. That's a great sport for a young man. It teaches them to be polite and mannerly. There's no bad element on the golf courses. If they have too much time on their hands, they'll just get into trouble."

Lara rubbed her chin. She couldn't see Josh playing golf or baseball. He wasn't the type. But Irene had a point about keeping Josh busy. She remembered his desire to be a weight lifter and thought they might join a health club after they moved back into the house in Irvine. "Thanks, Irene," she said.

The other woman looked at her and then moved close and collected her in her arms. "Honey, I'm so torn up over what's happened to you. It just breaks my heart. You're such a good person to go through all this tragedy."

Once Irene had stepped back, Lara shrugged her shoulders. "Just life, I guess. You have to learn to take the bad with the good. Unfortunately, there hasn't been much good lately."

Irene put all the containers in a grocery sack and carried them into the living room, leaving them by the door. They stood there for a while, both of them deep in thought. "This thing about Evergreen, Lara . . . I think you have to convince yourself that this detective is leading you astray. If I were you, I would distance myself from these accusations and distance myself from this man. He could destroy your career with this foolishness."

Lara's face flushed with emotion. "How can I distance myself, Irene? My sister was murdered."

"Okay," Irene said, "let's run through the cases

we've handled. In most of mine, they've had some novel way to attract young children. I had one man who was a Boy Scout leader. Leo just doesn't fit the profile. I don't know about Phillip. You might have the police look into his affairs if you think there's something questionable there, but not Leo. How in the world would an older man like Leo attract young children? Can't you see how illogical this whole line of thought is?"

It was like a million flash bulbs were popping in Lara's mind at one time. An image flashed in her mind of Josh at the computer console—the revered video games he was always talking about, the games he was playing right now with Emmet. "I've got to go, Irene," she told her.

The other woman looked at her as though she'd lost her mind. "What do you have to prove this, Lara? Do you have some evidence? Let me see it and then maybe I'll take this whole thing in a more serious vein."

"No," Lara said, her face flushed with excitement, wishing she could tell Irene about the pictures, "but I have an idea." She almost pushed Irene out the door and closed it behind her. "You go on home," she told her. "I'll call you later. And don't mention this to anyone. Promise me." Irene mumbled a response, but Lara didn't listen. She was sprinting across the courtyard in her stocking feet, leaving the other woman standing there with her mouth gaping open.

The door to the model condo was open and Lara let herself in, walking straight to Emmet's bedroom. What she saw and heard there stopped her right in her tracks. It's the little things in life that make a person think there's really someone up there surveying the damage, she told herself—like a god.

Emmet and Josh were glued to the computer screen, little flashing images darting everywhere. Emmet would tap out something really fast and the images would move. Then Josh would laugh and do the same. Laughter. She was actually hearing laughter on this gray day, this day of death. She had never even heard her nephew laugh.

"What are you two doing?" she said lightly, stepping up behind Josh and peering at the computer screen.

"We're playing Lemmings," Josh said enthusiastically. "Emmet's got Super NES. You know, Super Nintendo. He's good, man. He's got everything over here." He looked up and smiled. "Every video game in the world . . . all the latest stuff. And he's got a modem too. He can do all kinds of things, get almost any kind of information you want. He's got this thing called Prodigy. It's rad, totally rad. You can get sports statistics on it, order concert tickets. You said you'd buy me a computer."

Lara waited until the game was over and then sent Josh out on his bicycle. He didn't want to go. He wanted to stay and play with Emmet. Josh certainly didn't try to speak for Emmet. As far as she could see, Emmet's disability was nothing to Josh. They talked the language of common ground. "Go," she said after he ignored her first request. "Leave us alone a minute."

"What's going on?" Emmet typed out as soon as Josh left.

"Emmet, I have this thought. We've looking for a man who may be a child molester. He has access to a computer. Is there any way he could lure children with his computer?"

"Lure . . . ?" Emmet typed out. "How?"

"You know, you mentioned that message board. Could he talk to them that way, get them to meet him somewhere?"

"Anything is possible," Emmet typed. "How old are the children?"

"Prepuberty . . . eight to, say, thirteen."

"If they were older, there would be more possibilities. I need to think this through," he typed. "Give me time. I'll work on it. What's his name?"

"There's two names, two people. One's a well-known public figure. He'd never use his own name."

Lara knew that both Evergreen and Phillip had a computer.

"I . . . see," Emmet said, then continued typing. "People are peculiar, Lara, even people with something to hide. I read a lot. I like true-crime stories. Many times they use part of their own name, their initials, something similar so they won't forget. If you want me to help you, please tell me his name."

"I'll tell you," she said, "but you must not mention these names anywhere. No one must know, Emmet. Please, these people may be innocent and we can't be responsible for slandering them. That wouldn't be right."

"I . . . see," he said. "The . . . names, Lara?"

"Leo Evergreen and Phillip Ridley."

Emmet turned from the computer with a questioning look. "Phillip . . . your secretary?"

Lara nodded. She expected an interrogation. But Emmet was not Irene Murdock. He simply turned back to his computer.

"I'll . . . begin now."

As she watched, Emmet typed in the name Leo Evergreen. Then he tapped a series of letters and numbers, and the screen was covered with words containing some portion of the name. She let herself out and went to find Josh.

chapter 18

Madeline Murphy met Lara Tuesday morning at eight o'clock at the condominium and agreed to allow Josh to return. "We never wanted to cause a problem for you, Judge Sanderstone," she said politely. "We were just doing our jobs." The woman stumbled over her words a few minutes longer, making small talk about the weather. "You can pick your nephew up tonight. He should return to school tomorrow, however. I spoke with him and I think he's eager to be with you. See, this cooling-off period served its purpose. I told you a little time—"

"Right," Lara said, cutting her off, rolling her neck around as she locked the door to the condo. Her neck was so stiff that she could barely move. "Excuse me, but I must run or I'll be late for court."

After the morning session, the jury panel on the Adams matter had risen to four people and that was because they were moving fast, extremely fast for some reason. Voir dire, the process of selecting a jury, is the very essence of courtroom monotony. A lot of judges actually fell asleep. By noon, Lara had a splitting headache and couldn't wait to put the day behind her.

"Your friend Emmet is a nice man," Phillip told her at lunch. Rickerson had told her to avoid Evergreen, so she'd had him bring a salad to eat in her chambers. He set down the salad and then stood in front of her desk. "You know, I'm in the Big Brothers' program, Lara. Maybe I can spend some time with your nephew, take him to the movies or something. I'm sure this has been very difficult for him. My father died when I was twelve, so I know how he feels."

"You never told me you were in that program, Phillip," Lara blurted out, her fears and suspicions soaring now. Being a Big Brother was the perfect way to reach children. Her back stiffened and she dropped her hands in her lap, willing herself to appear calm. "How do you manage being a Big Brother with law school and a full-time job?"

"It's just one day a month. Besides, it looks good on my resumé." He smiled. "I come from a big family. I'm the oldest of five kids."

"Are you seeing someone, Phillip? You know, a girl?"

His eyes looked right through her as if he knew exactly what she was thinking—that he was gay. "I was, Lara," he said, just a touch of sarcasm in his high-pitched voice, "but we broke up recently. I have a little too much going on with my life right now to get involved in a serious relationship."

"So do I, Phillip. Listen," she said, changing the subject, not wanting to be too obvious. Eager to tell Rickerson the information she had just heard, Lara said, "Are you absolutely certain the Detective Rickerson hasn't called me?" Discounting the case, Lara couldn't get the detective out of her mind. Every night before falling asleep, she let her thoughts drift to him. It was a way to push the demons aside, she thought. But with each day her fantasies were more real, her desires more pronounced.

"No, it's really been quiet around here for a change."

"If he does and it's something urgent, get me off the bench," she told him as she walked out the door to return to the courtroom.

"No problem," he said, picking up the paper plates. "If the man calls, I'll get you right away."

No more than two feet from the door to her chamber, Lara ran into Irene Murdock. Right in the same corridor, walking in her direction, was Leo Evergreen.

"Lara," Irene said, "I was just coming to see you. Can you talk a few minutes?"

Lara glanced at Leo. He was headed her way, but his head was down. She didn't want to see him. "Gosh, Irene, I have to be back in court right now. How about later? Call me later." Lara was already walking off when Irene called out to her.

"Can I borrow Phillip a few minutes? My secretary is out ill and I need some things typed."

"Sure," Lara said, entering through the rear door to the courtroom. She quickly climbed the three steps and the bailiff spoke: "All rise."

The afternoon session commenced.

Lara listened to the defense attorney asking the same questions for the twentieth time that day. "Do you have children? Has any one of them ever been injured? How did you feel about that? How would you feel if someone removed your children and placed them in a foster home? How would you feel if they were sexually abused in a foster home?" On and on it went. Then at the end of the day, after the last potential juror had been interrogated, the district attorney pitched a fit over a discovery motion that he'd filed and the defense had not answered.

"Mr. Steinfield over here is attempting to withhold evidence in this case," the district attorney barked. "That motion was filed three weeks ago."

Lara looked sternly at the defense attorney. "Mr. Steinfield, have you responded to the people's motion?"

"No, Your Honor, I haven't. For the past two months I've been in trial on another matter. The psychological evaluation is complete, but the psychologist hasn't mailed me the report yet. He promised it would be in my office by the end of the day."

The district attorney sprang to his feet. "This is a contrived plan to buy time and undermine the prosecution," he said. "Mr. Steinfield should be found in contempt for failing to comply with a court order."

Lara glared at the D.A. "I'll decide if someone is in contempt." Her gaze turned to the defense attorney. "Mr. Steinfield, you have until tomorrow at three o'clock to comply with the terms of the discovery motion." She tapped the gavel lightly and looked out over the courtroom. "This court's adjourned until nine o'clock tomorrow morning. Good evening, gentlemen."

Rickerson had finally called, but when she called him back, they informed her that he was out again. It was late; Phillip had already left. As Lara was rushing out the door to get Josh, she ran right into the detective.

"We've got to quit meeting like this," he said, giving her a big smile. Then the smile vanished. "We have to talk."

She spun around and was headed back inside her chambers when he seized her arm. "Not in there. Evergreen might have a listening device. He's the big boss. Richard Nixon did, so . . ."

Lara rolled her eyes. "That's ridiculous. Where do you want to go?"

"How about your court? No one's in there, are they?"

"No, but . . ." He kept staring at her and she gave in. "Follow me."

Walking quickly, she entered again through the judge's door and they took seats in the back of the court, Rickerson tossing his long legs over one of the seats. Lara just stared out over the room. Courtrooms used to be full of wood paneling and had tile or wood flooring so the voices echoed. They also had windows, fans, and no air conditioning. Defendants would sweat, she thought, really sweat, the way they should sweat when they stood in a room like this, in front of a judge and jury. When she was a teenager, she used to ride the bus to the courthouse during summer vacations and imagine she was one of the attorneys, even going so far as to imagine she was the judge. This courtroom had bright blue upholstery on the seats, pale mauve carpeting, and the windowless space was climate-controlled. Judges didn't need booming voices that would carry; they had microphones. Lara really liked it better the old way. This way was too efficient, too pretty, too neat. In her eyes, justice had become too modern. It was losing the flavor.

This was her domain, her little kingdom, she told herself, glancing at the American flag by the bench. She didn't want to lose it if she was tossed off the bench for impropriety. She'd lost enough as it was.

"Wait until you hear what I learned today," she said, her voice echoing in the large, empty space. Rickerson had been sitting there quietly, deep in his own thoughts. "Phillip is a Big Brother."

"You mean the organization that helps kids?"

"Yes," she said loudly, emphasizing the word. "Now do you think we should consider him a suspect?"

"I'm ahead of you, Lara. I got his personnel jacket today. He has no criminal history, but that's not surprising. He lives with his mother in Costa Mesa, not far from where you are staying at the condo."

"His mother? He never mentioned living with his mother."

"He never mentioned being a Big Brother before either. Maybe he just manufactured that to get his hands on Josh."

"Why Josh?"

"Josh might know more than you think."

"Believe me, Phillip won't get within a mile of that kid. Not now. What about the money, the loans?"

Rickerson frowned. "Takes time—oh, I went to the D.A. today. Not too promising."

"Who'd you see? Did you go to the top, to Meyer?" Lawrence Meyer was the actual District Attorney of Orange County. Everyone else were assistant district attorneys who worked under his supervision.

"Yep. He's an asshole."

Lara turned to him. According to Rickerson, everyone was either a child molester or an asshole. And these were the people who controlled the criminal justice system in Orange County. "I never encountered any problems with him when I was working there. He's an outstanding prosecutor, an excellent supervisor. His record is impeccable."

"Told me I was out of my fucking mind about Evergreen. When I persisted, he threatened to have me removed from his office."

"Great," Lara said, cutting her eyes to the detective. "You shouldn't have gone to him. I told you it was premature. You didn't mention me, did you?"

Rickerson took his legs off the back of the seat. "No, but he did."

"What do you mean?"

"Here's what he said, practically verbatim, okay? Lara Sanderstone released Packard Cummings. We argued against it, meaning whatever D.A. was in court that day. She was using judicial influence and privilege to cover her brother's—" Rickerson stopped and looked at Lara. "He thought Perkins was your real brother. Anyway, he went on to say that the next day after Cummings's release, he killed someone and you were to blame. He said we should investigate your activities instead of Evergreen's if we wanted to investigate someone."

"That slimy bastard," Lara spat. "I can't believe he said that. Did he think I released Cummings so he could murder my own sister? That's horrible, that's vile."

"Told you he was an asshole."

"Now what?"

"We need to wait for the lab reports, something linking Cummings to the homicides. I'm pushing them, but they can only move so fast. They're completely buried."

Lara stood and climbed over Rickerson's long legs, pacing in the aisle. "So, that's it?" Her arms dropped by her sides and she stopped short.

"Well, we have the appointment book. It's pretty interesting."

"How? Tell me. And Ted, I have to pick up Josh, so

make it fast." Lara glanced at her watch. As soon as they moved back to the house in Irvine, Lara was going to look into changing Josh's school. She certainly couldn't keep up this frantic pace, driving him back and forth every single day.

"Everyone uses their own shorthand or code in books like that, even people who aren't prostitutes. Whatever kind of system your sister used, however, is pretty cryptic, no real rhyme or reason. But she had regular customers, which is something to go on. There's a client booked for every Wednesday afternoon. She penciled in the letters *LS* in his time slot. There's another appointment scheduled for the evening hours of July seventh, the night she came to your apartment. That was also a Wednesday, for whatever that matters. This man is penciled in as *LW*. After that date the book just stops."

"Really?" she said. "Well, the *LW* could stand for Leo something. He might have used his real first name and a phony last name."

"I already thought of that, but then what does the *LS* stand for? I was told by an expert that *LS* meant that the trick likes sex, and *LW* that he likes whips. What do you think?"

Lara just shrugged her shoulders.

"I guess once they started extorting money, Ivory stopped turning tricks. The book just stops after the night she came to your house back in July. Also, a lot of her appointments were scheduled around the seventh, eighth, and ninth every month. I have no idea what that means."

"Probably because the house payment was due," Lara said. "That's when she always used to hit me up for money. Someday I'll let you see my checkbook. Sam must have pushed her to ply her trade around then." Particularly after she had quit giving them money, Lara thought, cupping her hand over her mouth. If she hadn't cut them off, they might both still be alive.

"Well, I talked to another hooker who worked with

her. She's my expert. Maybe they all used the same shorthand."

Lara looked up. "Another prostitute? Ivory was working with another prostitute? What did she tell you?"

"Not much. Just that she had one regular client that might have been a student of some kind."

"Phillip's a student," Lara shot out. She stopped and they exchanged penetrating glances. Rickerson already knew that fact. "I need to ask you something."

"Shoot."

"Are you absolutely certain Josh wasn't in any of those photographs?"

Rickerson stood, stepping close to Lara. He turned sideways and his jacket brushed against her. They both leaned back against the railing. "What makes you ask?"

"Just a thought, that's all. I know he's been abused. I just don't know how." This had been dancing in Lara's head ever since the day with Josh and the discussion of the bloody T-shirt. She'd held back on bringing it up to him again, but it was troubling her. He had said whatever happened was embarrassing. Lara kept thinking that he could have been involved with this child molester, even sodomized or injured in some way. Eventually she knew she had to confront Josh.

The detective leaned even closer to Lara. She knew he did it on purpose. They were now shoulder to shoulder, and she was having trouble focusing on the conversation. All she could see was the slender gold band on his left hand.

"There's a slim possibility that Josh could have been the photographer, the one taking the pictures, but I personally doubt it. Because I'm convinced your sister stole the pictures, I don't really see how the boy could have been involved."

Lara pulled away and started to leave. Rickerson walked up to her and put two strong arms on her own. "We're gonna get this bastard," he said. Then he ran his finger down her nose and touched her lips. Before she could say anything, he had turned and walked off, exiting through the front of the courtroom.

That one touch of his finger to her lips had left her almost panting. It was like a kiss—a delicate, fleeting kiss.

Lara headed back down the corridor leading to her office and the judges' elevator. The building was quiet now, almost empty. She walked fast. Josh was waiting.

She punched the button on the elevator and the door opened. Lara gasped and stepped back a few feet in a state of shock.

"Lara," the man inside said, "My, you're working late."

For a few minutes she just stood there, uncertain what she should do, perspiration popping out on her brow and upper lip. Then she stepped inside the elevator with Judge Leo Evergreen and the mechanical doors shut.

"Yes, I am, Leo," Lara said. "You know, the Adams case . . ." She felt herself trembling and willed herself to remain calm. She couldn't stop herself from staring, however. He was wearing a black trench coat and carrying an expensive leather briefcase. He looked awful. His normally plump cheeks were caved in, and there were dark circles under his eyes. "Are you feeling better?"

As if she had given him a cue, Evergreen started coughing, removing a white handkerchief from his pocket and covering his mouth. "Not really, to tell you the truth. This flu is a nasty one. You better drink a lot of fluids and stay warm. This one can really put you down."

Right, Lara thought bitterly just as the doors opened and Evergreen shuffled off. He might know a lot of things that could put a person down. Someone had certainly put Ivory down. Right now she was six feet under. She jerked her head back around and watched him walk across the concrete garage floor. This man didn't limp. He was old and he walked slowly, with almost a stilted, stumbling gait.

But as far as she could tell, Judge Leo Evergreen did not have a recognizable limp.

chapter 19

The evening traffic leading into downtown Los Angeles was almost at a standstill, the sky blanketed with smog. Rickerson had stopped after he left Lara and purchased a hot dog and a Coke to eat in the car.

"Dinner," he said, disgusted, shoving the hot dog in his mouth and consuming it in two bites. Then he guzzled the Coke and tossed the paper cup over his shoulder into the backseat. He was meeting Dr. Gail Stewart at the crime lab. One of these days, he thought, he was going to actually have to deliver on all those steak dinners, movie passes, and long-stemmed red roses that he was always promising. But not today.

"Okay," she said, "sit your ass down in the chair and let's get going. Have you had dinner?"

"Yes," he said. "In the car."

"Lucky boy. I'm starving. Let's get this over with so I can go home."

She killed the lights and flicked on the slide projector. "Here's what you've got: The man in the small photograph with the woman is the same man in the picture you had sent over yesterday. See, watch how their features match perfectly when we superimpose the two images. Of course, he's holding his head at a different angle in this photo, so we had to recreate, but there's no doubt that this is the same man. Who is he?"

"Evergreen's son."

"Hot damn, buddy, you're on a roll now. Evergreen's the man in the photo?"

"From all appearance, he has to be. That's his son."

Dr. Stewart took a seat next to him, reaching a

chubby arm behind her to a drawer. "Here," she said. "Dessert." She tossed him a candy bar and started eating one herself while she spoke. "If you don't eat dinner, you can eat all the candy you want and never gain a pound."

"What kind of diet is that?" Rickerson asked, placing the candy bar in his pocket.

"The candy diet, of course. I just invented it." Once she had finished the candy and tossed the wrapper away, her face became serious again. "The man doesn't have to be the boy's father, you know. It could be a family friend, neighbor, anything. Just because these photographs were taken in someone's home doesn't mean anything."

Rickerson grimaced. "It's Evergreen. Believe me, I've never felt so strongly about anything in my life. It all fits, Gail, and every day it fits a little tighter."

"Did you bring me a tape of him walking?"

"Nah, not yet." He twirled the hairs in his mustache. "I guess I could get one, though, maybe coming out of the building or something. Look, Gail, are you certain that this disease or whatever it is would make him limp? Judge Sanderstone doesn't recall him having a limp like that. She claims he has a distinctive walk, but no limp."

Gail bristled slightly. She didn't like people to question her theories. She'd put a lot of hard work into that computer profile. "I told you the man in that photograph limps. I guess he could have had surgery. There's a new procedure where they insert a steel rod and straighten the spine. Anything is possible."

Rickerson was thinking of how he could get a film of Evergreen walking. The problem was, Evergreen didn't come out of the building. To tape him, they'd have to get Lara to let a cameraman hide in the underground garage where the judges parked.

Dr. Stewart continued: "What I really need is a naked shot of him from the back. Then we'd really give you something to take to the bank. We could confirm that spinal curvature, and you'd know without a doubt that he was the man in the photographs. And if he did have surgery, we'd see the scar."

"Sure," the detective said, standing and shoving the small metal chair back to the desk. "Just walk up to him and ask him to take off his clothes and pose for the camera. Give me a break, here, Gail. That's pretty stupid."

She leaned forward in the chair and stared at him. "Cops," she said. "Nothing but dummies." Then she flopped back. "Bet he works out at a health club or something. You know, plays golf, squash, gets massages, swims. You try hard enough, you can get a picture of about anyone naked. All you have to do is hang around in locker rooms. Everyone in this state goes to some kind of club. Californians are fitness crazy." She stopped and smiled. "That is, everyone but me. Dentist says I have rotten teeth. I want to die before they all fall out."

"Good idea," Rickerson said, shuffling to the door, deep in thought, her humor sliding right past him.

"And another thing . . ." she shouted when he was out in the hall.

Instead of returning to the room, Rickerson merely stepped up close to the window, his breath smoking circles on the glass. "Yeah?" he said.

Dr. Stewart walked over to the glass, her voice elevated so he could hear. "Find the son. Bet he molested him too. They usually do."

Rickerson tapped his forehead and smiled. "Smart."

"It's the candy," she said. "Trust me."

Removing the candy bar she'd given him from his shirt pocket, Rickerson stood right at the window and ripped it open and then shoved the whole thing in his mouth and ate it. She laughed. Then he turned and walked away.

Lara couldn't keep Josh away from Emmet. After missing so much school, he had books stacked two feet high on the kitchen table, but they just sat there while he played video games with his new pal across the courtyard. Lara brought home Kentucky Fried Chicken and carried the sacks to Emmet's.

"That's it," she said, stepping inside Emmet's bedroom and speaking to Josh. He was avidly jumping around in his seat pushing buttons on a hand-held control. "No more games, guy."

"But Mom . . ." Josh said without turning around. After that the room fell silent. Lara was flattered, but she quickly realized that Josh had just slipped back in time. She didn't try to stop him when he got up from the computer terminal and left the room, but after glancing at Emmet and shaking her head, she went to find him.

He was outside the condo, sitting on the grass under the weeping willow. Lara approached slowly and just stood there. Finally she said, "You shouldn't sit there. You'll get grass stains on your pants."

He stood and dusted himself off.

"I wish your mother was still alive, Josh—that none of this had ever happened." He nodded. She continued, "To be honest, I was very flattered in there—flattered that you would even accidentally call me Mom." She turned around to head back to the condo. There was nothing more to say.

"I . . . have . . . something," Emmet said once Lara had returned. "Working . . . all day on it." He hit a button on his chair and spun back to the screen, blanking off the game they had been playing and pulling up a menu.

"See," he said, "they . . . have . . . free services." He selected something from the computer menu and a list of what looked like businesses with toll-free numbers flashed on the screen. He moved the cursor down until he found what he wanted and hit another button with the pen attached to his head. Lara was leaning over his shoulder, reading.

SUPER SECRETS—THE GAME MAN, it said, listing an eight-hundred toll-free number to call. The caption under the title read, "If you want to be the best on your block, call the toll-free number on your screen for tricks and insider information on video games. No charge for this service. Nintendo, Super NES, Sega . . ." It went on to list all the different systems and games. Then it listed the person to contact: Tommy Black. The phone number was good only in the state of California.

"What are you saying, Emmet?" Lara asked him.

Emmet blanked the screen again and typed, "There are many numbers like this, help lines and things, but most of them are provided by the manufacturers of the games or the systems themselves. First, I explored the others and found they were all legitimate. I picked this one for the following reasons: It's an independent company or individual, and I'm not sure how they profit from this unless they try to sell other things, like accessories, magazines, or something related to video games. And it is also listed in several different directories for maximum exposure, particularly the directories that young people might respond to, where they have information on sports and movies, things like that. Most of these toll-free numbers are national. Even though this one mentions the state of California, it is really only good in this immediate area. You know, Los Angeles and suburbs."

Lara became excited. It was feasible that a young boy might call a number like that to find out how to win at a game or improve his score. "This is great, Emmet. But the man's name? We don't know anyone named Tommy Black."

Emmet typed, "I thought you said the child molester would use an assumed name. Want to call him?"

"Call who?" Josh said, entering the room. "And when are we going to eat? It's almost eight o'clock. My stomach's growling."

Lara looked at Josh and then had an idea. "Emmet, wouldn't it be better if Josh called? Then we'd know how he handled a child. If I call, he might just fluff me off."

They decided to wait until Josh had finished his dinner. Emmet's nurse had already prepared his meal before they'd arrived and Lara wasn't hungry. They sat around the table and discussed what he was to say. "Just tell him you're calling about getting better at a game. Do you have a favorite game that you can talk about?"

"Yeah," Josh said. "I love Joe and Mac. My friend has it. It's great. Emmet has it too."

"You can't give your real name, you know?" she told him. "This is something regarding my work, a little detective work."

Lara didn't set her hopes too high. Even if the killer was an active pedophile, it was doubtful if he was still trying to recruit victims after what had occurred. But then she ran through all the cases she'd handled in the past and knew that stress seemed to make these people's needs even greater. Some of them even molested children while they were awaiting criminal prosecution. It was a compulsion, almost like an addiction to heroin. This man might be desperate now for the companionship of a young person. It probably made him feel more powerful, more secure.

"Maybe we should wait," she told them just as Josh was about to go to the condo for the cellular phone. She recalled Rickerson's admonition not to run off on tangents on her own. This was a dangerous game. Three people had already died.

"Why?" Josh said. "It sounds like fun. Let me call."

She was being silly, she decided. Nothing was going to come of it anyway, and it was only a phone call. "Okay," she finally said. "Do it. Go get the phone and come back."

Once he returned, he dialed. They waited anxiously beside him. "It's a machine," he said.

"Quick," Lara said, grabbing the phone out of his hands. She wanted to hear the voice on the machine, knowing she would recognize it if it were Evergreen or Phillip. It had a strange, metallic sound. It didn't even sound human. The machine clicked off, and Lara hung up and then redialed. This time she handed the phone to Emmet. "Listen to this, Emmet," she said. "Is the tape worn out or something?"

Emmet listened only a few moments and then the phone dropped involuntarily in his lap and his muscles jerked, tossing his arm off the side of the chair. "It's . . . not a . . . real voice," he struggled to say. "It's . . . a . . . voice-synthesized . . . computer."

"A talking computer?" Lara said.

"Yes," Emmet answered.

They agreed that Josh should call back and leave a name and the number to the cellular phone. He did, using the name of his best friend, Ricky Simmons.

"Well," Lara said, thinking that the whole thing was an exercise in futility. The chances of this working out were a million to one. "It's time for you to hit the books tonight, Josh. No more games or you'll be repeating this grade next year."

"Not hardly," he said, indignant. "I have a 3.9 average. A week's worth of work will take about four hours and I'll be caught up."

Lara was embarrassed. She'd never even asked Josh about his grades at school, or what classes he was taking. For some reason she had decided that he was a weak student, possibly because of Ivory's learning disabilities and his lackluster appearance and demeanor. Now as she looked at him, she saw him in an entirely different light. He was an extremely bright young man, probably more so than anyone knew. More than anything, she doubted if his mother or Sam Perkins had even noticed.

"I'm impressed," she said. "Really, Josh. I am extremely impressed that you're such a good student, but why the 3.9? Can't we make it a 4.0?"

He smiled and there was a silent exchange between them. If he had done this well in school with no one to encourage him, they both knew he could do that much better with Lara's guidance and support. She bent down and kissed Emmet goodbye on the forehead, and they headed out the door. As they started across the grassy courtyard, Emmet appeared in the door. "Back," he said as loud as he could manage. "Phone . . . ringing."

They had left the cellular phone on the kitchen table. Josh sprinted back to the condo and seized it on about the fifth ring. Lara then ran right up behind him and whispered that if it was the game man, he should remember to use another name.

"Yeah," he said, talking now, nodding to Emmet and Lara that it was the man. He headed to Emmet's desk in the bedroom, Lara and Emmet following behind him. "I have Super NES. My favorite is Joe and Mac." Josh became silent and listened to the man talking. "Okay," he finally said, "you said I should save my keys and open the secret area for extra one-ups. Then what?"

Lara was frustrated. There was no line for her to listen in on and hear the man's voice. She held her breath.

Josh was cool, tossing his leg on Emmet's desk and leaning back in the chair as though he were talking to one of his friends. "Right," he said. "Then I can collect all the food and get four extra men. Wow! That's cool. That's cool . . . really." He glanced at Emmet like the man knew his stuff. Then the caller apparently started asking Josh questions, like how old he was and where he went to school. Lara grabbed a piece of paper off Emmet's desk and scribbled some words and held them up for Josh. He nodded acknowledgment.

"Yeah," he said. "I'm twelve." He sneered at Lara, hating to make himself younger. "San Clemente Elementary," he told the man and then gave his friend's name. "Ricky," he said, "Uh, Ricky Simmons." He fell silent, listening. "Sure, that would be great," he finally said. "Free . . . really? You'd let me have those games free? Prince of Persia, Smart Ball . . . Universal Soldier too. What do I have to do?"

Lara put her hand over her chest. This was getting better every second. She was flabbergasted at how sharp her nephew really was. He'd realized that he couldn't say he was in junior high school as he actually was and had told the man he was in elementary school. That was thinking on your feet. Even she hadn't thought of that one.

"My parents?" Josh repeated, glancing at Lara and making a face. "Yeah, I . . ."

Lara leaped right in front of him and then scribbled as fast as she could on the paper: "Your father's dead. Live with your mother." She knew how these people operated from experience. They looked for single family homes, particularly where the boy was deprived of a father's love and attention. These young people made perfect victims for pedophiles, and in many cases they stepped right into the family, convincing the child's mother that they were attempting to help the young boy, take them off her hands every now and then.

"No," Josh continued, taking Lara's cue, "my dad's dead. I live with my . . ." He paused and swallowed. This was not easy for him. ". . . my mother." Then he listened intently and answered again. "She works . . . yeah . . . works at the hospital." He made an expression with his eyes to see if Lara approved. She nodded. A few moments later, he hung up.

"What did he say?" Lara asked eagerly. She wished she'd grabbed the phone and listened to the man's voice, but it was too late now. They'd call him back another time, she decided.

"He gave me some pointers on the game. Pretty good, really. Then he said he could get me a bunch of games free, like demos or something. He never really said how or when, just that I should call back when I get home from school tomorrow."

"What about the other questions?" Lara asked. "The personal questions. And how did his voice sound? Was he young or old?"

"I don't know. It was just a voice. I can't tell how old someone is by their voice. All the dude asked was about my family, my parents, if my mom worked, if I like movies, arcades, all kinds of things. You know . . . you heard."

"Okay," Lara said. "You're out of here guy. I'll see

you in a few minutes at the condo. And I hope I don't have to tell you, never and I mean never call that man back without my knowledge."

"What's this all about?" Josh said. "What kind of case is this you're doing? I didn't think judges did this kind of thing. Isn't this cop stuff, trying to catch people?" He paused and then continued undaunted. "What do you think this man did anyway? It's just a con or something. He isn't going to give me those games for free."

"Go," Lara said, shooing him away with her hands. "Homework, remember?"

Once Josh left, she sat there and tried to put it all together. She sincerely felt they were on to something and thought of calling Rickerson, but then set that thought aside. The poor man couldn't work twenty-four hours a day. She'd call him in the morning. Besides, Benjamin England had called earlier and asked if he could stop by later. She'd decided to give him another chance.

What she really wanted was to purge herself somehow of her growing infatuation with Ted Rickerson. The way to do that would be to focus on someone else.

"Trace . . . number," Emmet said at the door.

"For sure, Emmet," Lara answered before heading back across the courtyard to the condo. "You can bet on it. This man might not be Evergreen or Phillip, but he sounds exactly like a child molester. No matter who he is, we're going to check him out." She paused and looked at the little man. "This could actually be the man who murdered my sister. It sounds unbelievable, but it's possible. Thanks, Emmet. You're a genius."

"I . . . know," he said.

Lara laughed. Emmet might be gravely disabled and frail, but he still had a pretty big ego.

When she turned around, Josh was standing there, listening to every word they said. "I thought I told you to go to the condo and do your homework," she said, her voice sharp, hoping he hadn't heard what she'd said about Evergreen, that he could be responsible for his mother's death.

His eyes were dark and intense. "I forgot my key," he said. Then he turned around and left, waiting for Lara in the courtyard.

Josh was in bed and Lara was sitting in the living room of Emmet's condo with Benjamin England. "I'm sorry," she told him. "Pretty austere, huh?" He was in the one black and gray upholstered chair with the ottoman, and she was sitting Indian-style on the hardwood floor. It was sort of stupid to call it Indian-style when she was a real Indian. She and Ivory used to laugh about that when they were teenagers. They were sipping wine. Lara wasn't really drinking hers. She was just swirling it around in the glass, lost in the past.

"It seems impossible that all this has happened," she finally said. "Only a few weeks ago, my sister was alive. I had no idea she was selling her body, doing the things she was doing."

"Well," England said, "what she was doing for a living isn't the problem. The fact that she got herself murdered is something altogether different. And you think she was blackmailing someone? A high-placed official. Tell me, Lara, who is this man?"

"I can't tell you. We don't really know who it is anyway. I mean, we have suspects, but nothing concrete."

"Come on, you can tell me. You know I'll keep anything you tell me in utmost confidence. I'm dying to know who this person is. Tell me."

"No," Lara said. "I wish I'd never mentioned it. I'm really not in a position to tell you about it right now."

He'd been leaning forward in his chair, thinking Lara was about to reveal the secret. When she didn't, he slapped back and looked disappointed. "Then you shouldn't have mentioned it if you weren't going to tell me. That's like a tease."

Although he was smiling, she knew he meant it. In a lot of ways he was like an overgrown child.

"We could go in your bedroom," he said suggestively. "I mean, at least there's somewhere to sit."

"Oh," she said, "I guess you're right." Even though she had wanted to see him, now that he was here, she just wanted him to leave. Her mind was reeling, filled with visions of catching the killer. And if they were right and this game man was him, they might be able to catch him red-handed—right in the act of seducing a child. But she couldn't use Josh. She'd never put him at risk, and she doubted if there was any child they could use. It was just too dangerous a game right now. She put that thought aside.

As soon as they stretched out on the bedspread in the bedroom, Benjamin reached for her and pulled her to him. "I really desire you, you know. I've been thinking about you ever since that last night we were together. You're so small and delicate, Lara. Your body's like a really young woman's. You gonna be my little girl, huh?" he said, sliding into baby talk and stroking her arm.

He looked at her and she promptly melted, allowing him to run his fingers through her long dark hair. Then his hands started roaming, reaching under her shirt for her breasts. She closed her eyes and imagined it was Rickerson's soft, padded hands. There was no comparison. Even in her imagination, England simply wasn't desirable anymore. Besides, he was grabbing, not stroking. "Stop it," she whispered. "This isn't going anywhere. Not with Josh in the next room."

He ignored her and slipped his hand under the hem of her skirt, his eyes filled with lust. "He's asleep. He can't hear."

His hands were sliding up the silk of her nylons, reaching the area between her legs. It had been so long. She moaned and in seconds he was on top of her. "Unzip me," he said just as he shoved his hand inside her panty hose and raked his fingernails through her pubic hair.

"No," Lara said softly, closing her legs, trapping his hand so it couldn't go any farther. "I told you we can't do anything here. The walls are so thin. Another time. We'll go to your place next time. Just be patient." She turned her head toward the wall where Emmet's file cabinet and computer equipment were located. "It's too soon, Benjamin. I'm not ready for this yet. Try to understand. And Josh . . ."

His hot breath was on her neck, and he was grinding his hips into her. This was definitely not sexy, she thought. The man had not even kissed her. Besides, it wasn't her he desired. It was any woman, any warm and wet port in the storm. He had started unbuttoning her blouse when Lara pushed him off and sat up in the bed. "I said no," she said, her voice forceful but still low. She didn't want Josh to hear.

"Come on, Lara," he said passionately, completely undaunted. "What's the big deal? I want you. I want to show you that I can please you this time. I've been thinking about this all day, thinking of what I was going to do to you." He stood and dropped his pants. "The kid's asleep anyway."

Lara's mouth fell open and she hissed at him, "Stop that. Another time, I said. I have Josh now. I just buried my sister, for chrissake."

Benjamin glared at her and then jerked his pants up and zipped them. "Can't someone else take the fucking kid?" he said. "Why do you have to get stuck with him? Is he going to live with you permanently?"

He was a nice date, Lara thought, seeing him standing here like a spoiled and petulant child, but it seemed to stop there. Once you passed dinner and light conversation, he transformed right before your eyes into the epitome of an asshole.

And his comment about wanting to please her was nothing but an outright lie. There was only one person Benjamin England strived to please: himself.

"Go home, Benjamin," she said, angry at herself for ever starting up with him again. She should have known better. She hadn't purged the detective from her mind. Just the opposite. England's inadequacies made Rickerson's strengths seem even more pronounced.

"And yes, he's going to stay here with me permanently. The kid has no one else and I care about him. For your information, I care about him a hell of a lot more than I care about you right now."

"I see," he said with a sneer. "I guess you don't give a shit about my feelings . . . don't care what I want?"

Now she didn't even feel anger. This man might be a Rhodes scholar, but he was such a jerk that she could feel nothing for him at all. "Get out," she said, narrowing her eyes and fixing him with a cold stare from her slate gray eyes, the kind of look she used when things got out of hand in the courtroom. "And don't call me again. Go track down your murderous client Thomas Henderson. I hear he's out on the streets again."

"Fine," he snapped. "And that was uncalled for, the remark about Henderson. Once a prosecutor, always a prosecutor, Lara darling. Have you forgotten? You're supposed to be a judge." He did a pivot turn on his expensive Italian shoes and stomped out of the condo, his footsteps echoing on the wood flooring, slamming the door behind him.

Lara jumped when the door slammed and then she fell back on the bed. She pulled the pillow to her chest and hugged it. Possibly she was looking too high up the social ladder, dating high achievers like England. Their egos were simply too inflated. They didn't need her; they were in love with themselves. She'd always identified with people who were more down to earth. Her parents were good, basic people. Rickerson was . . . she had to stop it.

She recalled all the Friday nights she'd sat home alone through the years, all the New Year's Eves that came and went. Years ago, she used to peek through the curtains and watch Ivory get into the car with Charley. Lara never had a date on Friday night, and Friday night was date night. Even when she did go out with a boy, he wanted to take her out on Monday or Tuesday, any night but Friday. Ivory was gorgeous. Ivory dated the handsome football player. Her big sister had all the confidence in the world in the classroom, and absolutely none when it came to socializing, particularly with the opposite sex.

Lara stopped herself. Ivory was dead and she was alive.

Josh came into the room in his pajama bottoms, rubbing his eyes. "What happened?" he said. "I heard the door slam."

"Oh," Lara said. "Don't worry about it. It was Benjamin. He's gone."

Josh turned to go back to bed and then paused in the doorway a few moments with his back turned. "I wanted . . ." he said, and then stopped.

"Yes, Josh?"

"I just wanted to say that it means a lot to me that you got me out of that place—that foster home—and that you care, you know." He turned his head around and looked at her over his shoulder with Ivory's piercing blue eyes. A second later, he disappeared.

Rickerson called Lara at eight o'clock the following morning, just as she was rushing out the door to drive Josh to school. It was a long drive and she'd barely make it back in time for court. She told him she'd call him back later unless it was urgent, thinking she'd fill him in on the "game man" when they talked.

"I need you to help me," he said quickly. "I need to find out where Evergreen's son is, and it's not in his personnel jacket. I managed to get my hands on it, but the son was still young then and in school. None of that information is valid now. It hasn't been updated in years."

"I don't know anything about where he is now." Then she recalled her conversation with Irene Murdock. "Look, let me go or I'll be late. I'll check it out and call you, but Ted . . ."

"Yeah."

"You've got to drop this thing with Evergreen. He doesn't limp and the whole thing is just a bunch of bullshit. I go along with you that it has to be someone at the courthouse, but it just isn't Evergreen. It could be anyone, absolutely anyone.

"Shit," she said, hanging up on Rickerson and rushing out the door, where Josh was waiting for her. "I'm going to be late for court."

Then she let the tension go and walked slowly with him through the parking lot, enjoying the morning air, the sun. Let them wait, she said to herself, glancing at the young man next to her. There were priorities in life, she decided, and she'd finally captured one for herself that really mattered. A career was a career and a man was a man, but a person who really loved you as she knew Josh could, in time, and asked nothing but that you return their love was a real rarity.

Her heart swelled. She didn't really need a man anymore. She had Josh. It was almost as if she had a son.

And Josh was dealing bravely with the tragedy that had been forced down his throat. He was trying to go on with his life.

He wasn't alone in that quest. Lara was doing the same thing. Some nights she thought of Ivory and cried alone in her bed.

After she dropped Josh at school, she headed back to the government complex. She parked in the underground garage and quickly made her way into the building.

Picking up her messages and a cup of coffee from Phillip, Lara went into her chambers and closed the door. She wondered what Rickerson had uncovered regarding Phillip. Having him right outside her door was agonizing; she was having trouble concentrating on her work. It was already nine-fifteen and they were calling from the courtroom. "Tell them another fifteen and I'll be there," she said, immediately dialing Evergreen's extension.

"Louise," she said when his secretary answered, "this is Lara Sanderstone."

"Yes," the woman said with her scratchy voice. "He's not in today. He took the day off."

"Oh," she replied slowly. "You know, Louise, I was going to see his son perform, but I misplaced the date and the address. Do you have that information?"

"Just a minute," she said, putting Lara on hold.

A few seconds later, she returned. "I have the symphony calendar right here. He's very good, you know. A very accomplished musician. The next performance is Friday evening at eight o'clock. Of course, you know where the concert hall is in Santa Barbara, don't you?"

She didn't but she would find out. She thanked the woman and hung up and called Rickerson. "He's a flutist with the Santa Barbara Symphony. I don't have his first name, but there's a performance on for Friday evening at eight o'clock."

"You got a date Friday?" Rickerson said.

"You want me to go with you?" she said. "What if Evergreen is there?"

"Hey, it's a free world. We can buy tickets and go to a concert like anyone else. Maybe it's time to make him sweat anyway. He could do something rash."

"Right," Lara said, her hand flying to her neck. Something rash could mean her career. "I don't know if I like that."

"Look, it's doubtful that Evergreen travels all the way to Santa Barbara for every performance. I want to try to talk to his son, and he might be more willing to talk if there's a woman there. When he learns I'm a cop, he might clam up and we'll be wasting our time."

"Why do you want to talk to him? I thought you just wanted to confirm he was the person in the picture."

"Tell you Friday," he said. "I'm about to get the address to that apartment he rents. It's a tough one. They're going through all their cancelled checks to see what apartment they apply his money to every month. Evergreen must have leased it under another name, but has the balls to pay for it with his own checks. Guess he thinks he's invincible. Never thought anyone would start looking under his bed. Kinda know what I mean?"

The whole time they were talking, Rickerson was smacking gum in her ear.

"God," she said, "that gum is annoying."

"Better than cigars," he tossed out. "We got a date or not?"

"We've got a date," she said. She started to hang up and then thought of something. "Didn't he write the apartment number on his check? If he didn't, how would they know how to apply the funds?"

"How the hell do I know? But he didn't. You saw the checks. There was no apartment number on them. Maybe he encloses a note or something."

"I guess that's possible," Lara said. "Did Evergreen's account reflect any large withdrawals?"

"Nada," Rickerson said, "but he might have a safety deposit box somewhere loaded with cash. Or he could have an out-of-state bank account."

Lara lowered her voice to a whisper and kept her eyes glued on the door. "Did you find out what Phillip was doing with the money he borrowed? The name of his bank is Orange National. I just remembered."

"Lara, I wasn't going to tell you this until Friday, but it was Evergreen's son in the photograph. We verified it yesterday."

"No," she said, shocked.

"I told you he was involved in this mess. I've been telling you all along."

"No," Lara said again. After taking a few moments to digest what she had heard, she continued, whispering, "Even if it was his son in the pictures, that doesn't mean Evergreen is a killer—or even a pedophile, for that matter. Phillip could have been one of those young men in the photos like I've been saying all along. Maybe he and Evergreen's son were both victimized by this unknown man in the pictures. You said the man would have a limp and Evergreen doesn't limp. Also, Phillip used to work for Evergreen. That's not such a wild assumption that he knew Evergreen's son."

Rickerson was silent. "Orange National Bank, right?"

"Right."

He hung up and Lara raced to the courtroom.

chapter 20

During noon recess, Lara brought a sandwich and walked into the park across the street, sitting there and eating it alone, enjoying the sunshine. No matter what was going on right now, she decided, she was going to stop and smell the roses. Life was too damn short. Look what had happened to Ivory.

Before her sister's death, Lara had worked through most of her lunch hours. But then she had worked through most of her life, coming down to the courthouse on weekends, staying late every single night, taking work home all the time. What did she think would come of it—that someone would give her a medal, pat her on the back? In San Francisco, members of the Judicial Counsel were probably right now deciding her fate. But these fears were not the ones haunting her, causing her to wake up in the middle of the night in a cold sweat. Even the suspicions about Evergreen she could handle. There was only one thing that Lara could not accept, would never accept. She'd released a man who had murdered her own sister.

"This arrived today," Phillip said, handing Lara a letter when she walked through the door.

"Shit," Lara said, reading the text. It was a letter from the Judicial Counsel stating a review date in two weeks on the charges of impropriety. Her breath caught in her throat. She had prayed it would just go away. She had been wrong. "You read this?" she asked. She knew he had.

"Uh, yes . . . I'm sorry," he said. "But look, I'm sure everything will be fine. They might issue an official reprimand or something, but they're not going to remove you from the bench. I mean, you didn't do anything everyone else doesn't do. I know. I've worked for a lot of judges, remember?"

Lara glanced at the clock. "There's only one thing you don't know, Phillip. The budget came out last month and it doesn't look good."

"What do you mean?"

"Next fiscal year, we'll be minus one position. It calls for substantial cutbacks, even on the bench."

"Really?" he said. "We're already shorthanded. How can they do that?"

"Easy," Lara said, staring down at the paper in her hands. "They can get rid of me. I'm the low man on the totem pole anyway. Now, with these charges, I don't know if I stand a chance." She walked past Phillip, reached for her robe on the hook, and then stopped. "And do me a favor please. Here's my keys. Get my briefcase. It's in the trunk of my car. I need it to take some files home tonight on this case." They now had a full jury panel, and the Adams trial was well underway. Lara needed to review all the details.

"Gonna burn the midnight oil, huh?" Phillip said.

"You got it," she said, heading out into the corridor. "If I want to keep my job, I better be damn good at it."

"I object," the district attorney said. "He's leading the witness."

"Sustained," Lara said quickly.

The witness was the school psychologist who had first reported the sexual abuse of the Adams child. The district attorney tried a different approach.

"Mrs. Mendelson, can you tell the court the circumstances around your report that Amy Adams was being sexually abused by her father?" the D.A. asked.

"The child told me her father spanked her the night before. I asked her how he spanked her and she said, 'With his hands.' I went on to ask her where on her body he had spanked her, and she pointed to a place between her legs."

"Her genitals? Is that correct?"

"Correct. I even showed her an anatomically correct doll we have just for situations like this, and she again indicated her genitals."

"In your eyes, you fully believed this child had been sexually abused and was at risk for additional abuse? Is that correct?"

"Yes, it is."

"No further questions," the D.A. said, sitting back down at the counsel table.

Lara leaned over the bench to the woman, who was standing to leave. "You're not excused yet. Please remain seated." She turned to the defense attorney. "You may begin your cross."

"Mrs. Mendelson, isn't it true that you showed Amy Adams this doll prior to her telling you that her father had touched her genitals? Didn't you actually hand her the doll and point to the doll's genitals, saying, 'Is that where your daddy touched you?' "

"No, I didn't," the woman replied flatly.

"Mrs. Mendelson, isn't it true that you have reported over fifty cases of possible sexual abuse at your school, and of those fifty cases, only eight have been substantiated?"

"Yes, that's true, but there were—"

Lara leaned over and peered at the witness. "Please confine your answers to the questions. Answer yes or no."

"Yes," she answered, her mouth compressed in a line.

"We have no further questions, Your Honor."

Lara felt she could have rendered a ruling now, but this was not a court trial. They had a jury impaneled. It had gone faster than Lara had ever imagined, primarily because the defense had used up their peremptory challenges the first day and the people appeared satisfied with just about everyone. Even the D.A.'s office appeared to be sympathetic to this man and his plight, and they were the ones charged with prosecuting him.

Other than instructing them and overseeing the attorneys, ruling on specific points of law, Lara's greatest impact on this case would occur at sentencing. Adams had committed the crime under great duress, but he had no means to deny it. There were, however, numerous mitigating circumstances. Lara knew the case would fall under the interest-of-justice section of the law, allowing her substantial leeway in imposing sentence. The system had fucked up and their fuck-up had destroyed many lives. The school psychologist had been overzealous and had led the small child in her statements. She was either lying or didn't remember. This kind of mistake was not an easy one to admit.

"Will counsel please approach the bench?" Lara said while the witness stepped down.

When the two attorneys were standing there, she leaned forward and whispered, "I'm going to call recess now. I want to see both of you in my chambers."

"Why?" the district attorney said. They were just getting started, had just this morning delivered their opening statements.

Lara glared at him until he turned and walked back to the table. "This court's in recess for thirty minutes," she said, tapping the gavel lightly and slipping from the bench. The jurors filed out of the courtroom and were escorted by the bailiff to the jury room.

The attorneys followed Lara into her chambers. "Gentlemen," she said once they were all seated facing her desk, "I think this trial is a waste of the taxpayers' money as well as Mr. Adams's money. As he is presently unemployed, I don't see the point of this." She turned to the district attorney. "From what I've read and heard so far, this case should be disposed of by means of a negotiated deposition. Adams is going to be convicted and I'm going to suspend his sentence. This whole thing has been nothing short of a disgrace. We all have egg on our faces—the whole system that allowed this to happen."

Parker Collins, the district attorney, was a hyperactive young man. He sprang from the chair in an uproar, his voice a high-pitched whine. "We already approached them with a plea agreement. We even offered a suspended sentence and they refused. Even the victim in this case just wants it to go away. Steinfield here wants a new Mercedes and doesn't give a shit who pays for it."

"You're out of line, Collins," Lara said, giving him a stern look. It used to be people worked for recognition, honors. Now everyone worked for expensive toys. "Mr. Steinfield, can you tell me why your client failed to accept the people's offer?"

"My client worked in the aerospace industry with a top-level security clearance before the state snatched his children and destroyed his life. If he ends up with a felony conviction, he'll never get another job."

"I see," Lara said, leaning back in her chair and removing her glasses, rubbing her eyes. "Did you advise him of the likelihood of conviction?"

"Of course I did," Steinfield said, insulted by her implication that he hadn't fully informed his client, or had exaggerated their chances for acquittal.

She turned to the district attorney. "Are you prepared to reduce to a misdemeanor battery?"

"Never," the D.A. said emphatically. Lara's small lamps with the green shades had bathed his face in shadows, giving his skin an almost greenish cast. "This woman is permanently scarred. I mean, we sympathize with what Adams has been through, and yes, it was a royal fuck-up, but Adams went crazy out there. A misdemeanor is totally unacceptable."

Lara sighed. "I guess we have nothing more to discuss," she told the attorneys. The trial would continue and Adams would suffer both the conviction and the staggering legal fees. Everyone wanted their day in court, it seemed, no matter what the penalties. The D.A. wandered out into the outer office, but the defense attorney lingered.

Raymond Steinfield was a distinguished man in his late forties with neatly trimmed brown hair, a thick mustache, and a face like Tom Selleck's. But he looked a lot better seated than standing. He was short and squat. Once he stood, any resemblance to Tom Selleck vanished.

"Yes," Lara said, looking up and seeing Steinfield. "Is there something else, Ray?"

He was leaning in the doorway. "Do you know they're trying to take his kids away again?"

Lara fell back in her chair and it squeaked on the plastic mat. "No," she exclaimed. "Social Services, you mean? Why would they do that? The abuse charge was unfounded as I understand it." For a moment she thought she was losing her mind. She'd read all the medical and psychological reports, but she'd been under a great deal of stress. "After all this, why would they try to take his children away again?"

"His wife was committed to Community Psychiatric Hospital last week. The woman's completely destroyed. They're medicating her, but no one knows when she will be released. They think she may have suffered a psychotic break or something." Steinfield paused a moment, frowning. "I mean, they had the poor woman convinced her husband was a child molester and that she had to divorce him to get her kids back. If she had continued to live with him, she could never have her children. She loved the man. It's been horrid for these people, just—"

"Go on," Lara said. "That still doesn't explain why Social Services feels they must remove the children again."

"Because Adams is on trial, pending almost certain conviction, and he's unemployed, a nervous wreck . . . well, you know . . ." He looked hard at Lara.

How well she knew. After what had occurred with Josh, she was beginning to think these people did more harm than good. "Their actions are unconscionable. Why are they harassing this man?" she said, consumed with the injustice of the whole situation, shaking her head. "Are you saying that they don't feel he's psychologically stable enough to care for the children?"

"Basically." Steinfield paused. "And of course, he did lose his cool that day."

Lara bit the corner of her lip. That was an understatement. The reports indicated the social worker would need extensive plastic surgery, but Steinfield knew that. "What about relatives?"

"His mother is alive but infirm. Her parents reside out of the state in a retirement village in upstate New York where they don't allow small children."

Lara felt for the man. She placed her head in her hands, thinking. A few seconds later, she looked up. "What about a live-in homemaker? Surely that would work?"

"He's had three. They've all quit. Evidently, the little girl who was abused in the foster home is seriously disturbed and acting out, screaming for her mother every day, tearing up the house. And no one wants to live with a single male. In addition, there's been tons of press. People think the man is violent. He *is* terribly despondent right now. I'm actually quite concerned."

"I can imagine," Lara said thoughtfully. "And you've fully discussed this with him, attempting to get him to accept a plea?"

"Believe me," Steinfield said, "I don't need another Mercedes. I already have one. Not only that, I'm handling most of this case gratis."

"Well, if he accepted a plea agreement, he could go on with his life, put this behind him, and possibly get Social Services off his back. Do you want me to speak with him personally? I will if you think it will help." This would be a highly unusual tactic, but Lara was a highly unusual judge.

"We'll see," the attorney said, glancing at the outer office, noting that the D.A. had already left and returned to the courtroom. "Maybe tomorrow. He just can't afford a felony conviction. He'll never get another job like the one he had. His career will be over."

They walked together to the courtroom, and Lara studied the man at the counsel table next to Steinfield. He was pale and drawn. As she watched, the muscles in his face twitched and he blinked his eyes about every five seconds. From all appearances, she thought, he was about to have a breakdown himself. As tragic as it was, Social Services might be doing the right thing by removing the children. The whole case was nothing but a nightmare.

By the end of the day, Lara was completely exhausted, both emotionally and physically. At least she didn't have to run to the school to get Josh. Ricky Simmons's mother had agreed to drive him home every day until they moved. She called him at the condo and told him she would be a few minutes late, then remained in her chambers reviewing the facts of the case. If only she could convince the district attorney's office to reduce to a misdemeanor, these people could resume their lives. The social worker, the victim in this case, wasn't the one pressing for the felony conviction. It was the D.A.

As much as she hated to do it, she picked up the phone and called Lawrence Meyer, the district attorney. How he could have said the things he did about her yesterday, she didn't know. But regardless of the mud-slinging and back-stabbing, many lives were on the line and she had to give it her best attempt.

Luckily, she caught him in the office. "Can I come over?" she asked him. "I need to discuss a case with you."

"Certainly," he said. He couldn't very well deny a judge. "I could come over there if you need to speak to me."

"No," Lara said. "I'll walk over now. I'm tired of sitting."

Unlike the courts, the district attorney's office was far from empty. Dozens of attorneys were still moving about the offices, and phones were ringing off the walls. Most of the D.A.'s spent so much time in court during the day that they had to utilize the evening hours to play catch up, prepare arguments, dictate motions, return phone calls.

Lawrence Meyer stood when Lara arrived, extending

his hand but shifting his eyes down to his desk. "Have a seat," he said. "What can I do for you?"

He was intelligent and well groomed, but needed exercise badly, Lara thought, noting that he had a pot belly that made it impossible for him to close his jacket. They'd once been fairly close when Lara was a D.A., and he was the second man in the agency. His harsh comments to Rickerson had stung.

"I think you should reduce to a misdemeanor battery on the Victor Adams matter and let this one go. The poor man is completely destroyed and about to lose his children again. I think he's been pushed as far as he can go."

Meyer bristled, staring hard at Lara. "When did you get to be such a bleeding heart? When you were a prosecutor, you were into nailing people to the wall."

Lara pressed back in her seat and didn't flinch. "Look, Larry I'm about as far from a bleeding heart as a person can get and you know it. But enough is enough. The system has to take some responsibility for what happened in this case and make some concessions."

"We are not prepared to reduce," he said flatly. "If we reduce on this, we'll look like fools. I don't care what the circumstances are, a person can't viciously attack someone and scar them for life and end up with nothing more than a misdemeanor on their record."

Lara stood. This had been a waste of her time. She started to leave and then turned around. "Why did you attack my reputation the other day?" she said impulsively. "I thought we were friends."

"Oh," he said, blanching, "that detective—what's his name—he repeated our conversation?"

"His name is Rickerson and yes, he did."

"Hey," he said, "talk to Evergreen. He's the one who called me and accused you of improprieties. He wanted our investigator to check out all your affairs, even on a personal level . . . and provide him with a full report."

"What personal affairs?" Lara said, trembling with

anger. She felt perspiration breaking out on her upper lip and blotted it with her hand.

"How do I know? You know, the usual dossier we prepare on any subject: associates, finances, romances, etc."

"Have you given him this report? Has it been completed?"

"Some time ago. Let me see." He rubbed his forehead, thinking. "A week ago, maybe two . . . something like that." His face turned bright red. "I'm really sorry, Lara. And yes, I do consider you a friend. I simply became enraged with this man Rickerson the other day, barging in here demanding that we get him a search warrant to gather evidence on Evergreen himself. Hell, he's the presiding judge. I thought it was some type of war between you and Evergreen, and we'd get caught in the middle. I bowed out, that's all."

"Thanks," Lara said facetiously. He certainly didn't bow out gracefully, not the way Rickerson had explained it. "And for your information, Rickerson might be a little rough around the edges and overzealous about Evergreen, but he's a fine investigator. I'm not completely convinced as to his suspicions about Evergreen either, but I don't think it's wise for either of us to simply discount them."

"Fine," Meyer said, standing to follow Lara out, grabbing his briefcase. "Bring me something concrete and we'll go after Evergreen with everything we've got. We don't care who he is; we'll get our sharp knives out without a problem."

He offered to walk Lara to her car, but she was parked in the underground garage. She left and trudged back to the courts by herself.

Lara packed her briefcase with the court file on Hobson, thinking she'd review it that night in greater detail, and headed down the elevator to the car. She might be able to dismiss on a technicality. The victim could always sue Adams for damages. That was the latest rage. Women sued rapists, families sued child molesters, sons sued fathers. Recently a child had sued his parents for divorce and actually won. Now they had three cases filed already in Orange County of children who wanted to dump their parents. It was absurd.

Certainly enough lawyers around, she thought. That was part of the problem. They could tie up the courts with litigation for the next fifty years.

She had nothing for Josh's dinner, her head was pounding, and she was still riddled with anger over Evergreen and the pending matter before the Judicial Counsel. With the proposed budget cuts, Evergreen could have decided to railroad her. She knew he would have a strong voice in this decision, and it was a difficult one. A number of judges would be competing for the same slot next year.

Only one car was left in the garage, and her footsteps echoed in the empty space as she walked across the concrete floor to the Jaguar. Digging in her purse for keys, she had a strange feeling and glanced behind her. She'd heard something, like a brush of a broom across the floor. And it was close, the sound—very close.

No one was there. She craned her neck and squinted, trying to see into the shadows of the garage, but still she saw nothing; it was completely silent. It was probably a rat or something, she thought, just wanting to get in the car and leave.

Fumbling with the keys and the briefcase, she finally dropped it on the ground and unlocked the car. Just as she put one leg inside and started to reach back for her briefcase, a hand snaked from underneath the car and her leg was locked in a steel vise. She fell forward, slamming her head on the roof, one leg out and one leg inside, her legs spread apart like a wishbone, the muscles in her groin stretching like salt water taffy. Pulling her leg out of the car before she was split in two, she suddenly found herself on her back on the concrete floor.

A huge man in dark clothing scurried out from under the car and kicked her onto her stomach. Seizing her leg again, he pulled her across the floor, like an animal taking his kill back to his lair.

"God," she screamed, her heart in her throat, trying to keep her face off the concrete with sheer strength of will, trying to wrench her head around, kicking out with her other leg. Her elbows scraped against the rough surface. She couldn't see his face, but he was tall enough to play professional basketball.

"Help me," she screamed, her heart beating even faster, the sound hammering in her eardrums, so loud that she felt she was under water. Her bladder emptied; warm urine spilled inside her panty hose.

She screamed again in terror. "God, someone help me. He's going to kill me. Help me." This couldn't be happening, she told herself. It just couldn't be happening. She was going to die just like Ivory.

As soon as she was out of range of the car, the man stopped and peered down at her. She quit breathing. She was so completely terrified, she thought her heart had stopped as well.

His face was distorted. He looked grotesque, like something from a nightmare, a horror movie. His nose, eyes, and mouth were squashed inside a woman's stocking, which was knotted on the top of his head. She saw his leg move back to kick her again and rolled across the concrete to escape. She couldn't.

The blow struck near her ribs, and a enormous gush of air left her lungs. Blinding pain seared through her body.

"Where are the pictures?" he yelled, his voice laced with venom, his lips barely moving under the tight stocking mask. "Give me the fucking pictures, bitch."

"In my briefcase," Lara said, panting. "Over there." Then she shrieked again, hoping someone, anyone would hear her. Her voice echoed in the underground garage, and she was surrounded by her own shrill screams.

In his hands was a large knife—a hunting knife or carving knife. Light bounced off the gleaming blade in the overhead light.

"No," she yelled again, completely panicked. "God, no. Please. Don't kill me. I'll do anything."

The knife was at her throat and she dared not move. His breath was hot and foul on her face, filtered through the stocking mask. He pressed down and she felt the cold edge of the blade on the delicate tissue of her throat. She was terrified beyond all reason. She gulped and gagged, certain he'd already cut her throat, imagining the perspiration dripping from her face and dampening her shirt was her own blood. The man was reeking in body odor. To Lara it smelled like death.

I'm dying, she thought. I'm going to die just like Ivory, and Josh will be alone. I'm going to die right in this garage—right underneath the courts. She prayed, her lips moving silently. She tried to think. She waited for death to take her or the man to plunge the knife into her heart. Her eyes darted back and forth frantically. She looked to the ceiling, the pipes crisscrossing and disappearing into the dark corners. She remembered that one car had been left in the garage. She prayed that someone might still be coming. But everyone had gone for the day. She'd never seen the car that was parked in the far corner before. There was no one—no one to help her, save her.

"If those pictures aren't there, you're fucking dead," the man spat in her face, removing the knife from her throat and standing, flipping her over on her side with the tip of his shoe like a sack of garbage.

Lara's hand went to her neck. She tried to get up and fell back down on the hard surface beneath her. For a second she thought she was going to pass out. Everything went black and then returned in blazing color. He was more horrifying than ever, larger than life, a monster sent from the bowels of Hell to destroy her, kill her, cut her into tiny pieces.

"Don't move," he ordered, panting. "Don't move or you're dead. There's nowhere for you to go and no one's coming, so you can stop all the screaming."

Lara was consumed with rage. It was vibrating, pulsing. She was a fighter. She wasn't going to let this man get away with this. She sprang off the garage floor and lunged at him, trying to stick two fingers in his eye sockets and poke his eyes out. Her fingers just struck the panty hose and the man laughed, knocking her back to the ground. Again she leaped up and managed to jump on his back. She tried to press her arm against his carotid artery in a choke hold, something she'd seen police officers do. She even let all her weight go, actually hanging from his body, but he didn't budge. While she was holding onto him, the man started walking off. Lara fell to the concrete floor, landing on her feet, feeling impotent and helpless. The man was a giant. She could never take him down.

"You're a stupid bitch," he said. "Get down and stay down or I'm going to slice your pretty pussy." He turned around and lashed out with the knife, almost connecting with her body. She started to reach for the knife and then realized it was sheer madness. She had felt the blade. It would cut right through her hand. He kept swinging the weapon at her, bent over, reaching out from the level of his waist. When she screamed and stepped back to avoid the knife, she fell backward to the floor. He started cackling again.

This time she did as he said, holding her body rigid, her arms locked at her side, her legs straight out in front of her. The man's disgusting laughter was echoing in the empty garage. Don't fight, she told herself. Don't fight or he'll kill you right now. What she had to do was stall for time. Her nose was running, but she dared not move. She watched out of the corner of her eye as he dumped the contents of the briefcase all over the garage floor and began sorting through them, tossing the papers in the air, searching the side pockets, snarling, growling, cursing.

Locked inside those few moments, memories from the past flooded her mind. She saw herself walking home from school with Ivory, her chunky little legs struggling to keep up with her older sister, her face beaming. She could almost smell her, smell the bubble gum she was always chewing, blowing big bubbles and letting them pop all over her face. Lara closed her hand, thinking she could feel her little sister's hand in her own. Then she saw herself at her graduation from law school, searching for her mother's and Ivory's faces in the crowd, consumed with pride and accomplishment. She saw herself when she was sworn in as a judge. Even though she'd had no family present that day, it had been the proudest moment of her life. She was going to change things, she had thought, actually make a difference. If she'd never become a judge, she would have never released Ivory's killer.

The man was making horrid noises now. Guttural sounds were emitting from the stocking mask. Lara knew he was going to kill her. She could sense it, feel it. Death was swirling all around her. When he'd held the knife to her throat, she had seen his excitement. He sounded and smelled like a wild animal. For a second she let her eyes drift to him and wondered if he was real or some terrible creature spawned from the filth of the city.

She asked herself what had gone through Ivory's mind those few moments prior to death.

Josh's face appeared before her and she tried to freeze it, lock it in. She whispered to him, hoping in some magical way that he could hear her, "I love you, Josh. All my life I wanted a child. Don't be bitter. Try to go on." Tears were stinging her eyes and dampening her face. Her time was evaporating. Soon it would all be over. She crawled inside herself. She prepared herself to die.

"They've not here. Fuck. You lying fucking bitch," he yelled, his voice booming. He kicked the papers away in a fury, heading in her direction with his shoulders squared and his head down like a bull on a rampage. Then he froze in his tracks.

The electronic gate opened with a loud cranking sound, and a white panel van headed down the ramp. The man turned and quickly disappeared into the shadows.

Lara sat up and screamed, "Help me. Over here. Please help me. God, someone please help me."

Just as the white van pulled up beside her and two men in white uniforms leaped out, another car roared past them up the ramp, its tires squealing. It was an older model blue Corvette, one side bashed in, the windows tinted so she couldn't see inside. Lara locked her eyes on the license plate and narrowed her vision so it was the only thing in sight. She committed it to memory, repeating the letters and numbers over and over. "347PJG . . . 347PJG . . . 347PJG." The men were beside her, trying to help her to her feet. She glanced at the name on their shirts: ORANGE COAST JANITORIAL.

"Call the police," she yelled. "Hurry, he's getting away. Call 911 and tell them someone tried to kill me. Blue Corvette," she stammered, gasping, "license number 347PJG."

The men stared at her and shook their heads.

"Hurry. Please. He's getting away. Run. Call the police. I'm a judge." She was standing now, wobbling, weak. 'Didn't you hear me?" she yelled again. "He tried to kill me. Call the police. What's wrong with you? Are you idiots?"

Finally the smaller of the two men spoke, "*No habla Inglés. No comprende,*" he said in Spanish. "*Policia . . . ?*"

Lara shoved them aside and staggered to her car. She used the car phone to call 911, repeating the vehicle description and her location. Razor-sharp pains shot through her side, and she leaned over the steering wheel gasping for breath. She was alive, she kept telling herself. It wasn't meant for her to die now, not when Josh needed her. There was a God, she thought. No one else could have saved her. She had prayed and somehow He had heard her. She could still taste her own demise on the tip of her tongue. She had been so close.

He was probably gone. She should have taken the gun when Rickerson offered it. If only I had, she thought, gritting her teeth against the pain, seeing his distorted face in front of her. If only I'd taken the gun, she kept repeating, imagining the gun in her hand, her finger on the trigger, the explosion reverberating inside the undergound garage. Finally, after all the years of dealing with violent crimes and violent offenders, Lara fully comprehended how a person could reach that point beyond reason. If she had taken the gun, she knew what the outcome would have been. There was absolutely no doubt in her mind.

She would have killed him.

chapter 21

Detective Rickerson didn't show up until the other officers were almost ready to clear the scene. Lara was sitting in the front seat of her car, turned sideways, the car door open, her feet on the garage floor. Her forehead was bruised and scraped, her blouse torn and her stockings ripped. On her neck was a thin red line where he had pressed the knife to her throat. In one spot the skin had actually been broken. The paramedics had treated the scrapes on her elbows and knees with antiseptic and covered them with bandages.

"Are you okay?" the detective said, rushing to the car. "I'll take you to the hospital. They should check you out."

"No," she said. "I have to go home. Josh is with Emmet, but I want to go home." She touched her side and winced in pain, lifting her blouse to look. There was an already darkening bruise right under her rib cage where he had kicked her. "The bastard kicked me," she said, still breathing hard. Every time she took a deep breath, her body was racked with pain.

"You might have a broken rib. Let me take you to the hospital. Josh will be fine."

"No," she said emphatically. "It's just a bruise. I'm fine. All I wish is that I'd had a gun. I want that gun now," she said, searching his eyes. "If I ever see that man again, I'll kill him. I promise I'll kill him."

"You did good, kid," Rickerson said, patting her gently on the shoulder. "You got the license plate. We'll get him. He's probably the same man that broke into your place when Emmet was there. The plate comes back to a Frank Door. If Frank Door was actually driving that car, he got out of jail the day of the break-in."

Lara's eyes grew wide. "What was he in for?"

Rickerson looked away. He'd hoped Lara wouldn't ask that question. "Attempted murder."

"Shit," she said. "Who did he try to kill?"

"Oh," Rickerson said, realizing she would find out anyway, trying to make his recitation casual instead of alarming, "just an ex-wife. He tried to put her in the crematorium at the mortuary where he worked. Nice guy, huh? Guess he didn't want to make alimony payments." He let forth a nervous chuckle.

"Not funny, Ted," Lara said. "Lord, he tried to put her in a crematorium? Really? I've never had a case like that in my life." Just thinking about it made her entire body shiver, and she wrapped her arms around herself. She'd certainly sized her attacker up accurately. If the janitors had not come when they did, she would almost certainly have been killed. "How'd he get out, then? Did the victim refuse to press charges or something?"

"Nope."

"Then he was out on bail?"

"Nope."

She glared at him. "All right. Want to tell me about it and quit playing games? I'm not in the mood, believe me."

"According to the jail, they received a court order the other day to release him. So they released him. We had someone check the court file, and the preliminary hearing is scheduled for tomorrow. There's nothing whatsoever in the file to explain his release. The charges weren't dismissed. He was being held without bail."

Lara was getting the picture. It was beginning to smack of the situation with Packy Cummings. Not only that, but it was beginning to give credibility to the detective's suspicions about Evergreen. "So it was probably Evergreen? Right? Whose name was on the order?"

"The jail says it came from Division Twenty-seven."

"That's the arraignment calendar. Hector Rodriguez is in there now. You think Evergreen called him, told him to release this guy like he did Packy Cummings?"

"I just don't know, Lara. It wasn't Hector Rodriguez's name that was on the order." He paused and his voice lowered. "It was yours."

She was shocked. All the blood drained from her face and she leaned against the door frame. "Mine? T-that's not possible," she stammered. "I didn't sign an order to release this person."

"Then I guess someone forged your name. Since the order was sent by computer from the court to the jail, I don't even know if there was an actual signature."

"My God, every day this gets more bizarre. Evergreen must have done it and put my name on it. That fucking bastard. If you'll give me that gun, maybe I'll just shoot him and get it over with."

Rickerson looked away. This man's record was far worse than Packy's. This man had been convicted five times on felony assault charges and once for rape. Lara was lucky, more so than she realized. If the janitorial service hadn't shown up, he might have raped her. With his last victim he'd said good-by by biting off one of her nipples. They'd convicted him by his teeth marks. He had an overbite.

"We tried to talk to Judge Rodriguez. He wasn't at home, but we'll get him in the morning and find out the particulars. Since the order came from his courtroom, he should know something about it. Pray that he does, Lara. Otherwise, we'll be up shit creek on this one."

"I'm praying," Lara said. "Believe me, I'm praying." She locked eyes with the big detective and filled her lungs with oxygen, then exhaled in one long, painful whoosh. "I can't take much more of this, I just can't, Ted." She fought back the tears. She didn't want the detective to see her crying. Then she thought of something: the budget cutbacks. "Ted, there's another possibility. I mean, it's farfetched, but no more so than your ideas about Evergreen."

"What?" he said, defensive.

"Just that there's going to be one less slot on the bench next year. Someone has to go."

Rickerson's eyebrows arched and he flicked the hairs in his mustache. "You mean someone would do this to get your position?"

"Possibly."

"That's dumb, Lara. Just plain dumb. They might want to destroy your credibility or something like that, but they wouldn't send a goon like Frank Door over here to beat the shit out of you. I'm right about Evergreen." He glared at her and his voice rose a few octaves. "When are you going to believe me? When he walks up to you and blows you away like Packy Cummings?"

Lara didn't answer. She looked away.

He bent down to help her stand. "How did this go down? Did he simply assault you? Did he say anything, give you any indication why he was doing this? Did he rob you?"

"He wanted the pictures. I guess whoever put him up to this told him I had the pictures. I lied and told him they were in my briefcase. When they weren't, he was going to rip me apart. I think he would have killed me with his bare hands. I don't think this man even needed a knife. I think he liked it. You know, the killing, the brutality." Her eyes rose to the detective's. The muscles in her face were twitching. Her voice dropped to a whisper, "I've never been that close . . . you know, to dying."

"Scary, isn't it?" he said. "I've looked down the barrel of a few guns in my life. It's not something you forget, let me tell you. But think about it. It's all related. The pictures, your sister's murder, the break-ins. This couldn't possibly have anything to do with budget cutbacks."

For a few moments they just gazed into each other's

eyes. Lara felt a sense of camaraderie. She knew now what it was like to be a cop. It was no wonder so many of them went off track, became brutal and hardened. Having someone you'd never even met try to end your life was the ultimate injustice.

The silence was shattered. Rickerson slapped his thighs. "It's obvious that this was Evergreen's doing. If the attacker demanded the pictures, then this certainly wasn't a random act. Now that they've searched both your house and the condo, they have to assume you have those pictures on you somewhere—that you're holding them yourself. Has Evergreen been in your office? He could have searched your office and didn't find them. Where do you generally keep your briefcase?"

Lara was silent for a few minutes, thinking. The other officers came over and told Rickerson they were clearing. He stepped aside and said a few words to them and then returned to Lara.

"I generally keep my briefcase in my office," she said. "It's one of the big ones, a litigation case. You know, it's a pain to drag around. But lately, since all this has happened, I haven't been taking any work home, so I had it in the trunk of the car. I just brought it in today. I was going to review the Adams case. And as far as Evergreen getting in my office, it wouldn't be a problem. But what about Phillip, Ted? He could have sent that order to the jail and forged my signature."

"I don't think so. It's Evergreen's son in the photographs, not Phillip. Look, get out and let me drive. I'll call for a unit to pick me up at your house." Then he tilted her head up and peered at her forehead, touching it gently with the tips of his fingers. "This one isn't that bad. It'll go away in a few days, but that one on your side looks pretty nasty."

He helped her to the passenger seat and they took off, Rickerson gunning the Jaguar up the ramp and down the street.

Josh was still at Emmet's. Lara was thankful. As soon as she walked through the door, she'd typed out a message on the computer telling him to come home for bed in an hour. She didn't want him to see her this way. The poor kid had been through enough as it was. She didn't want him to know that someone had almost killed the only relative he had left in the world.

She washed her face. She sniffed her clothes and tossed them in the trash can. Fear smells, she thought, trying to cover the place on her forehead with makeup. Rickerson wrapped a bunch of ice cubes in a towel. He handed it to her when she came out.

"Here," he said, "put this on your side. It will keep the swelling down."

Then he returned to the kitchen and poured them both a stiff drink from Emmet's cabinet. Lara was leaning back in the gray and black chair, her feet resting on the ottoman, her shirt hiked up and the ice pack on her side. Rickerson was wired, tossing the drink down in one swallow, going back to refill it, returning to pace back and forth in front of her chair.

"We're getting close, Lara, really close. Evergreen's got to know that we're on to him now. He's just got to know. And my guess is that he believes Ivory told you something. We know he thinks you have the photos, so he has to have come to this assumption as well. Maybe Frank Door was hired to do more than break into your car. He could have been hired to kill you."

Lara removed the ice and let it fall to the floor. Her blouse had become wet and she hugged herself to keep from shivering.

Rickerson continued, "I think Evergreen is trying to erode your credibility. By spreading rumors that you were using your position to protect your brother-in-law, and initiating an investigation, he's protecting himself. He figures by the time you come forward, no one will believe you. They'll just think you're retaliating in anger, trying to implicate him because he implicated you. He's setting this whole thing up like a pro."

"Yeah," she said. "He is a pro." Presiding Judge Leo Evergreen knew more about the ins and outs of crime than the majority of criminals, Lara thought. He's been a member of the California State Bar Association for over forty years: sixteen years as a prosecutor, twenty-four as a judge. And he was a master manipulator with tremendous power to get what he wanted.

"You know what I think he's doing?" she told Rickerson, finally falling into sync with him on his suspicions of Evergreen. "I think he's shopping for these goons like a person shops from a mail-order catalog. He has a computer in his office and he can pull up anyone's rap sheet, court date, release date, cases. You name it. Any agency in the country will tell him anything he wants to know. Nothing is beyond his reach. With a push of a button, he can manage anyone's release. He could have an army of these guys working for him, doing his dirty work. Not only that, he knows just how dirty they will get. You know, which ones are violent and which ones are not. Once he springs them, they need cash to get out of town before the court date comes up and we issue a warrant, enter it in the system. It's the perfect situation."

"Pretty scary," Rickerson said, looking hard at Lara. She knew that all too well after tonight. "But listen, we're getting close."

"Yeah," she said. "We're getting close, all right. I almost got killed tonight. I thought you weren't going to let anyone hurt me."

The detective's face flushed and his mouth fell open. Then he just shrugged his shoulders.

So much for the hero stuff, Lara thought. "Did you find out anything on the apartment?"

"Not what I wanted to find out. Seems Evergreen owns part of the building. It's an investment . . . something like a syndicate, they said. You know, a group of investors. I don't know a lot about that type of thing, but it sounds like a tax shelter to me. Anyway, he made an initial investment and then pays a certain amount every month."

"Shit," Lara said, sipping her drink and then setting it on the floor. Reaching up, she touched her neck where the knife had been. She could still feel the blade there, feel the cold edge against her skin. "What are we going to do now? We have to connect all these crimes to build a case. I don't want him on some minor charge. I want him for the whole ball of wax."

"I'm sending an undercover officer to his club tomorrow. He gets a massage every week. We're trying to get photos of him naked to match up with the pictures we have, to ID him from the spinal deformity. My man's going to hide in the ceiling, try to film through the air-conditioning vent. We could have gone for his medical records, but that would be a dead giveaway and we'd need a court order. Listen, his son is performing in a concert in Los Angeles tomorrow night. If you're up to it, we'll go then. I don't want to wait until Friday."

"Sure," Lara said. "Josh can stay with Emmet. He adores Emmet. They're inseparable."

"Oh," the detective continued. "Write me a consent to pick Josh up from school tomorrow. I'm going to take him down to the station and show him a photo lineup with Packy Cummings in it. He might have seen more than he knows. Maybe he saw the guy leaving or something that day and can't remember what he saw."

"Sure," Lara said. "Anything . . ."

Lara started thinking. If they could put Packy Cummings at the murder scene, then they would have a connection to Evergreen on the homicides. She suddenly thought of the game man. She went over the events of the previous night and told Rickerson what they had learned, explaining that she hadn't gone any further.

His face instantly flushed with excitement. "Emmet figured this out?" he said, remembering the frail young man. "This is brilliant, fantastic. Hot damn. He should go to work for us. I can't believe it. It could be him, Lara. Jesus fucking Christ, this game guy could be Evergreen himself."

He was smiling, slapping his thighs, practically coming out of his skin. Lara remained in the chair, reserved. "We don't know for sure it's him. Aren't you going a little overboard with all the enthusiasm?"

"You said his name was Tommy Black, right?" he said, a smile stretched his pockmarked face and making him look almost handsome, his rust eyes beaming.

"Right," she said, leaning back down to pick up the ice pack and finding nothing but a puddle of water and a wet towel. "So what does that mean?"

"Guess whose name is on the list of Ivory's clients? You know, calls made from that house. Guess, Lara. Just guess."

"I don't feel much like guessing. Why don't you just tell me?" she said, staring at him. His excitement was contagious. Her breath was coming faster.

"Tommy Black."

Lara's mouth fell open, and for a moment she couldn't say a thing. She was speechless. Then she let out a whoop and a holler that could be heard all over the complex, and Rickerson came over and picked her right up out of the chair and hugged her until she screamed.

"Put me down," she said, laughing in spite of the pain. "My side, remember."

Evergreen was not at the courthouse the following day. Lara called his office and his secretary said he was still out ill but might come in later. "Good," Lara said, hanging up the phone. "Hope you have a heart attack, you bastard." He was scared, too scared even to come to the courthouse. He had to know they were close. They had him on the run. For the first time since Ivory's death, Lara felt in control. Even with what had happened last night, she felt powerful. It could be, she thought, the very fact that she'd faced this Frank Door and survived that had given her renewed strength. With the threat of violence hanging over her head since Ivory's death, Lara had lived with tremendous fear. Although she had tried to suppress it, she had felt it growing with each day, about to consume her. Now that she'd met her worst nightmare, nothing could bring her down.

While she was in a ten-minute recess from court, Judge Hector Rodriguez stuck his head in the door to her chambers. He and Lara were about the same age, and he was a pleasant man, diminutive in size, his skin a dark brown, his mustache thin and wiry.

"I heard you were attacked in the parking garage last night," he said, rubbing his chin. "How in the world did they get in? Crawl under the gates? It's terrifying. Nothing is safe anymore." He paused and looked at her self-consciously. "The sheriff's office called me. They thought I released the man who did this."

Lara took a deep breath and tried to remain composed. "And did you, Hector?"

"Well, no, of course I didn't. I didn't even sit the arraignment calendar that day. I had to take care of some business in Los Angeles."

Lara had heard rumors that Hector was looking for an appointment on the L.A. county bench. Most of his family were up there. He wanted to transfer. She hoped he did before the budget cutbacks were implemented. That would mean a vacant slot. It could mean her job. "Then who covered for you?" She was holding her breath and felt her chest expand. Please, God, she prayed, let it be Evergreen himself. She waited.

"Irene Murdock," he said.

Lara was shocked, "Irene? Why would she release someone like this? My God, if anyone's a stickler for things like that, it's Irene. She would never have made this type of mistake.

"Uh, I don't know." Rodriguez was getting antsy, seeing the tension on Lara's face. "Why don't you ask her yourself?" He ran his hands through his dark hair and looked out over the room. "Anyway, I'm sorry. I'm sorry for all your problems. If there's anything I can do, let me know."

"Don't worry about it, Hector. It certainly wasn't your fault." She inhaled deeply. "I'll talk to Irene.

Don't tell her about this conversation. We're friends, you know."

As soon as he turned and started walking out of the room, Lara saw him favoring his right leg and almost leaped right out of her skin. "Hector," she yelled at him without thinking, "what did you do to your leg?"

"Oh," he said, looking down, "that . . . I pulled a muscle on the handball court a few days ago. Guess I'm not as young as I used to be."

She was getting completely paranoid. If she kept this up, she would end up in the funny farm. She was blanketing the entire courthouse with her suspicions. As soon as he'd disappeared from the door, she put in a call to Rickerson. With the throbbing pain in her side and now learning that her best friend had released this animal, she was about to put her face down on the desk and cry. "Look," she said when he came on the line, "Irene Murdock was sitting the felony arraignment calendar that day. I'm getting ready to call her and ask her if Evergreen was the one who told her to do it. The whole thing is pretty strange."

Rickerson sighed. "How do you explain your name being on the order?"

"Evergreen could have called and told her to release him. Then when the clerk prepared the order, they accidentally put my name on it. I was in that division a few weeks ago. I'm a female judge and so is Irene. Maybe they just weren't thinking."

"Doesn't something like that have to be signed?"

"Of course. Generally, we send it over on the computer and then follow up with the hard copy for their files—you know, the original, with the signature and all. A lot of times they release before they get the hard copy. They've been doing that for years. They can tell it's valid if it comes from our terminal. When we're really busy, we sometimes don't get the original over there for days."

"Then that's probably what happened. Evergreen called her, she cut the order, and then the clerk just made a mistake on the name. There you go."

Lara was silent. The door to her chambers was shut, so she put the detective on the speaker phone and put her head in her hands. "I told Irene that we suspected Evergreen. I don't know why she didn't call me or something. She knew I released Packy."

"You what?" Rickerson yelled in the phone. "Repeat what you just said?"

Lara felt her heartbeat quicken. She was about to be blasted. She grabbed the phone, taking him off the speaker, certain he was going to yell again. "Look, I didn't tell her about the pictures or anything. I just told her we thought Evergreen was a pedophile and possibly involved in my sister's death. God, Rickerson, she's my best friend and she's a judge. She knows Evergreen well. I thought she could give us some information."

"Judge or not, you're a fucking idiot," he said and slammed the phone down.

Lara listened to the dial tone and then called him back. Now she was angry too. "Don't you ever—and I mean ever—hang up on me again. Do you hear me?"

"Calm down," he said. "I'm sorry, okay, but what happened to everything I told you about keeping this to yourself? Christ, Lara, she might have run straight to Evergreen. You've compromised the whole case."

"I have not," she insisted. "Irene would never do that. She was genuinely concerned. I'm going to call her right now and see if Evergreen called her about Frank Door. And I've asked the jail to send me a copy of the court order. I'm going to get to the bottom of this."

"Go ahead," he barked. "Why don't you tell the whole fucking courthouse? Maybe you should run down there and tell Evergreen himself." Again he slammed the phone down in her ear.

Lara decided not to call. She was almost certain Irene was in chambers. She always took recess at this time of day. She marched down the hall and let herself in. Her secretary was evidently out somewhere.

"Lara," Irene said, peering at her over her glasses.

"Come in . . . have a seat. My God, what happened to your face? Were you in an accident?"

"Someone attacked me in the underground garage last night. His name was Frank Door. Ring a bell?" Lara didn't sit down. She remained standing in front of Irene's desk.

The woman looked away as she spoke, avoiding Lara's eyes. "Frank Door . . . name sounds familiar, but I can't recall from where. I think I sentenced him one time years ago."

"Well, according to the records, Irene, he was released the other day when you were sitting the arraignment calendar for Hector. The jail received an order from Division Twenty-seven. The man is a certifiable maniac." Lara grimaced. "You should hear the circumstances of this man's crime. God, Irene, he tried to cremate his ex-wife alive. Can you believe it? He actually tried to put her into the crematorium where he worked. He was supposed to be in court for a preliminary hearing today on an attempt 187. He certainly wasn't supposed to be released. Did Leo call you and ask you to do that, because if he did—"

Irene cut her off. "No, no, I don't think so." She thought about it a few seconds and then changed her mind. "I mean, he might have said something. I could have forgotten. Things were furious in there—a real zoo. I didn't do this, Lara. I swear. At least I don't think I did." She rubbed her forehead in dismay. She looked tired and strained. "If I did, it was a horrid error."

"Right," Lara snapped back, oblivious to her friend's distress. "A horrid error is an understatement. The man almost killed me."

Irene looked extremely distressed now. She was blinking and Lara could see her chest rising and falling. "I'm not used to the pace of the arraignment calendar. I just don't recall. I'm so sorry. What a terrible error. Did they catch the man?"

Lara didn't know what to say. "No, they didn't catch him," she finally told her. Then her face softened. Irene certainly hadn't meant to do something that would have caused another person harm. "Not yet. Anyway, forget it," she said.

The phone on Irene's desk started ringing. She looked at it and started to ignore it and then decided not to. "I guess I have to take that call," she told her. She punched the button and picked up the phone. Then she held the receiver away from her ear and whispered to Lara, "We'll talk later."

Lara headed to the door. She had to be back in court. She was already late. She headed straight to the courtroom. Once again she had lashed out when she should have remained silent. Irene was her friend. Everyone made mistakes. Maybe Evergreen was responsible for this anyway, she thought. He could have put a note in the file and Irene just forgot about it. About to enter the rear door to the court, she changed her mind and headed back to her office.

"Did that order come over from the jail?"

"Yes," Phillip said, handing it to her without looking up.

"Call the court and tell them I'll be another five minutes." With the computer printout in her hand, she made her way to the arraignment calendar. They were in session, Judge Hector Rodriguez on the bench. Lara crept in and bent down to talk to the clerk. Rodriguez glanced at her and then turned back to the courtroom. He was in the midst of an arraignment.

"Do you remember this order?" Lara whispered to the clerk, putting the paper right in front of her.

The girl looked at it and then looked at Lara. "No. Why?"

"Well, it was issued from this courtroom. It says Division Twenty-seven right there."

"But it's not our terminal. See?" She pointed to a series of numbers in the corner of the document. "That's not ours. I don't know who that terminal belongs to. Our number is 45892. This was transmitted on 45891. It's got to be someone in superior court, but it's not us."

Lara snatched the document away and crept back out of the courtroom. As she rushed down the hall, she repeated the number to herself. Then she remembered.

Terminal 45891 was on her own desk.

Evergreen must have entered her office, probably while she was out and Phillip was at lunch, and transmitted that order from her terminal. If she tried to do something about it, no one would believe her. They would assume she'd staged the entire event, possibly to attract people's sympathies, or to take the heat off herself because she was under investigation. Leo was smart. Every step he made was carefully orchestrated.

Bringing the court order up to her face as she walked, she stared at the typed lines. If she had typed this document, with her limited skills, it would have taken her hours. Could Leo Evergreen type? The words were all aligned perfectly. Not only that, what she was looking at was a form stored on the county's computer software with the specifics of Door's case entered in the blanks. Would the presiding judge know how to find this form on the county's massive computer system and execute it himself?

Lara exhaled and hit the back door to the court.

"All rise," the bailiff said as Lara took her seat on the bench.

She didn't hear the bailiff's words. She looked right over the heads of the spectators and attorneys as if they weren't present. Evergreen might not know how to operate the computer software, but Phillip certainly did.

chapter 22

Rickerson left Josh at the station in the hands of baby Bradshaw for the photo lineup and rushed home for an early dinner with the family. He had promised Lara he would pick up something for Josh and Emmet to eat on the way to the complex. As soon as he wolfed down his food, he got up to shower and dress for the concert.

After he cleared the table, Stephen followed his father into the bathroom and watched him shave. "Mom called today," he said, leaning back against the door frame.

"Oh, yeah?" Rickerson answered.

"She wants you to send her some money, and she's pissed that you haven't called her lately."

"Sure," he said, frowning in the mirror, "I'll rush right out and print some up. If she calls again, tell her we've got about fifty bucks until payday. She'll have to get a part-time job or a loan."

"I filled out an application at Baskin and Robbins today. They think they can use me a few days a week after school."

Rickerson dropped his razor in the sink and faced his son, hitching up his towel. "I don't want you working. First, I need you here in the house, and second, your grades are more important than the twenty bucks or so you could earn. It won't hurt your mother to get a job. She's the one who insisted on this whole thing." He rinsed his face and splashed on aftershave. "Besides, this next paycheck will put us over the top. I've been putting in a ton of overtime."

Heading to his closet, he took out his best sports jacket and laid it out on the bed, turning to the dresser for a dress shirt. "What tie would look best with this?" he asked his son, holding two or three ties in front of him.

"The brown paisley. Hey, Dad, where did you say you were going tonight?"

Rickerson looked at his son and saw the gleam in his eyes. "I'm working."

Stephen smiled broadly. "Really? You're working, huh? You're getting all dressed up like this to go to work? You've got a date, don't you? You're finally getting off your duff and going out on the town. Hot damn, Dad. 'Bout time."

Rickerson's face fell. "I'm working, okay? I'm working undercover. Who would go out with me anyway?"

"A lot of women. Leslie thinks you're a hunk. She even told me that the other day."

Leslie was a divorced neighbor three doors down. She was one of the few people that knew Joyce was gone. She was always coming over with casseroles and food for the kids. The woman weighed about two hundred pounds, was about four feet nine, and had four screaming little kids. "Thanks," Rickerson said, "but no thanks, kid. I'm hard up, but I'm not that hard up."

A few seconds later, Rickerson went in and spoke with Jimmy, gave him a hug and left.

Lara glanced at her watch and was relieved that the day was over. They had run past six o'clock. Poor Victor Adams looked more strained today than yesterday. He was teetering on the brink, but no one could save him, no one but the D.A. and he had refused. She instructed the jurors, tapped the gavel, and adjourned for the day, slipping from the bench. Rickerson had taken Josh to the police station for the photo lineup. She'd told him to drop him at Emmet's and then come to get her at the condo.

Back in her chambers, she was about to grab her

purse and leave. Phillip had already left. Then she looked up and saw Leo Evergreen standing in her doorway.

"Leo," she gasped, completely startled. "I thought you were ill."

"I was," he said, taking a seat in front of her desk. "I came in after lunch. I've been fighting this flu for a month now. I think the whole courthouse has it."

Lara walked backward to her desk. She felt safer there. Her heart was racing. She couldn't stop herself from staring. This man, she thought, her whole body trembling, could be the person responsible for her sister's death. Here he was—only a few feet away, in the same room, breathing the same air.

She forced herself to sit down and started moving papers around. "Uh, what can I do for you?" she finally said.

"I heard you were attacked yesterday. Terrible . . . bad business." He was shaking his head, not looking up. "You shouldn't stay late and go to your car alone. I know you do that a lot."

She didn't say anything. What could she say? Someone had let Frank Door into the underground garage. A person could crawl through the gates, but Frank Door had managed to get a car down there. For that he needed a connection. That connection might be sitting comfortably in a chair right in front of her.

He continued, "Something else has come up. I really hate to even mention it to you after what you've gone through, but I feel I must. Are you dating Benjamin England?"

Lara tried to read his eyes. They were expressionless—dark, watery pools that went nowhere. Her hands were trembling. She placed them in her lap so he would not see. She couldn't bear for him to know that she was frightened. Even in her lap, her fingers were dancing and fluttering. One foot started tapping involuntarily, and she held her knee with her hands. He was waiting for her to answer. His question had disappeared from her mind. "I'm sorry," she said. "What did you say?"

"England . . . have you been dating Benjamin England?"

"I've had a few dates with him," she said. "What's this about?"

"Oh," he said, pausing for a long time, breathing heavily. "I-I was hoping it wasn't true. The D.A. is filing a grievance. They heard you were dating England and believe you were prejudicial in your ruling of the Henderson matter."

Lara slapped back in her chair so hard that she slid across the plastic mat and had to use her heels to bring herself back to the desk. Then she couldn't contain herself and exploded, the tension racing from her stomach to her mouth. "That's insane. First, I wasn't even dating England at the time of the Henderson ruling. I would never date a defense attorney on a case I was hearing. Second, I would have made that ruling even if I'd been sleeping with the damn D.A."

"I see," Evergreen said, letting his mouth fall open and remain that way. Finally he closed it and said, "Relax, Lara. This is the type of thing you must deal with when you're on the bench. You have to watch every step you make. I've tried to tell you that ever since your appointment."

Lara's eyes were blazing, but she didn't speak. Perspiration was popping out on her brow, her upper lip, trickling down between her breasts.

"They want the ruling overturned and the matter brought back before the court," Evergreen continued. "I may have to oblige them. Are you lovers?"

Lara spun her chair around to the wall. This couldn't go on. She picked up a paperweight and held it in her hands, thinking in another second she was going to hurl it at him. "I don't think I care to continue this conversation any longer, Leo," she said in a firm, flat voice, one she hardly recognized as her own. "Whether England and I are lovers or not is no one's business but mine. I repeat, I wasn't dating him at the time of the

Henderson ruling. We started going out a week or so after. I'm no longer seeing him. If they want to open up a full-scale investigation, then so be it."

She didn't turn around until Evergreen was almost out the door. Then she slammed the paperweight down on her desk as hard as she could, and the older man glanced back at her before stepping through the door.

Tears were gathering in her eyes. She'd felt so strong earlier, so self-assured. Now she was shaken, enraged. Everywhere she turned, everything she did was now suspect. Somehow she had gone from being a respected professional to teetering on the edge of losing it all. She grabbed her purse and stood to leave, glancing around at her chambers, wondering if she'd be here much longer. There was only one good thing about it.

Right now she didn't really care.

The traffic was light and the condo close. Lara rushed back and jumped in the shower. When she got out, she stood there naked and studied her reflection in the mirror. She didn't really have a bad body. She was slender and her breasts had yet to start drooping. They would. She knew that. It was all just a matter of time. She turned around and looked at her backside. That would be drooping too before she knew it. Taking out all her makeup, she dumped it on the countertop and started painting. Tonight she wanted to look good. She wanted to look pretty and feminine. What she really wanted was to look like Ivory, but that was impossible. Sometimes she thought Josh's resentment stemmed from the fact that she did resemble his mother. He looked at her and maybe got angry—that she was alive and his mother was dead.

As she applied blush to her cheekbones, she stared into her own eyes. "You're going to sleep with him," she said.

Rickerson made her temperature rise, her pulse quicken. She darkened her eyebrows and then tossed the pencil onto the counter. Her sudden attack of vanity, the man constantly in her thoughts—she knew it was going to happen. She resigned herself to it. So he was married. She didn't want to wreck his home or steal him away from his wife. She certainly didn't aspire to marry him. She just wanted to borrow him for one night, one day, a few stolen hours. Was that so despicable? After everything she'd been through, didn't she deserve a few minutes of pleasure?

"Yes," she said out loud, "you're despicable." She didn't know when it would happen, but she knew she was willing.

"What will one little tryst with a cop do?" she asked her mirror image. "They're ready to fry me. Might as well go out in a puff of smoke."

"I want that gun," she told Rickerson in the car. When he'd walked through the door, he'd looked quite dapper. He was wearing a nicely tailored rust-colored sports jacket that flattered him considerably and looked great with his red hair.

"No problem," he told her, reaching down where he had the gun strapped to his leg with a few pieces of leather. He handed her a small-caliber pistol, the same one he had tried to give her before. "Be careful. It's loaded. It's my spare."

Lara turned it over in her hands, feeling how light it was. Such a small thing, she thought, wondering how much it weighed. But this little item was enough to end someone's life in a matter of seconds. It was amazing. She opened her purse and dropped it inside. They were stalled in traffic headed into Los Angeles. The concert began at eight.

"Rodriguez is a pretty straight shooter," she told him. "If you're a Hispanic judge in Orange County, you've got to be. I think he'll sign a warrant when we put everything together. I don't think he'd hesitate for a minute if the evidence is substantial."

"Sounds good," Rickerson said, a smug expression on his face. "Is that all you've got for today?"

"Guess so," she said. She'd already told him about

the court order, the fact that someone had issued it from her own terminal. And she'd told him about her conversation with Evergreen just before she'd left for the day. "I was really excited. I thought you would be too." She was disappointed. What she'd told him didn't seem to impress him at all. Getting a judge to cooperate would be a big accomplishment.

"Oh, I'm excited, lady. Let me tell you, I'm fucking about to piss in my pants."

She turned and leaned forward, bracing herself against the dash. "You look like the cat that swallowed the canary. Want to share it with me?"

He slapped the steering wheel. "We got lucky. I don't know why I didn't think of this a week ago, but I didn't. Josh identified Packy Cummings. Picked him right out of a photo lineup."

"No . . . really? How? He said he didn't see anything that day."

"That's because he didn't know what he was seeing. Evidently, he saw Cummings's face in a car coming down that hill. Every day he stopped and took a breather before going up. Packy was flying, speeding, burning up the roads. And guys like Josh love Camaros. They're hot cars, and a red one—not a teenage boy around isn't gonna take note. He looked, but of course he had no reason to remember. After he got to the house and saw the bodies, he forgot all about the man in the car. But today he remembered."

Lara put her hands together like she was praying and looked at the top of the car. "Thank you, God," she said dramatically. "I didn't think You were there, but I guess I was wrong." She then turned to Rickerson. "More, tell me more. This is better than sex."

"He might have seen him loitering around your street, over at the McDonald's. From what he said, it was around the time Cummings was shot. He said he saw a man on the phone and recalled seeing him somewhere before, but he couldn't remember where."

"Now he's made," Lara said. "Right?"

"Right, kid. Now he's made. If Evergreen talked you

into letting Cummings out O.R., which he did, then there's the connection we've been looking for. Not only that, but forensics put the finishing touches on it this evening. The skin samples found under your sister's fingernails came from Packy Cummings, and the semen sample is a match."

Rickerson saw an opening in the traffic and stomped on the accelerator. Then the line of cars braked. Not wanting to wait, he raced down the off ramp and then headed back up the on ramp. For the remainder of the drive, he repeated this technique, by-passing the traffic.

"Do we have enough for an arrest?" she asked, her spirits soaring, about to go right through the roof of the car into the stratosphere.

"Hey, you're the judge."

"What about Phillip?"

"Bradshaw says he looks clean. He did make two loans. One for ten grand a few months ago and a recent one for fifteen. We didn't match his phone number to any on the list. I think that rules Phillip out."

"I'm not so sure about that, Ted. He might have an apartment somewhere. Maybe he simply lists his mother's address on his employment records. A lot of people do that—young people who move from apartment to apartment.

"Lara, he made loans totaling twenty-five grand. Where'd he get the other fifteen? We found forty thousand in the safe, remember?"

"I don't know," she said. "Borrowed it from his mother."

Rickerson rolled his eyes around, giving Lara a look that said let it go. Before she could stop herself, she broke out laughing. Just being here with him, all dressed up and on their way to a concert, made Lara feel giddy.

"Does Josh get the forty grand?" she asked. "I mean, I could use it for his education. The killer's certainly not going to come back and claim his money."

Rickerson smiled at her. "I think you're right. I

didn't give it any thought. Do you think we have enough for an arrest warrant for Evergreen?"

"Yes," she said. "I say we do. I think we can go to Rodriguez in the morning unless you think we should wait until you trace the game man's phone number. I thought you were going to do that today."

"I let baby Bradshaw—you know, the chief's son—handle it and as usual, he fucked it up, had them trace the wrong number. Before I knew it, it was too late. We have the address, an apartment, for this Tommy Black, but we can't get in without a search warrant. I'm sure that's where the phone number will come back to—that apartment."

Lara sat back and closed her eyes. Rickerson was silent. Then she felt something. He had let his hand drift across the seat to hers and was lightly touching her fingers with his own. She didn't move; she didn't open her eyes. She relished the contact, the exchange of energy. She felt a rush of affection for this man. It wasn't even physical desire. It was real: genuine emotion and admiration. He was strong but sensitive. He had old-fashioned values. He was the kind of man who would make a great father for Josh. She stopped herself. She could reconcile her conscience to a brief affair. The way she was thinking now was completely off base. He had two kids, for God's sake. As if he could read her thoughts, the hand disappeared and the moment was gone. Rickerson steered the car into the parking lot of the concert hall and parked.

"This is it, kid," he told her, explaining his theory that Evergreen had molested his own son. Then he told her what he planned to do. "After the concert we'll go backstage. Watch the section he's in and see if you can spot him. We'll tell him something. I don't know. That we're music critics and we want to interview him. How does that sound?"

"I don't know a thing about music, Ted," Lara said. For a moment she leaned against the car, her bruised side throbbing from the long drive down. "I don't know if I can pull something like that off. Can't we think of something else? And why would he tell a music critic or a reporter that his father molested him? That's absurd."

It was dusk and people were walking past them, heading to the doors of the concert hall. Lara caught whiffs of cologne and men's aftershave. Rickerson joined her, standing right next to her and taking out a pack of gum. He offered it to Lara, but she waved it away. She sniffed. Even the detective smelled good. He was actually wearing cologne. And he wasn't smoking a cigar.

"You look really pretty tonight, Lara," he said. "I don't think I've ever seen you look this pretty."

She smiled. It was the makeup. She'd have to start wearing it every day. "I didn't really have much to wear at the condo," she said, looking down at her modest black jersey dress.

"I like it," he said. He glanced at her legs. Then his eyes rose to her chest. The dress was snug. It made her look more shapely than she really was.

She turned and touched his jacket, running her fingers along the lapels. "Nice jacket."

"You like, huh?"

"I like you," she said. As soon as she had said it, she wanted to take it back. She started walking across the parking lot to the concert hall. In seconds, he was next to her and another moment had vanished. "Go over again what we're going to do?"

"Look," he said. "We'll tell him this story—the music critics thing, get him to go for coffee with us, and then tell him another story. You plead and beg. Don't tell him about your sister. Make up another story about how your son was molested by his father. You know, something like that. Got it?"

"Got it," she said. "Hope this works."

Lara spotted Evergreen's son immediately. She had seen his picture on Evergreen's desk many times. She actually enjoyed the concert, sitting next to Rickerson, their thighs touching, everyone around them seeing them as a couple. On several occasions during the concert, he turned and just stared at her. She kept waiting for him to say something, but he never got the words out of his mouth. Once he picked up her hand and actually put it in his lap. She chickened out and pulled it away. She didn't even think he was aware that he had done it. Maybe he held his wife's hand like that, she thought. That was enough to put a damper on her feelings.

As soon as the concert was over, they scooted backstage. "Robert Evergreen," Rickerson said, pumping his hand. "This is my associate Shirley Brown. We're with *Music Today*. Can you give us a minute?"

He was in his early twenties, and it was obvious that he was painfully shy. Not once did he look either of them in the eye. "*Music . . . World?*" he stuttered. "I've never heard of that. Is it a magazine?"

"Yes, a new magazine. We want you for our first edition . . . want to do an interview. You were outstanding tonight. Tremendous performance. Inspired, actually. Didn't you think so, Shirley?"

The young man didn't speak. He shuffled his feet around and gripped his instrument in his right hand. "I-I don't think so," he finally said, his voice so low they had to strain to hear it. "Please, excuse me,"

"Wait," Rickerson said, touching the sleeve of his tuxedo. "Come on, give us a chance. We're a new magazine. We need the interview. Hey, it will advance your career."

The young man took a few steps forward and then stopped. Rickerson was blocking his way. "What do I have to do?"

"Great," Rickerson exclaimed loudly, turning to Lara. "Isn't this great? We're going to get an interview with Robert Evergreen. Boy, the boss will be impressed." He turned back to the man. "All you have to do is go and have a cup of coffee with us. We ask you a few questions and that's it. Then you're immortal—in print. Your father will be thrilled."

There it was. Both of them saw it. The moment they

mentioned his father, he completely froze and all the blood vanished from his face.

"What . . . are you talking about? Do you know my father? Did he arrange this?"

"We've heard of him, of course. He's an important man. I know he'd be pleased."

"I have to go," he said and again tried to walk away.

"Please," Rickerson said, looking for Lara for help.

"Yes," she said. "Please, they hired me on a trial basis. If I don't get an interview tonight, I could lose my job."

His eyelids fluttered and he finally looked up. "All right, give me a minute."

"No problem," Rickerson said. "We'll wait right here."

The man vanished into the crowd of musicians, and Rickerson took out another stick of gum. "Quiet, nervous man, huh?"

"Yes," Lara said. "Too quiet. You might just be right about Evergreen molesting him. He fits the profile."

They waited. Ten minutes turned into twenty. The lights went off on the stage, and most of the musicians had filed past them, exiting through the rear doors. "Think he went to take a piss and fell in?" Rickerson said. Then he stopped one of the musicians. "There's not a another door around here is there?"

"Yes," the man said, carrying a large cello case. "Right over there behind the curtain. It goes to the east parking lot."

"He skipped." The detective grabbed Lara's hand and pulled her behind him as he rushed to the back of the building. They looked in every room. Rickerson even checked the men's room.

Robert Evergreen was gone.

chapter 23

On the drive back to Santa Ana, Lara's side was throbbing, her elbows smarting from the scrapes, and she was exhausted. More than anything, she was annoyed that Rickerson had made her come on what had amounted to a wild goose chase. She should have known better.

"Why would Evergreen's son tell us anything?" she said sharply. She kept moving around in the seat, trying to get comfortable. "This was nothing but a waste of time."

Rickerson was silent. Rolling down the window, he punched his unmarked police car up to eighty miles an hour. The wind beat against his face. He wished he had a cigar and felt in his pocket even though he knew he hadn't brought one.

"I don't really feel like going home right now," he said. "Want to go for a little ride?"

She didn't answer. She was looking out the passenger window, lost in her thoughts.

"I guess that means yes. Right?"

Still she didn't answer. He took the next exit and headed for the beach. There was this one stretch of road, high on a hill near Long Beach, that looked out over the ocean and the city. He hadn't been there for years.

They climbed a winding, narrow road and Rickerson strained to see if they were headed in the right direction. Everything changed so fast around here. Sometimes he couldn't recognize a place in only a matter of months with all the building. The views were breathtaking up here, particularly on a clear night like this one. He wanted to stand there and look out at the lights, the moon reflecting on the water.

And he wanted to do it with Lara Sanderstone.

He pulled up near the edge and parked, cutting the ignition.

"I'm sorry I snapped at you," Lara said, turning to him. "I guess everything's been too much. You know, last night . . . Evergreen today . . . the whole thing. And then with this Frank Door . . . I think I'm handling it and then suddenly I realize I'm not handling it at all. Do you know what I mean?"

He did. "Let's get out. It's gorgeous up here."

When they were standing near the edge of the ravine, gazing out over the lights and the ocean, he reached for her, touching her fingers lightly and then letting the contact go.

"It is beautiful up here, Ted," she said, reaching her own hand out and lacing her fingers in his. "It's so peaceful, so calm."

He clasped her hand and pulled her closer. Then he draped his arm over her shoulder. Neither of them moved. They didn't look at each other. It was an awkward moment. They both knew it was the first step: a small gesture but a momentous one. Lara felt strange standing there with the detective's arm around her. She had wanted it, but now she was a bundle of nerves and apprehension. After untold moments had passed, he casually pulled her even closer, sheltering her under his arm. Even with the wind blowing, she could hear him breathing. It was heavy, labored. He was nervous too.

"'I panicked yesterday when I heard you were attacked. I wrecked the car." His voice was soft and low. Lara had to strain to hear him.

"The police car?"

"You got it. I ran right into the back of a woman with three kids in the car. Damn. Thank God, there were no injuries."

He wasn't looking at her while he was talking. His eyes were locked on the ocean, the view. Lara couldn't believe it. He was actually that concerned for her, shook up enough to wreck his police unit. He must be terribly embarrassed, she thought. Then she wondered if he'd have to pay for the damages. She pressed her head down to his shoulder and felt the coarse grain of his jacket. Someone really cared about her.

Suddenly he faced her and gathered her in his arms. She didn't resist. He didn't kiss her. It was an emotional embrace, the way a person hugs a long-lost child, a husband coming home from the war, a parent they haven't seen in years. He squeezed her even tighter, placing his own cheek next to hers. Except for his mustache, his skin was soft and smooth, clean-shaven. She forgot all about the acne scars. Right now he was the most attractive, masculine, and appealing man she'd ever known. Right now he was a long-lost love finally returning.

Her breasts were against his chest. She inhaled his cologne, the scent of his hair. They were up quite high and the wind was blowing, the evening air chilly. But she was warm, protected.

"Ted," she said softly.

"Don't say anything," he said, his voice scratchy. "Please, just let me hold you. I've wanted to hold you like this for days now . . . almost since the first day I saw you in that house in San Clemente."

They stood there in each other's arms. Moments passed. With his hands he turned her around and pulled her back against his body and wrapped his arms around her waist, trying not to touch her bruised side. He didn't want her to see the look on his face, in his eyes. He didn't want her to see the acne scars. What he wanted was for her to imagine that he was handsome, rich, and successful. More than anything, he wanted her to want him.

"Lara," he whispered, his face next to hers. "I've never cheated on my wife. Not once. Believe me. Not once in all these years."

"Then you shouldn't start now," she said softly.

"I only want to hold you, be close to you for a few minutes. Then we'll go back."

"Do you love your wife?" Lara asked, leaning even farther back against his body, feeling his genitals through his pants, asking herself if he was already aroused or if what she was feeling was normal. Whatever it was, it felt good. She moved her hips around. He grew. Her heart was racing. She wanted him. It was obvious that he felt the same. She was tempted to reach behind her and just grab him. She couldn't wait much longer.

"I loved my wife, Lara, and I tried to give her a good life, but she wanted more. She—she left me."

Lara jerked out of his arms and turned to face him. "You're divorced?" she said, her heart in her throat.

"No," he said, "I'm not actually divorced, but my wife moved out over three months ago. The way it looks now, she's not coming back."

"But you—you wear a wedding ring," she stammered. The wind was whipping her hair in her face. She took the clasp off and let it fly free. What she wanted to do was take all her clothes off and let them just blow away in the wind, then stand there completely naked with this man only an arm's reach away. Her heart was soaring. He was separated. He was on the verge of a divorce. "If you're lying to me, Ted, I swear to God I'll kill you."

"I'm not lying," he whispered. "Why would I lie about something like that?"

They were facing each other, the moonlight throwing shadows over their faces. His hair didn't even look red. It looked dark brown. The shape of his face, the slant of his nose, his large expressive eyes, all made him look unbelievably handsome.

"I want you, Lara." His voice was not the voice she recognized. It was softer, deeper. It was crackling with emotion and desire.

"Ted," she said, throwing herself into his arms, practically knocking him to the ground. He started kissing her face, her nose, her cheeks. His mustache tickled. She loved it.

"You're so beautiful," he said, lacing his fingers through her dark hair, placing his face there so he could smell it, taking a strand and twirling it around his finger.

"No, I'm not," she said softly, pecking again and again at his face with small, delicate kisses. She felt sixteen again; she felt like screaming and jumping up and down. She had never been this excited and stimulated in her entire life. She latched onto his earlobe and almost took a bite. She'd wondered what his skin would taste like; it tasted salty and sweet at the same time.

"Yes, you are. Maybe because you don't realize how pretty you are is what makes you beautiful."

This time his mouth connected with hers. His lips were so soft, the inside of his mouth so clean. She slid her tongue over his teeth. Briefly she asked herself if he had quit smoking cigars in anticipation of this one moment. He didn't reach for her breasts or grope between her legs as most men would. He just engulfed her body in his arms and held her as tightly as he could.

"Just tell me one thing," he said, panting with desire. "Tell me you feel the same way—want me as much as I want you."

"Yes," she said, her caution gone. "God, yes. Can't you tell? Are you blind? I've been dreaming about you. I thought you were happily married. I thought—"

Instantly he picked her up in his arms and carried her to the car. He placed her on the hood, her legs open, positioning himself between them, running his hands from her ankles to the top of her thighs along her nylons. She sighed. He lifted her around the waist in the air with one hand and pushed the hem of her skirt up around her waist with the other. Then he put her back on the car and started tugging on her panty hose. When he couldn't get them off, Lara pulled them off herself. She could feel the cold metal of the car on her skin, on her buttocks. "Here," she said, reaching for his crotch, wanting to please him, touch him.

"No," he said, breathless. "Not yet."

She could barely see his eyes in the moonlight, but she glimpsed the passion there. They were dark, fluid.

"I've waited too long for this to make it go fast," he panted, moving closer into the center of her legs, spreading them even wider. "I want it to last. I want to explore every inch of your body."

His hand came from out of nowhere and was suddenly between her legs. The soft, padded fingers slowly stroked her, arousing her, making her wet. Her head fell over onto his shoulder and she closed her eyes, let her arms hang limp. She only wanted to feel the sensation, block out the pain of the past week. It was as if he was playing a musical instrument—one he knew well. With his other hand he touched her hair, lifting it off her neck and tickling the tender spot with his fingernails.

"God," she said. Between her legs, she was on fire. He was so gentle, his touch delicate and sensuous. It was torture and pleasure at the same time. She pushed him back. She wanted to please him as much as he was pleasing her.

"No," he said, shoving her back onto the hood of the car, pulling on her dress until it was over her head and gone somewhere on the ground. He unsnapped her bra and tossed it as well. Now she was completely naked, staring up at the stars. Rickerson buried his head between her legs.

She was embarrassed. This was brazen. She tried to sit up, but he pushed her back down. The cool, moist air brushed across her nipples. They were hard. His hand found them and caressed them—delicately, tenderly. Lara was floating; between her legs was throbbing now. Never had she felt such exquisite pleasure, such passion. It was more than she could bear. Everything disappeared: Ivory, Josh, Evergreen, Phillip, England. She didn't want it to stop; she wanted it to go on forever.

It almost did.

Finally she sat up and jerked him to her chest. Then she slid off the car and unzipped him, taking him in her hand and relishing the feel of him. She had wondered about this part of his anatomy. Would he be small? Would his pubic hair be as strawberry red as the hair on his chest? In the darkness she couldn't tell. But what she felt in her hands was the essence of this man's masculinity. His skin there was as soft as a baby's skin. She dropped to her knees on the ground and took him in her mouth. He was clean, almost delicious. She was impervious to the gravel on her scraped knees. She was impervious to anything but pleasure.

He tried to pull her to her feet, but she knocked his hands away. She let him slide in and out of her mouth, completely into it. He moaned. Then he cried out, "Oh, my God . . . that feels so good." He put his hand on her head and pressed her even closer to his body.

When she could tell he couldn't wait a moment longer, he pulled her up with his arms and leaned back against the car. Then he lifted her in the air and let her slide down until he was inside her, kissing her mouth, probing with his tongue. She wrapped her legs around his waist, her arms around his neck. With his hands he moved her body, but it was slow, an inch at a time. And it was good. He started pushing her buttocks up until they had almost disconnected, and then he let her slide down again until he was deep inside her. She felt small, delicate, weightless. She felt wanton, without a care in the world.

Again and again he moved her up and down. His big, padded hands were on her buttocks. "Oh, Ted," she said. She suddenly opened her eyes and saw nothing but flashing white light. She flung her upper body backward, arching her back in pleasure, feeling her own hair grazing her back. He had to hold her tight to keep her from falling. She was impervious to the ground beneath her, secure in his grip. His own face was twisted with passion. "Now," she panted. "Now, Ted. Right now."

"No," he said. "Not yet."

Carrying her in his arms, he placed her in the backseat of the car and moved on top of her, his long legs sticking out the car door. She wrapped her legs around his waist. Then he pulled his body up and she placed them around his shoulders, lifting her pelvis up high, as high as it would go, wanting to feel him push right through her.

Outside she could suddenly hear the ocean, the waves crashing on the shore beneath them. It was as though they were on an island somewhere. She couldn't contain herself any longer. She was seconds away, holding back, not wanting it to end. He stopped. Withdrawing from her, he again put his mouth between her legs, holding her upper body down with his strong arms. She was writhing, moaning, crying out. Then in an explosion of pleasure, it was over. Her arms fell off the side of the seat, her body melted in satiation. She couldn't speak.

He was on top of her again and moving faster, harder now. Her arms and legs were like rubber, but the feeling began building again and she couldn't stop it, control it.

"Jesus," he cried in a voice from the center of his throat. He was sweating. Their stomachs were wet with perspiration, slick. There were funny smacking noises as he moved even faster, like they were stuck together, like suction.

Lara cried out again, tossing her head, never having felt such intense pleasure in her life. Just at that moment he plunged deep inside her and his body froze like a statue. He didn't cry out. He appeared to be holding his breath, locking the pleasure deep inside him. A second later, he collapsed on top of her.

"I love you, Lara," he said.

Tears started to fall from her eyes. He couldn't love her. As wonderful as it was, it was only sex. She didn't answer. She just held him, smelled him, let herself swim in the sensations. "You're the best lover I've ever had," she whispered. "And I mean that, Ted. The best."

"You're the most exciting woman I've ever known," he said.

They sat up. He got out and left Lara there while he found her clothes and brought them back to her. He leaned against the car door and watched as she dressed. "I'll never be able to look at another judge without wanting to undress them," he said lightly.

"Oh, yeah," she said, smiling. "Better make sure it's a female."

"You've redefined the law," he said. He was watching her struggle to get her clothes back on in the backseat of the car. He was grinning from ear to ear. "You're pretty cute too."

Then he repaired his own clothing: his shirt was unbuttoned, his jacket gone; he'd kicked his pants off by the car. Lara didn't think he had worn underwear. If he had, it was gone now.

He turned on the headlights and found the last remnants of their clothing: his jacket, her shoes; the panty hose had evidently blown away.

They stood for a long time in silence at the edge of the cliff looking out over the ocean, he with his arm around her, she leaning into him. The fantasizing was over. It had been better than she'd ever dreamed. Never had a man thrilled her, titillated her, completely satisfied her like this one. And the words—the words of love—they played in her mind again and again. Could it be real? Did she dare to let herself go, let herself really care about this man?

"Tell me about your kids, Ted," she said, pulling away. "Tell me everything."

"My kids . . . well, Jimmy is fourteen and Stephen is seventeen. They both go to St. Catherine's Catholic School in San Clemente. They live with me, Lara."

"Why?" she said. She was hungry for information and she wanted it fast. She felt like a prosecutor with a witness on the stand.

"Because Joyce—my wife—went back to college.

She attends Long Beach State. She's studying engineering."

"Must be smart," Lara said. "Have you filed for divorce?"

"There wasn't a reason. Before tonight, before I met you, I was actually hoping she'd come back." He looked over at her, but she was staring out over the ocean, the lights.

"Are you going to file now?" She couldn't look at him, but she had to know. She couldn't afford to climb on an emotional roller coaster.

"Yes," he said softly, reaching his hand out to her. "I'm going to file now."

Both their hands were sweating even though it was almost cold. He wasn't stupid. He knew what this conversation was all about. "Does it bother you that I'm just a cop? I mean, a judge is a pretty lofty position."

"Hell, no," she said, not having to think about it for more than a second. "And you're a damn good cop. You're a damn good cop, a damn good lover, and a wonderful man."

"I know," he said, laughing nervously. "I'm also a good father. Wonder why my wife didn't figure that one out?"

"She's dumb," Lara said, facing him.

"You just said she was smart."

"I was wrong. Ted," she said, serious now, "did you really wreck the police car when you heard I'd been attacked?"

"No," he said. "But it worked, didn't it? Sounded awfully good to me."

Lara punched him on the arm with her fist. "You little shit." Then she started laughing. Rickerson began laughing and neither of them could stop. Their laughter echoed in the canyon below and returned to surround them. Tears started rolling down Lara's face, but still she couldn't stop. She was the sophisticated judge. He was the street cop. And the man had completely seduced her, set it all up every inch of the way. All these days she had wanted him and thought she couldn't have him. "You know, lying to me could be considered perjury."

"Not hardly," he said. "Didn't I tell you the other night that you could be had?"

She was still laughing. She knew he was only joking. Besides, he was right. She had been ripe for the taking. The irony was that she had actually planned to seduce him. He had just been smarter and quicker.

"Let's go," he said once they both stopped laughing.

She stepped up to him, gazed into his eyes, and again he took her in his arms. He was so big; she was so small. While the chilly air whipped around them, they stood there together in silence. For those few moments, time stood still. "I think I love you too," Lara finally said.

"You think? You don't know for sure?"

"No," she said. "Not yet."

He yanked her arm playfully and she stumbled along behind him to the car. He opened the door and she stepped inside. "You'll know soon," he said, closing the door.

Once he was in the driver's seat, they headed down the hill.

On the ride home, Lara fell asleep. At first she faked it, leaning back and closing her eyes, wanted to savor everything that had happened and commit it to memory, sort through her thoughts. Then exhaustion overtook her and she fell into a deep slumber, slipping even farther down in the seat, her head rolling to the side against the window. Rickerson turned the volume on the police radio up where he could hear it, glanced to see if Lara would awaken, but she was oblivious to anything now.

He listened to the dispatcher. They were dispatching an officer on a barking dog. Having been out of patrol for years, he couldn't imagine sending officers out on such stupid calls. But that was part of the job, like it or not. He'd done his time, handled the family fights, the loud parties, the neighborhood squabbles. It wasn't all action and excitement. He kept glancing at the woman next to him. Her hair was tousled, her makeup smeared. He felt exhilarated.

Then he heard something that made his hair stand on end. An officer came on the air, screaming, his siren blasting in the background. You could even hear the roar of his unit's big engine as he raced through the night. He was in pursuit.

The car he was chasing was Frank Door's Corvette.

Rickerson, almost in Santa Ana, looked quickly at the freeway off ramps. He wasn't that far away.

Lara had no idea where they were when she opened her eyes. The car was barreling down the road, Rickerson sitting up close to the steering wheel, gripping it with both hands. The police radio was blasting, the volume turned all the way up.

"Seat belt on?" he asked Lara, having to yell over the radio. She nodded, rubbing her eyes. Then the detective slapped the steering wheel and almost lost control of the speeding car. "I should have never left the freeway. Fuck. I think we've lost him now."

Lara was dazed, just trying to figure out what he was all excited about. He cut through a dirt lot, dust churning in clouds, the unit bouncing up and down like a jeep, the windows rattling and shaking. "What the hell?" Lara screamed. "Tell me what's going on."

"Shut up," he barked. "Just hold on . . ."

"Shut up? You stop this car . . ."

Out of the dirt now, he flew over the curb, the front fender scraping against the road, fishtailed onto a side street, and again he stepped on the accelerator. "There," he said, "see it—there it is. Got the sucker. Hot damn. Snuck right up on him."

About two car lengths ahead of him was a blue Corvette with dark tinted windows. "My God, the car," Lara said, grabbing the dashboard and seeing if she could make out the plate. "That's it," she yelled, her heart beating faster and harder. "It was 347PJG. That's it. How did you find it?"

Rickerson was closing the distance. "I didn't find it," he screamed. "Another officer spotted it and went in pursuit. . . . Then he lost him and we were nearby. I found him. Good thing I drove the police unit tonight."

Rickerson grabbed the microphone. "Station One, this is 654. I have the vehicle. I repeat, I have the vehicle in sight. We're northbound on . . ." He paused, looking frantically at the street signs. "We're on Harbor . . . passing Orangewood. Get me a backup. Advise them to take the Harbor exit off the freeway."

The Corvette was exceeding the speed limit, but still wasn't aware they were following him. Then when they were practically on his bumper, the Corvette took off in a burst of speed, making a sharp right turn down a side street.

"Hurry," Lara screamed, totally into it now. "Get him. Get the bastard."

"I need a backup," Rickerson screamed into the radio again. "I have a civilian in the unit." He gripped the steering wheel and turned to Lara. "Shit, that 'Vette is souped. There's no telling what's under the hood."

He glanced at the speedometer. They were flying down a residential street at about eighty-five miles per hour, Rickerson desperately trying not to hit the parked cars in front of the houses and get them killed, maybe even run over some poor soul crossing the street in the dark.

Down another street they raced, this one a divided roadway with two lanes. Rickerson kept trying to pull up alongside the man on the left. While Lara's eyes were peeled on the road in front of them, he yanked his gun out of his shoulder holster and steered the car with one hand. "Get down in the seat," he ordered her. "And don't get up, no matter what happens."

For a moment, she didn't move.

He yelled again, "Get down." Then he shifted the gun to his left hand and shoved her head down with his right. The engine roared, the car vibrated. "Here it is," he yelled. "Put your face into the upholstery. Hold on."

No sooner had the words left his mouth than the car

jerked violently to the left and smashed into the other car, metal jarring metal with a loud metallic crunch. Then the police unit started spinning out of control, making a complete circle backward at tremendous speed. Rickerson wrestled with the steering wheel, trying to steer into the skid and bring the car to a stop. Lara dug her fingernails into the seat and screamed.

The car stopped.

Rickerson bailed out, leaving the door standing open. She could hear him yelling, "Police. Stop right there, you mother fucker. I'd just love to blow you away."

Lara unfastened her seat belt and crawled to the passenger window, only her eyes and the top of her head showing as she peered out at the scene. The detective had a gun trained on a man on the ground. The Corvette was upside down and the wheels were spinning, the engine still running, steam and smoke rising from the hood. Keeping her head down, she cracked open the car door and yelled, "Can I get out?"

"You okay?" he said, never taking his eyes off the man.

"I think so," Lara said, standing. Her legs were wobbling and her knees knocking, but she didn't think she was injured. "I'm fine. Is it him?"

"Take a look," Rickerson said, stepping closer to the man. He was on his face on the asphalt. Rickerson kicked him with his foot, and the man rolled onto his side. Blood was streaming from a cut on his chin, and his arm was bent at an unnatural angle.

"My fucking arm's broken," the man said. Then he spat on the sidewalk. His mouth was full of blood.

Since he didn't appear to be armed, Lara took a few steps closer. "That's him," she said. He didn't look as menacing without the stocking, but she knew it was him. He was tall and thin; his legs looked like stilts. She recognized the black polyester pants. They were about two inches too short.

"You bastard," she hissed at him. "You fucking bastard. I should shoot you myself."

"Want to rough him up?" the detective said, his shoulder twitching, the strain of holding the gun in front of him causing it to move up and down in his hand. He hadn't even brought a set of cuffs. He'd gone out to a concert, not expecting to end up in a pursuit. "You've earned it," he urged her. "Go ahead. Kick him or something. Kick him in the balls."

Lara froze.

She'd never purposely hurt another human being in her life. He was vile and contemptible, but she couldn't do it. She just stared at him, watching the blood drip from the cut on his chin. He started laughing at her. A few seconds later he was coughing and hacking, then rolling over and spitting up more blood.

"I'm fucking dying, man," he said. "My arm . . . my arm."

Rickerson looked back at Lara. "Do it. Do it now. Kick his arm and see how he likes it. See how he likes to be on the receiving end."

Lara continued to stand motionless. She finally took a few steps forward. Every second of that horrible night in the garage returned and she moved her foot around, started to pull it back and kick him. She was breathing hard. This was her chance for revenge. She could hurt him. She could kick in his face, kick him in his balls.

"Go on," Rickerson said. "We haven't got all night."

Stepping close to the detective, she whispered, "I can't. I just can't."

"Didn't think so," he said, smiling. "To be honest, I'm not into that type of thing myself, but thought I'd offer."

"I'm in pain, man," Frank Door screamed.

"Go to the phone and make certain they're sending a black-and-white. The radio's disabled." He looked around, trying to spot a street sign. "Take your purse and the gun. This isn't the best area. Check the street sign on the corner and give them the cross streets. Hurry." He paused and then added, "I guess you better get an ambulance too." He yelled at the man on the ground. "That is, unless you want to make a run for it, asshole, and let me put a hole in your fucking back."

Lara grabbed her purse and started jogging down the street toward the street light. On the opposite corner was a Stop 'n' Go. They should have a phone.

Lara stayed with Rickerson while they waited for a tow truck and then had to go to the police station to give her statement and make a positive ID that Door was the man who had attacked her. Rickerson still had to complete his report and transport Frank Door to the county jail. He arranged to have a patrol unit drive her home. Having consumed about five cups of black coffee, he was wide awake and wired. Before Lara left, he snuck her into the captain's empty office and closed the door. He kissed her, held her.

"Tonight was probably one of the best nights of my life," he told her. "I don't want to let you go."

"You're not going to let me go, Ted," she said, running her fingers through his hair. "But I do have a trial tomorrow. I have to get a few hours' sleep." She started for the door and he jerked her back.

"I could make love to you again—right here, right now."

"No, Ted," she said, pulling away forcefully. "Not here. Don't worry, I'm not going to disappear. Believe me, this meant as much to me as it did to you. Next time we'll try a bed. I'm a little too old for the backseat of a car."

"Tomorrow," he said. His eyes tracked her as she left the room, leaving him standing there in the dark.

A few seconds later, she stuck her head back inside and whispered, "Tomorrow. Better rest up."

Then she found the patrol officer and he took her home.

It was four in the morning before Lara fell into bed. Josh had slept on the floor at Emmet's in his sleeping bag. When she didn't get up in time after he'd returned, dressed, and had his breakfast, he went and woke her. "Are you sick?" he said, concerned that she was still in bed.

"No," she told him, forcing herself to put her feet on the floor by the bed. "I'll be ready in five minutes."

They walked to the parking lot together, her mind replaying the events of last night. They'd certainly chopped Frank Door down to size. In a way it had been quite gratifying, even if she didn't have the gumption to kick his face or rupture his balls. Just seeing him bleed had been worth it. She thought of Ted Rickerson. Just thinking about their lovemaking on the bluff gave her a warm, satisfied glow. Everything was a little brighter, sharper: the sun, the smell of the flowers planted near the front of the complex, the soft, warm air on her face.

She drove Josh to school. There was no reason to tell him what had really transpired last night with Frank Door. Josh didn't even know about the assault in the garage. She glanced in the rearview mirror, checking her face. The bruise on her forehead was fading, and she had covered it with makeup.

Frank Door was safely in jail; he'd refused to waive his rights and had demanded an attorney. Unless the D.A. offered him a deal, Rickerson doubted he'd ever talk. Was it really Leo Evergreen behind her sister's death? With Josh's ID, they now had a connection between Packy and the murders. Evergreen had told her to release him. Additionally, Evergreen's son was in one of the obscene photos. Even though she found the whole thing incomprehensible, she had to admit the evidence was beginning to stack up. The one thing that kept appearing in her mind was the court order to release Frank Door. She couldn't see Leo sneaking into her office and figuring out how to produce and transmit that document. He could have had another secretary or clerk do it for him, she thought, even though that would have put him at risk of exposure.

A thought flashed into her mind. If Evergreen was the game man, he'd be proficient in computers. Then another thought surfaced. Phillip loved video games.

Several times she had walked into her office and found him playing games on his terminal. Phillip could be the game man.

Clearing her mind of these thoughts, she made an attempt to converse with Josh.

All he talked about now was Emmet. Lara really felt she could have moved back into the house in Irvine several days ago, but she had stalled, hating to take Josh away from Emmet. They had bonded, became fast friends. In many ways they had merged into something similar to a family. And Lara knew Josh needed this companionship—to be surrounded by people. As far as she was concerned, Emmet had done more for the child than Dr. Werner could have done in a hundred sessions. He was talking more. He wasn't hurling insults at her. She was beginning to see the fine young man that he really was surface—the angry young man was finally fading away.

"Emmet's so smart," Josh said. "He's a genius. And he never complains. I mean, he never complains about anything."

Lara reached over and clasped his hand. "You don't complain a lot yourself, Josh. Guess you and Emmet have a lot in common. Neither one of you has had a lot of breaks in life, but you're a fine young man."

"Yeah," he said, his eyes clouding over, his fingers tightening on Lara's. "Way I see it, you have to take whatever comes along and make the best of it. That's what Emmet says. Did you know his mother dumped him when he was diagnosed? She just up and left. He hasn't seen or heard from her since."

Lara sighed. She hadn't known. In reality, she wasn't even certain how old Emmet was. From what he'd told her, she estimated his age in his late twenties or early thirties. He'd graduated from MIT. Then he'd gone on to get a master's degree at Long Beach State. But the way Josh was talking, she might be mistaken. Emmet might be only in his early twenties. He was probably a child prodigy who had gone to college at fourteen. In many ways the little man seemed ageless.

One moment he seemed like a child, almost helpless, and another he seemed to know all there was to know in the universe.

"Emmet says he gets scared sometimes," Josh continued. "He's afraid he's going to die alone. Sometimes in the middle of the night, he told me, he wakes up and thinks about it—about what happens when you die. You know what Emmet believes? He believes he will come back after he dies in a different body, a healthy body. Because God has made him suffer so much in this life, he thinks he will have a much better life next time. But his mother? . . . How could she leave him like that?"

"Well, Josh, some people can't handle illness. Some people are weak, but that doesn't mean they're bad. Possibly it's because they haven't had enough love or people have hurt them. I don't know."

"Is that what happened to my mother?" Josh said in a soft voice, his eyes turned to Lara. They were exiting the freeway, almost in San Clemente.

"No, no, your mother was very loved, at least before she married Sam. Our parents were loving people and your father certainly loved her. But she was insecure, afraid. She wasn't that sophisticated, and I think sometimes the world was too complex for her, had too many sharp edges. But she was a good person, Josh. No matter what happened, what she did there at the end, she loved you very much."

He was silent. He turned the radio on and tuned in a rock station. Then he started talking again over the noise. "I hope Emmet is right," he said.

Lara turned to him. They were stopped at a light, almost at the school. "About what?"

"About people coming back when they die. I hope my mom comes back in a new body—that she's happy now."

"I do too, Josh," Lara said. "I do too."

"Some people at school said some nasty things to me."

Lara gasped, locking her fingers on the steering

wheel. She had been afraid of this, but until now Josh had sworn everything was okay at school. "What did they say?"

"That my mother was a dirty whore and I was a bastard."

She didn't know what to say. She pulled up in front of the school and parked. "Honey, whoever said that is the one with the problem. They have to make other people feel small so they can feel big." She paused. "Can you handle it? If it persists, I can go to the principal. Or we could change your school. We'll probably transfer you anyway once we move back to the house in Irvine."

"No," he said, his hand on the door handle. "I can handle it. Are they about to arrest the man who killed my mother? I picked out this guy last night from a bunch of pictures. I saw him coming down our street that day . . . the day it happened. But Detective Rickerson told me the man was dead, that someone else was behind what happened to my mom and Sam."

"We're close, honey. Everything is getting close. We just don't have quite enough evidence yet to make an arrest, but soon."

After stepping outside, he turned back and gave her a weak smile that moved only the corners of his mouth. She watched as he walked away. Kids were congregating, laughing, jostling with one another. How could they be that cruel? she thought. Then she saw Josh walking back to the car and her heart jumped. Was there a problem? Did one of those stupid kids say something else to him? He opened the car door and climbed back in. "What's wrong?" Lara said, her voice full of concern.

"Nothing," he said. "I forgot something."

Lara tried to remember if she'd given him money for lunch. She had. "What? I gave you lunch money. Did you forget your books?"

For a long moment he looked straight ahead. Then suddenly he jerked his head to the side and leaned over and kissed her on the cheek. "That . . ." he said, smiling nervously.

Lara blushed. She felt her entire body surge with pleasure. Here—he had kissed her right here where all the kids could see. Teenagers didn't do that type of thing.

No man in the world could make her feel the way she felt right now, infused with such pride and joy—not even Rickerson.

She didn't say anything. She was lost in the moment, flooded with warmth. "I-I . . . Josh," she started stammering.

He got out and leaned back in the window, a wide smile on his handsome face. "In all my life," he said, the smile vanishing as he spoke, "my mom never once drove me to school."

Then he pulled his head out of the window and disappeared into the crowd of kids.

When Lara got to the courthouse and parked, she saw something white lying on the passenger seat. It must have fallen out of Josh's notebook. It was a piece of paper. She opened it and read. "I wanted to tell you about the T-shirt," it said in his small, neat handwriting. "I was too embarrassed to tell you before, but I want you to know. Sam made me eat a TV dinner. He made me eat the foil tray. I tore it up in little pieces and ate it with the mashed potatoes. The next day I started bleeding at school. I didn't know what to do, so I put my extra T-shirt in my pants. I didn't want the kids to see blood on my pants. They would have teased me. They would have said I was a girl. You know, having what girls have every month. So that's it. Don't worry. I'm fine now. Foil isn't that good to eat, though. In case you ever wonder." He signed it, "Josh. Your nephew."

Lara put her head on the steering wheel and cried. In his short life this young man had suffered more than she had in all of her thirty-eight years. And he had suffered alone—just as Emmet suffered alone. She would never complain again. Last night Ted had given her more love in one night than Nolan had in their entire marriage. And today Josh had kissed her, a clear indication that he cared. Even if they tossed her off the bench, she decided, she would just have to deal with it. That was her commitment.

chapter 24

Detective Rickerson arrived at the San Clemente police station at eight o'clock that morning. What with the evening with Lara, apprehending Frank Door, the pending investigation, he'd had less than three hours of sleep, but he was infused with energy. A natural at stalking his prey, he had the scent of the kill in his nostrils.

Pouring himself a cup of black coffee in the detective bureau, he thought of the magnitude of their undertaking. It was one thing to haul in small-time hoodlums. Arresting a man like Evergreen was a real coup. As he saw it, it was his one chance to climb the mountain all the way to the top. It was the chance he'd been waiting for all his life.

His task force had risen dramatically since the onset of the investigation. He had several officers from patrol working full-time on the case in plainclothes, baby Bradshaw, who did more harm than good, along with numerous reserve police officers. Reserves were men who wanted to be cops but had been smart enough to pursue other, more lucrative occupations. They were trained, given uniforms, weapons, and allowed to ride with regular officers so many days per month. If they ever had a disaster such as an earthquake, a flood, a major fire, they called on these men. Some of them were professionals, like doctors, dentists, accountants. And some of them were outright fools, wanting to play cops and robbers like children.

He couldn't afford to be picky. He'd taken whatever he could get, and the extra help had paid off.

Even though there were many leads left to follow and the investigation was in no way complete, he felt time was of the essence. Lara had already been attacked once. The next time she might end up in the morgue. He couldn't take the chance. They had to make their move.

He'd informed Lara that she should set up a meeting with Judge Rodriguez for twelve o'clock the next day. He didn't want to do it at the courthouse right under Evergreen's nose, so the meeting would take place at the police station. He contacted Gail Stewart at the lab, and she agreed to drive down and make a presentation.

Now that Frank Door had been arrested, they had to move fast. They had him in isolation at the jail, but they couldn't deny him phone access. The first person he'd more than likely call to spring him would be the good judge himself.

•

Lara made an appointment to see Judge Rodriguez during the lunch-hour recess. As soon as she got out of court, she called Evergreen's office and his secretary advised Lara that the judge had suffered a relapse of the flu and was out ill again. She was beginning to get frightened, afraid he was going to skip town. "Did he tell you when he thought he would be back?" she asked the woman. "I have something important to discuss with him. Is he at home?"

"Well, yes," she said curtly. "Where else would he be? He's sick."

Maybe on a plane to New Zealand, Lara thought, replacing the phone in the cradle and heading down the corridor to Judge Rodriguez's chambers. Either that or he was at home watching the shopping network, maybe looking for a few new goons.

"Hector?" she said at the door. The small man stood and waved her in, indicating she should take a seat.

Hector Rodriguez was far from neat. His desk was covered with papers, open files, law books, coffee cups. The credenza behind him was even worse, with periodicals and files stacked at least two feet deep.

Cardboard boxes with personal effects he'd never got around to unpacking stood gathering dust in the corners of the room. Only three months ago, he'd been appointed to a position on the Superior Court. Prior to that, he had been in Municipal Court—traffic court, to be specific. And he was already looking to get out, transfer to L.A.

Lara went over everything with him slowly, repeating many facts several times. Rodriguez listened, nodded, made notes on a yellow pad of paper. If he was shocked, he was keeping it under wraps. The telling over, Lara leaned back in the seat and waited. The next move was his.

"Tomorrow?" he said tentatively. "You want me to go to the police station?"

"Yes," Lara said, sitting forward in her seat. "I don't expect you to make a decision on the basis of my statements. Detective Rickerson is preparing a presentation, bringing in experts to outline the evidence. I want you to see it all with your own eyes." It was really more than that, Lara thought. She wanted it to be Rodriguez's call instead of hers. If he thought the detective had compiled enough evidence for a warrant, then so be it.

He swiveled his chair sideways, staring at the flag by his desk. "I think we should call the Judicial Counsel, have someone fly down for this presentation. This is serious business, Lara. Extremely serious business . . . and it affects all of us. Think what the press is going to do with this when we go public. It won't just be Evergreen who suffers. Public opinion of the legal system is at an all-time low. We'll all look bad."

"That's fine with me," she said. "You can have the pope come if you want. I just want to get this thing moving, get a warrant and serve him with it before he leaves town."

Judge Rodriguez turned his chair back to his desk and opened a law book, bending down and flipping the pages until he found what he wanted. "If you review section 1029 of the penal code, it states clearly that the

Judicial Counsel must be notified whenever a judge is charged with a criminal act. And, of course, if the D.A. agrees to prepare the case, file a complaint, it will have to be transferred to another jurisdiction. None of us can sit the trial."

"Okay," Lara said, standing. "I'll call Lawrence Meyer and advise him, have him come tomorrow, and you contact the Judicial Counsel."

When Lara was at the door, she looked back. Rodriguez was still deep in thought. "Listen, Lara, maybe we should even call the FBI in on this due to the child pornography. They have extensive records on this type of thing."

"Good idea. I'll handle it. And Hector," she said, "thank you for being so receptive. Some people would back off, want to keep their hands clean. They'd be afraid to go head to head with Evergreen."

The little judge smiled. His front teeth were crooked. Obviously, his family couldn't afford an orthodontist when he was a child. "Where I come from," he said, "basically the streets of south central L.A., the barrio, going up against anyone without a gun or knife in their hand is nothing." He paused and smiled again. "Besides, I never liked Evergreen that much. Something about him just rubbed me the wrong way. I think underneath that slick veneer, he's prejudicial against minorities. That's one of the reasons I want out. I think when the slot is eliminated next year, I'll be the one to go."

Lara smiled back and left. He might be small in stature, but Judge Hector Rodriguez looked pretty big right now.

Josh got a ride home with Ricky Simmons's mother. The first thing he did was drop his books in the condo and head to Emmet's, grabbing a bag of cookies on his way out the door and the cellular phone in case Lara called him. He knocked, but Emmet didn't answer. He had a key. Emmet had told him he could come over any time he wanted. Then he remembered. Today was the day Emmet went to the physical therapist. They were trying desperately to maintain his condition, keep the strength he had in his muscles from deteriorating further.

Josh sat down in the bedroom and loaded up the computer. He munched cookies and played video games. He was playing Wanders from Y's. He couldn't seem to get the hang of it and his points were low. The following night he was spending the night at Ricky's, and he wanted to beat him. Of course, Ricky was much better. He had his own computer and tons of games. Never once had Josh beaten him. On a piece of paper by the console was the number to the game man. On a lark, he dialed it and a man answered.

"Hi," he said. "Uh, this is Ricky Simmons. I called you the other day. I thought you could give me some pointers on Super NES's Wanders from Y's."

The man began talking and Josh listened intently. He blanked the screen and started over. He repeated the man's instructions. "Okay, I have the manufacturer's name up. It's American Sammy. Press up, down, up, down, select. I did that. Now what?" Josh had the phone clamped between his ear and his shoulder. "Start on the second controller? Okay. It looks just the same. This is just the beginning of the game." He was a little disappointed. The man continued giving him instructions. "Okay," he said, "I have the status screen. Press select on the second controller? Yeah. Did it. It says 'Debug.' "

"Now when you're damaged," the man's voice said, "and your hit points drop to zero, you can still come back to life."

"Cool," Josh said. He couldn't wait to show Ricky. "Thanks." He was staring at the computer screen, ready to hang up when the man began speaking again.

"I have all those demos for you," he told Josh. "They're new . . . all the newest games."

Josh was getting nervous. Lara had told him not to call this man, but he couldn't see what harm it would do, not just one quick phone call. But if she found out some way, he thought, she would be angry. "Hey, I have to go. I have homework."

"Wait," the man said, a tinge of panic in his voice, "don't go yet. Let's talk a few minutes. You called me, remember, and I helped you. It's not very nice just to hang up on me."

"Sure," Josh said. "Sorry. We can talk." He had no idea what the man wanted to talk about.

"Do you have a girlfriend, Ricky?" he said in a wispy voice, almost childish.

"I like this one girl in my math class, but she won't even talk to me." He thought of Heather Reynolds with the long blond hair and the big blue eyes. He'd almost fallen over his shoelaces when he'd seen her this year. During summer vacation she'd grown breasts. It was incredible. Heather Reynolds had been great just the way she was, but Heather Reynolds with tits was heaven on earth.

"I see," the man said slowly, a little smacking noise coming over the phone line.

"Look, I said I have to go," Josh said.

"Will you call me again, Ricky? Don't you want those demos?"

"Yeah, sure," he answered. Then he quickly hung up the phone and left Emmet's condo, crossing the grassy courtyard to Lara's place and beginning his homework.

Once he had done his math and his English, Josh called Ricky and made sure they were all set for tomorrow night. "I could get you some free games," he told him. He was certain the game man didn't have anything to do with his mother's murder. The man was really pretty cool. He knew everything there was to know about video games, even more than Emmet knew.

"And how are you gonna do that?" Ricky asked. "Hey, are you gonna rip them off from the store?"

"Do you want Smart Ball?"

"Shit, yes. I've been saving my allowance to buy it."

"I'll see if I can get it." Josh clicked off the phone. He was bored. Emmet had taken his TV to the model condo. Once his homework was done, he usually went over to Emmet's and stayed there until Lara got home. He thought about going out on his bike and then decided against it. After about an hour of sheer monotony, he called the game man back.

"I'd like those games, man," he told him. "What do I have to do to get them? I don't have any money. You said they were free."

"Yes, Ricky, they're free just like I said. All I have to do is fill out this questionnaire about you. The company I represent likes to know what their buyers are like . . . sort of a profile."

He started asking Josh questions. Some of them he'd already asked, like where he lived, if his father was alive, where he went to school. Then he asked him physical things: what color was his hair, his eyes, did he have bad skin? Josh answered them all. Some of them he lied about. He felt bad about that, but he had lied the first time he'd called him. He couldn't tell him the truth now.

"Do you like movies, Ricky?"

"Sure," Josh answered.

"Do you like to play miniature golf?"

"Yeah, sure."

"What about bowling? Do you like to bowl?"

"I don't know how."

"I see," the man said. "Have you ever had sex with a girl?"

"What?" Josh asked. He didn't know what this had to do with video games.

"You know, put it to her, stuck it to her."

"No," Josh said, completely mesmerized, lulled by the man's soft voice, thinking what it would be like to do that to Heather, to actually touch her breasts. She had this one white blouse. Every time she wore it to school, he could see her bra through the thin fabric. Last year she hadn't even had a bra. This year it was filled.

"I have some movies at my place," the man said in

that same funny voice. "You know, dirty movies. What does this girl look like?"

Josh felt himself perspiring. He moved around in his seat. His jeans were pinching between his legs. He was getting turned on. Normally, this only happened to him late at night, in his bed. Sometimes he touched himself, had nasty thoughts. This guy on the phone didn't even sound like a grown-up anymore. He sounded like Bart Miller at school. Bart always had dirty pictures of girls ripped from his father's *Penthouse* magazine. "She's got this long blond hair. It's really shiny."

"You should see this movie, Ricky. I'm looking at it right now. There's this girl in it with long blond hair and huge tits." The man giggled like a child. "She's touching herself. You should see her. She's putting her fingers right inside there. I bet she looks just like your girlfriend."

Josh snapped out of it. He felt dirty and disgusting. What was wrong with this man, anyway? He shouldn't be saying these things to him, offering to let him see dirty movies and all. That just wasn't right. "I've got to go, man," he said quickly and slammed the phone back. Now he'd have to tell Ricky he couldn't get the game. Ricky would be pissed. He looked out the window and saw Emmet's wheelchair at the front door of the condo.

He crossed the courtyard and waited while Emmet said good-bye to the lady who always drove him, and then called to him. "Hey, Emmet. Can I come in?"

Josh and Emmet played video games for about an hour. Josh couldn't concentrate and Emmet beat him every time. All he could think about was the man's funny voice, how he'd giggled so silly like a kid or something, the things they had talked about. Finally he turned and faced Emmet. "I'm going to tell you something, Emmet, but you have to promise you won't tell Lara. If you don't promise me, I won't tell you."

"I . . . promise," Emmet said.

Josh related his experience with the game man, and Emmet listened quietly. Then Josh told him what he thought. "This is a sick man, you know. I'm not a retard. Adults aren't supposed to talk about sex and stuff with kids. He's a pervert, isn't he? One of those child-molester people everyone's always talking about."

"Yes," Emmet said. "Do . . . not . . . call this man."

"He's a bad man." Josh got up and started walking around in small circles. He stopped and swiped his long bangs off his forehead. "You've got to tell me the truth, Emmet. We're friends. Did this man have something to do with what happened to my mom and Sam? Is that why Lara wants to catch him?" Suddenly the conversation he'd overheard between Emmet and Lara came back, and he knew he was right.

At first Emmet didn't answer. Then he said, "Maybe."

Josh flopped down in the chair again. It was one of those little chairs on rollers, and it slid a few feet on the hardwood floor. "I don't believe it," he kept saying. "I just don't believe it. They know it's him, but they don't have enough evidence." His eyes clouded over and he started thinking. They sat there without talking for a long time, maybe fifteen minutes, Emmet thinking too. Josh would look at Emmet and then look away. A few minutes later, Emmet would eye Josh and then his eyes would drift away involuntarily.

Outside, a couple of little kids were fighting over a Big Wheel and screaming at each other. Josh went to the open window and yelled at them. "Shut up, you little creeps. We're trying to think in here."

He sat back down and continued staring at the wall. "I've figured this whole thing out. They have to catch him, don't they? They have to catch him doing something bad. Otherwise, they would have already arrested him. Right?" he said, looking straight at Emmet. "Right?"

Emmet pushed a button and the chair spun around. He blanked the game off the screen and stuck his head in the wire contraption. A second later, words were flashing across the screen, Emmet tapping like mad. "I will not tell Lara that you called this man. I made a promise. But you cannot call him again. They are not certain he was involved in your mother's death, but he could be a very dangerous man. Let the police handle this. Now, you make a promise to me. Promise me you will not call this man again."

Emmet stopped typing and spun around to face Josh. He was about to walk out of the bedroom, leaning against the door frame. "I can't promise you that, Emmet. It was my mother. You understand, don't you? It was my mother."

Before Emmet could speak, Josh was out the door. Emmet hit the high speed on his electronic chair, but by the time he got to the living room, Josh had closed the front door. "Shit," Emmet said. He pushed the controls and his chair moved forward. Then he pushed it again and it moved backward. Back and forth he moved, the chair squeaking on the plastic runners.

"Shit," the little man said to the empty room.

At eleven-thirty the following morning, Rickerson walked into the squad room and checked everything. They had a slide projector, a screen, and a video setup. Next to the screen were two blackboards where they had outlined the facts of the case in chalk. There was also a cork board and baby Bradshaw had placed all the photos found in the San Clemente house on it with push pins. While he was standing there, one of the reserve officers came in carrying a large coffeepot. Another followed behind him with paper cups.

They were ready.

He took a seat and stared at his own writing on the board. Was it enough? He couldn't be sure, but they were not charged with gaining enough evidence to convict him, just enough to get a warrant for this arrest and start the wheels of justice rolling.

Gail Stewart was the first to arrive. "Too bad we don't have a computer set up," she said.

"You think we need it?"

"Nah, we got enough." She walked over and poured

herself a cup of coffee. "You should have brought in lunch or something," she told him.

"If all goes well, I'll buy you the best lunch of your life, doll," Rickerson told her.

"Sure," she said, sipping the coffee, holding it with both hands up close to her face. "Where have I heard that line before?"

Lara and Judge Rodriguez walked in at twelve-fifteen. Right behind them was a tall, thin man in a suit and tie. Rickerson didn't recognize him, so he assumed he was the justice from San Francisco. A few minutes later, the FBI agent arrived and took a seat, first stopping to pour himself a cup of coffee and chat with the chief. Lara was dressed in a plain white blouse and a black skirt, her hair again tied back in a clasp with a bow. She smiled at Rickerson and took a seat in the front row. Someone offered Rodriguez a cup of coffee, but he declined.

"Let's begin," Rickerson said, standing. As soon as everyone stopped talking and moving around in their seats, he began. "Okay, we are going to try to put this together chronologically. On July seventh, Ivory Perkins, Judge Sanderstone's sister, came to her residence in Santa Ana in the early morning hours claiming that she was being followed. She refused to tell her sister any more than that and left some time later with her husband, Samuel Perkins.

"On September seventh, Judge Leo Evergreen approached Judge Sanderstone and suggested that she release a man named Packard Cummings on his own recognizance, even though the man had an extensive record, advising her that he was working as a confidential informant for an unidentified law enforcement agency. She complied. As of this date, no agency in the state of California, or any federal agency, has been able to verify this information."

He waited, scanning the faces in the audience before continuing.

"The photos on the bulletin board behind me were found in the crawl space at the residence in San

Clemente where Ivory and Sam Perkins were murdered on September eighth." He noted the small judge leaning forward and squinting to see the pictures. "If you bear with me, we'll show you slides of the enlargements of these photos."

He paused and then continued, "Only a day prior to the homicides, Judge Sanderstone's place was ransacked, as was the murder scene, the killer evidently looking for what you see on the board behind you. Prints lifted from her residence by the sheriff's department's crime-scene unit subsequently came back to Packard Cummings.

"On September twelfth, Packard Cummings was shot and killed in the parking lot of the Sea Breeze Apartments in Santa Ana, only a few blocks from Judge Sanderstone's residence. There were no prints on the vehicle, but it appeared that he knew his assailant. His own weapon was found in the glove box.

"Three days ago, Judge Sanderstone was attacked in the underground parking garage at the courthouse, the suspect demanding that she give him these photographs. She copied down the license plate and vehicle description, and the suspect was apprehended last night. His name is Frank Door. He's in custody. Judge Evergreen must have entered Judge Sanderstone's chambers and typed out the order to release this man on her own computer terminal. He was a serious violent offender.

"Yesterday, Josh McKinley, the murdered woman's son, positively identified Packard Cummings from a photo lineup as the man he saw leaving the scene of the murders on September eighth in a red Camaro. We also have forensic evidence such as tissue and semen from the victim that matches samples from Cummings. This is an important fact, since it connects Judge Evergreen to the homicides.

"Ivory Perkins had a client that went under the name of Tommy Black. The phone records of calls from the house in San Clemente revealed this, and the phone number comes back to an apartment, also rented under this name. A search of DMV records, however, reveals about fifteen Tommy Blacks in this immediate area. We've eliminated most of them. One got killed in a traffic accident, one's in jail, another in a nursing home, and another is a seventeen-year-old boy, et cetera. Therefore, we believe this is a fictitious name adopted by Leo Evergreen. We need a warrant to search this apartment. Ivory Perkins's fingerprints could be inside.

"Tommy Black also advertises himself as a video game expert and lists a toll-free number for young people to call for tricks and pointers. This phone number has been traced to that apartment. It appears that he lures young people this way, offering them free video games and other enticements. Then he gains their confidence, befriends them, and molests them." Rickerson paused, facing his audience.

"Gentlemen," he said, "what we are dealing with is a desperate man who has now become a dangerous man. To be in a position such as Evergreen and be exposed and ultimately prosecuted for sexually abusing children, especially young boys, would be a certain disgrace. In addition, a fact Evergreen knows all too well is that child molesters do not fare well in prison. They are the scum of the prison system, the lowest of the low, and they are many times brutalized and even murdered inside the prison walls."

Rickerson let his eyes fall and then looked back up. "We intend to prove to you that Judge Leo Evergreen and Tommy Black are one and the same, that Judge Evergreen is a pedophile, and that Judge Evergreen conspired to murder Sam and Ivory Perkins." He nodded to Gail Stewart. "This is Dr. Gail Stewart of the Los Angeles County Crime Lab. She's going to take it from here."

Someone in the back dimmed the lights, and Rickerson took a seat next to Lara. "How am I doing?" he whispered.

"Great," she said. "You sound like a prosecutor. You've almost convicted the bastard."

The slide projector clicked and the first slide fell into place. "What you are seeing," Dr. Stewart said, "are enlarged and enhanced images of the photographs on the board, the ones taken from the San Clemente house. As you can see, some of these are solo photos of nude prepubescent males. We have not identified these boys." She stopped and another slide clicked into place. "This is the back of a nude male fondling the genitals of a young boy while someone else operates the camera. Although you may not be able to see it with the naked eye, this man suffers from scoliosis or curvature of the spine. Watch this next slide and you can see it better in enlargement. See," she said, "note how the spine curves. If we had Judge Evergreen in custody, we could render a positive ID."

A few moments later, Dr. Stewart was flicking through the slides until she came to the one she wanted. She stopped for a moment and took a sip of her coffee. "The next slide was developed from a mirror image enlarged from one of the photos found in the residence in San Clemente. What you are looking at is a photo on someone's dresser, enlarged from one of the shots with the man we think is Evergreen and the boy. The man and woman in that photograph are Leo Evergreen's wife and son." That slide vanished and another dropped down. "This is a recent picture of Robert Evergreen. He's several years older, but obviously it's the same individual as in the first photo. Hit the lights," she said. "That's all I have."

When Gail Stewart had taken a seat, Rickerson stood. "What this all adds up to should be evident by now. Judge Evergreen was seeing Ivory Perkins. Ivory Perkins was a prostitute. She called on him, somehow came across the compromising photos, and then she and her husband proceeded to blackmail him. He must have paid them some money, at least over forty thousand, because this is the sum we found in the safe at the pawnshop. Then they must have demanded more and he decided to put a stop to it. That's when Evergreen arranged to have Cummings released and contracted the murders. We believe he killed Cummings himself, meeting him in that parking lot, probably for a payoff. Exactly why he killed him we aren't certain, but it was more than likely to cover his tracks. Possibly Cummings was trying to raise the stakes and he feared exposure.

"Evergreen had to get the photos back. Even though his back was turned to the camera, he has to fear we will identify one of the victims and implicate him in that manner, or he is aware that his own home is reflected in those pictures. So after he eliminated Cummings, he shopped for another offender to spring, met him outside the jail, and hired him to break into Judge Sanderstone's residence again, this time the condo she was hiding in. When he still didn't recover the photos, he had Judge Sanderstone attacked in the underground garage, thinking the photos were in her car or briefcase. If the janitorial service had not arrived when it did, it is my belief that Judge Sanderstone would be dead right now."

Rickerson turned to speak directly to Judge Rodriguez. His signature on a warrant would be the green light they needed. "We are seeking an arrest warrant for Judge Leo Evergreen for a violation of section 187, first-degree murder in the death of Packard Cummings, for contracting a murder for hire in the deaths of Ivory and Sam Perkins, for conspiring to commit assault with a deadly weapon in the beating of Judge Sanderstone. This could even fall under section 217.1 of the penal code, in that he was attempting to murder or impede Judge Sanderstone in proceeding with her duties, and for conspiring to commit two residential 459's or burglaries of Judge Sanderstone's residences." He stopped and took a deep breath, his eyes locking with Lara's.

Rickerson sat down next to her. Gail Stewart chatted a few minutes and left. Judge Rodriguez, the justice from San Francisco, the D.A., and the FBI agent all stood in the corner of the squad room and conferred among themselves in hushed voices. They walked up and studied the pictures pinned on the cork board. They read again the facts of the case outlined in chalk on the blackboard. The justice from San Francisco glanced at Lara and then back to the other men. He was shaking his head. Then he shook Rodriguez's hand and left the room, walking fast like he had to catch a plane, his head down. A few minutes later, the FBI agent broke from the group and left. Now there was only Lawrence Meyer and Rodriguez in the huddle. Finally they arrived at a decision.

By five o'clock that evening, Rickerson was told, he would have the warrants in his hands.

Rickerson turned to Lara and smiled. They were on their way. For Presiding Judge Leo Evergreen, the most powerful justice in Orange County, it was to be the beginning of the end.

chapter 25

Josh went to Ricky Simmons's house after school. No one was there but the two of them. Ricky's mother was out.

They grabbed several cans of sodas and some potato chips and headed to Ricky's room. Josh had always envied his friend. He had it all. A nice home, always neat and clean. He had a mother and father that loved him, were even active in school activities. Ricky also had a huge collie named Viceroy that Josh adored. He dropped to his knees in the hall and hugged him, letting him lick his face with a red sticky tongue.

"I can't believe you let him do that," Ricky said. "He licks his balls, you know. He even licks his asshole."

Ricky had rock posters plastered all over the walls, two twin beds with brown chenille bedspreads, a desk covered with books and papers, and of course, the computer. He had told his mother he needed it desperately for his schoolwork. All he'd ever used it for was games. When he wasn't vegetating in front of a video game, Ricky lifted weights like Josh. He wanted to build up his body, but not to beat someone up. He wanted to do it to attract girls. Ricky was almost fifteen. He was in heat. There was only one problem with that, Josh thought, glancing at his friend. Ricky was a nerd. He was short and skinny, wore thick glasses, and in the past year his face had erupted in angry pimples. There wasn't a girl in school who would even look at Ricky Simmons, much less let him touch her. Even Josh knew that and the boy was his best friend.

The curtains were drawn in the room. Ricky liked it that way. Dark. When he wasn't playing video games, he was reading Stephen King books. In one corner he had a big tank filled with exotic fish, and the pump made a constant gurgling sound. Every day his mother made his lunch and cleaned his room. She even ironed Ricky's clothes. Anything he wanted he got. But Ricky took all this for granted, Josh thought, looking around him. He'd certainly never take it for granted. But then, he'd never had the chance.

"You really going to do this? Call that man and everything?" Ricky said, tossing a handful of chips in his mouth and crunching them. "I want to listen when he talks dirty. He talks about tits and everything? Wow. What else did he say to you? Tell me, man."

Josh gave him a nasty look. "This is not a game, dick head. This is serious stuff."

"Fuck you," Ricky said, tossing a few chips at Josh. "Since when did you turn into some kind of Sherlock Holmes?"

"Since someone murdered my mother." Josh had the phone in his hands. There was a black look in his eyes. Since his conversation yesterday with Emmet, all Josh had thought about was the game man and how they could catch him.

"I'm sorry," Ricky said quietly, shoving his glasses back on his nose. "Sometimes I forget. I mean, you never used to talk about them, so I just forget."

"Well, either shut up or get out. Go in the bathroom and jerk off or something."

He shut up.

With Ricky sitting on the edge of one twin bed and Josh stretched out on the other, Josh called the toll-free number and the game man answered.

"Hey," Josh said, sitting up straight and avoiding Ricky's eyes, "this is Ricky. You know, from yesterday. Say, I've been thinking and I'd really like those free games. My mom's gone today, so I could come and get them if you tell me where you live."

"Did you have a wet dream last night, Ricky?" the man said slowly. "Did your little pecker stand up?"

Josh turned bright red and Ricky leaned farther over his knees. "Let me hear," he whispered. "Shit, you used my name." Josh glared at him and he was silent again.

"Y-yeah," Josh stammered. "You gonna let me see that movie you were talking about? The one with the blonde?"

The man's voice became almost businesslike, the suggestive tone of before vanishing. "Do you have transportation?" he asked.

"I have a bike," Josh answered, glancing at Ricky. He didn't, but Ricky did.

"I see," the man said slowly. "If you come over, this has to be our little secret. When do you have to be home?"

"Anytime I want, man." Josh held his breath, hoping the man would agree to see him. "I can come to your house."

"No, that would be too far. You live in San Clemente, don't you? Why don't you come to the corner of Avenue Palizada in San Clemente? Isn't there a convenience store there?"

Josh though for a moment. That was a long street. "You mean right near the freeway? That one?"

"Yes," the man said. "I'll be in a gold Lexus. How will I recognize you?"

Josh looked at his clothing. "I'm wearing a blue T-shirt with Iron Maiden on the back. You know, the band. And I've got long hair."

"Oh," the man said, his voice laced with excitement, almost breathless. "Is it as long as a girl's hair, Ricky? I like that. I like long hair. Did you bathe today?"

Josh's stomach was flopping around like he'd swallowed a bowl of goldfish. He answered, "Yeah, I bathed. Why don't I meet you in about thirty minutes?" This guy was sick, he thought, really sick. He'd seen bad things before, but never had he heard anything as sick as this. It sounded like the man wanted to cook him for dinner. Asking him if he'd taken a bath and all. When he talked, he made these little smacking sounds. It made him want to throw up. The line was silent and then the man spoke.

"I'll be waiting, Ricky."

The Adams trial was still in session and Lara was watching the clock, counting the seconds. She'd made Rickerson promise that he wouldn't arrest Evergreen without her. Because they were late beginning the afternoon session, they were running past five o'clock. It was now after six. In the front row behind the defense table were two lovely little girls. Lara knew they were Victor Adams's daughters. She'd watched as a babysitter had delivered them to the courtroom about an hour ago. They were unruly and disruptive, jumping up and running down the aisles, pulling each other's hair and screaming. Their father turned around on several occasions and tried to subdue them, but they were bored and tired of sitting. Lara felt such compassion for the man that she had let the disruption continue. "This appears to be a good stopping point for today. Let's adjourn and resume at nine o'clock tomorrow morning." She tapped the gavel.

Lara glanced at the defendant. His mental condition seemed to be deteriorating a little more each day. His hair looked unwashed, his shirt was wrinkled, and he didn't appear to be following the proceedings. One of the little girls leaped in his lap while the other dumped a cup of coffee on the counsel table, soaking all the papers. Adams sat there motionless, as if they weren't even there, his eyes empty and unseeing. The attorneys were packing their cases and the jurors had already filed out, but Lara didn't leave the bench.

"Mr. Steinfield," she said. "Could you approach the bench a moment?"

Once he had, she leaned over and spoke in hushed tones. "Your client cannot bring his children to my courtroom. They're cute, but extremely disruptive."

"Believe me, I know that." He glanced over his

shoulder. "That soggy stack of paper over there is a brief I need for another case. He's having trouble with baby-sitters."

"I see," Lara said thoughtfully. "I have a thought. Would your client be willing to submit to a competency test?"

"I don't know," he said. "Why?"

"Well, I'm not certain he's mentally competent to stand trial right now. Perhaps we could suspend the proceedings and get him some type of treatment. Then he could get his life together and return at a later date. It makes sense. I could refer him for a court-ordered psychological evaluation."

Steinfield stood there a few moments and then glanced back at his client. "He's not going to go for it. We're halfway there, you know. He just wants to get it over with."

"I understand," Lara said, her voice still low, the D.A. eyeing her suspiciously, wondering what she was discussing with the defense. "But is he able to cooperate in his defense, Counselor?"

"Probably not," he said, glancing back at the defense table. "He's hardly speaking lately, and when he does, he's incoherent."

Lara noticed that the clerks, the bailiff, the court reporter, and the D.A. were standing around waiting, uncertain if they were adjourned or were about to continue. The court reporter had started to put away her machine and then stopped.

"We're no longer on record," Lara told them. "Mr. Steinfield and I are just discussing something. You may all leave."

Now there was a lot of shuffling of papers and people started spilling out of the courtroom, ready to hit the rush-hour traffic, go home to their families.

"Well, Mr. Steinfield," Lara said, "what do you think?"

"I'll ask him."

"Fine," she said. "Advise me tomorrow before we resume."

Lara left the bench and headed to her chambers. Rickerson was waiting. His face was flushed and his eyes wild with excitement.

"You go with me," he told her, smacking an enormous wad of gum. "The others will meet us at Evergreen's house. He lives in Anaheim Hills. The traffic's going to be murder."

"Did you get the warrants?" she asked, tossing her robe on the hook. Phillip had already left.

"Right here," he said, patting his jacket pocket. "Hot off the presses. D.A.'s coming too. And, of course, we have a warrant to search the residence and to search that apartment. You know, the one rented in the name of Tommy Black."

Lara faced Rickerson, her hands at her sides. "This is it, huh? I can't believe it. I know it's happening, but I just can't believe it. I can't wait to see his face when we walk up. God," she said, her eyes glued on the detective's, "I'm so nervous. I want this so bad. You'll never know. You'll just never know."

The detective stepped up close and brushed a strand of hair off her forehead. Then he bent down and kissed her gently on the lips. "When this is over, we'll celebrate."

Lara smiled at him. "I want to meet your boys. Jimmy is the same age as Josh. That's nice, you know? Think they'll like each other?"

"Sure," Rickerson said, dragging out the word. He knew a lot more about kids than Lara did. His boys would be jealous of Lara. Josh would be suspicious and jealous of him. Jimmy and Josh would more than likely hate each other the moment they met, but other than that, everything would work out fine.

"Just let it ring," Rickerson said when Lara's phone started ringing. "We've got to get moving. Everyone's waiting."

"It could be important," she said, seizing the phone. It was Emmet.

"Where's . . . Josh?" he said.

"Oh, I'm sorry, Emmet. He went to his friend's house. I should have told you."

"What . . . friend?"

"Ricky Simmons. Why? Is something wrong, Emmet? Do you need something?"

"I . . . need to . . . call . . . him," he said. "He . . . messed up . . . my computer."

"Oh, Emmet, I'm sorry. Hold on." Lara looked at Rickerson. He was pacing and anxious to leave. She dug Ricky Simmons's phone number out of her purse and went back on the line with Emmet. Once she had given him the number, she disconnected and headed to the door.

"You were great up there today," she said affectionately to the detective as they walked down the empty corridor. "Really, Ted. I mean it. I was very impressed."

His chest swelled with pride and his eyes flashed. "Nah," he said. "You're the one, Lara. You've been a trooper through this whole thing. Even with the threats on your life and your nephew to deal with, not once have you backed down or turned into a sniveling female. That asshole attacked you and you never missed a day of work. I admire you, you know." He stopped for a moment and cleared his throat. His face flushed bright red. Just then the doors to the elevator opened and they stepped inside. They were alone. "What are you going to do about Josh's school?"

"I don't know," Lara said, sighing, leaning against the back wall. "I guess I'll transfer him to a school in Irvine."

"Shouldn't really do that, you know. At least not right away. Everything else has changed in his life. Leave him there with his friends."

Her eyes drifted down. He might be right. "I'll think about it. Thanks."

They emerged from the building and walked to his police unit. "And Emmet," he said, changing the subject once they were at the car, "I owe that fellow a cup of coffee."

Rickerson's tie was crooked. Lara stepped closer and fixed it. "Coffee, Rickerson?" she said. "You owe him a dinner. Got that? Let's not be cheap here."

"What are we waiting for?" he said, throwing the car door open. "Let's go get that big fish and reel him in. I think he's beginning to smell."

As soon as Emmet hung up with Lara, he dialed Ricky Simmons's number. He was in his own condo, so he had access to a phone. At first Ricky couldn't understand him and thought it was a wrong number. Then he told Emmet that Josh was gone. "You're Emmet, huh?" Ricky said. "Josh said you have Prodigy. That's so cool. I wanted my mom—"

"Where . . . did . . . he . . . go?" Emmet said, cutting the boy off. He was nervous and having even more difficulty speaking. He was tremendously concerned about Josh. He had given thought to telling Lara what he knew, but he had promised the boy.

"To get some free video games, man. Hey," he told Emmet, "that's all I know. Some creepy guy is gonna give them to him."

"Ricky," Emmet said, his words coming faster, using every ounce of strength he had, "you must tell me . . . where Josh is. This man . . . is . . . dangerous. Please."

"All I know is he was supposed to meet him at the 7-Eleven by the freeway. The one off Avenue Palizada. He took my bike."

After thanking the boy, Emmet hung up. His fears were confirmed. This was bad, extremely bad. He had to do something. No matter what he had promised, he simply couldn't let Josh get hurt. He tried to call Lara back at the court, but there was no answer. His frail body was shaking. He dialed the police.

"I . . . I . . . need to report . . ." Emmet said.

"Sir," the dispatcher said, the recorded line beeping every few seconds, radio traffic in the background. "You'll have to speak up. I can't understand you."

"I . . . boy . . . San Clemente." It seemed the harder

Emmet tried to make himself understood, the less he could say.

"I'm sorry," the dispatcher said. "We must have a bad connection."

Emmet was in the throes of frustration now. "Help him. He . . . will . . . be . . . hurt."

"Did you say your name was Burt? I need your last name and your address. Then I'll dispatch an officer. Is there someone else there I can talk to? Your mother maybe, because—"

Emmet dropped the phone in anger. The stupid woman thought he was a child. By the time he got her to understand what he was saying, it would be too late. He hit the high speed on his chair, heading toward the front door. There wasn't much time. He had to stop Josh. He couldn't afford to wait another second. Moving fast down the walkway, he stopped at the door of the woman who normally drove him, but she wasn't at home. Then he headed straight to his van in the parking lot. It had hand controls. Until last year Emmet had been able to drive. He put the key in the rear door and activated the lift. He was counting seconds under his breath. Finally he was inside and behind the wheel. Sweat was dripping off his face and his wasted muscles were twitching with fatigue. He mustered up strength he didn't know he still had, seizing the hand controls with one hand, the steering wheel with the other. In seconds he was on the road to San Clemente, his head braced on the door window, his eyes straight ahead.

Josh pedaled as fast as he could. Ricky Simmons lived near his old house, in the foothills, and the location where he was meeting the game man was in downtown San Clemente. He tried not to look at the familiar surroundings as he hit the hill and coasted down, the wind blowing his hair. His life had split into two separate sections. One was his life before the murders and now there was his life since. When he thought of his old life, when his mother was alive, he tried to imagine that Josh McKinley was not him, that those people were not his relatives, his loved ones. Those people whose bodies he had seen that day.

It wasn't that he didn't love his mother, because he did. But sometimes he was angry at her, even now, even after her death. Once she had married Sam, she had almost stopped being his mother. And she had gotten herself killed—did things that were wrong, things he just couldn't understand. She had been so beautiful when his father was alive. It was more than the way she looked on the outside. It was something inside her. It was the way she laughed, the way she smiled—the way she smelled when he was young and she used to bend down over his bed to kiss him good night. She smelled like baby powder. It was fresh and clean. He could never forget that smell. Once his father died, she hadn't kissed him good night anymore. When she got close to him, he could smell beer on her breath and a sickening too-sweet perfume.

He would always miss her, dream about her, cry for her. But she was gone and nothing would change that. No amount of crying or pleading or screaming would ever change that.

He had a system. Every day he tried to let a little of the past go, let it run through his fingers like water. All the bad times particularly. They were the first ones to go. He worked at it, sitting in study hall during the day talking to himself under his breath, telling himself that he must not think of the bad times. All he wanted to remember were the days when his father had been alive, the days when they were all happy and together.

He was beginning to love Lara Sanderstone. He couldn't tell her yet, but he was. Not like his mother, but different. Maybe he loved her the way he would love his grandmother if she'd been alive, or an older brother or sister. He wasn't sure, but he knew the feeling. It was love built on respect. She was so smart, so sure of herself. She was determined in everything that she did. Sometimes he watched her, studied her face and saw her features settling into an expression he knew all too well.

He'd seen that expression in the mirror.

They were alike. He didn't know exactly how, but he knew they were alike. They crawled inside themselves, braced themselves against the bad times. They went on when they thought they couldn't go on.

That's how they were alike.

When he'd first come to live with Lara, after his mother and Sam were murdered, he'd hated her. Every time he looked at her, he saw his mother in her face, her hair, her eyes. And she wasn't quite as pretty as his mother. She was also sterner—a far more serious person. It had annoyed him for some reason that she was so like his mother and so unlike her at the same time. But lately those feelings had disappeared. Sometimes he actually pretended that she *was* his mother.

This game man had something to do with his mother's death. He didn't know what, but he knew he did, knew Lara was after him for exactly that reason. He was a dirty pervert. His mother had been a prostitute. There was a connection there, even if he didn't understand it.

He stopped and rested, checking his pocket and removing a piece of paper. He had the number of the police department written down—the number where that Detective Rickerson worked. He wasn't afraid. He wouldn't allow himself to be afraid. He was going to do something brave, something important. It would be his final gift to his mother.

Climbing back on the bike, he continued. He was almost there. Off in the distance he could see the freeway. Right past the freeway was the convenience store.

He watched television so he knew what he had to do. Almost every station had a cop program or a true-crime program. He liked *Top Cops* and *America's Most Wanted*.

What he had to do was get this creep to do something wrong. He had to let him do something wrong, something bad. Then they could arrest him. He drew lines in his mind as to just what he'd let him do. He could touch him. That Josh felt certain he could handle, as long as he wasn't totally gross and scary, didn't look like he'd cut him up and eat him. Lots of bad guys did that now. He saw it on the news. He'd seen one guy who had heads of people in his refrigerator. They'd carried out the heads and things in boxes.

And that guy had liked teenage boys too.

Josh was perspiring. His hair was soaking wet, and sweat was dripping down onto the handlebars. He didn't think it was just from the exertion of riding a bike. He knew he was scared. Stopping by a bunch of shrubs, he went behind them and urinated. He was so nervous that he couldn't hold it even though he had gone at Ricky's right after school. Then he wiped his hands on his jeans and started off again. He crossed under the freeway and rode straight to the convenience store.

He waited.

The black-and-white police units were parked a block down from Evergreen's residence. The FBI had insisted on being present, wanting to search the residence to see if there was any child pornography inside or any reason to believe that Evergreen had been producing his own films. Lawrence Meyer, the district attorney, was present in an unmarked car. He'd brought another D.A. and one of their investigators. The chief and his son were present. They were all waiting for Rickerson.

"I think we should go in now," the chief said, having got out of his own unit and walked down to the others. He was antsy. It wasn't every day they arrested a presiding judge. "He could destroy evidence, attempt to flee. Let's go."

Meyer spoke up from inside his car. Several of the other officers had stepped out onto the street. "Why don't we wait for Rickerson?" he told the chief. "He's probably tied up in traffic. Hell, this is his case. Let's not steal his thunder."

The chief stood there a moment, thinking, running his hands through his white hair. "You're right." He turned and walked back to the police unit, his son right behind him. Then the other men returned to their vehicles, and they all continued to wait.

About twenty minutes after Josh arrived at the 7-Eleven, a gold Lexus with a man at the wheel pulled up. He glanced at Josh and then his eyes scanned the parking lot. Josh had the sleeves of his T-shirt rolled up and his muscles were bulging. Even though he hadn't been lifting, he thought with pride, he was still pretty buffed. If the guy tried anything really weird or looked like he was going to eat him, cut him up or something, he'd beat the shit out of him. He watched him through the windows of the Lexus. He could take him. He didn't look like Sam or anything. He was a lot older. And there was something soft and weak about his face.

"Hey," he said, pushing the bike up to the car window once he felt confident, "are you the game man? I'm Ricky."

The man's face turned white. He stared at Josh, a funny milky look in his eyes like he'd been sleeping. "You're Ricky?"

"Yeah," he said, "didn't you hear me? I'm Ricky."

"You're not twelve," the man said indignantly, his face turning a bright red. This was a mature boy, with developed musculature. He was past puberty. It was obvious.

"Yeah, I am," Josh insisted. "I'm just big for my age. Aren't we going to your place? You told me you'd give me those games."

The man was silent, staring out the window. Josh didn't know what was wrong with him. He seemed to be in another world. He'd asked him to come here and now he was acting like he had seen a ghost or something. Finally the man turned to him. "Get in the car," he barked.

"What about my bike, man?"

They both turned back to the convenience store at the same time. There was a bike rack there and Ricky had a lock. Josh walked over and chained it to the rack and got in the passenger side of the Lexus. The man pulled out into the street, but he didn't speak. He acted disappointed.

"What's wrong?" Josh asked. "Don't you like me or something? Did I say something wrong?"

"No, no," he said suddenly, as if his mood had changed. He let his hand roam across the seat and touched Josh's hand. "I think you're a fine young boy. You just look a lot older than I expected."

Josh remembered Lara making him tell the man he was only twelve. He had no idea why. It didn't make sense. He studied the man's face. Josh inhaled and then let it out, allowed his body to sink deeper into the leather seat. He didn't look like a killer. But he did look spooky. It was just something about him. He was dressed nice, in a sports jacket and knit shirt. He smelled of strong cologne. His hair was neatly styled, but he still had a strange look. He seemed nervous, tense. Josh thought he saw his body trembling and thought perhaps he was excited instead of tense—terribly excited. And he was breathing heavily, his nose expanding and contracting, his tongue coming out almost like Ricky's dog. If the man had a tail, Josh thought, it would probably be wagging.

"Where do you live?" Josh asked as the man entered the freeway and headed north, back toward Los Angeles. Suddenly Josh felt the fear climb from his stomach to his throat. What if he took him somewhere far away, somewhere where there was no phone and he couldn't call for help?

The guy could kill him.

"Look," he said, his voice cracking no matter how he tried to steady it, "I made a mistake. I do have to be home tonight. I should be home by eight o'clock or my mom will go crazy and start looking for me. She might even call the police."

"Fine," the man said without looking at Josh. His hands were tight on the steering wheel.

Josh couldn't see his eyes for his dark glasses. They rode in silence, the only noise inside the Lexus the man's raspy breathing.

"Can I call you Rick?" the man finally said. "You seem more like a Rick to me than a Ricky."

"Yeah," Josh said. "You can call me anything you want." When the man turned his head, Josh forced a smile.

Emmet was panting, struggling to keep the van on the road. Thank God, the traffic was light, for he was headed away from Los Angeles. Even when he had driven, he had always traveled slowly and used the side streets. Now he was flying down the freeway, pushing the hand control for the speedometer and holding it down all the way. He saw the exit for San Clemente and steered the van down the ramp. Then he saw the 7-Eleven. His eyes started searching for Josh. A car was pulling out of the parking lot. Emmet stared at it. His heart leapt in his throat. He saw Josh in the passenger seat, a man at the wheel. He tried to turn the van around and ended up with the rear wheels on the curb.

He was going to lose them.

chapter 26

Although it wasn't that far from Santa Ana to Anaheim Hills, they hit rush-hour traffic on the 405 freeway. Rickerson tried to contact the chief and advise them that they were on the way, but he was out of radio range. "Let's try the sheriff's frequency," he said, punching buttons on the police radio. "The chief usually monitors their radio when he leaves the city just in case something heavy goes down and he's sitting right on top of it. They can relay a message to him. Let him know we're running late."

They listened to the radio traffic. It was fast and furious. Before Rickerson could try to transmit, he had to wait his turn. They were dispatching ambulances and paramedics. "They've got something going on," he told Lara. "Probably a big accident with bodies all over the road. Glad I'm not working traffic."

Lara heard something she recognized. She sat up straight in the seat and strained to make out exactly what they were saying. The voices were crackling with static. "Ted," she said quickly, "did you hear the address they just mentioned, where they're sending all the emergency vehicles?"

"Nah," he said, "I wasn't listening. Why?"

"I thought they said Fairmont—820 Fairmont. Can you check? It's important." She held her breath. If she wasn't mistaken, 820 Fairmont was Victor Adams's address. She prayed she was mistaken.

Finally Rickerson found a lull in the air traffic and seized the mike. "Station three, this is unit 654, San

Clemente. Repeat the location you are responding to. We're in the area."

"Eight-twenty Fairmont," the dispatcher said. "We have a triple 187 working. Adult male and two small children. One may be a suicide." Before the words were even out of her mouth, she was dispatching a crime-scene unit and other units to direct traffic, seal off the area.

"Oh, my God," Lara exclaimed. She was ashen and beads of sweat appeared on her forehead. "That's Victor Adams's address. He has two children. Please, Ted, find out what happened. They said a triple homicide . . . possible suicide. Jesus, he must have killed himself and the children. He just left my courtroom. I knew something terrible was going to happen. I just knew it." An hour ago, the precious little girls had been alive.

Rickerson got the dispatcher on the air and asked her to scramble the transmission. He knew she couldn't advise names of victims over the air. He flipped the button on his console and activated his own scrambler. Then they waited until the woman had a free moment of air time.

"San Clemente 654," the dispatcher said. "We have a Victor Adams at that location and his two daughters. All three are DOA. Nothing further at this time. Units are at the scene."

While tears streamed down Lara's cheeks, Rickerson continued. "Cause of death?"

"Shotgun wounds. Neighbor called it in. Occurred about ten minutes ago."

Lara couldn't believe it. She felt sick to her stomach, about to throw up on the floorboard of the car. Sensing something horrid hanging like a dark cloud over the courtroom, she'd had a terrible feeling when she'd looked at Adams sitting there today. He was at the end of his rope, completely destroyed. And the system had done it. They were the actual murderers. They had taken his life and ripped it apart, a virtual annihilation. Those two darling girls, dead, at their own father's hands. Lara looked out the window at the string of cars ahead, the tacky billboards, the debris by the road, the thick layers of smog hanging on the horizon. It was still light outside, only about seven-thirty, but all she saw was blackness and blood red death. She saw wasted dreams: two beautiful little girls who would never wear makeup, never go to a high school dance, never get married. She saw them running down the aisles, so full of life, giggling and laughing.

"Shit happens," Rickerson said, taking the next off ramp and speeding down the surface streets. He reached his hand across the seat and clasped Lara's. "This was the guy on trial, right?"

"Right," she said, sniffing, reaching into her purse for a Kleenex. "Why didn't Evergreen shoot himself instead of Victor Adams? And why did he have to kill the children? Good Lord."

"Never works out that way, doll. The bad ones live to be a hundred and the good ones die."

A few minutes later, they pulled up alongside the units and Rickerson leaned out the window. The chief walked over. The other officers remained in the car.

"Let's go," Rickerson said to the chief. "Let's get this show on the road."

Lara was sitting quietly beside him. Evergreen didn't really matter to her right now. All she could think about was Victor Adams and his little girls.

The man in the Lexus pulled into a parking lot. Josh leaned forward in the seat and tried to figure out where they were. From what he could tell, they were somewhere in Irvine and the building looked like an apartment complex. They weren't far from the freeway. Most of the buildings around there were skyscrapers housing technical companies and medical offices.

The man glanced at Josh lovingly and filled his lungs with the essence and odor of youth. The boy had been perspiring. He could catch the delicious scent floating by his nostrils. The boy might be older than he thought, but he didn't yet manufacture foul body odor.

It was warm and clean and fresh, this scent. If he took his tongue and pressed it to his flesh, it would be slightly salty.

This young man was only beginning his life, he thought. He envied him. Sometimes he believed his desires were actually a longing to return to his youth. By loving these young men he was traveling back in time, capturing some of their youth for himself. It was almost like a mystical experience, as if their life force, their vitality, became his own. When he was with them, he felt young again. He felt alive.

He pulled to the back of the complex and parked in his assigned spot. "Come on," he told the boy. "I have a wonderful surprise for you."

"What's wrong with your leg?" Josh asked, watching the man hobble across the parking lot. "Did you hurt it or something?"

"No," the man said, glancing back over his shoulder at Josh. "I have a spinal deformity."

"Oh, yeah?" Josh said, genuinely sympathetic. "I have a friend who has ALS. Do you know what that is?"

"Lou Gehrig's disease," the man tossed out without a second thought, trying to find the right key on his key ring. "That's unfortunate. He's not a young boy like you, is he? That disease usually strikes when a person is older."

"No," Josh said. "He's older, but he's still my friend."

The man opened the door to the apartment and hit the light switch. The room came alive. He'd recently purchased a fortune in computer equipment, had it installed right in the apartment. No one knew about this place. He'd paid a year's rent in advance.

He was seeing a psychiatrist. He was even taking medication. But it only made him sleepy. It didn't take away his desire to be with young men. Nothing would take that away.

He knew that. He'd fought this alone for years. Finally he had learned to accept it. At first he'd thought he was homosexual and had been filled with self-loathing. Then he realized this was something totally different. He had no desire to have sex with men. He only desired sex with young boys—boys so tender and fresh that they were untainted by life. Boys who looked up to him, admired him.

Besides, he didn't hurt these young men. He loved them. To him, it was real—the love. He became their friend and confidant; he taught them about life. Most of the boys he had been involved with over the years had no father in the home. He was their role model. He gave them gifts, took them on wonderful outings, counseled them about their future. And then, at last, he pleased them. That's where his own pleasure was derived: from giving them pleasure, seeing that expression of bliss on their bright young faces for the very first time.

Sometimes he didn't even need the sex. Just being around these young men was enough to give him real pleasure. Their very presence chased the demons away—his ever present fear of death, his fears of inadequacy.

He couldn't stop. It was a compulsion, an addiction. The only way he could stop was to kill himself, and he didn't have the courage. In the past he had been consumed with guilt, even attempted to take his own life on several occasions. Some nights he prayed that someone would kill him, end it for him, do what he couldn't find the strength to do.

He had reconciled himself that he would never be cured. For the illness he suffered, there was no such thing as a cure.

Most of the equipment was on and lights were flickering on the consoles. Quickly he walked through the room turning on the television monitors. "Well," he said, putting his hands together in pleasure, "what do you think?"

For a moment Josh didn't speak. He'd never seen a room like this one except on television, or in war movies when they showed command posts. "Wow," he said, truly awed, "it's great, man."

On every monitor was a different channel. One whole wall was computer equipment. "My friend Emmet would go crazy in a place like this." The man was smiling. Josh turned around and looked at him.

The man placed his hand over his mouth and giggled. When he removed it, he said, "I knew you would love it. But you haven't seen the best."

Strolling across the room, looking back over his shoulder at Josh, he suddenly pulled a sheet off a large object. "*Voilà,*" he said with a little wave of his hand. "Meet Henry."

Josh couldn't believe it. The man had a real little robot. While he was crossing the room, the man did something behind the robot's back and it sprang to life, lights blinking on top of its head, its eyes a funny shade of red.

"My name is Henry," the robot said. "How may I serve you?"

"This is so cool," Josh exclaimed. "My God, this is the coolest thing I've ever seen. How much does something like this cost? What can it do? Where did you get it?"

"I got it at the Consumer Electronics Show in Las Vegas last year," the man told him. "It was a gimmick. You know, they built it to attract people to their booth. I convinced them to sell it to me."

Josh was so impressed with the whole setup that he couldn't believe it. Maybe they were all wrong about this guy, and he was just a high-tech nut or something. He seemed nice enough. He had a problem walking. It reminded him of Emmet. Sometimes people didn't understand people with problems. He knew that now.

But the hand-holding stuff in the car had to go, he told himself. That was weird.

The robot started walking across the floor like a giant vacuum cleaner. "Would you like a cold drink or something?" the man said. "Or maybe a nice cold beer? I also have wine coolers."

"Yeah," Josh said. "I'll take a wine cooler." He'd always wanted to try one of those things. They were real popular with all the kids in high school.

The man disappeared and the robot scooted across the floor behind him. A few minutes later, the robot appeared in the door with the wine cooler on a little tray. "Your drink," it said in that strange computerized voice.

Josh laughed and picked up the wine cooler. His throat was parched from the long ride from Ricky's to downtown San Clemente. It tasted like Kool-Aid. He drank it in almost one gulp. When the man came back into the room, he was wearing a velvet smoking jacket and a little pair of silk shorts. Josh stifled a laugh. He looked so funny. Although his upper body was almost chunky, his legs were real skinny and white.

The man saw the empty bottle set on one of the tables and immediately picked it up, checking to make certain it had not left a ring. "Young men should always put their glasses on coasters. See," he said, holding up a coaster, "there was one right here. Do you want another?"

"Yeah, sure," Josh said. He was still thirsty. Either that or his throat was dry from nerves. "Do you have Smart Ball?" he asked. "You said you did. I promised my friend."

"Certainly," the man said. "All the games are right in that box by the computer. Go ahead, start playing and I'll give you some pointers. Then when you leave, you can take the games."

Josh loaded up the computer and the game began. The man leaned over close to him and told him how to raise his score. Josh was enthralled. Wait until Ricky sees this, he thought. The game finished, Josh looked at his score. "I can't believe it," he told the man. "Wait, I want to enter my name. I bet my score's right up at the top."

"I can teach you a lot of things, Rick," the man said. He pushed his chair even closer to Josh and leaned toward him. He put his hand on his thigh. Josh didn't even notice it.

"Can I play again? I bet the next time my score will be even better."

"I'll get you another wine cooler," the man said.

The man returned and handed Josh the wine cooler, his fingers making contact with Josh's and a funny, silly look in his eyes, as though he had a secret and was about to tell. "Want to see that movie?" he said, arching his thin eyebrows.

Josh would have preferred just to play the games, but he remembered why he had come to begin with. "I guess," he said. The man headed off toward the back of the apartment and Josh followed him. He stopped in the door to a bedroom. It was dark in there. He wasn't going in there in the dark with this guy. No way.

Josh remained in the doorway as the man fiddled with the VCR and the movie came on the screen. Then the man walked over to Josh and Josh stepped aside, letting him pass. "I have some things to take care of right now, so you just enjoy the movie." He walked down the hall into another section of the apartment.

Josh flopped down on the bed and began watching the movie, tossing the new wine cooler down his throat in almost one gulp.

Stopping in the living room, the man started to turn the computer off. He hated to waste electricity. That was one of his good points. He'd always been frugal. Then he saw it. The boy's name was flashing on the screen next to the name of the game distributor.

"Josh," he said, repeating the name, panic setting in.

The boy had lied to him. He'd said his name was Ricky. The man felt sharp pains in his chest. His breath was shallow. This boy lived in San Clemente. The horrid prostitute and her husband who had stolen the photos and blackmailed him lived in San Clemente. Even the name sounded familiar. He fell forward over the computer terminal and held his chest. He waited for the pressing pain signaling a heart attack, but it didn't come. Finally he sat up and with trembling fingers opened a drawer and took out the newspaper article he had saved on the deaths.

There it was: Josh McKinley was the surviving son of Ivory and Sam Perkins.

Emmet managed to catch up to the gold Lexus at the stoplight. He stayed at least one car length behind as he followed them to Irvine. If he stopped to call the police, he thought, they would get away and he had no idea where the man was taking Josh. When the car turned into the apartment parking lot, Emmet couldn't navigate the van fast enough.

He lost them.

"Shit," he muttered, feeling desperate and angry, cursing his weakened body, wishing he was strong and normal. "Shit," he said again. Around and around he circled in the parking lot, wrestling with the steering wheel, his exasperation rising with each second, consumed by exhaustion yet determined to go on. Something was going to happen to Josh, and he would be responsible. He should have told Lara the truth.

He found the Lexus, but it was empty. They were already gone. He fell forward against the steering wheel. His glasses slid off and ended up on the floorboard where he couldn't reach them. He had no idea what apartment the man lived in or where he had taken Josh. There was only one thing to do. He needed help and he needed help fast.

He simply had to call the police.

Josh sat on the bed in the dark room and watched the adult movie. He was beginning to get drowsy and almost fell asleep several times. But he sure wasn't going to fall asleep in this house with this man, he told himself. He set the empty wine cooler on the end table. Even though it tasted like Kool-Aid, Josh was beginning to feel the alcohol. He was dizzy and almost felt like he was going to be sick to his stomach.

The movie was dumb. He'd seen these kind of

things before anyway. Sam had always had a whole drawer full of them in the bedroom.

All of a sudden the video clicked off and soft music started playing. It was old-timer music, with lots of violins and things. It gave him the willies. Sometimes they played music like this in horror movies, he thought. The room was completely black since the movie had gone off. Josh tried to see in the dark. This was turning into a horror movie as far as he was concerned. He was about ready to split. This whole thing might not have been such a good idea, he told himself, his fear escalating. He might have bit off a lot more than he could chew.

Then he saw the man in the doorway.

He was naked. He appeared for only a second and then disappeared inside the room. Josh held his breath; his heart pounded in his ears. He had to get out of here, call the police. Then he heard rustling near the bed and saw the outline of the man.

"You lied to me, Josh," the man said. His voice was not at all the voice of before. Now he sounded like his school principal. He sounded stern and angry.

"I didn't lie to you, man," Josh said, getting up, ready to bolt from the room.

"Ricky Simmons? You're not Ricky Simmons."

Shit, Josh thought. How did the man find out? And what was he doing without his clothes? "Sure, I am. I told you I was. Anyway, I have to go home. My mom will be looking for me."

"Your mother won't be looking for you, Josh. Your mother is dead."

Sweat sprang from every pore on Josh's body. He was terrified. This had to be the man who had killed his mother and Sam. He rolled off the side of the bed and started crawling in the dark to the door. Then he heard a flurry of rapid movement and felt a sharp pain in his hand. He tried to keep moving, but he couldn't. It was as if his body was nailed to the floor. The man was standing over him and had stepped on his hand.

"Please," Josh cried. "Let me go. You're breaking my hand."

"And you," the man said, "you think it's just fine to lie to me, trick me, deceive me. People are always doing that to me. Boys like you, in fact. They take all the gifts I give them and then they turn against me, ridicule me, call me disgusting names. They use me, Josh. They don't appreciate me."

"No," Josh pleaded. "I didn't mean to trick you. Please, let me up. I won't call you names. I won't do anything. I promise."

"You're just like your mother, little Josh. Like mother, like son. She used me and then demanded I give her money. Even when I did, it wasn't enough. She wanted more, more, more. She was greedy. You know what happened to her, don't you? You know what happens to people who lie and cheat, who use people, don't you?"

Josh was crying. His hand was killing him and he was consumed by fear. "Please, just let me go home. I won't tell anyone. I promise. Please."

"No," the man yelled. "No. Because of you, because of what you've done, you can't go home. I can't let you go home." He bent down and pulled Josh up by his hair. "You must pay me back, Josh. You must do exactly as I tell you. Then we'll talk about you going home."

"I'll do anything, man," Josh said, rubbing his hand, glancing furtively around the room for something he could use as a weapon. "Just don't hurt me anymore."

"Get on the bed," the man ordered Josh. Then his voice dropped to a low rasp. "Be still and close your eyes. Unzip your pants. I won't hurt you. I'm going to love you."

It didn't matter what he did with this boy, the man thought. He could indulge his every desire. Josh McKinley knew far too much ever to walk out of this apartment alive.

* * *

Before they pulled in Evergreen's driveway, Rickerson had flipped the radio back to the San Clemente frequency. They were close enough to pick up the signal. Almost the second he did, the dispatcher advised him that Dr. Gail Stewart had called from the crime lab.

"Station one," he responded, "did she advise the nature of the call? I'm tied up right now."

"Unit 654, she said it was urgent. I've been trying to raise you. She's in her office waiting."

"Damn," Rickerson said, turning to Lara. Then he radioed the chief and told them to stand by. They were only a few feet from the entrance to Evergreen's driveway. He tried to contact Gail Stewart on his cellular phone, but she had already left for the day.

Calling the chief back and telling him they were ready, they drove into Evergreen's driveway. Just as Rickerson was getting out of the car, a white county car roared up and screeched to a halt. Gail Stewart leaped out and jogged toward Rickerson's vehicle on her stubby legs, her breasts jiggling, her face flushed.

"God," she said, panting, leaning over and holding her side. "I found you. You don't know the strings I had to pull to get Evergreen's address. You haven't gone in yet, have you?"

"This better be urgent, Gail," he told her. "We're about to arrest the S.O.B. He's probably watching us through the window right now."

"Well, you be the judge. I'm just the conveyor of fact. Your man finally came through with the film of Evergreen nude. They shot it in the locker room at the Sports Club in Irvine. He went there for a massage yesterday." She paused, then spat it out. "Evergreen's not the man in the photos."

"What the fuck?" Rickerson exclaimed. Lara was standing next to him and placed her hand over her chest.

"Evergreen's not the man?" Lara repeated, incredulous. "Then who is? My God . . . what's going on?"

Rickerson ignored Lara and glared at Gail Stewart. The other men were out of their units and standing around on Evergreen's circular driveway, waiting for Rickerson to give them the signal. He spoke low, stepping to a corner of the yard under a big tree. Lara followed them. "Okay, Gail, want to tell me how you manufactured this atomic bomb?"

"He doesn't have scoliosis. He's simply not the man in the pictures, the man with the boys." Gail shoved a tree branch out of her face.

"But that's his son. You verified that was his son and his wife. It has to be him. You must be mistaken." Rickerson was sweating. His eyes took in the string of police cars. They were about to come down like the marines on the presiding judge of Orange County, and now she was telling him he wasn't the right man.

"I can't believe this," Lara said, glancing first at Gail Stewart and then back to Rickerson. "I thought you were certain."

"Gail," Rickerson barked, "are you going to tell me what's going on? We were all set, I thought. This was the guy. Remember?"

She became indignant. Her chunky cheeks froze into solid rocks. There were no dimples now. "Look here, Rickerson, I told you the man in the pictures might not be related to the people reflected in the mirror. And I told you that on several occasions. You're the one who kept insisting that he was. He might have just used their house, be a friend or something. It was Evergreen's son. There's no doubt about that, so I guess he has to be involved in some way. And he did release that Cummings guy." She was breathing heavily. She paused before continuing, becoming defensive. "Hey, don't jump all over me. You're the cop. I'm just a criminologist."

"Fuck," Rickerson said, stomping on a snail as it inched its way across the driveway and listening to it crunch. Then he just stood there, staring out at the men, trying to comprehend what he'd just heard, his chest heaving. He was flustered and angry.

"My God," Lara said, "what are we going to do now?" She waved her arms around, on the verge of outright hysteria. "They're going to throw me off the bench for sure. I'm going to look like a fool. And what about all these men . . . the warrant?"

Rickerson was silent, trying to collect himself, regroup. For a few moments he didn't answer. Finally he spoke, the decision made. "It was Evergreen's son in the pictures and Evergreen gave the order to release Cummings. If he didn't contract these killings, he knows who did."

He paused and looked over at Lara. "We're going in."

Emmet opened the rear door to the van. Not wanting to wait for the lift, he shoved his wheelchair out. Then he climbed down from the van and fell the rest of the way onto the concrete. That's when he saw the number painted on the curb in front of the gold Lexus. It read 212. Instantly he realized that was the apartment number, that the man had an assigned parking spot.

He managed to get the chair open and hoisted himself into the seat. Hitting the high speed, he took off across the parking lot, his eyes scanning the numbers on the doors, leaning forward to go even faster, searching frantically for unit 212. He had to get Josh out of that apartment. If he called the police, it would take forever just to get them to understand him. Then he would have to wait for an officer to arrive. All the while Josh was in grave danger.

Emmet decided he had to rescue Josh himself.

If the man attacked him, it might give Josh a chance to escape. And Emmet had little to lose. If the man beat him, it would be nothing new. Life had already taken that shot, beat his once strong body to only a shell of his previous self. If he killed him, well, Emmet thought, he was going to die in the near future anyway. Josh was young and healthy. Emmet was not. And Josh had brought something into Emmet's life: laughter, friendship, a sense of belonging. Josh accepted him completely as he was, overlooked the ravages of his illness.

Finally Emmet saw unit 212. His eyes drifted up and his body compressed even farther in the wheelchair. What Emmet saw in front of him was the icy north face of Mount Everest. He looked for an elevator, but there was none. Then his eyes returned to the obstacle: steep, despicable stairs.

Unit 212 was on the second floor.

They knocked and announced that they were the police. Then they rang the doorbell and waited. If Evergreen didn't answer in a few seconds, they were prepared to kick the door down. Lara was sitting in Rickerson's unit in the driveway, looking out the window. A few seconds later, Evergreen came to the door. He was in his robe—an old motheaten brown and green flannel. An odor assaulted their nostrils. It was Vicks. Rickerson moved closer to the door. "Judge Leo Evergreen," he said, knowing it was him, having to go through the motions, make the identification.

"Yes," he said, pulling his robe closed in the front and peering out at the police units. "What's wrong? Has something happened to my son?" He blanched and looked as if he was about to faint, grabbing onto the door to steady himself.

"Uh, no, Judge Evergreen," Rickerson said. "Your son's just fine. We have a warrant for your arrest and a warrant to search your residence. May we come in?"

What they were saying didn't appear to register. Evergreen looked old and tired. He began coughing. "A warrant for my arrest?" he repeated once the spasm passed, stepping farther inside the house. "What in the world is going on, Officer? Yes, come in. There must be some type of mistake. Do you know who I am?"

Evergreen stepped back and they entered. The men flared out and started heading for the back of the house to conduct the search. Evergreen watched them in dismay. Rickerson read him his rights. "I'm sorry, but we're going to have to take you down to the station," he told him once he was finished and the little card he'd read from was back in his pocket. He stood to handcuff him.

"But—but I can't believe this. This is an abomination. What in the heavens is this about? This has to be a mistake . . . some dreadful error."

Rickerson read off the charges and then faced the judge. "Do you waive your right to an attorney?" he asked him. "Because if you do, we can discuss this right here."

"Yes—yes," Evergreen stammered. His body was racked by another fit of violent coughing. "I've done nothing to need an attorney. I have nothing to hide. Explain this situation to me right now, Officer."

Rickerson did. They took a seat on the living room sofa. It was a yellow brocade, probably twenty years old. On the end table were pictures in small silver frames, the silver tarnished. Evergreen was speechless, deep in thought. His voice was low and thin when he answered. "I've never molested a child. I'm a judge of the superior court. I've never in my entire life even broken a law. This is ludicrous. Who made these accusations?"

"Judge Evergreen," Rickerson said in a consoling voice, "didn't you ask Judge Sanderstone to release a Packy Cummings, telling her he was a confidential informant?"

Evergreen thought hard for a few moments, rubbing his forehead. Then he looked up at Rickerson. "I remember that name. I believe that was the man Irene Murdock called me about, telling me that he was a police informant and asking that I arrange his release, which of course I did." His pale, watery eyes searched the detective's. "We always try to accommodate you fellows in your work." From the look on his face, that wouldn't be the case in the future.

Rickerson stood. Things were spinning in his mind. "So Judge Murdock is the one who wanted this man released? Packy Cummings. You're absolutely certain?"

"Well, yes, I am. I have a very good memory, Officer." He paused and looked up at the detective as if wondering if Rickerson thought he was senile. "Really, I do." Then he began coughing again.

"Fine," Rickerson told the judge, walking straight out the door to the police unit where Lara was waiting. He got inside and sat there, trying to put it together in his mind.

"They've been calling you on the radio. I didn't know how to work it, so I didn't answer."

Rickerson picked up the mike.

Emmet was waiting at the foot of the stairs right by the trash container, praying that someone would walk by and he could get them to call the police. If not that, they could help him get up the stairs to unit 212. He saw people pulling into the parking lot, but they all headed in other directions. He tried yelling, but his voice was too weak and no one heard him. Peering into the trash can, he picked out an empty aluminum can of peas, ripping the sharp-edged lid off. He would use it as a weapon. Someone had thrown away an old, stained T-shirt, and he tore it and then wrapped the round jagged lid in it and stuck it into his shirt pocket. "I've never asked for much, God," he said in his mind, "but just this once, give me the strength I need to do this and I'll never ask for another thing." He propelled his body out of the wheelchair onto the walkway, his eyes on the steep flight of stairs. He had to get to Josh. His illness wasn't going to stop him. This might be the last thing he ever did in this world, but he was going to do it.

Taking a deep breath, Emmet started crawling, pulling his frail body a step at a time up the stairs, oblivious to the pain as his elbows scraped against the concrete, only one image in his mind: Josh.

Josh was on the bed in the darkened room. He had unzipped his pants as the man had told him. Then the phone started ringing and the man stepped into the other room. Josh sprang from the bed, picking up a statue off the dresser. He could hear the man talking in the other room. He heard him mention his name. He was telling someone about him. Josh positioned himself behind the door and waited. When the man walked back in, Josh was going to bash him.

He waited. His hands were sweaty and he was afraid the statue was going to slip out. He was trembling with fear. He peered out from the door and saw the man walking back in his direction, wearing the smoking jacket again. He raised the statue over his head and held his breath. Suddenly the man stopped. There was a funny sound at the front door. It wasn't a knock. It was like a cat scratching or a dog. The man glanced at the bedroom and then back at the door. The scratching turned into a pounding. He stepped a few feet forward.

"Stay in there," the man said at the door to the bedroom, not realizing Josh was no longer on the bed. "Don't come out until I tell you. Don't make a sound."

Josh was ready to bring the statue down on his head just when the man spun around and headed for the front door. Josh stood in the shadows and watched.

The man looked through the peephole. Then he called through the door, "Who's there?" After waiting a few more seconds, the man shoved the dead bolt aside and opened the door. He stared out and started to close it when a hand reached out toward his leg.

It was Emmet.

"What the . . ." the man yelled, seeing Emmet on the ground to the right of the door. He started kicking his foot, but Emmet held on. Then he screamed, "My ankle. What have you done to me? What are you anyway, some kind of filthy beggar?"

Josh raced toward the front door. He ran right into the coffee table and jabbed his thigh on the sharp edge. The statue fell from his hand and shattered, but he just kept going. He had seen Emmet. No way was this man going to hurt Emmet.

Josh growled and tackled the man from behind, both hands around his lower body, his legs. The man fell forward over the doorstep, landing on his face right next to Emmet. Blood was oozing out of a deep cut in his ankle, staining the landing. He tried to get up, but Josh pulled back and slugged him right in the face. He fell back down. Josh then threw himself on the man's side and pressed his entire body weight down to hold him.

"Emmet," he panted. "Are you okay?"

"Josh," Emmet stammered. "I . . . was . . . so . . . scared."

The man was silent, a glazed look in his eyes. Both Josh and Emmet looked at him and then looked away. "Here," Josh said, reaching for Emmet's hand, pulling him closer. "Want to give me a hand here, Emmet? Shit, you didn't look scared to me. I was the one who was scared, man. Believe me, you never looked so good, Emmet. Thought I might want to kiss you right on the mouth." Josh took a breath and then continued, "What did you cut him with?"

Emmet was sitting on the man's legs while Josh sat on his chest. He smiled with pride. "This," Emmet said, holding up the bloody rag containing the lid to the can of peas and showing it to Josh.

"Cool," Josh said. "Totally cool, Emmet. You took this guy out with a tin can lid. Wait until I tell Ricky. That's wild. I love it."

Seeing a woman staring up at them from the downstairs apartments, Josh yelled at her, "Hey, call the police. Can you do that, huh? Can you call the police? We've got something for them. We need a little help up here." He paused and then yelled again, "And tell them to make it fast. We don't want to sit on this guy all night. We've got other things to do, you know."

Then he turned to the little man and smiled.

Detective Rickerson finally raised the dispatcher and she began speaking. "The S.O. has been trying to reach you. They're at an address in Irvine and would like you to 11-98 with them there. They have a Josh McKinley there and he was asking for you. The call came through their switchboard as a suspect in custody being held by a civilian—a citizen's arrest."

"Josh," Lara started screaming, hearing nothing other than his name. "Josh is supposed to be in San Clemente with his friend. Something must have happened." She punched Rickerson's shoulder. "Quick, find out if he's okay. Find out what's going on."

"Station one," Rickerson continued, ignoring Lara. He was in the middle of the biggest mess of his life, and now he had to deal with some kid playing cop. "Get a phone number. I'll call them."

A few moments later she returned with the number, and Rickerson called the sheriff's deputy on the portable phone. He listened and then his eyes got wide and his mouth fell open. "You're shitting me?" he said.

Lara yanked on his sleeve, about to rip it right off. "Tell me," she yelled, completely beside herself. "Is he okay?"

"Yes," he snapped at Lara. "For God's sake, calm down." Then he returned to the conversation. "John Murdock, huh? The man was John Murdock? What's his wife's name?" He listened and then answered, "That's what I thought. Judge Irene Murdock. We'll be there as soon as we can. Keep the boy there. An Emmet Daniels? Yeah, I know who he is. He's there too. Shit, this is a fucking carnival here." As soon as he hung up, he hurled the phone against the dash. It struck and tumbled to the floorboard.

"Irene and John," Lara repeated. "Tell me what this is about! Now, Rickerson. Has something happened to Irene and John? And you said Emmet . . . did something happen to Emmet?"

"Stay here," he barked, his composure gone, his case against Evergreen dissolving right before his eyes. "Josh is fine. Emmet is fine. And I wouldn't worry right now about your good pals the Murdocks," he said sarcastically. Then he took a deep breath and looked at Lara. "I need to check something and then we'll go get them."

Rushing into the house again, he found Leo Evergreen still sitting on the yellow sofa. "Judge Evergreen," he asked, a lot more politely than he felt, "did you ever loan your house to someone? You know, possibly John Murdock?"

Evergreen lifted his head and his chin jutted out. "That's Irene's husband. He's a physician. They're very good friends. Why would I loan anyone my home?"

"Yes, that's Irene Murdock's husband," Rickerson said. He knew who the man was. He didn't need Evergreen to tell him. "Did they ever house-sit when you were away—you know, look after things?"

Evergreen looked down at his hands and thought about this for some time. Then he said, "Well, yes, I believe they did, but it was many years ago. I went to Europe after my wife passed away, took a leave from the bench. Everyone told me to do it. I didn't want to go." He was regressing, returning to those sad days of grief. "Irene and John took care of my dogs and watered the plants, things like that. They looked after our son. He was only sixteen then. He was adopted, you know? My wife loved that boy. She wanted children so badly." His breath seemed to catch in his throat. "She would be brokenhearted if she knew how things have turned out. We're not very close—my son and I."

Rickerson suddenly felt sorry for the man sitting before him. From the look on his face, he didn't have a lot to live for. He seemed so alone in this huge house. He was nothing but a sick old man still grieving for his dead wife.

"What's this all about?" Evergreen said, searching the detective's face, regaining a measure of authority. "Officer, I demand you explain this to me this second or leave my home."

"Look, Judge Evergreen, we've made a serious mistake here. I can't divulge all the details now, but we'll inform you of everything in time." Rickerson started yelling at the men, trying to get their attention. They were rifling through everything, tearing the house apart. "We were only trying to do our jobs," he said to the judge as he left the room.

He found the chief in the bedroom. He wasn't going to be happy. Rickerson told him. "Evergreen's not our man. It's John Murdock."

The chief looked up. "Who in the hell is John Murdock?"

"He's married to Judge Irene Murdock. The S.O. has him in custody. Let's clear. Just leave some of the guys to smooth things over, try to put the place back together."

The chief glared at him, tossing some of Evergreen's property back into the drawer where he had found it. "This better be good, Rickerson," he said, his mouth a thin, hard line. His eyes flashed behind the thick glasses. "This better be damn good."

Three hours later, Josh, Emmet, and Lara were waiting in the lobby at the San Clemente Police Department. John Murdock had been sequestered in an interview room for over two hours with Detective Rickerson and his attorney. The chief had called Irene Murdock and instructed her to come to the police station, where they were holding her husband. They informed her he had a minor injury, refusing to tell her anything more. As yet, she had not arrived.

Josh and Lara were huddled together in a corner in the lobby. Emmet was exhausted and sitting quietly across the room, his head drooping to the side of the wheelchair. On several occasions he had dozed off.

Lara was guzzling black coffee and chastising Josh. "I can't believe you did that. You went against what I told you and got yourself in a terrible mess. There's no telling what he could have done to you. You could have been killed."

He smiled, unfazed by Lara's ranting. She'd been saying basically the same thing for hours. "We got him, though, didn't we? Wasn't Emmet cool? Can you believe he cut the guy with the lid from a can of peas?"

Lara sighed. "Yes, we got him. And yes, I'm totally

impressed by what Emmet did, but Josh, if you ever do anything like that again, I'll ground you for the rest of your natural life."

"Oh, yeah," he said, the smile a permanent part of his face. "Emmet and I are heros. You can't ground a hero."

"Oh, yeah," she said. "You're a hero, all right. But I can still ground you anytime I want and don't think for a minute that I won't either." Then she set the coffee cup down and seized him, locking him in a bear hug. "I couldn't stand it if something happened to you." She whispered in his ear. "Do you understand? Do you know how much you mean to me?"

"Yes," he whispered back. "I love you too, Aunt Lara."

When she finally pulled away, her eyes were filled with tears. But she was smiling.

They waited for another hour, but Irene Murdock didn't appear. Finally Rickerson came out of the interview room and approached Lara and Josh. "He spilled his guts, even though his attorney advised him not to. I think in some ways he was relieved it was over. He's been under a psychiatrist's care—a Dr. Werner."

"Werner?" Lara said. "That's the psychiatrist that Irene recommended for Josh. Christ, you think he knew about this?"

"He certainly knew Murdock was a pedophile, but I doubt if he knew about the crimes. Even if he did, he was in a bad position. You know, patient confidentiality and all. He couldn't come forward."

"What about Irene?" she said. "Don't tell me Irene knew what John was doing. It's hard enough to believe that John was who he was, but Irene . . ." Lara played it over in her mind. She walked to the wall and looked at the pictures there. They were portraits of the officers who had died in the line of duty. Then she turned and faced Rickerson.

"Tell me everything," she said and then glanced at

Josh. "I guess he can hear too. I mean, he's involved up to the hilt."

All three sat on the sofa in the lobby, Rickerson sitting on the edge turned sideways. Emmet pushed a button on his wheelchair and joined them, all eyes and ears. "Murdock's been molesting young boys for years. How many we can't possibly venture to guess. For quite some time, he's only seen patients in his medical practice in the mornings. The afternoons he spends in that apartment, taking calls from young kids."

"I've known Irene and John for years," Lara said, shock and disbelief registering on her face. "Naturally, I knew Irene better than John, but still I would have never known. He was a doctor, for God's sake. They were pillars of the community."

"Yeah, well, he claims he had nothing whatsoever to do with Packy's killing. He's sort of pussy-whipped. It's obvious Irene wears the pants, wields the power. When your sister started blackmailing him, he tried to handle it alone. But there was a problem. All of their assets were in joint accounts, requiring both their signatures, and all the banks knew Irene was a judge. They certainly didn't want to make a mistake with her money. Murdock said he managed to withdraw the first fifty thousand without Irene knowing, but when he went back for the next fifty, the bank contacted her."

"The next fifty?" Lara said. "Want to explain that?"

"First, your sister and Perkins demanded the fifty G's. Then once he paid, they must have decided to press for another fifty. The bank got nervous because Murdock was asking for a huge sum of money in cash and with all the divorce cases—you know, one spouse cleaning out the bank account—they notified Irene. Murdock said he had to tell her. Your sister and Sam were threatening to take the pictures to the police. I guess she was pretty shocked, even threatened to divorce him. She insisted he enter therapy with Werner. But according to John, she was mortified that their sons would find out and it would destroy them, that her career would be ruined and her standing in the community. She told him she'd handle it. Evidently one son's in medical school, the other in Harvard. She dotes on them, I guess." Rickerson paused. Her efforts had been in vain. The young men would know it all now. "She must have sprung Packy, and from what Murdock says, Packy just went wild in there. He raped your sister and then ended up killing them both. When the Murdocks figured out Sam and Ivory were related to you, Lara, and Packy raised the stakes, demanding more money, it's my guess that Irene killed him."

"Irene?" Lara said, completely shocked. "No. That's not possible. Irene is my friend. She would never have killed someone. Not Irene. No, you must be mistaken." Lara walked over to the wall and leaned her forehead against it. "Then it was Irene who came into my chambers and typed up that order to release Frank Door? God, he could have killed me and she didn't even care."

Rickerson continued, "John Murdock doesn't know for sure, but it's my guess that Irene herself met Packy that day and shot him through the window of the car. Her husband didn't even know he was dead. That is, if we can believe what he's telling us. Anyway, that's why Packy was caught off guard. Irene made John hire him and arrange everything—to get the photos back. All she did was make the phone call to Evergreen. It's my guess Packy knew nothing about Irene, only that someone high-placed in the system was involved. When she showed up that day, he probably had no idea who she was."

"Jesus," Lara said, turning around, facing both Rickerson and Josh. "This is beyond belief. I would have never dreamed . . . never in a million years. And John used Evergreen's house to molest children?"

"At one time. He did more than that, Lara. He molested Evergreen's own son. According to him, it was Robert Evergreen who took most of the pictures. He started molesting the boy when he was about eleven, even before Evergreen's wife died. He used to go over and get him, take him out to play miniature golf, things like that. Evergreen was older. The boy was adopted. He didn't spend a lot of time with his son. John Murdock became like a substitute father, having raised two sons of his own."

"What about his own sons? Did he molest them?"

"He says no. One boy was in college when this all started. Another in high school. My guess is they were too old to be appealing. Once Robert Evergreen passed puberty, Murdock stopped molesting him. Then he had him be the photographer. He helped Evergreen recruit other victims. It's really very sad. From what he says, Robert Evergreen is a homosexual now and lives with another man, a musician. He and his father seldom speak. The old man couldn't handle it."

"Does Leo know about this . . . the child molests? Does he know what happened to his son?"

"I'm sure Leo Evergreen knows nothing about this," Rickerson said.

"Should we tell him?" she asked, thinking of all they had already put the poor man through. They surely owed him an apology. "It could kill him."

"No," Rickerson said. "Not unless we have to. What we have to do now is find and arrest Irene Murdock. We sent a unit to the house, but she was gone. We've notified the airports. My guess is she's trying to leave the country. When John Murdock learned who Josh was, he called Irene. She was on her way to the apartment, evidently to decide what to do about it, when Emmet came." He paused. His eyes met Lara's. They were both thinking the same thing—that the Murdocks might have taken drastic measures. They had everything to lose at that point. Those drastic measures could have meant killing Josh.

Rickerson continued, "We probably should have never called her, tipped her, but then at the time, I wasn't certain of her involvement. A woman . . . I never figured the killer to be a woman. I think after Packy killed your sister and brother-in-law, Irene Murdock went completely insane. They only wanted the pictures back. I don't think for a moment she arranged to have them murdered. Realizing how dangerous Packy was, what he had done, she became incensed and decided to kill him. She certainly couldn't call the police and have him arrested. That would have been suicide. And if he was arrested, he would have surely implicated her husband and herself. I mean, she arranged his release. She had to fear it would come back to her eventually."

Lara was silent. It was so hard to comprehend. "How did this Packy person get into the house? Remember, you kept driving that point home to me, that there was no forced entry."

"Oh," Rickerson said. "I forgot to tell you. We figured that one out about three days ago. Under the front seat of his Camaro, the S.O. found a phony badge. He must have bought it at a police supply store or a novelty store. We assume he just flashed it at your sister, told her he was a cop, and she let him in. It's my guess that she somehow managed to call Sam at the pawnshop, thinking she was about to be arrested, and when he came home, Packy killed him. From what the coroner says, Ivory was already dead by then."

Emmet was shaking his head. Josh was looking at the ground. Lara put her hand on his shoulder. She was sorry now that she'd allowed him to listen. It wasn't easy hearing these things about his mother.

"Oh," Rickerson said, "guess who suffers from scoliosis?"

"Murdock, right? I never saw him limping. Explain that, Rickerson. You and your people kept telling me that whoever the man was, he would limp."

The detective stood. He needed to return to the interview room. They were typing Murdock's statement and he was ready to take it in for his signature. "Up until a week or so ago, Murdock wore special shoes with a lift. Then he developed a problem with his heel, a bone spur or something, and stopped wearing them."

"This is still so hard for me to swallow," Lara said. "I mean, Irene should have known it was me. She knew I bought a house in Irvine."

"Did she ever come over there?" Rickerson asked.

"No, we usually spent time together at the office or at her house in Newport. She had dinner parties now and then. Come to think of it, I don't think I ever even told her the address. I didn't entertain much. But you would have thought . . ."

"What? That she looked up your address, got it from personnel or something? Think, Lara. She had no earthly reason to connect you to this situation."

"I guess you're right." Lara sighed and stood. "You mean we can finally go home? To my house in Irvine? We don't have to stay at the condo anymore?"

"You got it, kid," Rickerson said with a smile. "And rest assured, we'll get her. Every cop in the city's been alerted. She can't get far." He paused. "It's over. You can finally go home. Like Dorothy in *The Wizard of Oz,* huh? There's no place like home."

"That's for sure," Lara said, draping an arm around Josh and turning to Emmet.

Rickerson walked up to the little man and pumped his hand. "I guess I owe you more than a dinner now, Emmet. You're quite a man. My hat's off to you, buddy. It was a lid off a can of peas, huh?"

"I . . . try," Emmet said modestly. Then he smiled with pride. "You know . . . a person . . . has to be resourceful."

"And Lara," he said, turning to her, "if you had never asked Emmet to work on this, we might have never known it was Murdock. Leo Evergreen would be in jail right now, faced with defending himself against these charges."

Lara didn't say anything. She didn't want the detective to feel worse than he already did. But it was a horrifying thought: that Evergreen might have faced prosecution for a crime he hadn't committed. They were about to leave. Rickerson couldn't take his eyes off Lara. He would turn toward the hall and then stop and face her again.

"Oh, by the way, Lara," he finally said, as if he had

forgotten something, "can I speak to you a moment in private?"

"Sure," she said. She followed him down the hall to a vacant interview room. He closed the door and they stood there staring each other in the eye. A lot of things were said in those moments, things they couldn't say with words. "Thank God it's over," Lara said, looking away. "I mean, Irene isn't in custody, but just knowing . . . you know?"

"Yeah," he said pensively. "Still think I'm a great cop? Right now I feel like an idiot."

Lara reached over and hugged him, grinning up into his face. "Yes, you're a great cop. I was certain it was Phillip, remember? How much longer do you have here before you can leave?"

"I just have to get Murdock to sign the statement. I'll get a unit to transport him to the jail. Why?" His eyes were twinkling. "You got something in mind?"

Lara pulled back and played with his lapels. "I thought you could join us for dinner. Then later . . . who knows?"

"I'll have to meet you when I finish."

"No problem. We'll wait," Lara said. "Carl's Junior right down the street? Can you live with that?"

He held her in his arms. He didn't kiss her. He just held her. After a time he said, "Yeah, I can live with that."

She slowly pulled away and headed for the door, glancing back over her shoulder for one more look at the detective. "What? About fifteen minutes?"

"You got it," he said.

Then she walked out of the interview room into the lobby.

"You ready, fellows?" she said to Emmet and Josh. It was time to get on with the process of living. At least she didn't have to worry about the budget cutbacks. Irene had taken care of that. "Hey, are you hungry? How about Carl's Junior for dinner? You know, a really good bacon cheeseburger with an enormous mound of fries?"

"You're on," Josh said, snaking his arm around her waist as they walked side by side to the front door of the police station, Emmet rolling along right beside them. "We're going to move back into your house in Irvine, right? Does that mean you're going to actually cook one of these days? I mean, I don't mind fast food, but don't forget, Emmet and I are heroes."

Lara laughed, tossing her head back and letting it all go. The nightmare was over. "Who knows, Josh, maybe we'll get you that motorcycle you want so bad. You know, like a reward. And Emmet, you just might get a real award of some kind, maybe something from the city."

"Not . . . me," Emmet said.

Lara looked at Josh.

"Nah, I don't want a motorcycle," he said thoughtfully. "I've decided I want a dog. Then we'll be a real family. All we need is a dog. I never had a dog."

"A dog?" Lara said. This was the first time she'd heard this one. All he'd ever talked about was the motorcycle.

He looked up, completely serious. "That's how my father got killed—on a motorcycle."

Josh helped Emmet into the front seat of the Jaguar and climbed in the backseat. So, Lara thought, Josh has learned what most young people don't learn until it's too late: the value of that fleeting thing called life. Three lives had ended this evening in senseless tragedy: Victor Adams and his two daughters. Her closest friend had been responsible for her sister's death. A man she had known for years, had respected, had been a practicing pedophile. Lara looked up at the sky. She wondered why these horrid things happened, how people could go so far off track. But there were no answers. She knew that. All a person could do was struggle toward acceptance, keeping fighting the fight. As her father used to tell her, you just had to keep marching.

Lara opened the trunk and hoisted Emmet's wheelchair inside and then glanced through the rear window of the car. Josh and Emmet were chatting and laughing. No, she thought, nothing would bring back Ivory or Victor Adams and his little girls. But somehow in the midst of it all, Josh, Emmet, and Lara had stumbled upon a new beginning. And she had found Ted Rickerson. The powers that be had somehow moved them all into position, moved them where they were supposed to be. She thought briefly of the pending hearing on charges of impropriety. All they could do was officially reprimand her; the charges couldn't possibly be deemed serious enough to remove her from the bench. It was a mark on her record, but after all she'd been through, she decided it was nothing to lose sleep over. Getting into the Jaguar, she pulled out onto the street.

An hour later, Judge Irene Murdock was arrested and charged with murder as she was attempting to catch a flight at John Wayne Airport. In her purse was the tiny .25 caliber handgun she had used to kill Packy Cummings, purchased years before to protect herself from irate defendants. She had tried to carry it through a metal detector.

In her haste to avoid apprehension, Irene Murdock had completely forgotten the gun was in her purse.

They handcuffed her and walked her through the crowded terminal. It was just about the time Josh, Lara, Emmet, and Rickerson got their cheeseburgers.

You are invited to
Preview an Excerpt from
Nancy Taylor Rosenberg's
Latest Triumph—

FIRST OFFENSE

A Riveting Legal Thriller
Sizzling with Suspense

The courtroom was armed and waiting. The Assistant district attorney Glen Hopkins was making notes in his file and sipping a cup of coffee while the defense counsel, Harold Duke, glanced at his watch anxiously. Two court clerks and a uniformed bailiff were staring straight ahead like statues. A probation officer, Ann Carlisle, an attractive woman with short blond hair and classic features, had her head braced in her hand and intermittently glanced over at the well-built district attorney, waiting to catch his eye.

Judge Hillstorm took another look at the clock and then glared at the defense attorney. Originally from Georgia, the white-haired judge still spoke with a distinctive southern accent. "Your client is late, Mr. Duke," he chided. "This here hearing was scheduled for five o'clock. In exactly sixty seconds your client will forfeit his bail, and a bench warrant will be issued for his arrest."

A small, wiry man, Harold Duke gulped and swallowed. He turned toward the double doors for the hundredth time and then let out an audible sigh of relief when they were thrown apart by a lanky, long-haired young man wearing black jeans, a black shirt, and black leather boots with jangling chains and fake spurs. He strode into the courtroom as if he owned it, marched straight to the counsel table and flopped down in the chair between his attorney and the probation officer. Duke's relief quickly dissipated when he saw the entourage that followed.

The judge had the gavel in his hand and opened his

mouth to call the court to order when he froze. Four striking young girls pranced into the courtroom, each one flashing a smile at the judge. They looked like recycled hippies: bell-bottom pants, bare midriffs, breasts bulging and jiggling, platform shoes, long straight hair. They slipped into the back row and huddled together.

Following them was a tall, handsome Chinese man in his early twenties. He rushed up to the defendant at the counsel table, dropped down on one knee and whispered something. As soon as he was finished, he took a seat several rows up from the girls, glancing back and smiling at them over his shoulder.

Judge Hillstorm's face flushed, and he slammed the gavel down to call the courtroom to order. As he did, the back doors opened again and another attractive young man, this one with blond hair, burst through the doors, scanned the courtroom and then quickly took a seat next to the young Chinese man.

"Well," Judge Hillstorm said nastily, "now that we're all assembled under the big top, why don't we try a little law on for size? People versus James Earl Sawyer II." He nodded his head at the probation officer, and the sentencing hearing was officially on record.

"Mr. Sawyer spent six days in custody subsequent to his arrest and prior to the court setting bail," Ann Carlisle said, her words clearly enunciated as always. "According to the felony disposition, the defendant should receive credit for time served of twelve days, pay a fine of one thousand dollars, and be placed on twenty-four months probation. Since the original charge was a felony and involved narcotics, it's our recommendation that the defendant be placed on formal probation with full drug and search terms."

"I see," the judge said slowly, turning toward the district attorney. "Mr. Hopkins."

At that moment Glen Hopkins was leaning over the counsel table, gazing across the room at Ann Carlisle. A tall, muscular man in his late thirties, his face was more rugged than handsome. Fine lines radiated out from his eyes and clustered around his mouth from too much time spent in the sun. Raised in Colorado, he had once ridden bulls on the rodeo circuit. That wildness of spirit had not left him either. No matter how expensive or well tailored his suits were, he always looked uncomfortable in them, constantly pulling his starched collar away from his neck as if it were strangling him.

Ann Carlisle flushed when she realized he was eyeing her. Several months ago, after a year of fencing and flirting, she had finally given in to his advances. Sex with him was an adventure, she had quickly found out. Knowing he could see her long legs under the table, Ann slowly crossed and uncrossed them. Then she stiffened her back and stared straight ahead, annoyed at herself for having such thoughts in the courtroom.

"Mr. Hopkins, we're in session here. Could you please give us your full attention?"

"What? Oh," the district attorney said, instantly collecting himself and facing the judge, a sly smile on his face. "I think Ms. Carlisle is mistaken. We agreed on the fine and the credit for time served but not supervised probation. The negotiated disposition states summary probation."

Judge Hillstorm looked down at his file and riffled through the papers. "Ms. Carlisle, do you have a copy of this agreement?"

Ann looked up, "Yes, Your Honor, I have the documents right in front of me, but the agreement only states twenty-four months' probation. It doesn't specify summary or formal. My agency is recommending formal."

"It was an oversight," Hopkins said impatiently, speaking to Ann instead of the judge. "The typist just failed to type the word summary next to the word probation."

"Mr. Duke," the judge said, "would you like to comment?"

The diminutive attorney stood formally to address the bench. "This is a first offense, Your Honor, and my client is an earnest young man who unfortunately bowed under peer pressure. He has never used drugs before and is preparing right now to enter college. All he did in this matter was accept what he thought were 'smart pills' from a stranger, not knowing they were controlled substances or in fact hallucinogens. This same individual then told Mr. Sawyer that they would help him concentrate at a higher level. Mr. Sawyer, after ingesting these—"

"Mr. Duke," the judge said, interrupting the attorney's dissertation, "we're only discussing one point here, and we wouldn't be discussing even this point if there hadn't been an oversight. I mean, you are aware that this case has already been settled. You're not in the wrong courtroom, are you?" Hillstorm smiled as chuckles rang out.

"Of course not," Duke said, shifting his jacket uncomfortably.

"Well, then," Hillstorm said, "this is what we're deciding: will your client be on summary probation to this court, basically unsupervised, or will he have a probation officer? Once we determine that, we can all go home."

Duke continued, his voice carefully modulated, showing no hint that he was annoyed. "There's no reason to submit my client to supervised probation."

Judge Hillstorm played with his glasses, taking them off and putting them back on again while he made his decision. "James Earl Sawyer," he finally said, "in case number A5349837, I hereby sentence you to twenty-four months *modified* probation. As a condition of this here modified probation, you will have what we call drug terms, and you will pay a fine of five thousand dollars by October 23rd, exactly one year from today. Now, I know this here fine is more than this agreement stated, but the agreement between you and me was that you were to appear in this court promptly at five o'clock and you failed to honor that agreement. That," Hillstorm said, chuckling, "is what we call breach of contract. Running this operation costs what a young fellow like you'd call *big bucks.* As for your probation, you'll have to report once a month to your probation officer, Miss Carlisle. She's the pretty little lady sitting right next to you. Do you understand?"

"Yes, I understand," Sawyer answered stiffly, not looking at Ann, whose mouth was open in outrage.

"This court's adjourned, then," Hillstorm said, standing and quickly exiting the bench down the back stairs.

As soon as the judge disappeared, the court reporter began folding up her machine and the court clerks bolted from the room to beat the rush-hour traffic. Ann remained at the table, incredulous. Hillstorm had done it again. The older judge had developed an annoying habit of making up the rules as he went along. A judge could modify the terms of a person's probation, but there was no such thing as modified probation per se, and Ann did not supervise probationers. Judge Hillstorm, however, was a dinosaur. He thought every offender should have his own private probation officer. It simply wasn't possible. The field supervision officers now handled only the most serious offenders, and their caseloads were still mammoth and unmanageable. This was the second time Hillstorm had done this to Ann, sticking her with a probationer to supervise personally, and she was hopping mad. Her desk was piled sky-high with files as it was.

"What did that mean?" Jimmy Sawyer asked her. "You know, what the judge said?"

Ann looked over her shoulder—let the man's attorney explain it to him—but like everyone else, Harold Duke had made a run for the hills. Everyone, that is, except Glen Hopkins. The district attorney was still seated at the counsel table, packing files in a larger black litigation case, a scowl on his face.

"I guess it means I'm your probation officer, Jimmy," Ann said, her expression making it clear that she was not happy about the situation. "Call me tomorrow to set up an appointment, okay? Then I'll get your terms and conditions typed and go over them with you." She picked up her files and started to leave.

Sawyer held out a hand to her. "I understand about the probation part. But the drug terms, what does that mean?"

"It means you have to urinate in a bottle once a month any time I ask you. If the test comes back dirty, you go to jail for a violation of probation." He flinched as she bore in on him. "You also have search terms. They go along with the drug terms. That means I can come out to your house and search for narcotics without notice, anytime I wish. Any more questions?"

"Yeah," Sawyer said, his face ashen, "you mean you can just walk in my house any time you want? Isn't that a violation of my constitutional rights?"

"What constitutional rights?" Ann said harshly. "You're on probation now, Jimmy, you don't have any rights."

As she headed down the aisle, Glen Hopkins fell in beside her. "Can you believe it?" she said. "Hillstorm did it again. I wanted this guy supervised, but I didn't want to be handcuffed to him for life. That stupid old fart."

Outside the courtroom, Ann stopped, turned to face the district attorney. "And your office simply has to stop busting felony drug charges down to misdemeanors. Sawyer had a ton of dope on him, an extensive juvenile record, and he ends up convicted on a paraphernalia charge." She gave him a querulous look. Normally he hated to settle for less than the top count. "Give me a break, Glen. Why don't you just give the guy a medal and the address of every elementary school in the city so he can ply his trade? He's a damn dealer."

She looked over and saw that Jimmy Sawyer had trailed closely behind, listening to every word they said. Their eyes met briefly before Ann turned her back on him. A few moments later, she heard Sawyer's chains and spurs clanking down the hallway.

"It was his first adult offense," Hopkins said softly,

his eyes following Sawyer down the hall. When he turned his gaze onto Ann, his voice was unusually sharp. "Look, I don't like it any more than you do. Tell me one person who works harder at putting these people away than I do, huh? But you have to look at the big picture, Ann. We've got four murder trials in progress, seven rapes and God knows how many gang-related shootings and stabbings. We can't take the time to try every first offense that comes through the doors any more than you can supervise them." He frowned as he recalled something, then went on. "I thought you'd be overjoyed that I asked for summary probation. You really threw me for a loop in there, Ann."

Ann stepped back, a bit off balance. They had frequently debated the inadequacies of the criminal justice system, yet Glen had never fired off like this. As in the courtroom, he was always cool and loose, making his points effortlessly. Ann was the one who got hot and started hammering at him, just as she was about to do now. "That's a crock and you know it. By the time a person gets their first conviction—not their first arrest, mind you, but their first actual conviction—they may have committed dozens of crimes. Just look at Sawyer's juvenile record."

"It's sealed, Ann," he said, shrugging, regaining his cool. "You know we can't use it. Most of the charges were dismissed anyway. Look, if you don't want to deal with Sawyer, just carry the case on the books and ignore him. That's what all the other probation officers do."

"Well, I certainly don't," Ann said, her eyes narrowing. "Sawyer will be sorry he was ever born by the time I get through with him. I'm going to crawl right up his asshole. Hillstorm wants him supervised, believe me, he'll be supervised. If he so much as dispenses an aspirin, I'll drag him back to court." As Ann leaned back against the wall, though, she looked at her lover and saw his face shift into hard lines. Suddenly she realized she had been pushing him too hard. "I'm sorry, Glen. I just needed to let off steam." She laughed. "Guess I'd make a lousy prosecutor. Good thing I never went to law school. If I lost a case, I might go over and punch someone out."

"Oh, yeah?" he said, not really listening, rubbing his temple as if he had a headache.

Ann became concerned. "Are you all right? Is something bothering you? You seem--"

Glen loosened the knot on his tie, grimacing as he did so, as if he wanted to yank it off. "I'm fine, Ann."

She saw a glint of perspiration across his forehead and upper lip. "Well, you don't look fine."

"It's Delvecchio," Glen said sourly.

Ann waited until four or five people passed. "I thought that case was going well. Did something happen?"

Hopkins raised his eyes and shook his head. "Fielder declined to file on the homicides: insufficient evidence." Robert Fielder was Glen's boss, the elected district attorney of Ventura County.

Ann put her hand over her mouth in dismay. Randy Delvecchio was on trial for raping four women, all in their sixties and seventies. Although they had as yet to prove it, the district attorney's office and the Ventura Police Department were certain he was responsible for two unsolved homicides, also of elderly women. They had been brutal, savage slayings, and Glen was determined to put this man away. His fervor was understandable, Ann had thought, for he was very close to his elderly mother, a supreme court justice in Colorado.

A sea of people swirled around as another court spilled out for the day. Wanting privacy, Ann took Glen's hand and led him across the hall, through a heavy steel door to a landing of a fire escape.

"You're going to get convictions on the rapes, though?" she said, her voice echoing in the stairwell. "Isn't that want you told me just the other day?"

"I want the homicides, Ann. I can't let these kinds of maniacs kill people and get away with it."

"It's just a case, Glen," she said, trying to get him to

look at her. Just then she noticed that Glen's hair had fallen forward onto his forehead, and she reached over and tenderly brushed it away.

"It's not just a case," he shouted, flinging his hand up to brush her away. "One of the victims was my high school English teacher. Shit, these women are the same age as my mother."

No wonder he was tense and distracted, Ann thought, wanting to comfort him. Because she was handling Delvecchio on an underlying offense, a violation of probation, and would also be assigned the presentence report following conviction, Ann was not only familiar with the case, she would have considerable influence at sentencing. "Just get the rapes," she said firmly. "With the enhancements for the weapons and a recommendation for consecutive sentences on the sodomies, I'll recommend at least twenty years."

"He'll be out in ten years," Glen responded. "And that's if he gets the full boat. The judge may impose the mid-term and he'll be out in five years. Delvecchio's only twenty-six, Ann."

She moved closer and ran her fingers along the lapels of his jacket, wanting to coax him out of his funk. "He'll get the max, Glen. The court always follows my recommendations. You know that. He was even on probation at the time of the rapes. That's an aggravating factor." Seeing the tension in his face ease, Ann carried it a step further. "And don't forget, he's an African-American with an established record."

Glen smile weakly. "You really believe the court imposes higher sentences on minorities, don't you?"

"Of course," Ann said. "I know it for a fact, Glen, and it makes me sick, but hey, when they're guilty of crimes as nasty as these, it can work in our favor."

The smile on his face expanded, one corner of his lip curling up and exposing a tooth.

Luring him on, Ann idly trailed her hand over the metal railing for the stairs, then ran it down the side of her neck, stopping right over her breasts. "Guys like Jimmy Sawyer glide through the system because they're white or their family has the bucks to buy a first-rate defense," she said, her hand now circling her breasts seductively. "But believe me, Delvecchio is going to sit in prison for a long time."

Even though Glen was still smiling, he shook his head. "You're wrong, Ann. The only reason minorities get stiffer sentences is that they commit more serious crimes. Hey, I believe in the system, remember?"

"Yeah," Ann said playfully, "you're the last Boy Scout. You showed me that on the beach last week." With her foot, she kicked the toe of his boot.

Glen chuckled. "I'd rather be the last Boy Scout than the Angel of Death. I hear that's what they call you at the jail."

Ann stiffened. "Where did you hear that?"

"From one of the deputies. He says you go over there and sweet-talk those animals, get them to tell you all kinds of incriminating shit. Then you turn around and use it to aggravate their sentences. Is that true?"

"Of course not," she said quickly. "My God, they're criminals. I wouldn't be surprised at anything they say about me."

Glen tilted his head and winked. "Oh come on, Ann. I know it's true."

Ann tried to keep a straight face, even though she wanted to break out laughing. She was cautious, however, about admitting her private war on crime: getting criminals to talk, tell her things they had never told anyone else. It was a skill she had honed for years. Defense attorneys frequently tried to cry entrapment, but not one of Ann's cases had ever been overturned on appeal. Just as some officers generated hostility and apprehension, Ann had a disarming, innocent way about her that garnered trust from almost the moment she walked in an interview room.

She was turning to leave when Glen pulled her into his arms. "I need you, Ann," he said in an urgent tone she was starting to know well.

"I have to get back to work," she said, her breath catching in her throat, memories of the last time they had made love igniting her body. Glen had taken her to the movies and slid his hand up her dress. By the time they'd walked out of the theatter, Ann was both wildly excited and mortified at the thought that someone might have seen them. Glen had driven straight to the beach and talked her into making love in the open. Conservative Ann, who people said looked like a school teacher in her pastel sweaters and white cotton blouses, had discovered a side of herself she'd never known existed. And Glen made it all seem so natural. Hemmed in a stuffy courtroom all day was agonizing, he told her. Passion should be spontaneous, even a little dangerous—not delegated to a bedroom.

"You don't have to go back to work," he said, his voice low and sexy. "It's almost six. Everyone is gone by now."

"I have a report to dictate," Ann said, gently pushing him away.

"Please, Ann, I want you," he said, placing his hands on her buttocks and pressing her even closer to his body. "You're begging for it," he said, emitting a husky laugh. "You should see the look on your face."

"No, Glen," she protested, looking up and meeting his mouth and then trying to slip away. "Don't do this . . . not here."

"I can't wait," he said, keeping her close, his eyes dancing in anticipation. "No one's going to come in here."

She could feel his chest expanding and contracting, feel his erection through her clothing. She should never have brought him in here, never acted so suggestively. It was just so new and exciting, she thought, this feeling, this man.

Fingers tickled the back of her thighs. Hands slid the hem of her skirt over her nylons covertly, an inch at a time. Anne felt the cold surface of the wall against her buttocks through her pantyhose as he raised her skirt to her waist.

"I hate pantyhose," Glen panted, his fingers inside now, ripping right through the nylons to reach the spot between her legs, touching her, stroking her.

"Please, Glen," Ann said, torn now between her urge to run and her growing desire to do anything and everything he wanted.

He kissed her neck again along her collarbone, then sucked her left breast right through her silk blouse, leaving a small wet spot. Ann laughed nervously, "Now you've made sure I can't go out there. You're incorrigible."

Opening his jacket, Glen leaned his torso into her and pulled her head gently onto his shoulder. The sound of their clothes rustled up and down the stairwell. He began rubbing the small of her back. "Relax, Ann. Look at me. I like to watch your face when you get turned on."

Ann's mouth was open and her eyes closed. If she didn't open them, she thought, then she could possibly forget where they were. "I can't," she protested, her eyes springing open. "Someone's going to see us."

"Yes, you can," he whispered. "You loved it the other night on the beach."

"Not here," she said, eyeing the surroundings. Everything in the stairwell was painted gray, like the interior of a battleship, ugly, industrial. Huge rolled ducts laced across the ceiling. They must have just painted the whole area recently because Ann could smell the paint . . .

"Oh," she exclaimed, feeling him push inside her.

Lifting her legs, Glen held them as he moved inside her slowly and sensuously. "I adore you, Ann," he said, finding her eyes and probing there. "You know what turns me on the most?"

"Mmmmm," was the only sound she could make. His words were falling around her while she responded with her body, pushing forward to meet him.

"You look so prim and proper . . . that little gap between your front teeth. Even Mother will adore you." Ann's legs were locked around his waist now, and he placed a palm over her stomach, right above her pubic hair. "But down here you're hot," he said sensuously, "incredibly hot."

Holding her breath, Ann was adrift, her inhibitions stifled by her state of arousal. She didn't cry out, but she felt a jolt of liquid pleasure and her body trembled and then stiffened. Silent and intent, Glen began moving faster, her lower body striking the wall again and again until he exploded inside her.

All at once, Ann heard a noise and looked up just as the door leading out into the corridor slowly closed. "Glen . . ." she said, panic rising.

Ignoring her, he kissed her on the mouth and pinned her arms against the wall, chuckling while she tried to twist away. Then he released her arms and sighed, running his fingers through his hair and looking around in a daze.

"Christ, Glen, someone came in. Someone saw us." She shoved her skirt down, saw her nylons in shreds where he had ripped them. "The door just closed. Why did I let you talk me into doing this?" she said, her face flushed and damp with perspiration.

"Great, wasn't it?" Glen said, slumping back against the wall. Then he saw the alarm in her eyes and became alert. "Are you serious? Someone saw us?" He quickly zipped up his pants, shoving his shirttail in at the same time. "Who? Did you recognize them?" His tie had been flipped over his shoulder, and he pulled it back down, smoothed his hair and straightened his jacket. "You just imagined it."

"No, Glen," Ann insisted, "I saw the door closing. If it was closing, it had to have been open. It's too heavy to open by itself."

She glared at him as she would an errant child. Although he was concerned, she could see he was also titillated by this public exposure. When she spoke, her voice was low but cutting, "I have a son, Glen. I can't afford to carry on like this in public, subject myself to ridicule. Especially not here at the courthouse."

He tried to take her in his arms, but she pushed him away and reached for the heavy fire door.

"Don't you think David has been through enough?" she tossed out, her voice shaking. "He certainly doesn't need to hear that his mother is screwing in the stairwell at the courthouse."

"Ann," Glen said, trying to get her to calm down, "even if someone did see us, it's not going to get back to David. Aren't you overreacting? So, maybe it was a bad thing to do, but it's not a four-alarm fire."

She sighed, letting the tension go. He was right. There were more serious things to be concerned about. David was one. "I just want him to accept you, get to know you before he finds out we're sleeping together. And he will, Glen. He might even suspect it now. He's very observant for a twelve-year-old."

Glen held up his hand, irritated. "It's not like I haven't tried," he said.

They stood there facing each other without speaking. Ann felt sorry for him. He'd made every effort to gain her son's approval. A week ago, she'd casually mentioned that Tommy Reed, a homicide detective and old friend, was taking her son to a Raiders football game. Glen had insisted on tagging along. Not only had the boy remained aloof, barely acknowledging Glen's presence, but Reed and David had purposely excluded Glen from every conversation. Glen had even bought David a Raiders pennant, but when the game was over, David had left it on the stadium bench, telling Glen that he didn't like pennants. Ann had scolded him, but beyond that there was little she could do.

Ann knew she had to give the man credit. Faced with a hostile kid and a woman recovering from the loss of her husband, most men would have walked away. "David will come around, Glen. You just have to give him time." She glanced at her watch, reaching for the door handle again. "It's late. I have to get home and start dinner."

With that, she touched a finger to his lips in a mock kiss, smiled, and walked through the door.

Back in her office, Ann saw out the window that it was dark. She thought of calling David and telling him she was running late, but after the frenzied coupling in the stairwell, she was in a strange mood—pensive, inert. Picking up her briefcase, she had decided to forgo the call and leave when her gaze landed on her husband's picture on the desk. Setting the briefcase down, Ann brought the photograph close to her face. He would always look like this, she thought. No gray hair, no wrinkles, not a day older. Sometimes the only image she could remember was the one she was holding.

The time had come, she decided, sucking in a breath and then letting it out slowly. She opened her desk drawer and gently slid the glass frame inside, knowing this was a significant moment. Funny, she thought, sometimes milestones in a person's life came and went in the most mundane ways. A picture placed in a drawer. A letter tossed in a mailbox. A key removed from a key chain.

Thank God for Glen's persistence, she thought, grabbing her briefcase and heading for the elevators, feeling lighter and younger than she'd felt in years. Without Glen she would still be mired in the past, sitting home every night feeling sorry for herself. Seven times over the last year, the district attorney had asked her out, and each time Ann had turned him down. But he was patient and polite, continuing to ask until she finally said yes, expressing his concern for her and her son each time they spoke.

"Yeah, sure," Ann said, chuckling at herself as she pushed the button on the elevator to go down. Now that she knew him, she wondered if the fact that she had consistently turned Glen down was what had fueled his interest. Who cares? she thought, kicking off her shoes and peeling off what was left of her pantyhose in the elevator, something she would never have had the courage to do in the past. When the doors opened, Ann stepped back into her pumps and tossed the balled-up hose in the nearest trash can. Glen might be brash and a little wild in some ways, but he made her feel alive. Now all she had to do was get her son to let go and move forward with his life.

That could take some doing, though. The boy was as stubborn as his father.

A highway patrol officer, Hank Carlisle had been nicknamed "Bulldog" by his fellow officers. Although he had been six feet tall, his stockiness had made him appear closer to the ground. As Ann walked along, the image became clearer to her. He had worn his light brown hair in a military style crew cut, but the "Bulldog" handle developed due to his thick neck and small, cunning eyes. That and his explosive temper. Ann had accepted her husband's fierceness along the lines of security. Unlike the average police spouse, she hadn't worried about him getting injured on the job. Of course, Ann's father had been a police captain, and Ann herself had started her career as an officer with the Ventura Police Department. She wasn't exactly the run-of-the-mill police wife.

She'd always seen Hank as indestructible. She even used to crack jokes around the office that it was the people on the streets that she worried about, not her husband.

Then, four years ago, the incomprehensible had occurred: Hank Carlisle had simply vanished off the face of the earth.

His police cruiser had been found abandoned alongside the Interstate just outside the Arizona/California state line—that long, dusty stretch of road highway patrol officers call no man's land. The car doors as well as the trunk of the police unit had been left standing wide open, and no blood or other evidence was found in the vehicle. He'd made no radio transmissions the hour prior to his disappearance.

The investigators had put it together only one way: Sergeant Hank Carlisle had made a routine traffic stop that summer night four years ago, probably to issue a speeding citation. The motorist he'd stopped was a wanted criminal. Knowing the policy of the highway patrol was to check wants and warrants on all traffic stops, the person or persons had jumped Carlisle as he walked back to his unit to use his radio. The most likely scenario was that he was struck from behind with something heavy, the butt of a weapon perhaps. Then when he was unconcious, he had been disarmed, transported to another unknown location and executed.

After months of digging in the miles of barren, sandy earth, the authorities had failed to locate the body. They'd used dogs and helicopters, the most sophisticated aerial photography, canvassed the area on foot and in four-wheel drive vehicles. But they found nothing. No body, no evidence, not a single thread they could pursue.

Ann had suffered through grueling interviews from highway patrol investigators, question after question about their marriage, their finances, their friends and associates. They had to rule out everything, they told her, even the possibility that her husband had purposely staged his disappearance for some reason they had as yet to uncover.

Thank God, Ann thought now, the ruling of foul play had officially been entered in the file. The ruling was important for more reasons than her peace of mind. Although the department had been issuing Ann small checks each month from Hank's retirement fund, they had as yet to release his life insurance money. She could use that money to put David through college.

Ann reached her '87 black Jeep station wagon, nearly alone in the parking lot. Once she was in the driver's seat, she turned the key in the ignition. There was only a click. "Damn," she said, trying it again. Her response met with another metallic click; the engine wasn't engaging at all. It couldn't be the battery she told herself, getting more annoyed by the second. She'd just replaced the battery last week. This time it had to be something more costly—like the starter. Getting out of the car, she slammed the door and tried to figure out what to do.

Glancing back at the court complex, Ann thought of returning to call the emergency road service. For a few moments she just leaned back against the car and let the cool evening air brush across her face, telling herself that she mustn't let little things like this get to her.

Her eyes rested on the windows of the jail, and she watched as shadowy figures moved around inside. The complex took up an entire city block, housing almost every official agency in the county. During the day it was next to impossible to find a parking place, though Ann estimated there were enough slots for five hundred or more cars. The county had also sprung for some decent landscaping. Oleander bushes formed a tall hedge all around the parking lot, filtering the noise from Victoria Boulevard, a major divided thoroughfare in Ventura. Ann thought they were nice, since they softened the concrete and gave her a little greenery to look at from her window.

Deciding the road service could only tow her to the nearest garage if it was the starter like she suspected, Ann decided to walk home. It wasn't that late, and David had probably snacked all afternoon anyway. In the morning she'd ask her supervisor's husband if he would have someone look at her car. He was the service manager of a local car dealership and frequently had Ann's car repaired for free. Besides, she told herself, her house was only five blocks up Victoria. If she walked briskly, she could be home faster than if she returned to the building and hailed a cab.

Ann began walking toward the exit that she normally used when driving and then changed course. She'd spotted an opening in the oleanders in the far corner of the lot that would place her right on the sidewalk for Victoria Boulevard. From there she could walk straight up the hill to her house.

Just as she reached the opening, Ann heard a loud pop and jerked her head around. It sounded like a gunshot. She scanned the empty parking lot and then peered through the foliage to the street. There was nothing. Steadying her nerves, she decided it must have been a car backfiring. People were always mistaking cars backfiring for gunshots. When she had been a cop, she'd responded hundreds of times to these type of false alarms.

Bending down, she ducked inside the bushes. As her heels sank into the mud, she scowled, thinking her shortcut might not have been such a good idea after all. The automatic sprinklers had just gone off, and the ground was soaked. "Shit," she said, squatting down even lower to inspect her shoes. Mud was oozing out around them. She'd have to remind herself to clean off her shoes before she went in the house, or the carpet would be ruined.

Pushing back the branches of the tall shrubs, Ann was about to step out onto the sidewalk when she heard another loud crack.

Her shoulder . . . her left shoulder.

"Oh, God," she cried. Her mind began spinning, and she couldn't catch her breath. Instinctively her hand flew to the spot where the pain was, and she touched something wet. When she brought her hand to her face and saw the blood, she screamed. "I've been shot . . . God, help me . . . someone's shooting at me.

She heard an engine roar, tires squealing, and smelled the distinctive odor of burning rubber.

Get down, she told herself, but she was unable to move, paralyzed with fear. Stumbling forward, lashing out at the bushes with her hands, Ann fell forward onto the concrete sidewalk, her good arm cushioning her face from being badly scraped. "I've been shot. Someone help me. Please . . . get an ambulance . . . police."

Even though Ann was desperately trying to scream and draw attention to herself, she could hear her own words mumbled against the sidewalk. Like boiling water poured over her back, she felt the hot blood spreading, dampening her blouse.

She tried to slow her racing heartbeat, tried to find strength inside the panic. The bullet could have struck an artery. Stretching her fingers forward, fighting against the pain and raging fear, she found them resting in a spreading puddle of her own blood.

As her life pumped out on the sidewalk, Ann could hear her internal organs with unnatural clarity: her lungs straining for oxygen, her heart pulsating and pumping, pumping, like the sound an oil rig made. She was going to die. But she couldn't die. It wasn't fair.

She'd already paid her dues in suffering . . . her precious child. He needed her. She was all he had in the world. If there was a God, she kept telling herself . . . He just couldn't let this happen.

Cars were zipping by on Victoria Boulevard, the exhaust fumes choking her as she gasped for breath. Without success she tried to make her cries louder, attract someone's attention before it was too late and she passed out. "Help me . . . please help me . . . I've been shot."

As soon as she uttered the words, her face fell back to the cement, the coarse surface scraping her chin. Black spots were dancing in front of her eyes. She was nauseous, both hot and cold at the same time. "I can't pass out," she told herself. If she passed out, she would bleed to death for sure.

Gritting her teeth and pushing with all her might, Ann managed to get up on all fours. Then she collapsed again and had to struggle all over.

Ann could hear noises: cars passing, people's voices and laughter, a siren somewhere in the distance, a jet streaking over her head. "I'm right here," her mind kept screaming. People were all around her. Why couldn't they see her, hear her? "Help me," she cried again, this time louder. "Please help me."

Turning her face toward the sound of voices, Ann realized the parking lot for Marie Callender's was right across the divided parkway. People were walking in and out of the restaurant. She was so close—yet not close enough. The traffic, the wide divided roadway, Ann's position right outside the line of shrubbery made her all but invisible in the darkness.

"Help me," she called again, fixing her line of sight on a couple with a young child who were about to get into a dark blue station wagon. The woman was laughing and talking to the man, the little boy's hand clasped in her own. Just then the boy turned and walked across the street toward Ann. "I'm here . . . over here," she yelled, lifting her head off the concrete. "I've been shot . . . get help."

While Ann watched in agony, the little boy's mother

jerked his hand. Not breaking stride, the family got inside their car and were soon pulling out onto the street.

"No," she cried, a pathetic wail. "Don't . . . leave . . ."

She was going to die.

As the puddle of blood increased and the pain intensified, Ann tried to focus on the image of her son's face, use it to fuel herself, give herself strenth. Once again she tried to push her weakening body to her feet, blocking out the pain. It's not an artery, she told herself. You're going to be fine. Maybe it wasn't even a bullet. Maybe she'd backed into a jagged metal wire . . . something sharp.

"Stay calm," she could hear her father say. He'd told her that right after she graduated from the police academy and had seen her first dead body—that of a child. She'd come home and told her father she couldn't do it, wanted to resign. She was too young, too sensitive to be a cop. "Everyone is sensitive to death. If a person wasn't sensitive to death, they wouldn't be human. Take some deep breaths and call on your inner strength," he'd said firmly.

Ann suddenly felt herself fully upright. Her vision was blurred and distorted, perspiration streaming from her forehead into her eyes, but she was standing. She knew now what she had to do. She had to make it across the street.

"Are you hurt?" a concerned voice said from behind her. "Is something wrong?"

"I'm . . . I've been . . ." She tried to hold on, to turn around, to speak. Help was here . . . it was going to be all right now.

Ann felt her strength evaporating. As soon as she felt an arm brush against her side, felt the comforting warmth of another body against her own, she allowed the person to lower her back to the ground.

"You?" Ann mumbled as a disembodied face floated in front of her. Gentle, caring eyes looked down into her own, the most beautiful eyes she'd ever seen.

"Get an ambulance," a voice yelled so loud she was startled. "Quick, she's hemorrhaging. She's going into shock. And . . . blankets. Get blankets. Look in my trunk."

The next second the voice was calm and soothing, and Ann saw a man leaning over her body, his shirt brushing against her face. "We have to apply pressure. The bullet struck an artery. Be still and relax. The ambulance is on the way."

The man moved to the other side of Ann's body and she felt his hands on her. She kept watching his face, lost in his eyes. From somewhere far away Ann remembered them, knew she had seen them. She was swimming now somewhere between consciousness and blacking out, aware but not really awake—a murky wavy world, almost as if she were under water. She heard other voices, heard other feet pounding in her direction. All she could see was this face, hear this reassuring voice, feel the warmth of this person's touch on her body.

Through the fog Ann heard a shrill siren piercing the night. With his free hand the man stroked Ann's forehead, gazed down in her eyes again. Hair brushed across her face. "Your hair . . ." Ann said. It was like a soft blanket.

"You're going to be fine," the voice assured her. "The bullet entered near your shoulder."

Ann strained to see, hear. The face was becoming distorted. She felt a rush of emotion—love—mixed with a feeling of complete peace. "Hank," she whispered. "I knew you'd come back."

Her eyelashes fluttered and then closed involuntarily. She felt an unknown force pulling her down into the darkness. She desperately held on to the image of the man in front of her, refusing to let it go. It was the only thing between her and the nothingness that was calling. Then she was sinking, unable to hold on. She heard Hank's voice, smelled his body next to her own, recognized his firm touch. Hank was here. Her son would have his father. She could let go.

A few seconds later, she let the darkness take her.